EXPLORING REVOLUTION

Exploring Revolution

Essays on
Latin American Insurgency and Revolutionary Theory

TIMOTHY P. WICKHAM-CROWLEY

M. E. Sharpe, Inc.
Armonk, New York
London, England

Copyright © 1991 by M. E. Sharpe, Inc.

Library of Congress Cataloging-in-Publication Data

Exploring revolution : essays on Latin American insurgency and
    revolutionary theory / Timothy P. Wickham-Crowley.
        p. cm.
    Includes bibliographical references and index.
    ISBN 0-87332-705-5
    1. Revolutions—Latin America. 2. Insurgency—Latin America.
3. Guerrillas—Latin America.   I. Wickham-Crowley, Timothy P., 1951–
JC491.E96   1991
321.09′4′098—dc20   90-41547
                                                                      CIP

Printed in the United States of America

                    ∞

MV   10   9   8   7   6   5   4   3   2   1

For Kelley

Contents

Tables and Figures

Preface

Two decades ago, Eric Hobsbawm brought into high relief the study of bandits—a topic whose study, to put it mildly, had not been central to previous historical research.[1] The history of rural banditry had been something that took place in the shadows of everyday life, yet Hobsbawm managed to put a substantial degree of empirical flesh upon the lives of bandits in medieval and early modern Europe. He also did something more: employing a particular set of theoretical lenses, in his case tinted red by an undogmatic brand of what C. Wright Mills would surely have called "plain Marxism," he added a substantial theoretical skeleton to that flesh. In so doing, he gave sociologists like myself pause for thought about the social conditions and historical changes that produced bandits on a large scale, about the kinds of peasants likely to become bandits, and about the nature of the relationship between "social bandits" and the local population.

For some time now, I, too, have been a scholar in a shadowy area, the study of guerrilla warfare in Latin America. Indeed, one observer has aptly termed such conflicts "War in the Shadows."[2] In the course of my own research and writings to date, I have tried to zero in on two central aspects of Latin American insurgencies; their origins and their outcomes, including successful social revolutions in Cuba and Nicaragua.[3] To adduce adequate arguments on behalf of, and as evidence for, my theoretical conclusions, I found myself studying almost a dozen cases of "attempted revolution," Latin American sociopolitical history over a third of a century and more, and the body of social scientific theoretical writings on revolution as well. The combination of multiple cases, multiple theories, and multiple empirical complexities produced a fat book, whose sheer size left little room for exploration of empirical and theoretical side roads. I was often tempted to pursue those roads not taken, but wisely decided to keep my focus on more narrowly circumscribed, if still vitally important issues.

Yet the issues that went unaddressed, or at best fleetingly addressed, in that monograph are important as well, and merit detailed, if separate, treatment, which I will attempt to supply herein. It seems to me that two types of issues concerning guerrilla warfare had escaped my systematic attention. (My further sense is that other scholars have done little in filling the lacuna with regard to the first issue below.) First, while I was giving systematic attention to the origins and outcomes of revolutionary movements between 1956 and 1989, the sociological treatment of the interim *processes* of revolutionary (and counterrevolutionary) mobilization and demobilization received only tangential analysis. Second, while I did discuss the contributions of various theorists to the study of revolution, I did not give revolutionary *theory* per se the fuller and more nuanced analysis it deserved.[4] In particular, I only suggested, rather than strongly supported, my arguments for the integration and complementarity of several influential theories of revolution. Many theoretical issues, of particular importance to sociologists who have studied revolutionary phenomena closely, I chose to gloss over with an appeal to Latin American empirics; in this work I shall stay a while, and strengthen my conclusions concerning and my conceptualization of revolutionary theory, while still keeping mainly to a Latin American context.

For comments on earlier writings leading to these collected essays I would like to acknowledge the helpful advice of several scholars. First and foremost, Susan Eckstein has read at least a few of these pieces over the years, as well as small truckload of my related writings, and I would like to thank her for her inevitably stimulating, sheerly logical, and rigorously organized commentaries; they have always improved the flow of argument of the finished topics. Chapter 7 began as two different conference papers;[5] for critical and useful commentary on them I thank Charles Tilly and Manuel Antonio Garretón. Chapters 2 and 3 appeared previously—in slightly different form—in *Sociological Forum* and *Comparative Studies in Society and History*,[6] respectively. I thank their anonymous (or not) reviewers and in-house editors, whose commentaries substantially improved the inferior early versions, especially for chapter 3. I also thank my colleague Elizabeth Andretta for urging me to put down in an organized form the less coherent thoughts, presented in a visiting classroom lecture to her Hopkins graduate students, that were the basis for chapter 4. A 1979 Graduate School Summer Research Grant from Cornell University also allowed me to spend several months at the Library of Congress. That research enriched greatly the primary and secondary sourcework on Latin America, for the years 1956–70, on which much of this book (especially Part 1) and my earlier dissertation were based.

All translations from Spanish, French, German, and Italian are my own. Being a (necessarily) modest polylector rather than an accomplished polyglot, I take full responsibility for infelicities that enter the resulting texts. I deem them, however, preferable to leaving them in the original and forcing the readers into resorting to a spate of dictionaries—anyone kind enough to spend much time with this book deserves more courtesy than that.

TW-C
Washington, D.C.
July 1990

Notes

1. E. J. Hobsbawm, *Bandits* (London: Trinity, 1969).

2. Robert B. Asprey, *War in the Shadows: The Guerrilla in History*, 2 volumes (Garden City, N.Y.: Doubleday, 1975).

3. See particularly my "Winners, Losers, and Also-Rans: Toward a Comparative Sociology of Latin American Guerrilla Movements," chapter 4 in *Power and Popular Protest: Latin American Social Movements*, ed. Susan Eckstein (Berkeley: University of California Press, 1989); and my more detailed and slightly altered conclusions in *Guerrillas and Revolution in Latin America* (Princeton, N.J.: Princeton University Press, forthcoming 1991), especially chapter 12.

4. The clearest treatments I provide of competing revolutionary theories are in *Guerrillas and Revolution in Latin America*, including the opening comments to chapter 6; part 2 of chapter 10; and chapter 12. Each of those discussions is topic-specific rather than comprehensive.

5. The first half of chapter 7, dealing with Paige and Skocpol, and with agrarian structures and "mafiacracy," is a revision of "Revolutionary Theories and the Latin American Experience: The Cases of Cuba and Nicaragua," paper presented at the Meetings of the Eastern Sociological Society, Boston, 1–3 May 1987; the second part, on comparative regimes, is a revision of "Failure and Success among Latin American Guerrilla Movements: The Forms and Reforms of the State," paper presented at the Congress of the Latin American Studies Association, New Orleans, 16–20 March 1988.

6. "The Rise (and Sometimes Fall) of Guerrilla Governments in Latin America," *Sociological Forum* 2, no. 3 (Summer 1987), pp. 473–99; "Terror and Guerrilla Warfare in Latin America, 1956–1970," *Comparative Studies in Society and History* 32, no. 2 (April 1990), pp. 201–37 (reprinted with permission).

Part One

THE BÉRET AND THE SANDAL: EXPLORING THE GUERRILLA-PEASANT ENCOUNTER

1

The Revolutionary Process
and Theories of Social Movements

After more than a few years studying revolutions—years in which I read the Soviet-line *World Marxist Review* as carefully as I read the U.S. armed forces' *Military Review*—I inevitably encountered a great diversity of approaches to the topic. Indeed, I now feel qualified to suggest a taxonomy of approaches to that difficult, ideologically tendentious field of study (and endeavor).

For example, one can approach the study of revolutions themselves in the stance of the social scientist, as ''specimens'' for sociological, historical, or political scientific analysis, with objectivity advocated as a primary value, and understanding as one's primary goal. Such studies are typically comparative in approach (to avoid the sociological Scylla of studying *any* phenomenon where $n = 1$), and include key contributions by Brinton, Davies, Johnson, and Gurr.[1] I would place this work largely within that tradition.

A second group of scholars is closely related to the first group, inasmuch as they also pursue the objective analysis of revolutions. They differ somewhat, however, in that they place their values on their sleeves, so that readers may know from which personal stance they approach the study of revolutions. This particular need to assert one's ideological persuasion in preface or text seems to be characteristic of scholars self-located on the left. Theda Skocpol clearly identifies herself as a socialist in her book on revolutions, and textual and subtextual messages in the writings of Eric Wolf, Charles Tilly, and Walter Goldfrank also suggest a position squarely on the left. Susan Eckstein's work may be the most interesting special case in that, by its method and its style it is in the ''objectivist'' camp, but by its conceptual approach, topics, and conclusions—argued with great comparative rigor—it falls toward the "left-objectivist" direction.[2]

In our third case the focus of intellectual attention has shifted somewhat, and seems to be on the revolutionary process and struggle, rather than on the outcome itself, as in the first two "schools." One can, as Norman Gall once acerbically suggested of a rival's work, approach revolutions largely as a "cheerleader," certainly taking note of the facts (or at least some of them), yet lustily applauding the advances of one's coreligionists while deprecating the goals, tactics, and honor of one's opponents. I hasten to add that such cheerleading occurs on both sides of the barricades, in both strongholds of theory and operation. One of the most obvious locales to find such cheerleading is among the political left within Latin America itself, especially in its Marxist-Leninist and even Maoist camps, and often but not exclusively in universities. Within that laudatory context, however, resides a purely intellectual, even scholarly, core of Marxist-Leninist theory and debate concerning the best strategies that will practically advance a society from its dependent capitalist present to its (necessary?) revolutionary socialist outcome. As Andre Gunder Frank once responded to a group of Chilean students who greeted with loud applause his ringing cry for socialist revolution, "*La revolución no se aplaude; se hace!*"[3] ("One does not applaud the revolution; one makes it!") Hence the Leninist position must move beyond sheer cheerleading to the analysis of revolutionary opportunities, which leads it in the direction of a kind of applied sociology. Those practical steps, in any version of Marxist-Leninist theory attentive to Lenin's contribution, certainly involve the formation, promotion, and expansion of a revolutionary movement.

There remains yet a fourth identifiable group, again concerning itself more with social movements than with revolutions, but this time as scholars rather than as cheerleaders. There is a long and substantial tradition of social movement analysis in sociology,[4] but of late the field is clearly dominated by the school known as resource mobilization theory, which focuses on the social conditions that support the expansion of opposition movements. Can such works, based largely on studies of formal and legal protest organizations in the United States, fruitfully inform the study of subterranean and illegal Latin American revolutionary movements?

Moreover, can these last two perspectives—strange bedfellows indeed—tell us how the organization, expansion, and tactics of social movement organizations contribute to the revolutionary process in Latin America? Or do we instead have to resort to other, perhaps more traditional, forms of social-movement analysis to understand the mobilization of revolutionary activity in that region? In this and the next three chapters I will concern myself with those questions of revolutionary movements and revolutionary mobilization, and will reserve the study of revolutions per se for chapters 5 through 7.

Reflections on Resource Mobilization Theory and Leninism

As a theorist studying both revolutionary movements and the regnant sociological literature on social movements, I have had a peculiar *aha* type of phenomenological experience.[5] Again and again, as one reads the interviews with or proclamations of guerrilla leaders, ranging in time from Fidel Castro in the 1950s to Joaquín Villalobos in the 1980s, and from the Caribbean to Argentina, one cannot but be struck by the ubiquitous and pervasive sense of *agency* in the guerrillas' views of revolutionary struggle, and the consequent playing down of social structural limits on the opportunities for successful revolution, particularly those limits imposed by different types of regimes or social structures. When utter failures or temporary setbacks happen to the armed left, a recriminatory emphasis on wrongheaded agency has come regularly to the forefront, at least among those who stay within the "armed struggle"; those who return to civilian life are rather more ready to engage in sociological analyses of society and regime to account for their failings. To employ their own vernacular, the guerrillas overwhelmingly attribute their failures not to the "objective and subjective conditions" that were so central to an earlier generation of orthodox Marxists, but to a failure of "organization," specifically a failure to act intelligently and cohesively in mobilizing the population for revolutionary struggle.[6] All such thinking contains very strong echoes of the writings and life of Vladimir Lenin from roughly the 1890s until the Russian Revolution, and we may perceive leftist guerrilla activity in Latin America as a latter-day, rurally oriented union of Leninist theory and *praxis* (as the cognoscenti put it).

The Leninist stress on intelligent organization clearly comes from the debate between the *foquista* theorists, who followed the 1960s theses of Ché Guevara and Régis Debray, and the post-1970 guerrillas who pursued prolonged wars, Maoist-style.[7] Despite those ideological differences, in both periods guerrillas have generally assumed that the masses are there, waiting to be mobilized, and that the guerrillas simply have to push the right buttons and mobilization will come. The later generation of guerrillas, those who drew on Maoist inspiration and spoke of patiently nurtured "prolonged popular wars," have been distinctive mainly in their willingness to *wait* for a supportive response from the civilian masses. (I refer to the long-term and patient preparation for insurrection that took place in the 1970s, prior to military encounters, in Nicaragua, Guatemala, and Peru.)[8] Now, it makes perfectly good ideological sense that these revolutionary vanguards, who see themselves in relation to the peasantry as the Leninist party is to the proletariat—that is, as *necessary* mobilizing agents—would believe that agents of mobilization are crucial to the ultimate triumph of the revolution. Yet there are inherent, and quite similar, theoretical limitations in both perspectives—*foco* and "prolonged popular war"— which I have theoretically dissected elsewhere. Briefly, if one's goal is to understand why some nations undergo successful social revolutions while other nations do not, those two "revolutionary" viewpoints emphasize far too much the behavior of revolutionaries, and systematically discount the contributions of peasant culture and social structure, on the one hand, and the strengths and weaknesses of various regimes, on the other, in contributing to such outcomes.[9]

The *aha* experience came about as I reflected on the literature of the resource mobilization (RM) school of social movements, and its perspective on the birth and fortunes of movements for social change. RM theorists have from the beginning deemphasized the role of discontent in the formation of social movements. They do not believe that higher levels of discontent naturally generate social opposition movements. Instead they believe that there is always a lot of discontent floating around in social systems. Social movement organizations (SMOs, in their standard abbreviation) rather are faced with the task of mobilizing resources—people's money, energy, time, other material contributions, even their lives—that is, putting those resources at the service of movement goals, rather than into workaday existence. The imagery in the RM theoretical literature is that of the citizenry picking and choosing among SMOs and deciding, in a manner akin to selecting housing or fresh vegetables, to which, if any, they will commit their resources. The SMOs themselves, in turn, seek to secure their own survival and the furtherance of movement goals by guaranteeing themselves a steady flow of resources in the face of competition with other SMOs.[10]

In terms of its intellectual parentage, RM theory seems to be inspired largely by two other schools of thought: the sociology of organizations (N.B.: not social movements), and the orthodox economics (N.B.: not economic sociology) of supply, demand, and interfirm competition, as well as the orthodox microeconomics of consumer choice. Given those forebears, we may better understand why RM theory has systematically devalued the *causal* role of (greater or lesser) discontent in fomenting movements, in favor of describing (only?) the *processes* of mobilization. They seem to have replaced the "why?" of an earlier generation of movement theorists—along with the crucial historical questions of "when?" and "where?", all central to the study of movement origins—with a "how to?" that sounds more than a bit like applied sociology. Indeed, one sympathetic yet critical observer of RM theory has acutely observed that "Resource mobilization theory generally views social movement activity as a craft, requiring practical knowledge to perform," and it seems empirically accurate to observe that many (not all) RM–sympathetic theorists are deeply involved in ongoing social movements, even to the point of hosting "workshops" on the nuts-and-bolts of movement logistics at professional conferences.[11] In general, RM theorists have been intensely, and perhaps increasingly concerned, unlike most sociologists, with the relationship between their sociological theories and living practice. That this is but the first echo of certain classic themes in the Marxist-Leninist tradition—despite the strikingly different intellectual roots of the two "schools"—will now become clear.

Certain rough parallels between these two ways of thinking have probably already surfaced, and we can now enumerate those parallels, while simultaneously addressing the central issues that *both* of these perspectives, by the very nature of the approach they take, fail to address.

Causes and Origins?

The systematic causal analysis of the *origins* of social movements is downplayed in both perspectives, and the reason should be clear: if mobilization comes only through outside agency, then the implication is that without such agency mobilization of the populace to collective action will be considerably scarcer than the mobilizers would prefer.

Yet such particular human agency is a notoriously under-patterned, and *not* structurally determined phenomenon, as Parsons and Alexander have stressed in influential writings almost half a century apart.[12] RM and Leninist theories seem, by their very conceptualization of the issue, to have rendered themselves incapable of systematically addressing the causal question of origins. Nevertheless, precisely those earlier analyses of movement origins strike me as lying at the very heart of the classical sociological problem-center of social movement studies. No more, it would seem.

The Mobilizers, Not the Masses

It is more internally consistent in both perspectives to focus on the agents of the mobilizing process (Leninist "cadres," or RM's "constituents"), rather than on the characteristics of the populace to be mobilized. The Leninists view the latter as the "masses." RM theorists see them as potential "constituents," best recruited from ideological coreligionists, known as "adherents"; more generally they term the uncommitted masses "bystander publics." Each viewpoint does give some ad hoc attention to characteristics of the populace, but rarely is that attention systematized in a truly comparative and sociological way: why are *some* "populations" *more* responsive to attempts at mobilization, while *other* populations within that same society are *less* responsive to such attempts? Once again, we have a sociological issue with real "bite" to it, yet that issue is simply glossed in RM theory and Leninist theory.[13]

Movement Organization and Hierarchy

Due to the emphasis on the mobilizers and not the mobilized, we should not be surprised to encounter a heavy Leninist emphasis on party discipline. Hence the ill-named "democratic centralism" among the Russian Bolsheviks, or the military command structure of guerrilla armies,[14] and the corresponding RM theoretical stress on the movement professionals or cadres (especially resource-providing "conscience constituents"). RM theory, unlike any social movement theory that came before it (or after), has shown intense concern for the bureaucratization of social movements, and the tendency of some, but not all, to produce a relatively permanent staff, sometimes salaried.[15]

Lenin, of course, was famed for his insistence on a hermetic, conspiratorial, tightly disciplined, revolutionary party, and was opposed to the dominance of larger yet "flabbier" mass organizations. In one characteristic response to a plea for unity among revolutionaries, made in December 1914 prior to his irrevocable split with the Mensheviks and the Socialist International, Lenin argued, "I am more afraid at the present time of such indiscriminate unification than of anything else."[16]

The Cadres and Ideology

In both perspectives, it should be noted, these movement "professionals" seem to be less in need of mobilizing because their ideological commitments to the movement obviate the need to activate other forms of commitments; in particular, such professionals do not have to be promised or supplied with the selective material rewards that induce the rank and file (sometimes "beneficiaries," in RM theory's terms) to join the movement. The implicit assumption is that ideologues do not have to be lured by bread-and-butter issues. For Communist revolutionary movements in particular, Alvin Gouldner still has provided our best guide to the social and cultural forces that lead intellectuals ("the New Class") to overwhelming predominance in the leadership, despite the absence of specific material rewards inducing them to make such dangerous commitments.[17]

Expansion or Not?

The previous commonality suggests an implicit answer as to why the social movement (organization) has come into being: because some ideologically committed persons chose to create it. While such an answer makes a great deal of common sense, it fails to answer the previous objection: why do some such "creations" expand and grow, while others do not? To answer that they are more successful in mobilizing resources (Leninist version: in recruiting members/cadres) is to answer with a tautology. One cannot but recall here David Hackett Fischer's analysis of one essay by Eric Goldman, where the latter concluded that some social movements were successful because they were "moving with history." As Fischer noted, that sounds very like a description of "success."[18] The idea that differing characteristics of "the masses" might affect such expansion differentially is not an integral part of RM theory, although there, as anywhere, one can easily produce ad hoc explanations.[19] Yet precisely such attention to "the state of the masses"[20] has been the distinguishing feature of all other theories of collective behavior, including those of Marx, Turner and Killian, Blumer, Smelser, Davies and Gurr, and Tilly.[21] For example, and at a very general level of abstraction, perhaps such differing "states of the masses" provide differing degrees of cultural readiness or structured opportunities for social movements to secure resources from them.

An Economic Model: Competition for Mobilizable Resources

Oddly enough, both RM theory and Lenin's notorious diatribes seem to spill far more ink on the nature of "the competition" than on the characteristics of the potentially cooperative populace. RM theory focuses heavily on competition among SMOs within the Social Movement Industry (SMI), while Lenin's attacks on his revolutionary competitors are, of course, now legend. To summarize RM's perspective in brief: Since multiple groups sometimes seek similar goals we can think of those groups as competing organizations within a single industry, in the sense that they are competing for membership and resources from the target populations (adherents and bystander publics), whose sizes and resources are economically limited. The hidden assumption, derived from an axiom of the sociology of organizations, is that an organization, once brought into being, will try to persist, even if at the expense of other organizations.[22]

To continue, if this sounds more than a bit like Lenin's bitter rivalries with the Mensheviks and later the Socialist Revolutionaries, it also echoes the Latin American experience, where since 1956 multiple guerrilla organizations have contended for power *with each other* within the "revolutionary movement industry": in Cuba (mildly so); in Venezuela, Guatemala, Colombia, Peru, and Bolivia in the 1960s; and in Nicaragua, El Salvador, Guatemala, Peru, and Colombia since 1970. Revolutionary "unity" was clearly achieved late in Nicaragua, prior to ousting Somoza, and was mostly effected by a geographical and social division of labor among the three tendencies of the Sandinistas. Multiple revolutionary organizations also finally announced unity in El Salvador (1980), Guatemala (1980–81), and, after a quarter-century of rivalry, in Colombia (1988).[23] Still, the announcement of unity has not produced true unity in any of those cases, with the Salvadoran FMLN (Farabundo Martí Front for National Liberation) closest to accomplishing it despite, or perhaps due to, several internecine murders and a mysterious death.[24]

Despite such clear evidence of "interfirm competition" within the Latin American "revolutionary movement industry," a central weakness undermines any purely economic model that attempts to account for mobilization into (revolutionary) organizations, and especially weakens attempts to explain *any* kind of political mobilization under authoritarian or totalitarian political circumstances. We can still do no better than J. S. Duesenberry's epigram in summarizing our objection to choice-centered RM theory: "Economics is all about how people make choices. Sociology is all about why they don't have any choices to make."

It is no accident that RM theory began in the United States, a society (1) with a free-enterprise, capitalist economy, where people had (2) many free-floating resources, and (3) many possible social movement organizations to which they were free to commit those resources. With regard to the last point, the United States has long been distinctive in the sheer number and diversity of its "available" voluntary organizations, to which citizens might devote themselves and their resources.[25] The vast majority, if not all, of the supporting examples proffered in the first major statement of RM theory were drawn from the experiences of that one society.[26] RM theory's founding papers have since been collected in a volume with the indicative title *Social Movements in an Organizational Society*, proclaiming its focus on the United States alone. This parochial feature of RM theory clearly raises the question of generalizability. Now, in respect to certain social characteristics the United States is certainly not an unusual case (e.g., high levels of personal freedom, of GNP per capita, or of blue collar to white collar social mobility); yet in respect to the characteristics central to RM theory, the United States and Western Europe, with very few other cases, are historically and currently very unusual cases indeed. (Long-term governance under electoral democratic systems is one such trait.) Furthermore, RM theorists are increasingly aware of theoretically relevant differences even between European societies and the United States.[27]

The elaboration of RM theory may make a great deal of sense in a rich and free society; its unmodified application to a poor and/or unfree society is likely to produce nonsense. Since social movements respond to both threats and opportunities, as Charles Tilly has instructed us, we should also pay close attention to societies where threats are real and pervasive, and opportunities are limited by poverty of organizational or material resources.[28] RM theory has shown real tendencies, therefore, of raising American provincialism to the level of general theory; and here, perhaps unlike some other fields, the danger to our understanding of the broader world is truly substantial.

Outside Agitators?

We may have one final parallel between the Leninist and resource mobilization theories of movement growth. At the risk of considerable simplification, we might note that both theories look suspiciously like "outside agitator" theories of social movements; RM theorists have noted that resemblance.[29] It suggests yet a more profound *aha* experience, because such a perspective has been the usual "explanation" of collective behavior—whether short-term riots or longer-term movements pressing for change—adopted by the authorities when confronted with such unrest. From the Sierra of Peru to the streets of Chicago in 1968, the knee-jerk response of the police, the military, and governments in general to collective unrest has been to lay the blame on outside agitators who have stirred up the (stupid but) usually law-abiding populace.

The Contributions and Limitations of Resource Mobilization Theory

Resource mobilization theory has been most effective, for our purposes here, in pointing to the sheer needs of social movements for resources if they are to continue as effective "ginger groups" (as the English nicely term them). RM theory has further emphasized that resources are not solely measured in terms of dollars, but also in other resource units that SMOs might use. To wit, freely offered man- and woman-hours can be put at the disposal of SMOs in activities ranging from stuffing envelopes with propaganda to stuffing cartridges with gunpowder. RM theory's recurrent, though not universal, emphasis on external mobilizing agents strikes a second resonant chord with the empirics of guerrilla movement expansion throughout Latin America, where middle- to upper-class, university-educated persons have routinely been the leaders and mobilizers of peasant-based guerrilla armies.

RM theory is deficient, in our guerrilla context, in that it systematically underestimates how the degree and structure of mass discontent contribute to the growth of radical SMOs. As I have shown elsewhere, the comparative regional evidence throughout Latin America has consistently indicated that relative levels of (inferred) peasant discontent do correlate well with the peasantry's support for guerrilla insurgencies. Major disruptions of the moral economy, or the presence of a tradition of rebellion against central authority, have both influenced the propensity of peasants to rebel. Moreover, the (class) *structure* of cultivator discontent, and not merely its level, also correlates well with insurgent peasantries: regions with disproportionate numbers of sharecroppers, squatters, and migratory estate laborers have been havens for insurgency throughout Latin America; regions with many small-holder farmers, or many plantation laborers on capital-intensive estates, or strong patron-client ties between "serfs" and landlords have not been prominent in insurgent activity.[30]

What is RM theory missing? Perhaps we can find some clues in earlier work. Over a quarter-century ago, Neil Smelser offered sociologists a general theory of collective behavior, which since that time has been more widely criticized than employed. Without endorsing its tenets, we can note the multivariate, value-added structure of Smelser's model. Collective behavior, including social movements as a subtype, only occurs when a series of five social conditions converge: (1) structural conduciveness, which allows collective action of certain types to occur, like stock markets permitting panics to deepen; (2) strain, that is, some accentuated form of "discontent"; (3) the formation of a generalized belief (ideology if one prefers) that "identifies" the problem and hence tends to dictate the manner in which the collective actors will respond to the experience of strain (e.g., movements can be primarily economic, religious, political, etc.); (4) some kind of precipitating event; and finally, (5) mobilization of the collective actors to action itself.[31]

RM theory has essentially taken the fifth step of Smelser's model, and raised it to the level of a general theory. To reread Smelser, particularly on the intriguing idea of structural conduciveness, is to appreciate just how much McCarthy, Zald, and their cotheorists have glossed.[32] Let us note in admiration that their contributions to the conceptualization of the mobilizing process have been most important, for Smelser's own treatment of such processes is quite cursory. While acknowledging RM theory's contribution to that underconceptualized aspect of Smelser's model, we must reject its corollary assumption that strain and the other steps of Smelser's model are therefore unimportant in the origins and expansion of social movements. The time has therefore come to assess the contributions RM theory can and cannot make to our understanding of the mobilization processes involved in guerrilla warfare.

An Alternative View of Revolutionary Mobilization: Five Propositions

Why do some peasants join, or otherwise support, revolutionary movements, thus leading to the systematic expansion of such movements from a few dozen founders to numbers as high as ten thousand?[33] The crucial contribution that RM theory can make for us here is the simple observation that people are unlikely to mobilize by themselves, except under relatively unusual social circumstances. Therefore, a very common feature of social mobilization has been the interaction of a group of people with persons coming from outside that social system.

Proposition 1: The self-mobilization of the peasantry with revolutionary consequences has been very rare in world history.

The best examples to date remain those of Zapata's revolutionary movement in Mexico during the 1910s; the French rural insurrections whose rhythms pushed forward and finally constrained the French Revolution of 1789 and after; and the widespread peasant uprisings in the "Black Earth" regions of Russia that put paid to the old regime.[34] In each of these cases, one could make two very strong arguments: (a) the peasantry largely rose up due to a process of self-mobilization, and the insurrections were led by peasants who defined their own goals; (b) those partially successful insurrections were in good part made possible by a change in the threat/opportunity structure in society, especially by a (virtual) collapse of the coercive power of the state. Thus even where the peasantry rises up in "revolution," it has been responsive to the "field of power" that surrounds it, as Eric Wolf so nicely put it.[35]

I should also draw the reader's attention to my careful wording above, to the phrase "with revolutionary consequences." The ongoing debate over peasant consciousness—are they moral economic actors, rational actors, or something else altogether?—is one that I have just circumvented. If Eric Wolf is correct, it seems rather unlikely that the peasantry would share the ideologies of Marxist revolutionaries, for peasant utopias are those of self-governing villages independent of the extractions of states, landlords, or others.[36] Instead, all theorists would be well advised to look at the *consequences* of peasant collective action, and to waste far less ink on whether, when, and where peasants (and their states of mind) are per se revolutionary. If peasants are *anywhere* likely to be revolutionary—that is, envisioning the world turned upside down—it is likely to be in the circumstances of religious movements, specifically millenarian ones, where they anticipate that the lord or utopia indeed "cometh soon."[37]

Proposition 2: The success of revolutionaries in mobilizing the peasantry depends primarily on the preexisting nature of peasant culture and social structure, and only secondarily on the actions of the revolutionaries themselves.

It is here that revolutionaries and most RM theorists are likely to go astray, when they attribute both their failures and their successes to their own efforts at "organizing." A case of such blinders appeared in interviews with former Venezuelan guerrilla leader Teodoro Petkoff, who traced the FALN's (Armed Forces of National Liberation) early 1960s successes in securing peasant support in Lara State to the insurgents' organizing efforts there. Yet the undeniable peasant support they obtained therein could far more plausibly be traced to two other *preexisting* features of peasant life there. First there was the extant influence of the Communist Party (PCV), which secured over half of the vote in two Lara *municipios* during the 1958 national elections, while receiving only about 5 percent nationwide; the PCV later formed the FALN guerrilla movement in the early 1960s and used its local influence and infrastructure in those Lara *municipios* to secure backing for the nascent guerrillas. A second crucial contributor to organizational success also was intact before 1960: the leader of the guerrilla front there was Argimiro Gabaldón, son of locally revered *hacendado* José Rafael Gabaldón, who had led a peasant-backed uprising against the Gómez dictatorship in the Lara hills back in 1929. Argimiro, for his part, early in his youth had begun the organization of estate workers in the region, further adding to the *patron-client* relationships which already marked the guerrilla struggle in Lara; and he, too, was a member of the PCV.[38] In El Salvador, too, the guerrillas have been extraordinarily successful in mobilizing peasant support for the insurgency, and certainly feel that their correct "line" has much to do with their successes. Yet the regional distribution of their strengths strongly suggests two things: (1) they are strongest in the departments (equivalents of states) that are agriculturally most marginal to the nation—unsuitable for sugar and cotton, or even for coffee; (2) those regions, especially Chalatenango and northern Morazán, are the main homes of El Salvador's migratory estate laborers, a type of peasant whom Jeffery Paige has statistically and contextually shown to be responsive to nationalist revolutionary appeals.[39] Finally, there is at least prima facie evidence that regionally variant "cultures of resistance" influenced peasant responsiveness to guerrilla appeals in certain regions of Latin America, in particular in the hills of eastern Cuba and in the violence-ridden Colombian interior. The absence of any such regional tradition probably hampered Ché Guevara's *foco* in eastern Bolivia, an area markedly different from, and lacking the historic tradition of peasant revolts in, the *altiplano* and the Cochabamba Valley further west.[40]

If the primary impetus behind an expanding insurgency lies in the nature of the peasantry rather than in the organizing capabilities of the guerrillas, this does not preclude a significant contribution of guerrilla actions to the process of mobilization. After all, peasant discontent of a type similar to that found in guerrilla zones has existed elsewhere in the region without engendering the civil wars and near-civil wars produced by guerrilla-mobilized insurgencies. The primary contribution of the guerrilla leadership is to channel that discontent into radical and armed organizations. To put it succinctly: while peasant discontent proposes, mobilizing leadership generally disposes. However, leadership does not "dispose" simply through an ill-defined "organizing" process, but rather through quite specific kinds of social activities. Rather than talking about organizing, we should instead attend to three basic social processes—exchange, coercion, and (political) socialization—and assess their relative contributions to the successful or unsuccessful mobilization of peasants.

Proposition 3: Guerrilla leaders secure peasant supporters and rank-and-file combatants largely through macrosocial exchange processes.

Corollary 1: The most important elements in that exchange process are not selective benefits, but collective benefits.

Corollary 2: The collective benefits that induce the peasantry to support revolutionary movements are the classic collective goods supplied by governments: protection from external and internal enemies, the provision of legal and administrative order, and contributions to the material security, even prosperity, of the populace.

By providing real and promising future benefits to the peasantry—once again, typically only when the peasantry in question is already predisposed—guerrillas in effect secure a peasant following through asymmetrical bestowal of "favors" upon rural cultivators. This observation in effect stands RM theory partially on its head. RM theorists have written exhaustively about the manner in which social movements try to secure resources *from* the populace, and have paid only a little attention to the "[potential] beneficiaries" who join/support movements because they may individually benefit from membership or from the achievement of movement goals.[41] Contrariwise, guerrilla movements typically secure support by first providing valuable resources *to* the populace. In doing so, the guerrilla armies are creating and cementing a macrolevel exchange process with the rural populace in guerrilla zones. That exchange typically means that guerrilla armies provide to the peasantry protection, police services, material security (from theft, exploitation, and bandits), and even material prosperity (schooling, medical care, secure access to land). The peasantry in turn obeys guerrilla directives; often provides food and shelter; and regularly takes on logistical support, civil defense, and paramilitary duties, not to mention incorporation into the guerrilla army itself. I explore all these themes in detail in chapter 2 below.

Corollary 1. The publication of economist Mancur Olson's *The Logic of Collective Action* in 1965 stirred intense and still continuing sociological debate over the motivations that bring individuals to participate in social movements. In the book's central thesis Olson argued that if a movement will "deliver" collective, nondivisible ("public") goods to a population, then it is not in the self-interest of individuals in that population to commit resources to (i.e., join) such a movement, for they will benefit when the movement achieves its goals whether or not they have supported it, and can thus make more "profit" by withholding their scarce resources from the movement. That is, they can become what economists call "free riders."[42]

Several scholars have in fact employed this theory to understand why peasants might join revolutionary movements, but I believe it is misleading as to the true sources of the population's backing for insurgency. Indeed, Barbara Salert has lodged a severe critique of Olson's theory when applied to revolutionary movements, particularly noting its complete inability—acknowledged by Olson—to deal with any type of material benefit that cannot be measured in money, as well as its inability to capture psychological, moral, or social incentives. Olson's theory becomes effectively untestable unless rewards are viewed as a linear function of money.[43]

Quite apart from those specific objections, Olson's theory suffers from the more general deficiencies of all "rational actor" theories of human behavior, for he also implicitly assumes that an outside observer can easily identify an actor's "true" and rational interests. This is a most widely believed tenet in the social sciences, but is nonetheless nonsensical if we give it but a moment's clear thought. Human beings qua humans have multiple, not singular, goals (or values) which are not existentially given, but culturally and psychologically developed.[44] Given multiple values, action can only be deemed "rational" (or not) once we know the relative value placed on those various goals; since we do *not* have such knowledge, as a general thing, all such attributions of "rationality" (or not) to social actors become nothing but exercises in cant.

The comparative evidence from Latin American revolutionary conditions does not tend to support Olson's position, nor that of his theoretical followers, Joel Migdal and Samuel Popkin. For one thing, the *mass* participation, whether as combatants or supporters, witnessed in so many Latin American revolutionary movements of the last four decades does not, to put it charitably, give strong support to Olson's predictions about free riders in large-scale, collective action organizations (i.e., he would expect many more such than we observe).[45] Indeed, his view cannot deal with collective *solidary* action any better than most economists or rational-choice theorists. Observers have noted of Guatemala, for example, that the hermetic and solidary Indian villages, which for centuries had been essentially "closed" to Hispanic Guatemalans, at times during the 1970s and 1980s went over en masse to the EGP (Guerrilla Army of the Poor), rather than as individual joiners.[46] Such experiences belie the individualistic assumptions that continue to pervade and bedevil much economics (and social science more generally), for blinders to the *social* roots of solidary action do not really help us to understand better the nature of revolutionary collective action. Instead, that tunnel vision suggests that such theorists have read too much Adam Smith and John Stuart Mill, and not enough Durkheim or social anthropology.

One strong test of the model might be to ask ourselves *when* people tend to commit themselves to revolutionary guerrilla organizations. As I show in chapters 2 and 3 below, and as military practitioners of counterinsurgency now understand all too well, the central government's use of terror against the civilian populace tends to produce *more* immediate recruits for the guerrilla armies; Olson's theory would rather predict fewer such recruits in the face of the "negative incentives" terroristic governments can visit upon the peasantry. Furthermore, a second situation also tends to produce a wave of recruits for the guerrilla forces: successful guerrilla engagements against the government armed forces, where the insurgents show they are capable of delivering the most important (and the most classic) collective good of government, the defense of the populace against external enemies.

Corollary 2. Taken together, these two recruit-producing situations make sense only if we emphasize two features of the decision to join: (1) the sense of moral outrage involved in the decision, which Olson's model is utterly incapable of grasping, and which is regularly expressed by the new recruits (see my discussion in chapter 3 below); (2) the fact that guerrilla armies provide *collective goods* to the populace, first and foremost, in the form of *protection* from bandits, usurers, exploitative landlords, and (especially) government troops.[47] The evidence from Latin America that I amass in chapter 2—when systematically viewed from the selective vs. collective goods debate—more strongly supports my contention that guerrilla organizations gain the support ("resources") of the populace when they behave as *governments* do. That is, when they provide collective goods to the populace (like defense, peace, and order), or bestow goods on the populace that, while being individualized in their benefits, are in effect made available to all the local populace to whom the revolutionaries are able to minister (e.g., literacy training, cooperative agriculture, and medical care).

Proposition 4: Guerrilla movements do not secure peasant support through coercion or terror, although such techniques can be used to neutralize opposition. Instead, widespread use of terror is more likely to generate recruits for one's enemies, or lead the populace simply to withdraw from the armed struggle, where possible.

In effect, I have suggested a hierarchy of influences which bring people to social movements. Exchange processes are quite important in this regard; terror is insignificant in recruiting for oneself, but it may generate recruits for the enemy. In chapter 3 I provide evidence that terror can consistently provide recruits only for those who are fighting the agents of terror; at best terror used by itself can neutralize a populace into cowed and grudging submission. Since terror has been of little importance to the expansion of revolutionary movements, I have instead in chapter 3 sought to describe and then explain varying levels of terror, especially government terror, in guerrilla warfare. I also explore the nature and circumstances of guerrilla terror against the civilian populace, and draw certain parallels between government terror and guerrilla terror. Afterwards, I try to show some structural and ideological reasons why government terror tends to be vastly greater in scope than that committed by guerrilla armies. Finally, but in lesser compass, I also explore some of the consequences of terror for the populace, the insurgency, and the regime.

Proposition 5: Guerrilla movements do not secure peasant backing and recruits through unstructured attempts at "consciousness raising." If shifts in peasants' world views do take place—whether before or after recruitment into the guerrilla army—such ideological conversions will tend to take place through the operations of structured social networks, just as similar political and religious conversions have done elsewhere.

"Consciousness raising," or political socialization into new ways of thinking, is a rather more difficult force to assess in considering its importance to the expansion of revolutionary movements. Such successful consciousness-raising processes are rarely found in vacuo among individuals prior to joining social movements, as a substantial literature now confirms. I explore that literature and Latin American specifics in chapter 4. The image in the consciousness-raising literature usually is presented as something like this:

Figure 1.1 **Consciousness-Raising Model of Mobilization**

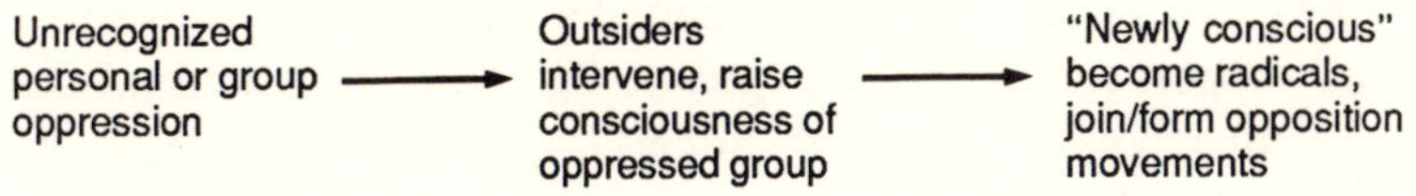

Unrecognized personal or group oppression	$\longrightarrow$	Outsiders intervene, raise consciousness of oppressed group	$\longrightarrow$	"Newly conscious" become radicals, join/form opposition movements

On the surface, this model may seem uncontroversial, but from a sociological standpoint this image has many flaws, which I detail in chapter 4. For our purposes here, however, we may simply suggest an alternative model, which is more consistent with both existing studies and with the guerrillas' own experience:

Figure 1.2 **Attachment-Network Model of Mobilization**

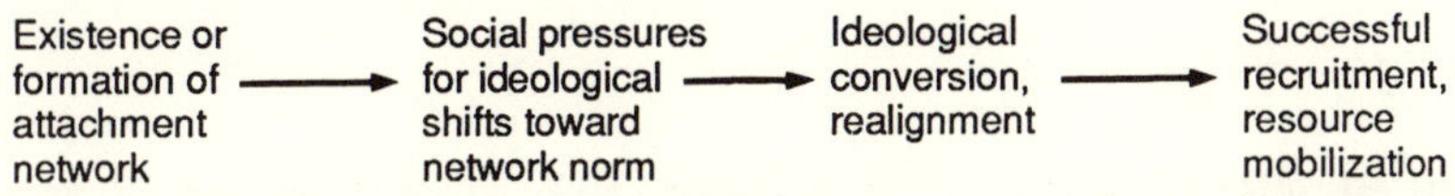

Existence or formation of attachment network	$\longrightarrow$	Social pressures for ideological shifts toward network norm	$\longrightarrow$	Ideological conversion, realignment	$\longrightarrow$	Successful recruitment, resource mobilization

This model is far more sociological than the consciousness-raising model, in linking itself to a wealth of sociological evidence that we form our political and religious beliefs in group contexts, often primary-group ones. Moreover, it does not rely on the highly dubious assumptions that there exist "true" and "false," or "higher" and "lower" states of consciousness, or on the corollary assumption that people are too stupid to understand their own situations. Finally, my alternative model also relies far less on the historical happenstance of external intervention ("outside agitators") to explain collective behavior. Most important of the three, and well worth reiterating, my alternative model zeroes in on the group contexts in which human beings make decisive, sometimes agonizing personal decisions about political or religious commitments.

To make the point as bluntly as possible: the revolutionaries' attempts at "organization" have generally been far more successful where they had a *preexisting linkage to peasant attachment networks, and/or could activate such linkages easily.*[48] However, as evidence will suggest, the authorities could often activate their own attachment networks to the peasantry and, where that was true, the guerrillas encountered severe difficulties in mobilizing the peasantry for revolutionary activity.

Thus we shall see in chapter 4 that the nature of preexisting social structural networks could either engender or constrain even the guerrillas' secondary influence upon the degrees and activation of peasant support for radical insurgency. (In some more unusual cases, the guerrillas could with great diligence construct such networks, a process both arduous and time-consuming.) As Anthony Giddens has argued, by its very nature, social structure can both enable *and* constrain the actions of individuals placed in different structural locations.[49] In this particular respect, then, guerrilla leaders have been constrained, not only by varying levels of peasant discontent (and hence "willingness" to rebel), but also by social structures themselves, which could funnel the two groups into revolutionary alliances or, instead, channel them into nonalliances, or even mutual opposition.

Notes

1. Historian Crane Brinton, *The Anatomy of Revolution* (New York: Vintage, 1965); sociologist James C. Davies, "Toward a Theory of Revolution," *American Sociological Review* 27, no. 1 (February 1962), pp. 5–19; and political scientists Chalmers Johnson, *Revolutionary Change* (Boston: Little, Brown and Co., 1966), and Ted Robert Gurr, *Why Men Rebel* (Princeton, N.J.: Princeton University Press, 1970).

2. The work of the scholars mentioned here is carefully considered at other points in this book, especially chapters 5 through 7. For two examples of Susan Eckstein's unusually careful analyses of issues central to human welfare, see "The Impact of Revolution on Social Welfare in Latin America," *Theory and Society* 11 (1982), pp. 17–42; and "The Debourgeoisement of Cuban Cities," ch. 19 in *Cuban Communism*, 3d edition, ed. Irving Louis Horowitz (New Brunswick, N.J.: Transaction Books, 1977).

3. For Gall's review of Richard Gott's sympathetic and fact-packed book on the guerrillas of the 1960s, see Norman Gall, "A Cheerleader's Report," *New York Times Book Review*, 28 March 1971, pp. 6+; for an anti-Communist cheerleader whose work is still very useful for its comprehensive quotations from the guerrillas themselves, see Donn Munson, *Zacapa* (Canoga, Calif.: Challenge, 1967). For some reason, the study of Guatemala seems peculiarly productive of this type of analysis, especially by the left. One such examplar, notwithstanding its many and varied virtues, is Concerned Guatemala Scholars, *Guatemala: Dare to Struggle, Dare to Win* (San Francisco: Solidarity Publications, 1982). For the anecdote on Andre Gunder Frank, I am indebted to my former teacher Gláucio Soares.

4. The works of Smelser and Turner and Killian that I discuss below are probably the most important early statements of social movement theory.

5. The notion of an *aha* experience—a serendipitous discovery that causes one to rethink old conceptions—comes from the work of Alfred Schutz; my indirect source is his former student Peter L. Berger, *Pyramids of Sacrifice: Political Ethics and Social Change* (New York: Basic Books, 1974), p. ix.

6. Examples of such rueful postmortems emphasizing wrong-headed agency include virtually every piece on Ché Guevara's Bolivian *foco*; the self-criticism sections of the quasi-official biography of the Colombian EPL (Popular Army of Liberation), in Fabiola Calvo Ocampo, *EPL: Diez hombres, un ejército, una historia* (Bogotá: Ediciones Ecoe, 1985); as well as the criticisms by an ex-member (later murdered by his erstwhile comrades) of the Colombian ELN (Army of National Liberation), found in Jaime Arenas, *La guerrilla por dentro* (Bogotá: Tercer Mundo, 1970). For Guatemala, left-wing critiques of the 1960s guerrilla movement have routinely focused on its choice of a *foco* strategy, and there is little variation in that commentary; see, for three such examples, NACLA (North American Congress on Latin America), *Guatemala* (New York and Berkeley: NACLA, 1974), pp. 180–88; Concerned Guatemala Scholars, *Guatemala*, pp. 18–21; George Black, with Milton Jamail and Norma Stoltz Chinchilla, *Garrison Guatemala* (New York: Monthly Review, 1984), p. 70. Venezuela, with several prominent guerrilla veterans, provides several good examples of such analytical retrospectives, which focus more on Venezuelan social and political structure, and less on the guerrillas themselves; in particular see the two-part interview by Norman Gall, "Teodoro Petkoff: The Crisis of the Professional Revolutionary" *American Universities Field Staff Reports—East Coast South America Series* 16, no. 1 (January 1972), pp. 1–19, and 17, no. 9 (August 1973), pp. 3–20; and Alfredo Peña, *Conversaciones con Américo Martín* (Caracas: Ateneo, 1978), esp. pp. 74–90. Petkoff's first interview veers back and forth between the typical revolutionary emphasis on wrong choices and more acute sociological analyses of the conditions giving rise to support for guerrillas in rural Falcón State and in the poor Caracas *barrios*.

7. For a good collection of writings by mostly uninvolved Marxists, see Leo Huberman and Paul Sweezy, eds., *Régis Debray and the Latin American Revolution* (New York: Monthly Review, 1968), where the principals mostly attack Debray's vade-mecum, *Revolution in the Revolution?* (New York: Monthly Review, 1967). For critiques of the *foco* theory by those intimately involved in the promotion or analysis of a particular revolutionary struggle, the sources noted above for Guatemala are excellent.

8. For patient, underground preparation in these various cases, see George Black, *Triumph of the People: The Sandinista Revolution in Nicaragua* (London: Zed, 1981), pp. 82–86; Mario Payeras, "Days of the Jungle: The Testimony of a Guatemalan Guerrillero, 1972–1976," *Monthly Review* 35, no. 3 (July–August 1983), reports the years of the EGP's (Guerrilla Army of the Poor) silent organizing, and was also published as a book; for ORPA (the Organization of the People in Arms), which underwent a very similar and simultaneous experience organizing near Lake Atitlán, see their own report, "Eight Years of Silent Organizing," in *Guatemala in Rebellion: Unfinished History*, eds., Jonathan L. Fried, Marvin E. Gettleman, Deborah T. Levenson, and Nancy Peckenham (New York: Grove,

1983), pp. 269–72; David Scott Palmer, "Rebellion in Rural Peru: The Origins and Evolution of Sendero Luminoso," *Comparative Politics* 18, no. 2 (January 1986), pp. 127–46.

9. See Timothy P. Wickham-Crowley, *Guerrillas and Revolution in Latin America* (Princeton, N.J.: Princeton University Press, forthcoming 1991), ch. 12.

10. The first major statement clearly outlining the main principles of resource mobilization theory was John D. McCarthy and Mayer N. Zald, "Resource Mobilization and Social Movements: A Partial Theory," *American Journal of Sociology* 82, no. 6 (May 1977), pp. 1212–41; that, and the other core essays of RM theory's founders, have now been conveniently collected in Mayer N. Zald and John D. McCarthy, *Social Movements in an Organizational Society: Collected Essays* (New Brunswick, N.J.: Transaction, 1987).

11. See William Gamson's introduction to (and quotation in) Zald and Mc Carthy, *Social Movements*, p. 4; at the 1989 meetings of the Eastern Sociological Society in Baltimore (17–19 March), William Gamson chaired a workshop-session on "The Peace Movement: Current Dilemmas and Opportunities." The women's, peace, and antinuclear movements seem to provide especially attractive activist venues for such theorists.

12. Talcott Parsons, *The Structure of Social Action*, 2 volumes (New York: The Free Press, 1968 [1937]), in particular his "model" for behavior embodied in the "unit act," vol. 2, pp. 727–43; Jeffrey C. Alexander, *Theoretical Logic in Sociology*, 4 volumes (Berkeley: University of California Press, 1980–83). In volume 2, Alexander argues that both Marx and Durkheim failed to move beyond theorizing that implied structural or cultural determination of social action; in volume 3, he argues that Weber failed in his attempt to synthesize the notions of structure and action, as did Parsons (volume 4), who came closest to success in integrating the two.

13. See McCarthy and Zald, "Resource Mobilization and Social Movements," pp. 1227–31, on federated and isolated structures among the constituencies; also see Roberta Ash Garner and Mayer Zald's discussion of "systemic constraints" on social movement sectors, in Zald and McCarthy, *Social Movements*, pp. 298–301. In the two key RM–theory pieces in which minor theoretical attention is given to the characteristics of the *populace*, there are two unusual features: one is a very early piece (the appendix to *Social Movements*, published in the early 1970s) where "grievances" are grudgingly conceded some role (p. 370); the other is coauthored by Roberta Ash Garner, who seems inclined to give such features their due. Much greater and systematic attention to the nature of the populace being mobilized can be found in a precursor to RM theory, Anthony Oberschall's *Social Conflict and Social Movements* (Englewood Cliffs, N.J.: Prentice-Hall, 1973), esp. ch. 4. Oberschall's many and sharp propositions about more- and less-mobilizable populations for some reason have not found their way into the core of RM theory, despite an elective affinity between the two viewpoints (here I rely on Zald and McCarthy's *Social Movements* as a guide to what is or is not in the RM theory of the late 1980s). The term "gloss" seems well advised, for there *is* an early (1977), one-paragraph reference to Oberschall's work which RM theory apparently never further developed; cf. McCarthy and Zald, "Resource Mobilization," p. 1237. As for Vladimir Lenin, we have a guide to Lenin's practical concerns in the classic study by Leonard Schapiro, *The Com-*

munist Party of the Soviet Union, 2d ed., revised and enlarged (New York: Vintage Books, 1971), part 1. Schapiro's narrative strongly suggests that Lenin's concerns focused far more on intraparty and interparty conflicts with fellow revolutionaries than on the nature of the Russian working class whose vanguard the Russian Social Democrats (later split into the Bolsheviks and the Mensheviks) claimed to be.

14. One offense meriting the death penalty in Fidel Castro's guerrilla army was "insubordination," while Castro himself always stressed that leadership was the crucial variable in the struggle.

15. For a focus on the "professionalization" of American social movements, see Zald and McCarthy, *Social Movements*, Appendix.

16. Schapiro, *The Communist Party of the Soviet Union*, pp. 148–49. See also his opposition to a loose federation of revolutionary parties, as distinct from a single centralized party; ibid., p. 151.

17. Alvin Gouldner, *The Future of Intellectuals and the Rise of the New Class* (New York: Continuum, 1979), pp. 53–73; I have confirmed the predominance of university-educated intellectuals in the leadership of Latin American guerrilla movements in *Guerrillas and Revolution in Latin America*, chs. 2 and 9; the one major (yet not complete) exception is Colombia's guerrilla movements, which were mostly rooted in the peasant violence of the 1950s, and hence often led by men from rural, lower-class backgrounds.

18. David Hackett Fischer, *Historians' Fallacies: Toward a Logic of Historical Thought* (New York: Harper and Row, 1970), pp. 31–32.

19. Once again, for two such ad hoc treatments see Zald and McCarthy, *Social Movements*, pp. 298–301, 370. For Lenin in 1917, there were two main concerns expressed about the state of the masses: (1) for the peasantry, the Bolsheviks were willing, alone among the contending groups, to recognize the ongoing land seizures that were bringing revolution to the countryside; (2) as to the urban soviets, Lenin was only willing to propose "all power to the Soviets" once those workers' councils had moved out of the Menshevik and Socialist Revolutionaries' camps, and largely into the Bolshevik fold; only then would Lenin be willing to sponsor a workers' uprising; cf. Schapiro, *The Communist Party of the Soviet Union*, pp. 161–62, 165–66.

20. This useful phrase became the basis of a book, itself useful in debunking a host of misconceptions about the concerns and attitudes of the American public vis-à-vis their jobs, their society, and their government; cf. Richard F. Hamilton and James D. Wright, *The State of the Masses* (Hawthorne, N.Y.: Aldine, 1986).

21. Ralph H. Turner and Lewis M. Killian, *Collective Behavior*, 2d ed. (Englewood Cliffs, N.J.: Prentice-Hall, 1972), take a broadly symbolic interactionist view, emphasizing the emergence of new meanings in understanding the origins of collective behavior; the views of Herbert Blumer, widely considered to be the "founder" of symbolic interactionism, are concisely set out in his "Elementary Collective Groupings" in *Collective Behavior and Social Movements*, ed. Louis E. Genevie (Itasca, Ill.: F. E. Peacock, 1978), pp. 67–87; Neil J. Smelser, *Theory of Collective Behavior* (New York: The Free Press, 1962), whose principles I outline below. The relative deprivation of the masses is the key variable in James C. Davies, "Toward a Theory of Revolution," *American Sociological Review* 27, no. 1 (February 1962), pp. 5–19, and, in its most complete defense, in Ted Robert

Gurr, *Why Men Rebel* (Princeton, N.J.: Princeton University Press, 1970). Charles Tilly provides a quasi-Marxist interpretation of collective resistance, one emphasizing the givens of class conflict and class resistance, plus the contingents of organization and repression, in *From Mobilization to Revolution* (Reading, Mass.: Addison-Wesley, 1978).

22. See especially Zald and McCarthy, *Social Movements*, ch. 7.

23. For the formation of the FMLN in El Salvador, see Robert S. Leiken, "The Salvadoran Left," in his *Central America: Anatomy of Conflict* (New York: Pergamon, 1984), pp. 111–30; for the unification document forming the Guatemalan National Revolutionary Unity (URNG), see Fried et al., *Guatemala in Rebellion*, pp. 269–72; for close parallels between those two unification statements, see Daniel Camacho and Rafael Menjívar, "De lo corporativo a lo político: Proyectos alternativos, Guatemala y El Salvador," in their *Movimientos populares en Centroamérica* (San José, Costa Rica: Editorial Universitaria Centroamericana, 1985), pp. 38–41; for references to the recently created Colombian guerrilla umbrella group, the Simón Bolívar Guerrilla Coordinator, see *Proceso* (Mexico City) 639 (30 January 1989), pp. 40–43.

24. In now well-known events, ERP (Popular Revolutionary Army) member Roque Dalton and an ally were executed by Joaquín Villalobos in 1975 for supposedly being both CIA and Cuban agents(!); those executions led to a split in the ERP, and the formation of the Armed Forces of National Resistance (FARN), whose leader Ernesto Jovel later died mysteriously while the two groups were still bitter rivals. Mélida Anaya Montes (Comandante Ana María) was killed in a vicious ice-pick murder in early 1983 while involved in attempts to set up and consolidate the FMLN's peace talks with the Salvadoran government; her killers were followers of the most important Salvadoran revolutionary leader, Salvador Cayetano Carpio (head of the FPL—Popular Forces of Liberation), who then guiltily committed suicide, perhaps under Nicaraguan pressure. For the first two events, see Gabriel Zaid, "Enemy Colleagues: A Reading of the Salvadoran Tragedy," *Dissent* (Winter 1982), pp. 17–19, 24–26; on Ana María's death and Carpio's suicide, see Leiken, "The Salvadoran Left," pp. 122–23.

25. Robin M. Williams, Jr., *American Society: A Sociological Interpretation*, 3d ed. (New York: Alfred A. Knopf, 1970), pp. 523–33.

26. McCarthy and Zald, "Resource Mobilization and Social Movements."

27. I have been told this in a private communication from my good colleague Sam Marullo, who has worked fruitfully from the RM perspective in the study of peace action movements in the United States.

28. Tilly, *From Mobilization to Revolution*, ch. 4.

29. Zald and McCarthy, *Social Movements*, pp. 337–38.

30. See my "Winners, Losers, and Also-Rans," pp. 146–55, or my *Guerrillas and Revolution*, chs. 6, 7, and 10.

31. Smelser, *Theory of Collective Behavior*, passim. In particular, critics have regularly zeroed in on Smelser's assertion that generalized beliefs constitute "short-circuited" views of social reality, and are "akin to magical beliefs"; cf. ibid., pp. 8, 82; for those who wish to annihilate a theory rather than to preserve its useful elements, the dubious nature of those assertions, especially when applied to reformist social movements (as opposed to, say, witch crazes), have been sufficient grounds for relegating Smelser's model to the trash heap of sociological

history. Why not simply alter Smelser's assumption by noting that *some* generalized beliefs may be "magical" while others may be reasonable, and see how the altered theory holds up? My view: while I am appalled by the turgid language in which the model is presented, along with some truly intimidating summary tables, and while I concede that the model is not a series of linked propositions whose concepts are clearly measurable (*strain* is particularly tricky), Smelser's model yet retains much to recommend it, mainly in its sheer comprehensiveness. No other general model of collective action, save for Charles Tilly's *From Mobilization to Revolution*, even comes close to recognizing the complexity of forces that lie behind the origins of social movements; and only Smelser's model even attempts to use that *same* model to predict collective behavior more generally—crazes, panics, and hostile outbursts—and not just organized social movement activity. Perhaps his goal of a general theory of collective behavior is a hopeless one, but who else has done better?

32. Smelser, *Theory of Collective Behavior*, pp. 15, 133–40, 175–76, 227–41, 278–87, 325.

33. Ten thousand is the figure commonly given for the number of combatants in the Salvadoran guerrilla movement by about 1983–84; the other major movements since 1975, in Colombia, Guatemala, Nicaragua, and Peru, also all fielded at least 2,000 combatants each, with Colombian revolutionaries perhaps reaching 7,000. The majority of combatants in all five cases, except perhaps for Nicaragua, were peasants. None of those totals includes other types of civilian supporters of the revolutionaries.

34. On the Mexican peasantry, the best guide remains a superb one, John Womack, Jr., *Zapata and the Mexican Revolution* (New York: Vintage Books, 1968); on the Russian peasantry, see Theda Skocpol, *States and Social Revolutions* (Cambridge, England: Cambridge University Press, 1979), pp. 128–40, and Eric R. Wolf, *Peasant Wars of the Twentieth Century* (New York: Harper and Row, 1969), ch. 2 (and ch. 1 on Mexico); on the elite-independence of French peasant uprisings, see Skocpol, *States*, pp. 118–28, who also notes how the character of French village life eventually put the brakes on the radicalism of those uprisings as well; in the latter respect, she echoes the conclusions of her former teacher, Barrington Moore, Jr., *Social Origins of Dictatorship and Democracy* (Boston: Beacon, 1966), pp. 70–92, 108–10, where he also argues that the historical situation increasingly tended to pit urban radicals against newly landed middling peasants, whose conservatism eventually doused rural France's revolutionary fires.

35. Wolf, *Peasant Wars*, Conclusions, esp. p. 290.

36. For a good guide to the revolutionary peasantry debate, see Theda Skocpol, "What Makes Peasants Revolutionary?" *Comparative Politics* 14, no. 2 (April 1982), pp. 351–75; Wolf discusses the peasants' utopia in *Peasant Wars*, pp. 294–95.

37. For two important, yet different, studies of such movements see Norman Cohn's classic on medieval Europe, *The Pursuit of the Millennium* (New York: Harper & Brothers, 1961); and Bernard Barber's brief but instructive comparative study of regions that did and did not experience the Ghost Dance and the peyote cult in the American Indian West, "Acculturation and Messianic Movements," pp. 382–85 in Turner and Killian, *Collective Behavior;* it was published earlier in

American Sociological Review 6 (October 1941), pp. 663–69.

38. On Lara, see Gall, "Teodoro Petkoff I," p. 13; Luigi Valsalice, *Guerriglia e Politica: L'esempio del Venezuela* (Florence, Italy: Valmartina Editore, 1973), p. 131; and V. L., "Venezuelan National Hero," *World Marxist Review* (England) 8 (May 1965), pp. 58–59. For an autobiographical account of one Communist's guerrilla organizing experience there, see Angela Zago, *Aquí no ha pasado nada* (Caracas: El Sobre, 1972). For a detailed and thorough theoretical and empirical guide to the political importance of cross-class, patron-client relationships and alliances, as opposed to class-conflictual relationships, see *Friends, Followers, and Factions: A Reader in Political Clientelism*, eds. Steffen W. Schmidt, Laura Guasti, Carl H. Landé, and James C. Scott (Berkeley: University of California Press, 1977).

39. Santiago Ruiz, "La modernización agrícola en El Salvador," *ECA* (Estudios Centroamericanos) 31 (April 1976), p. 156; Robert G. Williams, *Export Agriculture and the Crisis in Central America* (Chapel Hill: University of North Carolina Press, 1986), pp. 63, 218 n. 39; Jeffery Paige, *Agrarian Revolution: Export Agriculture and Social Movements in the Underdeveloped World* (New York: The Free Press, 1975), chs. 1–2, 4. In addition, see Paige's theoretical treatment of the Guatemalan insurgency, which he also links to that nation's migratory labor population, in his "Social Theory and Peasant Revolution in Vietnam and Guatemala," *Theory and Society* 12, no. 6 (November 1983), pp. 699–737.

40. Wickham-Crowley, "Winners, Losers, and Also-Rans," pp. 154–55.

41. McCarthy and Zald, "Resource Mobilization," pp. 1221–23.

42. Mancur Olson, *The Logic of Collective Action: Public Goods and the Theory of Groups* (Cambridge, Mass.: Harvard University Press, 1971).

43. The most important applications of the "selective-benefit" model to understand the radical behavior of peasants are Joel S. Migdal, *Peasants, Politics, and Revolution: Pressures toward Political and Social Change in the Third World* (Princeton, N.J.: Princeton University Press, 1974); and Samuel Popkin, *The Rational Peasant: The Political Economy of Rural Society in Vietnam* (Berkeley: University of California Press, 1979), ch. 6. For an acute and, I think, decisive critique of the applicability of Olson's model to the study of revolutions, see Barbara Salert, *Revolutions and Revolutionaries: Four Theories* (New York: Elsevier, 1976), chs. 2, 6.

44. Wickham-Crowley, *Guerrillas and Revolution in Latin America*, chapters 4, 12.

45. Olson's theory leads to slightly different predictions for small groups than for large ones, in good part because in a small group one's *own* participation might clearly be perceived as decisive in achieving the group's goals, quite unlike the nature of large-group activity; cf. Olson, *Logic of Collective Action*, pp. 22–36, 53–65.

46. Concerned Guatemala Scholars, *Guatemala*, pp. 42, 44, 54; on the hermetic history of Indian communities, dating back to their seventeenth-century "reconstitution" after a century of contact with Europeans, see ibid., p. 51, but especially Murdo J. MacLeod, *Spanish Central America: A Socioeconomic History, 1520–1720* (Berkeley: University of California Press, 1973), pp. 326–28.

47. On this issue, a far better guide to the psychology of rebellion is Barring-

ton Moore, Jr., *Injustice: The Social Bases of Obedience and Revolt* (White Plains, N.Y.: M. E. Sharpe, 1978).

48. For my already published arguments and evidence along these lines, see my "Winners, Losers, and Also-Rans," pp. 155–60, and *Guerrillas and Revolution in Latin America*, ch. 7, part 2, and ch. 10, part 4.

49. Giddens's general, developing perspective on social theory is conveniently summarized in Jonathan H. Turner, *The Structure of Sociological Theory*, 4th ed. (Chicago: The Dorsey Press, 1986), ch. 22, esp. p. 460; this useful summary partially obviates the need to consult Giddens's ongoing development of ideas on this topic, embedded in about one new book every year or two. For one good source, see his *Central Problems in Social Theory: Action, Structure and Contradiction in Social Analysis* (Berkeley: University of California Press, 1979), ch. 2.

2

The Rise and Sometimes Fall
of Guerrilla Governments in
Latin America

In his history of the Russian revolution, Trotsky wrote of situations of "dual power," where a substantial portion of the populace comes to treat a challenger for power as their sovereign and new legitimate government, simultaneously denying such legitimacy to the previous incumbent. Charles Tilly has updated and systematized Trotsky's views in his discussion of "multiple sovereignty," and the virtual identity in many cases between such a phenomenon and the revolutionary situation itself.[1] Yet the process through which such multiple authority and loyalty shifts emerge continues to be a murky one in writings about revolutions and their outcomes.

This chapter aims to contribute to our knowledge of how one government comes to succeed another in revolutionary situations, with special reference to the guerrilla movements which pervaded Latin American politics from the Cuban revolution until the late 1960s, and which are currently experiencing a revival. While the discussion is mostly confined to the earlier period, my ongoing research suggests that the principles elaborated in studies of the earlier period apply as well to the 1970s and 1980s.

Understanding Governors and Governed

When we ask, "Where do governments come from?" we enter the controversial historical area of the origins of the state.[2] Although there is no widely accepted explanation of those origins, the very posing of this question raises important issues about the nature of the social *processes* involved in acts of governance and acts of obedience to the directives of rulers. By posing the question in such terms we can perhaps avoid irresolvable and tedious debate.

At least since Socrates and Thrasymachus disagreed over the nature of the actions of rulers, social commentators have argued whether those who govern do so as representatives of the *consensus* of the governed, or whether governors rule as *coercive* agents, enforcing some narrower self or group interest upon an unwilling subject populace.[3] In these polar views, governments come into being in two rather different ways, the first through the establishment of some kind of "general will" made incarnate in government, the second through a seizure of power or coercive exercise thereof. This debate has come down to us in scarcely altered form in the modern, yet now-classic debate between Parsons and Mills over the nature of political power. Parsons saw power as a nonzero-sum medium of interchange in any social system, one used to achieve the collectively agreed-upon goals of society.[4] Mills, in contrast, saw power rather more in zero-sum terms, as a resource used by some persons or groups against others, even though the power-holders might do so in the name of the common-weal.[5] More generally, those hard-to-find functionalists supposedly have viewed the polity, and society itself, as based on some form of consensual process.[6] Classical Marxists, in contrast, view the state as an instrument to batter the masses into submission, either by outright coercion or through the establishment of a "false consensus" within society. The latter version, usually associated with the writings of Gramsci, sees consensus-making processes roughly as brainwashing writ large.[7]

It has been clear for some time now that these polar viewpoints do little to explicate the relations between rulers and ruled. No social scientist, to my knowledge, views the state or government as a simple projection of societal consensus, although it may be a view of democracy bruited about in high school civics classes. Perhaps the perspective closest to that view is pluralism, whose proponents emphasize the variety of groups that influence and benefit from actual decision-making patterns.[8] A not dissimilar view contrasts polyarchy—with multiple social groups contending for power and influence—with situations of more unitary political control.[9]

Marxism has fared no better, however. As one author noted, we can no longer speak of *the* Marxist theory of the state, and to continue to believe in it is to "live in cloud cuckooland."[10] To paraphrase Ché Guevara, we now confront two, three, many Marxist views of the state.[11] Most Marxist writers have abandoned the view of the state as a coercive "instrument" firmly in hands of the "executive committee" of the bourgeoisie. An alternative theory, emphasizing *ideological* coercion, has proven more appealing to latter-day Marxists faced with the acquiescence of the masses to capitalist welfare-state democracies in "The West." This newer view instead emphasizes the false consciousness of the masses (but not of the Marxists, unsurprisingly). Yet this view, too, has been subjected to severe theoretical and empirical critiques.[12]

Given this undisciplined state of affairs, and our desire to understand better the nature of government authority, perhaps we should shift our focus from the static concepts of coercion and consensus to another elemental social process, that of *exchange*. By focusing on the relations between governors and governed as a process of exchange, we can break out of this now-sterile consensus-conflict debate. A focus on exchange processes can help us to understand two vital distinctions, which are closely related: (1) governance by consensus vs. governance by coercion, which I treat as polar types of a continuum; and (2) legitimate vs. illegitimate authority.

A useful starting point is the discussion of authority and resistance in Barrington Moore's *Injustice*.[13] Authority, in his rendering, encompasses not only the relationships between formal government organizations/office-holders and the subject population, but also other, more informal situations of authority such as lord-peasant and patron-client relationships historically common in many world regions. Thus, James Scott has identified such informal "governance" relations throughout Southeast Asia in this century and before, while Perry Anderson has written of the weakness of the central state and the consequent "parcellized sovereignty" characteristic of Western feudalism.[14] In such instances, the absence of a state apparatus in direct contact with a subject populace does not, therefore, imply the absence of "government" in Moore's sense or mine. Instead, we can discern a continuum. At one end, the state can confront the citizenry directly as taxer and governor, with a weak or absent landed upper class, as in Wittfogel's hydraulic societies or most modern societies.[15] In the middle of the continuum is a mixed type, in which a landed upper class competes with the state for extraction from the peasantry, as in Skocpol's agrarian bureaucracies.[16] Last we encounter the cases discussed by Scott and Anderson, where the formal state is relatively weak, and the landed elite governs the countryside more or less autonomously.

Can we speak of these informal landlords/patrons, and not just the formal state, as "government" or "authority" in any meaningful sense? If so, can we additionally speak of an "exchange"—asymmetrical though it may be—between the upper class and the underlying population in such situations? It is certainly extreme to speak of the feudal lord-serf relationship as a symmetrical contract which either party could theoretically break off.[17] No scholar seriously questions the asymmetry of power in lord-serf, patron-client, or chief-follower relationships.[18] While some have seriously questioned whether one can speak of any "exchange" element in the case of landlord-dominated rural areas (notably Brenner), Barrington Moore has discerned at times distinctive elements of mutual obligation, with the landed upper class often providing some security and protection to the peasantry.[19] Where those protective, paternalistic elements were weak or absent, peasant rebellion was more common, as in China and Russia.

A fortiori, those exchange elements of mutual obligation were clearly evident in the patron-client relations discussed by Scott and Kerkvliet, and by many theorists of patron-client politics.[20] Therefore, for both formal and informal "governments" we encounter structurally similar phenomena: an asymmetrical exchange relationship between an upper class and an underlying population involving the exercise of authority by the former over the latter.

The common denominator in such affairs is that an upper class extracts a surplus from the underlying population and, in Moore's felicitous phrase, turns it into culture: the art, architecture, literature, and other forms of culture produced by "leisure classes" in history. Extending a discussion from his earlier work, Moore in effect suggests an exchange view of legitimate authority, which is based on an unstable and varying combination of coercion *and* exchange.[21] He further implies that "predatory authority" is based largely on coercion, while "rational authority" embodies a much larger element of popular consent, which arises from exchange processes. (Most notably, Marxist anthropologist Maurice Godelier has arrived at an almost identical view of the *origins* of the state.)[22]

In the course of ironing out such surplus-extracting relations, an *implicit social contract* emerges between the authorities and the underlying population. Where that contract is still intact, we may speak of legitimate authority; where the authorities are failing to keep their side of the bargain, yet still exercise power, we may speak of predatory or illegitimate authority.

Casting a wide net over world history, Moore argues that certain features occur over and over in that basic social contract.[23] The obligations of the authorities are as follows: (1) defense of the populace, especially against foreign enemies; (2) maintenance of internal peace and order, including protection from bandits and the resolution of civil disputes and strife; and (3) contributions to the material security of the populace (''prosperity'' is too strong a word here). In return for such actions, the populace is expected to contribute part of the surplus to the maintenance of the ruling authorities, to render obedience to appropriate directives, and to contribute to the defense of the ''nation'' in times of external attacks, especially through military service.

Violations of the social contract can and do occur. For our purposes we will focus on those that the authorities commit. Their failure to fulfill any of the three obligations would constitute a violation of this implicit social contract: e.g., allowing foreign armies or bandits to loot the countryside, or excessive taxation/extraction so as to make the people groan under its weight. An especially severe violation is the use of police or military forces *against* the civilian populace, rather than against foreign or domestic enemies of society.

What might people do in case of such violations? For most of history, they have simply had to endure the excesses of authority-turned-predator, since they lacked the resources to fight back. Perhaps their sense of injustice might find an escape valve in popular culture, in songs, tales, poetry, popular theater, and folklore that expressed veiled moral condemnation of the established authorities. In Southeast Asia, as well as among black Americans under slavery and Jim Crow laws, such cultural patterns appeared under conditions experienced as oppressive.[24] At other times, under certain conditions, people might instead rebel, in the course of which new authorities might emerge, creating Trotsky's aptly named ''dual power.''[25]

Five Propositions

I wish to suggest the following propositions, based in part on discussions by Moore and others.[26] I will elaborate each of them in fuller detail in the remainder of this chapter.

1. The greater the failure of governors (landlords/central govern-ment) to fulfill the social contract—and a fortiori severe violations of the contract—the greater the chance they will be converted into preda-tory authorities in the eyes of the populace.

2. The more extreme the decline or absence of legitimate authority in a region, the more the populace becomes "virgin territory" for those who would become a "counter-state" or alternative government. *Corollary:* The more legitimate authority persists in a region, the more likely the populace will reject the claims of the challengers.

3. The counter-state of a region establishes itself through exchange processes, in effect establishing a new "social contract" with the pop-ulace. (Rejected propositions: that legitimate authority arises largely through ideological conversion or through sheer coercion.)

4. New authority is constructed and maintained by providing the three classic contributions of government: defense of the populace; maintenance of internal peace and order (the police and administrative functions); and contributions to material security (the welfare func-tion). The more such services are provided, the more solidly new au-thority will root itself in the region.

5. Once established, the counter-state becomes subject to the social-contractual obligations of all governments. The greater the failure to fulfill those obligations, or the greater the active violation thereof, the greater the chance that the new rulers, too, will be viewed as predatory authorities.

Propositions 1 and 2: The Decay of Traditional Authority

Latin America since independence has had a pattern of centralized state authority, to be sure.[27] Yet such state authority has only weakly reached into the countryside, strikingly so in nations such as Colom-bia.[28] Classic descriptions of the Latin American countryside described the prevailing pattern as one of "feudalism," in which the landed elites became de facto the law on their rural estates. To the extent that cultivators experienced government in any form then, it was in the person of the *hacendado*, who often would even dominate local formal politics, assuming local positions of political power, where they ex-isted. Formal agencies of law enforcement, like the police and rural guard, would commonly be under landlord control or influence. Latin American evidence from Mexico to Chile, and from the seventeenth to the twentieth centuries, displays this recurring pattern.[29] Thus the Latin American pattern has fitted closely Anderson's image of a landed elite governing the countryside in the absence of stable, federal authority.

Apart from its coercive core, the classic hacienda often had elements of the paternal in the relationship between landlord/patron and peasant/client, a diffuse system of reciprocity in which landlord governance entailed certain social obligations, such as godfathering of peasants' children and other protective activities.[30] James Scott in particular has studied the breakdown of such reciprocal patron-client relations in rural areas under the impact of modern market forces, elaborating ideas which appeared in less systematic form in earlier work by Tilly and Wolf.[31] His description of those earlier patron-client relations shows clearly that the relation was not just economic, but also political. Other writers have summarized a vast literature showing that these relationships between patrons and clients are fundamentally political both in content and in consequence.[32] Scott and Kerkvliet argue that when the reciprocal element in the patron-client relationship weakens, so too does the claim to authority.[33] The consequent rejection of traditional landlord authority can easily broaden from the local landlords to the central government, whose taxation efforts can also cut into the peasants' subsistence minimum. Scott argues that both of these authority-rejecting situations arise in response to the "intrusion" of world market forces into areas previously shielded from the market.

The implications of his argument for Latin America are notable, for that region has participated for centuries in the world market, and we would have expected it to exhibit in strong form the "solvent" effect of the market on traditional patterns of reciprocity. That is, we would expect to find few areas where the traditional hacienda and reciprocal patron-client relations between landlord and peasant still remain. Where those relations do remain, they serve as a "protective wall" against revolutionary change.[34] Where, however, such reciprocity has broken down—as it did increasingly in the Southeast Asian cases Scott and Kerkvliet studied—we would expect to find a peasantry increasingly rejecting the claims of various authorities to "rights" to peasant surpluses, and ever more willing to shift their loyalties to a new sovereign, one willing to fulfill the "contractual obligations" of governments, the obligations which still-powerful yet illegitimate authorities—the landlord and the state—no longer perform.[35] Evidence suggests that just such a breakdown of traditional, paternalistic authority has become extreme in the Guatemalan highlands since the 1960s, in the very regions where guerrillas rooted themselves in the 1970s and 1980s.[36]

The most casual examination of the existing literature on landlord-peasant and government-peasant relations in Latin America reveals that government obligations—such as the defense and police functions—are regularly absent or even turned against poor cultivators.[37] Alliances between landlords and the local police or the "rural guard," as well as landlord control of the regional judiciary, are often used against the peasantry for land-grabs, criminal violence, and suppression of basic human and labor rights. We need not search far for examples. In 1956 and 1957, Cuba's Batista employed systematic police violence in Santiago and army attacks on peasant squatters, so that his legitimacy throughout Oriente Province was largely destroyed by 1958; at the same time, Fidel Castro's following there grew sharply.[38] In Nicaragua, Somoza's appointed *jueces de mesta* (the local constabulary) were involved in a variety of assaults on peasants and their lands in the mountainous interior for some time, and those areas later harbored the FSLN guerrillas in the 1970s.[39] A more common pattern was the simple land-grab. For various periods of time peasants were evicted or systematically uprooted from their lands in Cuba, Colombia, El Salvador, and Guatemala by legal decision, government decree, land-title sales, landlord violence, military action, or some combination thereof. Each of these instances was followed by a period in which guerrillas rooted themselves in those same regions among the peasantry.[40] Direct landlord attacks on individual peasants preceded partial guerrilla successes in Peru's Ayacucho department in 1965.[41] All of these are but examples of sustained, long-term processes by which hacienda lands have encroached upon and uprooted peasant villages and villagers.[42]

Many other examples could illustrate the basic point: in a rural milieu where power is exercised increasingly on a basis of pure coercion (predatory authority) rather than on an implicit exchange between the peasantry and the formal or informal authorities, an armed social group claiming to be an alternative authority or counter-state is apt to find a responsive audience.

If peasants alienated from various authorities are prime candidates for revolution, those still embedded in effective networks of patron-client reciprocity are less likely to respond to radical appeals. We can specify three different situations that work against the interests of radical mobilizers. First is the traditional hacienda, with strong patron-client ties, which acts as shield against revolution.[43] Second is the case of reform parties rooted in the countryside, whose promises and programs of land reform (and hence betterment of the social contract) have generated more or less widespread peasant support for *non*revolutionaries—sometimes in power—in Venezuela 1958–68, in Peru in the mid-1960s, and in Bolivia from 1952 until about 1970, including 1967, the critical year for Ché Guevara's guerrilla *foco* there.[44] Finally, civic action programs carried out by the army in rural areas, including medical checkups, school-building, well-drilling, and literacy campaigns, can be understood as government attempts to repair the violated social contract by increasing the third element thereof: contributions to material security.[45]

Each of these counter-instances, where the social contract is intact or promises to be repaired, has been associated with peasant indifference, resistance, and even hostility to the appeals of guerrilla protogovernments. In Venezuela, Bolivia, and Peru the guerrillas ultimately failed in the countryside because the incumbent government had more peasant support than did the guerrillas, extensive though the latter may have been in Venezuela. In Colombia, extensive civic action programs in the 1960s apparently succeeded in reducing guerrilla influence in some regions.[46] In Peru's 1965 counterinsurgency campaign, civic action apparently won the Campa Indians over to the army and away from the guerrillas they had previously supported, while similar events occurred in Guatemala in 1966–67, where the peasantry also turned in part against the guerrillas.[47] In Bolivia, civic action led by Colonel René Barrientos had been routine for the armed forces since the early 1960s, and he thereby secured a mass peasant following that later supported him as president when faced with Guevara's insurgency.[48]

Propositions 3 and 4: The Rise of Guerrilla Government

Given the decay or absence of legitimate authority in a region when guerrillas arrive, we would expect them to encounter a peasantry receptive to their aims. Guerrilla government, properly speaking, usually begins as the military responds with greater or lesser terror against the region. That terror usually encompasses the surrounding peasantry, whether or not they individually support the guerrillas, thus producing an especially severe violation of the social contract: the use of the defense and police forces against the very citizens they are supposed to defend. As in the case of Colombia, this straw may break the camel's back, turning the peasantry decisively against the government.[49]

Guerrillas consolidate their authority over the peasantry as they begin to provide the full array of social contract "services" to the local populace: defense, police/administration, and welfare. The first two functions are crucial in generating guerrilla *government*. For guerrillas to control a locale they must control the means of violence, a fundamental prerequisite of government. (Of course their authority has some moral or exchange basis; without their weaponry, however, they would just be nosy social workers.) Hence, even at its beginnings, rational guerrilla authority displays that distinctive mix of coercion and exchange which is the hallmark of government. Their perceived "goodness" combined with their perceived "strength" generates legitimate authority.

As Robert Merton has argued, one should first establish the existence of a social phenomenon before one seeks to explain it. Otherwise one may elegantly account for pseudo-facts in ad hoc fashion. In the present case, however, there is indeed massive evidence—for Cuba, Venezuela, Colombia, and Guatemala before 1970; perhaps in isolated cases in Peru; and fragmentary evidence for the post-1970 movements—that people came to perceive rural guerrilla movements as legitimate, governing authority in certain regions. Guerrillas did not usually announce themselves as the new regional authorities, yet in the literature we almost inevitably encounter the words "government" and "authority" to describe their presence, regardless of the ideology of the chroniclers.[50] Such a recurrent, largely invariant pattern suggests that we have tapped into a cultural regularity, a fundamental definition of "government." Indeed, there is striking evidence that peasants continued to recognize that they were the subjects of not one, but two authorities—a situation of dual power—and this situation was repeated in the 1970s and 1980s in Nicaragua, El Salvador, Peru, and Guatemala. A Venezuelan peasant nicely summarized the situation, distinguishing the guerrillas' *gobierno de arriba*, or government up in the hills, from the normal government down in the towns, or *gobierno de abajo*.[51]

Why did peasants come to view the guerrillas as government? The obligations of the peasants to obey the new guerrilla authorities may well be generated by the benefactions that the insurgents bestow upon cultivators during their initial contacts.[52] The order in which the guerrillas come to fulfill the obligations of government is readily apparent. First are contributions to the material security of the peasantry, various actions which raise peasant incomes or improve their quality of life. Next to come are defense and police activities, as guerrillas both maintain internal security and protect the peasants against retaliation where they can. In this situation the two functions are difficult to distinguish, for the "enemies" from whom one needs protection may be "foreign" to the region, but are usually fellow countrymen. Finally we are apt to encounter the administrative functions of authority, as guerrillas begin to establish the mechanisms and organizations we usually associate with formal government: formal executive and judicial power, often in the form of village committees the guerrillas have organized.

Most notably, *demands* upon the peasantry—the other side of the exchange equation of the implicit social contract—are relatively muted until the later stages of guerrilla government consolidation. Hence the exchange is heavily weighted toward "bestowal of gifts" upon the peasantry in the earliest stages, a situation that is apt to lead to the creation of a power or authority relationship.[53] (Peasants have, however, commonly supplied food to insurgents, often without payment.) Typically, a few working rules suffice at the start, such as "Thou shalt not inform." Only later do we find active intervention in village affairs, attempts to maintain the guerrillas' version of peace and order. In advanced (and perhaps poor) guerrilla movements we may finally encounter compulsory forms of taxation, as in the case of the Filipino New People's Army, or the use of corvée labor by the Viet Cong and Chinese guerrillas. Therefore, as the guerrilla government grows and strengthens itself, we can observe the shifting of the exchange equation toward a reciprocal set of obligations, and the emergence of a more clearly defined set of interlocking rights and duties for both governors and governed.

Contributing to Material Welfare

When the insurgents first arrive, they often rapidly increase local peasant incomes by buying supplies from the locals at two or more times the going rates.[54] They may also employ villagers to carry goods or give money for an overnight stay, as Castro did in Cuba. As one Venezuelan peasant noted, "When the guerrillas were relatively unknown, a peasant could coexist with them, getting good prices for his corn and hens, though most of those cooperating did so for fear of being killed."[55] At times, both guerrillas and governments tried openly to bribe peasants into cooperation, the former into silence, as Ché did in Bolivia, the latter into informing.[56]

After establishing their presence in an area, the guerrillas begin to make further contributions to peasant welfare. Ché Guevara, who served as physician for the peasants of the Sierra Maestra in Cuba, was the model for guerrillas who carried a medical kit in one hand and a rifle in the other. Later in the conflict, medical care developed to where a full-fledged field hospital operated there, complete with X-ray machine, while in the nearby front run by Fidel's brother Raúl, a complete department of health had been organized, staffed with five physicians and a nurse. Even broader achievements marked the history of the other Cuban guerrilla group, the *Directorio Revolucionario* in the Sierra Escambray.[57] Guerrilla movements in other nations also delivered medical care, but without such extensive and expensive facilities. In Venezuela, guerrillas at least once set up a roadside clinic to treat peasants, and similar features marked the 1960s Guatemalan movement as well.[58] In more recent years the Salvadoran guerrilla forces have brought medical care to residents of their control zones as well.[59]

The literacy campaigns of postrevolutionary Cuba and Nicaragua attracted considerable attention and outside support, yet they were only the more visible, widespread expressions of guerrilla activities that began while the war was still in progress. New guerrilla recruits to Castro's M-26 went directly to school, where some peasants learned to read and write, and schools were also set up in the other two major guerrilla regions.[60] Elsewhere in Latin America, guerrillas time after time began to teach reading and writing to peasants in areas where they established any kind of permanent presence.[61] This pattern, too, has reappeared in the 1970s and 1980s guerrilla movements, notably in El Salvador.[62] Even the peripatetic Guatemalan insurgents of the 1960s would teach peasants a few letters of the alphabet during their brief stays in each village.[63]

Most importantly, guerrillas at times may have been able to answer a basic peasant wish: the desire for land. Promises of a land reform appear to have been the most crucial element in securing peasant support in a region. In contrast, the Cuzco region of Peru in 1965 and Bolivia in 1967 knew no such land hunger; the absence of this factor was probably decisive in producing those two revolutionary fiascoes: little or no peasant support, and the annihilation of the guerrillas. In two other regions of Peru, in contrast, the guerrillas briefly acquired land for land-poor peasants by chasing the landlords from the regions, and gained some support thereby. Guerrillas promised future land reforms—after victory—in Venezuela and Guatemala in the 1960s, and later in Nicaragua, El Salvador, Peru, and Guatemala. In several of the above instances they drove landlords from a region or executed them.[64] The evidence from Peru for both the 1960s movements and even for the more recent case of *Sendero Luminoso* (Shining Path)— despite the Andean regional land reforms of 1968–78—also confirms the importance of land in guerrilla appeals to the peasantry.[65] In Cuba, the contractual element in guerrilla offers of land came most clearly into the open. Fidel Castro struck a deal with squatter leader Crescencio Pérez before he began his guerrilla campaign in the Sierra: squatter support in exchange for, among other things, land titles to squatters after Castro won. In fact, Camilo Cienfuegos began land reforms *during* the rebels' final offensive in Las Villas Province. Castro promptly began the promised land reform upon coming to power in 1959.[66]

Defending the Region

Guerrillas gained popularity by eliminating those perceived by peasants as the "scourges" of a region: rapacious landlords, usurious middlemen, and bandits. Landlords and bandits in particular—the former where they had become "predatory authorities"—were special targets for execution, as in the Guatemalan guerrillas' execution of the "Tiger of Ixcán."[67] Yet many more cases confirm the guerrillas' general tendency to drive out the previous authorities and assume for themselves such a mantle.[68] Most notable in this respect have been Peru's *Sendero* and El Salvador's ERP (Revolutionary Army of the People), who have recently engaged in executing, exiling, or kidnapping mayors and other local office-holders, much as the Viet Cong did in the Vietnamese countryside around 1960.[69]

Where the central government responded to the guerrillas' presence or support in an area with armed force, that force was usually indiscriminate, almost always killing more peasants than guerrillas: in Cuba, in Peru 1965, in Venezuela, Colombia, and Guatemala in the 1960s, and in the Nicaraguan and later movements since 1970, where the body counts have become enormous. Guerrillas typically responded by trying to protect the populace, as government should. Armed defense of villages was common, as were plans for the evacuation of villagers on the approach of the military (used by the Guerrilla Army of the Poor in Guatemala); smuggling out of villagers through holes in a *cordon sanitaire*; digging of foxholes, use of caves and camouflage, and other protection against aerial bombardment; or careful instruction of villagers on dealing with questioning by army patrols (e.g., "Tell soldiers you gave food to people dressed in uniforms because you thought they were army personnel"). Guerrillas of course also regularly took offensive actions against army personnel in order to make them fear coming into a region, such as ambushes of army patrols, attacks on army barracks, and the planting of land mines on well-traveled paths into an area.[70]

A striking feature of these wars, which suggests the increasing legitimacy of guerrilla government with decreasing support for the incumbent authorities, is that guerrillas receive the most new recruits after two types of military events. The first type follows soldiers' attacks upon peasant villagers, after which those seeking revenge join the guerrilla units, rather clearly rejecting government claims to legitimacy. The second type of wave usually follows successful guerrilla engagements against the military, where the guerrillas display the ability to protect the peasantry from its enemies.[71]

Providing New Police and Administration

Guerrillas usually begin as the very informal, yet very real (i.e., armed) authority in the regions they control. They typically impose few rules at the start, save that of silence. Later they tend slowly to become more involved and intertwined in local activity, organizing local peasant committees for village administration or working through already existing ones, as the 1970s and 1980s Guatemalan insurgents have done. Gradually they further involve themselves in local political and social affairs.[72] Most striking, of course, is the aforementioned execution of the previous local officials. More typical are the kinds of events Zago describes for Lara State, Venezuela in the mid-1960s, where, as a *guerrillera*, she was put in charge of a zone. She chronicled the guerrillas' attempts to police the area, trying to inhibit local violence (like stabbings and machete fights), and to control excessive drinking, truancy among schoolchildren, and "sleeping around."[73] In the Sierra Escambray in Cuba and more recently in El Salvador, guerrillas attempted to move peasants toward cooperative forms of agriculture.[74] In these and other nations the guerrillas tried further to "remake" the social order in their attempts to eliminate male chauvinism in guerrilla and village affairs.[75]

Finally, guerrillas may begin to organize formal governments, true counter-states, to control activity in a region, moving beyond Guatemalan peasant committees to the forms seen in Raúl Castro's guerrilla front in Cuba by mid-1958. There he set up three major "directorates"—Personnel and Inspection, War, and Interdepartmental—each with several subdirectorates, and governing such diverse activities as mapping, inspection, police, justice, finance, sanitation, and education. At the same time, in Las Villas Province, the guerrillas actually carried out a census in the Sierra Escambray, looking very governmental indeed.[76]

Constructing Guerrilla Government?
Cuba and Bolivia as Cases

Even if the preceding patterns are clear, they fail to fulfill the readers' need for a narrative of success or failure in constructing guerrilla government. We have more information for the cases of Cuba and Bolivia than for any others, and the latter only because of Ché Guevara's Bolivian diaries. Before proceeding with these two opposing outcomes, I would stress that the Cuban example was *not* the only successful example of such construction. Not only in Nicaragua, as some might well infer, but also in Venezuela, Colombia, Guatemala, El Salvador, and Peru at various times, guerrillas have succeeded in establishing themselves as legitimate authority in certain regions of each nation. Their failure to extend this achievement to a successful, nation-wide revolution in most cases was due to *national* political variations. Therefore, consolidation of guerrilla government at the regional level depended fundamentally on regional conditions, and was no guarantee of national success. It apparently was a necessary but insufficient condition for a national revolution.[77]

What evidence do we have that the area in which Castro's guerrilla government formed was "ripe" for supporting a counter-state? The entire province of Oriente had a long history of rebellion, first against Spanish colonial rule, then against central government authority following independence in 1898. No other region of Cuba had a rebellious past remotely resembling the intensity of that in Oriente. In addition, within Oriente, rebellion historically had rooted itself in the very hills where Castro's guerrilla movement located itself.[78] Culturally, Oriente harbored a "Wild West" type of mentality that made it the center for lawlessness in Cuba, a focus of banditry, a haven for refugees from the law. Meneses describes *orientales* as "obsessed by injustice and neglect," viewing their province as a supplier of raw materials to Havana.[79] In fact, *orientales* were the poorest, least educated, and worst housed of all Cubans.[80]

Just prior to Castro's arrival, conditions for the squatter population had worsened. Eviction cases in the courts were increasing, and landlords were especially likely to win those cases in Oriente, where most of the Cuban squatters resided.[81] Squatters were in constant conflict not only with the local branch of the rural guard, but with the foremen who ran the Oriente estates, and that conflict may have had racial overtones, for the peasant population of Oriente was strongly Afro-Cuban, and "foreman" was the whitest of Cuban occupations. Not only were landlord eviction attempts threatening the very lifeblood of the squatter population, but Castro's arrival led indirectly to an acute crisis. Local landlords directed Batista's army troops toward local squatter leaders, further threatening their lives. Throughout Batista's army campaigns against Castro from late 1956 to late 1958, the typical victims of army action were peasants of the Sierra, often killed in the foothills during village sweeps that supposedly were directed against "guerrilla" strongholds. Army troops avoided firefights with the guerrillas, who suffered relatively few losses during the war.[82]

Under landlord pressure, the squatters had independently formed armed antieviction bands before Fidel Castro ever arrived in the Sierra. Crescencio Pérez was the premier leader of those squatters; he was said to be "lawyer, judge, sheriff, counsellor, and patriarch of the 50,000 *guajiros*."[83] Prior to Castro's "invasion" of Cuba in December 1956, and in exchange for the support of Pérez and his followers, Castro promised land titles to the squatters, agrarian reform, education and health measures for the entire nation, and an end to crimes and atrocities committed by the authorities against the populace.[84]

The joint pattern of a guerrilla promise of protection and welfare, plus the incumbent government's terror against the peasantry, created a new government in the Sierra. "As a consequence of this campaign of terror, the *precarista* leaders sealed their alliance with the Fidelista rebels."[85] After gaining the support of the squatters, the guerrillas steadily spread their authority to other areas and other peasants in the sierras of eastern Cuba.[86] Other highly reliable chroniclers of the revolution (who, like Barquín, are not revolutionary sycophants) report a similar process:

> The guerrillas became the real and effective authority to whom the peasants referred all problems . . . the Sierras' peasants were well aware that their survival and security depended mainly on whether they helped the guerrillas or not. . . . Since the regular troops viewed the Sierra peasants as an enemy from the very beginning, the rural population backed the guerrillas so that they could keep the regular army out of the small villages. Reprisals were applied by the guerrillas, as well as the army.[87]

Yet the guerrillas were able to give their executions a far more defensible cast than could the army. Such differentiated relations eventuated in the stabilization of guerrilla authority:

> Toward the end of the insurrection, the rural inhabitants of the Sierra Maestra looked upon Castro's men as representatives of the law—but a law that was far more just than the one they had known, which generally had been used against them.[88]

Guerrillas in that role provided defense against the Rural Guard Corps and banished middlemen from the region, whom peasants viewed as exploiters. The justice that the guerrillas applied was not blind, but favored peasants whenever there was any doubt. After the first few months, the application of "revolutionary justice" became a benefit to peasants, and the sincerity of the guerrillas created a new revolutionary mystique about them, as comparisons to the nineteenth-century heroes of the independence struggles came to abound.[89]

Thus was a new guerrilla government constructed in the hills of eastern Cuba. As I have suggested above, similar patterns have occurred elsewhere in Latin America in the last three decades, but we do not yet have sufficient detail to chronicle them in fine-grained case studies. We can, however, consider the most notable failure of them all: Ché Guevara's Bolivian *foco* of 1966–67, at the end of which Guevara was wounded, captured, and killed.

Why did the guerrillas fail in their attempt to generate new patterns of support and authority in eastern Bolivia, prefatory to making that nation the heartland of a continental revolution that would sweep all of South America? On the surface, Bolivia showed features suggesting it was ripe for revolution, as some informed analysts have argued.[90] Bolivia's history of peasant rebellion and hostility to landlordism— over 2,000 rebellions or opposition movements from 1861 to 1944— suggests a pattern of predatory landlord authority comparable to the historical Chinese or Russian experience.[91] The revolution of 1952 also produced a pattern of armed and/or independent groups of miners and peasants who confronted the postrevolutionary governments almost as equals.[92] Surely this was a promising locale to construct a counter-state.

Such an approach ignores three fundamental features that undermined Guevara's revolutionary strategy: the consequences of the 1952 revolution; regional differences; and the nature of Bolivian governmental authority in 1967.

First, the revolution of 1952 had destroyed the old Bolivian landlord class almost overnight. While there was a formal process of agrarian reform, in the early 1950s that process often only validated a previous pattern of peasant land invasion or refusal to pay rents. Formal patterns of agrarian reform continued well into the 1960s, and were still in process in 1967. Therefore, if land hunger is the sine qua non of peasant support—as Ché Guevara once argued—then the fundamental cause of peasant discontent with informal governments (i.e., landlords) had largely disappeared when guerrillas came on the scene, while the formal government in La Paz was continuing the process of land reform which benefited the peasantry.

The pattern of Bolivian peasant revolts is certainly most impressive—more so than Cuba's Oriente—yet historically they had been heavily concentrated *outside* the area of Guevara's guerrilla *foco*. Whereas he began in Santa Cruz, near the Chuquisaca border, in a sparsely populated frontier area of Bolivia, peasant resistance had historically been located further west, in the highlands and in the

Cochabamba Valley. Guevara's chosen site had no such history of peasant rebellion, and in fact there had been a regional land reform there in 1878, which had made most of the locals small landowners.[93] Despite the absence of land hunger and peasant agitation there, the region's families had been disproportionately favored with land reform in the years up to 1966.[94] In such a situation, one critic remarked, "What, then, could Che offer the local peasantry? Still more land they could not use?"[95] The peasants in the region, usually living on poor but plentiful land, were generally not dissatisfied, and were well-disposed toward the central government.[96]

Finally, the character of the Bolivian government of 1967 militated against Guevara as well. President René Barrientos had come to power in a coup, but had later been elected in an election overseen by the OAS. There was little question of his popularity among the nation's Quechua-speaking peasants. Barrientos spoke Quechua himself, and had secured a strong personal following among the peasantry when he headed the Bolivian army's civic action programs in rural areas during the early 1960s, as even hostile observers have agreed. While Barrientos's personal following was largely in the highlands far from Guevara's *foco* site, even in the latter area the local peasant union leader was a Barrientos follower.[97] Despite serious conflicts with the nation's miners, the Barrientos government enjoyed the strong support and favor of at least large sections of the nation's peasantry. In the middle of the guerrilla campaign, in fact, a national peasant congress condemned the guerrillas and offered support to the government.[98]

Guerrillas in such situations have been known to claim support where none existed, posing a dilemma for journalists and historians. For Bolivia, such problems are fewer, for we can rely on Guevara's famous Bolivian diary to prove that, under such unpromising conditions, the guerrillas never approached the status of a counter-state in rural Bolivia. Not a single peasant ever joined the movement. And while some were cordial enough to the guerrillas when they arrived on the scene—often making a quick peso through high-priced food sales—many persons informed on the guerrillas throughout the campaign, one such action leading to the ambush that wiped out Joaquín's band.[99] Despite Guevara's diary notation that it would soon be time for both sides to employ terror against the peasants, such terror never came. Terror cannot explain the lack of peasant support or the failure of the guerrillas to become a working counter-state.

The counter-state could only develop with the greatest difficulty where peasants had tolerable, cordial, or even supportive relationships with their central government; the necessary state of alienation did not exist (Corollary to Proposition 2). Guerrillas were typically received, then, with peasant indifference and hostility, as every chronicler of the campaign has noted (Guevara himself compared them to stones). The guerrillas, moreover, fighting for survival against a hostile physical and social environment, were in no position to bestow benefactions upon the peasantry. Indeed, the government showered the guerrilla zone with leaflets, urging the peasants: "Defend your lands!" against these foreign agents who would take them away. In doing so, the government played simultaneously on the fact that peasants *had* land, and on the fact obvious to all Bolivians who met the leaders of the *foco*: they were not Bolivians. Bolivian nationalism had been quite strong since the 1952 revolution. Under any circumstances, let alone those, it was absurd to assume that Bolivian peasants would come to treat a band of Cuban-led guerrillas as a Bolivian counter-state. Under social circumstances where even a Bolivian-led guerrilla band would have failed to generate peasant support, the Cuban-led band saw its fate sealed from the start, just as less extreme ethnic distinctions between Hispanic guerrillas and Indian peasants had blocked guerrilla attempts to become counter-states in Peru and Guatemala in the 1960s.

Pairing the Cuban and Bolivian cases strongly suggests that Propositions 1, 2, and 3 are accurate. Where alienation from government exists, regional peasantries are responsive to guerrilla attempts to construct a counter-state. Where guerrillas additionally employ the proper governmental techniques—not excluding punishment where deemed appropriate—such counter-states come into being, sometimes with very strong support. Absent such alienation from central-formal or local-informal governments, however, peasants are far less likely to respond to guerrillas' attempts to establish one arm of "dual power" in the countryside.

Proposition 5: The Decay of Guerrilla Authority

Where guerrilla authority arose, it could also decline. When guerrillas do become the legitimate regional authorities in the areas they control, then we may assume that they have taken upon themselves the obligations thereof. Failure to defend the populace may be grounds for loss of such authority, and terror against one's own citizenry is an especially serious violation of the implicit social contract.

Military destruction rather than loss of legitimacy wrecked most guerrilla movements. Yet evidence suggests that failure to defend the populace damaged them as well. Evidence from the Chinese revolution suggests that regions that harbored the Chinese Communists in one period, and were later overrun by the Guomindang, did not harbor them in later periods. Hofheinz argues that such areas were "burned out" for future mobilization; the Communists' failure to defend the peasantry from enemy forces was probably at the root of this fact.[100]

Such a failure was a root cause of the guerrillas' 1965 failure in Peru as well, as guerrilla chief Héctor Béjar argued in retrospect. Their contemporaries, the Colombian ELN, twice withdrew into the hills when army patrols came to nearby villages, leaving the locals open to army violence; on their return they executed villagers who had informed under duress. Arenas describes the results: "two zones of the greatest importance were lost due to lack of combativeness."[101]

Where government armies employed terror *along with* civic action, support for guerrillas at times simply crumbled. Why? Because the central government was increasing its contributions to material welfare while demonstrating that the peasants' protogovernment could not defend its subjects from enemy violence. In addition, such terror raised the costs of supporting guerrillas to very high levels indeed. Confronted with just such a combination, the Campa Indians turned against their former Peruvian guerrilla allies in 1965, and Guatemalan peasants adopted what one guerrilla chief called "a counterrevolutionary position," as he, too, pointed to the insurgents' inability to defend the local populace.[102]

Evidence from the last five years in El Salvador suggests a bifurcated pattern of peasant support: strong support where guerrillas are relatively secure government (where terror is notably absent), while other peasants simply cooperate, out of fear, with any armed visitors, declaring their "support" for whoever is in charge at the moment. This pattern is almost surely traceable to the high level of *guerrilla* terror against the citizenry of El Salvador—many thousands of admitted "executions"—which, in conjunction with far more widespread government terror, has produced a peasantry that increasingly declares, "A plague on both your houses."[103]

This suggests that guerrillas, like governments, may be using terror in attempts to establish questionable authority, or to halt the decline of existing authority. Government terror has been mostly absent where the peasantry has clearly not supported the guerrillas: La Convención, Peru in 1965 and Bolivia in 1967. Elsewhere it has been a commonplace.

If terror, in fact, is a response of "government" to weakness or decline, then we would expect to find guerrillas using terror where their authority is decaying or challenged. Only the most fragmentary evidence exists, but it is consistent with this hypothesis. In 1965, Peruvian guerrillas were alleged to have killed peasants mainly near the end of the counterinsurgency campaign, when they were in flight from the military and most in need of support. More systematically, the peaking of guerrilla terror in Venezuela seemed to come at two inflection points in the struggle for power. In Caracas, urban terrorist violence peaked—22 to 34 civilian dead and more than 100 wounded—in the two weeks preceding the December 1963 national elections, which were the strongest single challenge to the FALN guerrillas' contention that they constituted a parallel, legitimate authority.[104] In rural Venezuela, official allegations of guerrilla terror were few in the period 1962 to 1963, as guerrilla groups consolidated strong peasant support in some rural areas. The number of such incidents—30 to 50 reported killings of peasants from May 1964 to November 1965—peaked in the very years in which the guerrillas' prospects and numbers fell most sharply due to army sweeps and air force bombing raids, and as evidence indicated a decline of support for insurgents in their strongholds, especially in Lara State.[105] This evidence, I stress, is fragmentary and suggestive at best, but is consistent with the view that terror by guerrilla "governments" is a response to weak or declining claims to legitimate authority, perhaps the last gasp of a dying counter-state. (For an expansion of this argument, see the following chapter.)

Conclusions

Where central government and/or landlord versions of traditional authority have decayed in Latin America, guerrilla movements are apt to find responsive audiences to their efforts to create a counter-state in the countryside. In the course of interacting with regional peasantries who are alienated from previous authorities, guerrilla movements develop some of the characteristics of legitimate authority. They can come to regard themselves, and be so regarded, as the legitimate, if parallel governments of the regions they control. In such circumstances, they have presented in microcosm the features that revolutionary governments later may display shortly after seizing nationwide power, as in Cuba and Nicaragua. If we focus on the "implicit social contract" that emerges between the guerrillas and the rural populace, we can better understand the emergence of "dual power" or "multiple sovereignty" in nations with large-scale revolutionary movements.

This is not to suggest that revolutionary movements can only come to power through such loyalty shifts within the populace. While such an image fits the Cuban and Nicaraguan revolutions well, a greater degree of sheer coercion apparently operated in China and Vietnam, while the access to power of the Cambodian Khmer Rouge involved yet a greater display of brute force. Despite those elements of coercion, terror itself has never been an important element in generating peasant support for guerrillas. Terror has been and can be effective in stifling open opposition, but is incapable per se of generating that positive sense of loyalty and endurance displayed regularly by the peasant populace under conditions of guerrilla warfare.

The most important theoretical issue is rather the basis for the mass mobilization of peasant opposition to the incumbent regime. The securing of peasant support and cooperation in Latin America has *not* come about through any process of "consciousness raising" or ideological uplift. False consensus and the whole problem of false consciousness are but red herrings in this debate. Instead, theoreticians and outside observers like Migdal, and Armstrong and Shenk, as well as revolutionaries like Cuba's Guevara, Colombia's Marulanda, and Peru's Béjar, all agree that peasants join guerrilla movements to pursue peasant interests, not due to ideological conversion.[106] Again and again, guerrilla leaders complained of the low level of "consciousness" of the peasant recruits, and of the consequent need to raise their "cultural level." If conversion to Marxist ideology ever comes, it comes after membership, rather than before.

Neither terror nor consciousness raising, then, can account for the pattern of widespread peasant support for guerrilla counter-states in Latin America. Instead, I have suggested that an asymmetrical pattern of exchange arises between guerrillas and peasants, leading directly to the formation of guerrilla governments. Moreover, since exchange processes are inherently dynamic, this perspective suggests situations in which these newly constructed governance relations can in turn collapse, since new social contracts can decay just as the old ones did. Perhaps such processes lay behind the partial successes of the Nicaraguan Contras in recruiting peasant followers. Indeed, the 1990 national election results showed that the opposition coalition received their highest vote percentages in precisely the same regions where the Sandinista rural insurgency had secured peasant support during the 1970s.[107] Thus, wherever and whenever surplus-extracting relations increasingly disfavor the underlying populace, we might well look for revolutionary potential in the countryside.

Notes

1. Charles Tilly, *From Mobilization to Revolution* (Reading, Mass.: Addison-Wesley, 1978), pp. 190–93.

2. Marvin Harris, *Cannibals and Kings* (New York: Random House, 1977); Robert Carneiro, "A Theory of the Origin of the State," in *The Pleasures of Anthropology,* Morris Freilich, ed. (New York: Mentor, 1983), pp. 40–53; Maurice Godelier, "Infrastructures, Societies and History," *New Left Review* 112 (November–December 1978), pp. 93–96.

3. Ralf Dahrendorf, "In Praise of Thrasymachus," in Morris Freilich, ed., *Essays in the Theory of Society* (Stanford, Calif: Stanford University Press, 1968), pp. 129–50.

4. Talcott Parsons, "The Distribution of Power in American Society," in *World Politics* 10, no. 1 (October 1957), pp. 123–43; and "On the Concept of Political Power," in *Class, Status, and Power,* 2d ed., eds. Reinhard Bendix and Seymour Martin Lipset (New York: Free Press, 1966), pp. 240–65.

5. C. Wright Mills, *The Power Elite* (New York: Oxford University Press, 1956).

6. William J. Goode, "Functionalism: The Empty Castle," in *Explorations in Social Theory* (New York: Oxford University Press, 1973), pp. 64–94.

7. See Ralph Miliband, *The State in Capitalist Society* (New York: Basic Books, 1969); Martin Carnoy, *The State and Political Theory* (Princeton, N.J.: Princeton University Press, 1984); and Frank Parkin, *Marxism and Class Theory: A Bourgeois Critique* (London: Tavistock, 1979).

8. See Robert A. Dahl, *Who Governs?* (New Haven, Conn.: Yale University Press, 1961); and Arnold M. Rose, *The Power Structure* (New York: Oxford University Press, 1967).

9. Charles E. Lindblom, *Politics and Markets: The World's Political Economic Systems* (New York: Basic Books, 1977).

10. C. G. Pickvance, "Theories of the State and Theories of Urban Crisis," in *Current Perspectives in Social Theory: A Research Annual,* eds. Scott G. McNall and Gary N. Howe (Greenwich, Conn.: JAI Press, 1980), p. 38.

11. Carnoy, *The State and Political Theory.*

12. See Nicholas Abercrombie, Stephen Hill, and Bryan S. Turner, *The Dominant Ideology Thesis* (London and Boston: G. Allen and Unwin, 1980); also, Peter

L. Berger, *Pyramids of Sacrifice* (New York: Basic Books, 1974), pp. 111–32; and James C. Scott, "Hegemony and the Peasantry," *Politics and Society* 7, no. 3 (1977), pp. 267–96.

13. Barrington Moore, Jr., *Injustice: The Social Bases of Obedience and Revolt* (White Plains, N.Y.: M. E. Sharpe, 1978), pp. 15–31; see also Ronald Rogowski, *Rational Legitimacy: A Theory of Political Support* (Princeton, N.J.: Princeton University Press, 1974).

14. James C. Scott, *The Moral Economy of the Peasant: Rebellion and Subsistence in Southeast Asia* (New Haven, Conn.: Yale University Press, 1976); James C. Scott and Benedict J. Kerkvliet, "How Traditional Rural Patrons Lose Legitimacy (in Southeast Asia)," *Cultures et Developpement* 5 (1973), pp. 501–40; Perry Anderson, *Lineages of the Absolutist State* (London: New Left Books, 1974), pp. 407–12.

15. Karl Wittfogel, *Oriental Despotism* (New York: Vintage, 1981 [1963]).

16. Theda Skocpol, *States and Social Revolutions* (New York: Cambridge University Press, 1979).

17. Robert Brenner, "Agrarian Class Structure and Economic Development in Pre-Industrial Europe," *Past and Present* 70 (February 1976), pp. 30–75.

18. See, respectively, Brenner, "Agrarian Class Structure"; Scott and Kerkvliet, "Rural Patrons Lose Legitimacy"; and Marshall D. Sahlins, "Poor Man, Rich Man, Big-Man, Chief," in *The Pleasures of Anthropology*, ed. Morris Freilich (New York: Mentor, 1983), pp. 383–99.

19. Barrington Moore, Jr., *Social Origins of Dictatorship and Democracy: Lord and Peasant in the Making of the Modern World* (Boston: Beacon Press, 1966), pp. 469–73, 253; and Moore, *Injustice*, pp. 17–31.

20. Scott and Kerkvliet, "Rural Patrons Lose Legitimacy"; Steffen W. Schmidt, Laura Guasti, Carl H. Landé, and James C. Scott, eds., *Friends, Followers, and Factions: A Reader in Political Clientelism* (Berkeley: University of California Press, 1977); and Robert R. Kaufman, "The Patron-Client Concept and Macro-Politics: Prospects and Problems," *Comparative Studies in Society and History* 16 (June 1974) pp. 284–308.

21. Moore, *Social Origins*, pp. 469–73.

22. Godelier, "Infrastructures, Societies, and History," pp. 93–96.

23. Moore, *Injustice*, pp. 20–23.

24. Scott, *Moral Economy*, pp. 231–40; and Charles F. Silberman, *Criminal Violence, Criminal Justice* (New York: Vintage, 1980), pp. 189–205.

25. Tilly, *From Mobilization to Revolution.*

26. Moore, *Injustice*; Daniel H. Levine, *Conflict and Political Change in Venezuela* (Princeton, N.J.: Princeton University Press, 1973), pp. 226–27; and Luis Mercier Vega, *Guerrillas in Latin America: The Technique of the Counter-State* (New York: Praeger, 1969).

27. Alfred Stepan, *The State and Society: Peru in Comparative Perspective* (Princeton, N.J.: Princeton University Press, 1978); and Claudio Véliz, *The Centralist Tradition of Latin America* (Princeton N.J.: Princeton University Press, 1980).

28. John M. Hunter, "A Testing Ground in Colombia," *Current History* 46 (January 1964), p. 10.

29. François Chevalier, *Land and Society in Colonial Mexico* (Berkeley and

Los Angeles: University of California Press, 1963), pp. 288–307; Eric Wolf, *Sons of the Shaking Earth* (Chicago: University of Chicago Press, 1959), pp. 202–12; Gláucio Ary Dillon Soares, *Sociedade e política no Brasil* (São Paulo: Difusão Europeia do Livro, 1973), pp. 97–144; and Brian Loveman, *Chile: The Legacy of Hispanic Capitalism* (New York: Oxford University Press, 1979), pp. 26–28.

30. Wolf, *Sons of the Shaking Earth*, pp. 206–9.

31. Scott, *Moral Economy*; Scott and Kerkvliet, "Rural Patrons Lose Legitimacy"; Benedict J. Kerkvliet, *The Huk Rebellion: A Study of Peasant Revolt in the Phillippines* (Berkeley: University of California Press, 1977), pp. 254–56; Charles Tilly, *The Vendée* (Cambridge, Mass.: Harvard University Press, 1964), pp. 20–22, 35–37; and Eric R. Wolf, *Peasant Wars of the Twentieth Century* (New York: Harper and Row, 1969).

32. Schmidt et al., *Friends, Followers, and Factions*.

33. Kerkvliet, *The Huk Rebellion*, pp. 254–56.

34. See F. Lamond Tullis, *Lord and Peasant in Peru* (Cambridge, Mass.: Harvard University Press, 1970), pp. 90–91, 115–18; and Fritz René Allemann, *Macht und Ohnmacht der Guerilla* (Munich: R. Piper, 1974), pp. 393–94.

35. E. J. Hobsbawm, *Primitive Rebels* (New York: W. W. Norton, 1965), p. 67; Kerkvliet, *The Huk Rebellion*, pp. 254–56; and Joel S. Migdal, *Peasants, Politics, and Revolution: Pressures toward Political and Social Change in the Third World* (Princeton, N.J.: Princeton University Press, 1974), pp. 34–42; Rogowski, *Rational Legitimacy*, p. 265.

36. Concerned Guatemala Scholars, *Guatemala: Dare to Struggle, Dare to Win* (San Francisco: Solidarity, 1982), pp. 22, 48.

37. Ernest Feder, *The Rape of the Peasantry: Latin America's Landholding System* (New York: Doubleday, 1971).

38. Ramón L. Bonachea and Marta San Martín, *The Cuban Insurrection, 1952–1959* (New Brunswick, N.J.: Transaction, 1974), p. 96; and (Col.) Ramón A. Barquín López, *Las luchas guerrilleras en Cuba*, 2 vols., (Madrid: Plaza Mayor, 1975), vol. 1, pp. 317–19, 327.

39. John A. Booth, *The End and the Beginning: The Nicaraguan Revolution* (Boulder, Colo.: Westview, 1982), pp. 117–21.

40. Timothy P. Wickham-Crowley, "Winners, Losers, and Also-Rans: Toward a Comparative Sociology of Latin American Guerrilla Movements," ch. 4 of *Power and Popular Protest: Latin American Social Movements*, ed. Susan Eckstein (Berkeley: University of California Press, 1989); Harald Jung, "Behind the Nicaraguan Revolution," in *Revolution in Central America*, ed. Stanford Central America Action Network (SCAAN) (Boulder, Colo.: Westview, 1983), p. 24; North American Congress on Latin America (NACLA), "Guatemala: Peasant Massacre," *Report on the Americas* 12, no. 4 (July–August 1978), pp. 44–45; and Harald Jung, "Class Struggles in El Salvador," *New Left Review* 122 (July–August 1980), pp. 5–7.

41. Héctor Béjar, *Peru 1965: Notes on a Guerrilla Experience* (New York: Monthly Review, 1970).

42. Feder, *Rape of the Peasantry*; David Browning, *El Salvador: Landscape and Society* (Oxford: Clarendon, 1971).

43. Allemann, *Macht und Ohnmacht*, pp. 393–94.

44. John Duncan Powell, *Political Mobilization of the Venezuelan Peasant*

(Cambridge, Mass.: Harvard University Press, 1971); Mercier, *Guerrillas in Latin America*, p. 149.

45. Willard F. Barber and C. Neale Ronning, *Internal Security and Military Power: Counterinsurgency and Civic Action in Latin America* (Columbus, Ohio: Ohio State University Press, 1966).

46. Richard L. Maullin, *Soldiers, Guerrillas, and Politics in Colombia* (Toronto: Lexington, 1973), pp. 69, 79; Jean Lartéguy, *The Guerrillas* (New York: World Press, 1970), p. 137.

47. Mercier, *Guerrillas in Latin America*, pp. 177–80; Camilo Castaño, "Avec les guérillas du Guatemala," *Partisans* (Paris) 38 (July–September 1967), pp. 144, 152.

48. Ernesto "Ché" Guevara, *The Complete Bolivian Diaries of Che Guevara and Other Captured Documents* (New York: Stein and Day, 1968), pp. 21–22; Ojarikuj Runa (pseud.), "Bolivia: Análisis de una situación," *Pensamiento Crítico* (July 26, 1967), p. 213.

49. Jaime Arenas, *La guerrilla por dentro* (Bogotá: Tercer Mundo, 1970), p. 191; Mario Menéndez Rodríguez, "Colombia (II): ¡Ni un paso atrás! ¡Liberación o muerte! (Fabio Vásquez Castaño)," *Sucesos* (Mexico City) 1778 (1 July 1967), p. 17; Jaime Velásquez García, *Contrainsurgencia y guerra revolucionaria* (Bogotá: Tinta Roja, 1975), pp. 97–98.

50. See Bonachea and San Martín, *The Cuban Insurrection*, pp. 91, 100–102, 180–82; Allemann, *Macht und Ohnmacht*, p. 76; and Mercier, *Guerrillas in Latin America*, pp. 78–79, for Cuba. For Venezuela, see Angela Zago, *Aquí no ha pasado nada* (Caracas: El Sobre, 1972), pp. 60, 82; Alberto Domingo, "Guerrilla in Venezuela," *Monthly Review* 15 (February 1964), p. 43; Régis Debray, *Strategy for Revolution*, ed. Robin Blackburn (London: Jonathan Cape, 1970), pp. 98–99; and Norman Gall, "The Continental Revolution," *The New Leader* 48 (12 April 1965), p. 5. For Guatemala, see Adolfo Gilly, "The Guerrilla Movement in Guatemala II," *Monthly Review* 17 (June 1965), pp. 16–17, 38–40; and Judy Hicks, "FAR and MR-13 Compared," *Monthly Review* 18 (February 1967), p. 31. For Colombia, see Mario Menéndez Rodríguez, "En Colombia: ¡Basta ya!" *Sucesos* 1779 (8 July 1967), pp. 41–43; and "Colombia: Única vía la lucha armada—¡Hasta la victoria final!" *Sucesos* 1780 (15 July 1967), p. 16. For Peru, see Manuel Castillo, "Las guerrillas en el Perú," *Estudios* (Buenos Aires) 581 (April 1967), pp. 60–61; and Richard Gott, *Rural Guerrillas in Latin America* (Harmondsworth, England: Penguin, 1973), pp. 460–61.

51. Gall, "The Continental Revolution," p. 5; also CBS Evening News (20 March 1984) for El Salvador.

52. Peter M. Blau, *Exchange and Power in Social Life* (New York: John Wiley and Sons, 1964), pp. 106, 124; also William Foote Whyte, *Street Corner Society* (Chicago: University of Chicago Press, 1955), pp. 256–58.

53. Blau, *Exchange and Power*, pp. 106, 124.

54. Norman Gall, "The Legacy of Che Guevara," *Commentary* 44 (December 1967), pp. 33, 38; Lartéguy, *The Guerrillas*, p. 244; Luis J. González and Gustavo A. Sánchez Salazar, *The Great Rebel: Che Guevara in Bolivia* (New York: Grove, 1969), p. 182; and Sara Beatriz Guardia, *Proceso a campesinos de la guerrilla 'Túpac Amaru'* (Lima: Impresiones y Publicidad, 1972), pp. 41–43.

55. Gall, "The Continental Revolution," p. 5.

56. Guevara, *Bolivian Diaries*, June 15, June 27, October 7, 1967; on government bribes see Bonachea and San Martín, *The Cuban Insurrection*, p. 105; Luigi Valsalice, *Guerriglia e Politica: L'esempio del Venezuela* (Florence, Italy: Valmartina Editore, 1973), pp. 126–27; Robert Rogers and Ted Yates, "The Undeclared War in Guatemala," in *The New York Times Magazine* (13 June 1974), p. 32; and Allemann, *Macht und Ohnmacht*, pp. 256–57.

57. Barquín, *Las luchas guerrilleras en Cuba*, vol. 1, pp. 329–30; Bonachea and San Martín, *The Cuban Insurrection*, pp. 191, 194; and Ernesto "Ché" Guevara, *Reminiscences of the Cuban Revolutionary War* (New York: Monthly Review, 1968), p. 102.

58. *El Nacional* (Caracas) September 17, 1962; Domingo, "Guerrilla in Venezuela," p. 43; Debray, *Strategy for Revolution*, pp. 100–101; A. P. Short, "Conversations with the Guatemalan Delegates in Cuba," *Monthly Review* 18 (February 1967), pp. 34–35.

59. Michael Schwahn, Michael Schornstheimer, and Ernst Meili, *El Salvador: Der Weg ist lang* (Zürich: Rotpunktverlag, 1982), pp. 196–201; Charles Clements, *Witness to War: An American Doctor in El Salvador* (Toronto: Bantam, 1984).

60. Z. Martin Kowalewski and Miguel Sobrado, *Antropología de la guerrilla* (Caracas: Nueva Izquierda, 1971), p. 58; Bonachea and San Martín, *The Cuban Insurrection*, pp. 177, 182–83, 195.

61. Debray, *Strategy for Revolution*, pp. 97, 103; Zago, *Aquí no ha pasado nada*, pp. 60–61; Adolfo Gilly, "The Guerrilla Movement in Guatemala I," *Monthly Review* 17 (May 1965), p. 14; Donn Munson, *Zacapa* (Canoga, Calif.: Challenge, 1967), pp. 112, 151.

62. CBS Evening News, 19 and 20 March 1984.

63. Rogers and Yates, "The Undeclared War," p. 32; Short, "Conversations," p. 35.

64. Gott, *Rural Guerrillas*; Gilly, "Guatemala II," pp. 15, 36; Munson, *Zacapa*, p. 118; George Black, *Triumph of the People: The Sandinista Revolution in Nicaragua* (London: Zed, 1981), pp. 120–22; Robert Armstrong and Janet Shenk, *El Salvador: The Face of Revolution* (London: Pluto, 1982), pp. 132–33; Jonathan L. Fried, Marvin E. Gettleman, Deborah T. Levenson, and Nancy Peckenham, eds., *Guatemala in Rebellion: Unfinished History* (New York: Grove Press, 1983), pp. 287–91.

65. Héctor Béjar, "Ne pas surestimer ses forces," *Partisans* (Paris) 38 (July–September 1967), p. 111; Cynthia McClintock, "Sendero Luminoso: Peru's Maoist Guerrillas," *Problems of Communism* 32, no. 5 (September–October 1983), pp. 29–30; and David Scott Palmer, "Rebellion in Rural Peru: The Origins and Evolution of Sendero Luminoso," *Comparative Politics* 18, no. 2 (January 1986), pp. 136–37.

66. Barquín, *Las luchas guerrilleras,* vol. 1, pp. 329–30; Bonachea and San Martín, *The Cuban Insurrection*, pp. 183, 195.

67. Béjar, *Peru 1965*, p. 94; and Mario Payeras, "Days of the Jungle: The Testimony of a Guatemalan *Guerrillero*, 1972–1976," in *Monthly Review* 35, no. 3 (July–August 1983), pp. 72–77; Payeras's report was also published as a book.

68. See Bonachea and San Martín, *The Cuban Insurrection*, pp. 100, 189–90 for Cuba; Debray, *Strategy for Revolution*, pp. 100–101 and Antonio Zamora,

Memoria(s) de la guerrilla venezolana (Caracas: Síntesis Dosmil, 1974), pp. 126–27 for Venezuela; Gilly, "Guatemala II," p. 11 for Guatemala; Armstrong and Shenk, *El Salvador*, pp. 202–3 for El Salvador.

69. McClintock, "Sendero Luminoso," pp. 29–30; for the FMLN's threats against incumbent mayors, see Horacio Castellanos Moya, "Terminar o no la guerra, en el fondo del proceso electoral" *Proceso* (Mexico City) 637 (January 16, 1989), p. 45.

70. Channel 4 (England), "The Front Line," (July 9, 1983); Fried et al., *Guatemala in Rebellion*, p. 277.

71. For example, see Menéndez, "¡Ni un paso atrás!"

72. See Zago, *Aquí no ha pasado nada*, for Venezuela; see Mario Menéndez Rodríguez, "Colombia: ¡Al ataque!" *Sucesos* (Mexico City) 1777 (June 24, 1967), p. 36 for Colombia; see Gilly, "Guatemala II," pp. 16–18 and Fried et al., "Guatemala in Rebellion," pp. 173–78 for Guatemala in the 1960s and 1980s, respectively; and see Black, *Triumph of the People*, pp. 79–82 for Nicaragua.

73. Zago, *Aquí no ha pasado nada*, pp. 56, 61, 64–65.

74. Bonachea and San Martín, *The Cuban Insurrection*, pp. 183, 193; Armstrong and Shenk, *El Salvador*, pp. 204–6.

75. Bonachea and San Martín, *The Cuban Insurrection*, pp. 183, 193; Fried et al., *Guatemala in Rebellion*, pp. 273–74; SCAAN, *Revolution in Central America*, pp. 379–434.

76. Bonachea and San Martín, *The Cuban Insurrection*, pp. 182–97; Barquín, *Las luchas guerrilleras*, vol. 2, p. 704-E.

77. For details see chapter 7 below; also see Enrique A. Baloyra, *El Salvador in Transition* (Chapel Hill and London: University of North Carolina Press, 1982), p. 85, for suggestive thoughts on the Nicaragua–El Salvador distinction.

78. Robin Blackburn, "Prologue to the Cuban Revolution," *New Left Review* 21 (October 1963), pp. 88–89; Hugh Thomas, *Cuba: The Pursuit of Freedom* (New York: Harper and Row, 1971), p. 523; Jorge I. Domínguez, *Cuba: Order and Revolution* (Cambridge, Mass: Belknap Press of Harvard University Press, 1978), pp. 435–36; and Cuba, Academia de Ciencias de Cuba y Academia de Ciencias de la URSS, *Atlas nacional de Cuba* (Havana, 1970), p. 129.

79. Barquín, *Las luchas guerrilleras*, vol. 1, pp. 317–27; Allemann, *Macht und Ohnmacht*, pp. 71, 394; Thomas, *Cuba*, p. 808; and Enrique Meneses, *Fidel Castro* (New York: Taplinger, 1966), p. 22.

80. Domínguez, *Order and Revolution*, pp. 429–37; Lowry Nelson, *Rural Cuba* (Minneapolis, Minn.: University of Minnesota Press, 1950), p. 20.

81. Nelson, *Rural Cuba*, pp. 20, 112; Domínguez, *Order and Revolution*, pp. 429–33.

82. Domínguez, *Order and Revolution*, pp. 436–37; Barquín, *Las luchas guerrilleras*, vol. 1, p. 317.

83. Meneses, *Fidel Castro*, p. 46.

84. Barquín, *Las luchas guerrilleras*, vol. 1, pp. 329–30.

85. Barquín, *Las luchas guerrilleras*, vol. 1, p. 317.

86. Barquín, *Las luchas guerrilleras*, vol. 1, p. 328.

87. Bonachea and San Martín, *The Cuban Insurrection*, p. 91.

88. Bonachea and San Martín, *The Cuban Insurrection*, p. 100.

89. Bonachea and San Martín, *The Cuban Insurrection*, pp. 100–102.

90. Gott, *Rural Guerrillas*, pp. 483–84; John Womack, Jr., "The Bolivian Guerrilla," *New York Review of Books* 16 (11 February 1971), p. 8+.

91. Gerrit Huizer, *The Revolutionary Potential of Peasants in Latin America* (London and Toronto: Lexington, 1972), pp. 88–105; Moore, *Social Origins*, pp. 469–70.

92. Allemann, *Macht und Ohnmacht*, pp. 219–21.

93. Dwight B. Heath, Charles Erasmus, and Hans C. Buechler, *Land Reform and Social Revolution in Bolivia* (New York: Praeger, 1969), pp. 36–49, 74, 120–22, 256–59; Robert F. Lamberg, "Che in Bolivia: The 'Revolution' that Failed," *Problems of Communism* 19 (July–August 1970), p. 30.

94. James W. Wilkie, *Measuring Land Reform: Supplement to the Statistical Abstract of Latin America* (Los Angeles: UCLA Latin American Center, 1974), pp. 41, 55.

95. Guevara, *Bolivian Diaries*, p. 59.

96. Lamberg, "Che in Bolivia," p. 30.

97. Guevara, *Bolivian Diaries*, pp. 18, 175; Edgar Millares Reyes, *Las guerrillas: Teoría y práctica* (Sucre, Bolivia: Imprenta Universitaria), p. 40; Runa, "Análisis de una situación," p. 213; Klaus Esser, "Guevaras Guerilla in Bolivien," *Vierteljahresberichte—Forschungsinstitut der Friedrich Ebert Stiftung* 37 (September 1971), p. 327.

98. Millares, *Teoría y práctica*, p. 40.

99. Guevara, *Bolivian Diaries*, pp. 48–49.

100. Roy Hofheinz, Jr., "The Ecology of Chinese Communist Success: Rural Influence Patterns, 1932–1945," in *Chinese Communist Politics in Action*, ed. A. Doak Barnett (Seattle, Wash.: University of Washington Press, 1972), p. 33.

101. Arenas, *La guerrilla por dentro*, pp. 151–52.

102. Guardia, *Proceso a campesinos*, p. 20; Castaño, "Avec les guérillas," pp. 144, 152.

103. Gabriel Zaid, "Enemy Colleagues: A Reading of the Salvadoran Tragedy," *Dissent* (Winter 1982), pp. 13–40 and "Gabriel Zaid Replies," *Dissent* (Summer 1982), pp. 357–59; R. Bruce McColm, *El Salvador: Peaceful Revolution or Armed Struggle?* (New York: Freedom House, 1982), pp. 23–24; Penn Kemble, "The Liberal Test in El Salvador," *The New Republic* (14 March 1981), pp. 17–21; Michael J. Englebert, interviewer, "Flight: Six Salvadorans Who Took Leave of the War," *The Progressive* 47, no. 3 (March 1983), pp. 38–43; Lydia Chavez, "El Salvador: The Voices of Anguish in a Bitterly Divided Land," *The New York Times Magazine* (11 December 1983), pp. 58, 81; CBS Evening News, 14 March 1984.

104. Colonel Edward F. Callanan, "Terror in Venezuela," *Military Review* 49 (February 1969), pp. 49–56; Norman Gall, "Teodoro Petkoff: The Crisis of the Professional Revolutionary—Part I, Years of Insurrection" *American Universities Field Staff Reports—East Coast South America Series* 16, no. 1 (January 1972), p. 16.

105. *El Nacional* and *Daily Journal* (Caracas), 1962–67 issues; Venezuela, Oficina de Información, *Six Years of Aggression* (Caracas: Imprenta Nacional, 1967?), pp. 36–49; Valsalice, *Guerriglia e Politica*, pp. 141, 216 n. 23, 221.

106. Migdal, *Peasants, Politics, and Revolution*; Armstrong and Shenk, *El Salvador*, pp. 204–8; Guevara, *Reminiscences*, pp. 192–94; Carlos Arango Z.,

FARC: Veinte años—De Marquetalia a la Uribe (Bogotá: Aurora, 1984), pp. 33–34, for Marulanda; and Allemann, *Macht und Ohnmacht*, pp. 209–10, for Béjar.

107. Compare the maps in Booth, *The End and the Beginning*, pp. 117, 149, to comments made following the February 1990 elections by a number of observers, who noted that the greatest voting strengths of the UNO opposition coalition were in the northern rural areas which had seen a great deal of Contra-Sandinista fighting; see, for example, *Newsweek*, 12 March 1990, p. 37.

3

Terror and Guerrilla Warfare in Latin America, 1956–70

Now is the time when terror will be used against the peasants by both sides, but with different objectives.
—Ché Guevara, *Bolivian Diaries*

Extraordinary waves of terror have swept many Latin American societies since 1970, most occurring in guerrilla-based insurgencies or even civil wars. Because of the massive body counts produced during these confrontations between revolutionaries and government-based or government-linked counterrevolutionaries, human rights organizations have issued a long series of reports about the terror, especially that carried out by incumbent regimes and death squads (reports supplemented by the guerrillas' own exposés). Amnesty International, the OAS Human Rights group, and Americas Watch have been the major international actors documenting the terror wave. Many independent national groups such as El Salvador's "Socorro Jurídico," and other church-linked human rights organizations, have undertaken that more perilous task at home.

Yet terror against the civilian population did not begin twenty years ago, but pervaded as well the insurgencies of the 1950s and 1960s throughout Latin America. The earlier wave of terror does not match the later wave in the size of its "bone heaps," to be sure, and I will try to account for those differences later in this chapter. Nonetheless, the very obscurity of the earlier terror morally and intellectually compels us to address it. More so than the "prolonged popular wars" characteristic of guerrilla warfare since 1970, the earlier Latin American guerrilla struggles were "Wars in the Shadows," as one author put it, and the time has come to bring light to those shadows, lest they be forgotten.

My purpose here is not solely historiographical, even though many sources here are known to and employed by few chroniclers of these events. Instead, my aim is ultimately sociological and theoretical: to employ the information we can retrieve about guerrilla warfare in order to arrive at a better understanding of the causes, concomitants, and nature of terror in guerrilla wars. Yet before we seek to explain any social phenomenon, Robert Merton has cautioned us, we should be quite sure that we are accounting for facts, not pseudo-facts. Since so much of the reporting on terror is ideologically freighted and tendentious, that caution will carry special weight herein.

The cases I will report on here are six: (1) Fidel Castro's own insurgency against the Batista regime from 1956 to 1959, which began with a boat landing in Oriente Province and ended with a triumphal march into Havana; (2) the Venezuelan insurgency of the Communist-backed Armed Forces of National Liberation (FALN), and the Movement of the Revolutionary Left (MIR), against elected *Acción Democrática* governments in the 1960s; (3) the Guatemalan insurgency of the 1960s, involving the Communists (PGT) and one or two—there was fission and refusion here—guerrilla groups, the 13th of November Revolutionary Movement (MR-13), and the Rebel Armed Forces (FAR); (4) three different Colombian insurgent groups posing revolutionary challenges to the 1960s coalition National Front governments: the Moscow-linked Colombian Revolutionary Armed Forces (FARC), the Castroist Army of National Liberation (ELN), and the Maoist Army of Popular Liberation (EPL). All four of the preceding guerrilla movements secured substantial peasant support in their areas of operation during insurgency.

The remaining two nations experienced insurgencies in which the guerrillas secured at best moderate (and at worst no) support from regional peasantries: (5) Peru, where two left-wing political splinter groups unleashed four simultaneous *focos* in the Andes in 1965 against the elected government of Fernando Belaúnde Terry: the MIR (Movement of the Revolutionary Left), and the ELN (Army of National Liberation); all four were eliminated in less than a year; (6) finally, there was Ché Guevara's *foco* in eastern Bolivia, providing at best a weak challenge to the popularly elected and peasant-supported regime of General René Barrientos. At the end of the insurgency, in October 1967, Guevara was wounded, captured, and killed.

Recounting the Terror

Government Terror

We will consider terror to be certain acts forbidden by the rules of war. Among these are: (1) beating, killing, robbing, bombing, or other assaults on a civilian population, including relatively unusual items such as forced relocation; (2) beating, torturing, or killing of combatants who have indicated a willingness to surrender; (3) the use of weapons that do not discriminate sufficiently among combatants and others. Such weapons include germ warfare, nuclear weapons, and punji stakes. The latter were used by the Viet Cong in Indochina, and a high percentage of casualties were due to people falling into pits filled with these sharpened, dung-covered stakes.[1]

First, some preliminary conceptual distinctions may help us analytically to sort out the empirical accounts to follow. Eugene Victor Walter has done the yeoman work in developing a systematic theory of terror. Walter distinguishes between a *regime* of terror and a *siege* of terror, carried on respectively by government and opposition. Either of these encompasses the *process* of terror, which has three distinct elements: (1) the violent act itself; (2) the victim of the violent act; and (3) the target of the violent act. This last element is fundamental to any system of terror, for the basic aim of terror is not to kill individuals but to frighten entire social groups.[2]

Using these criteria, the Cuban people certainly suffered intensive terror from 1953 to 1958, but the extent of this terror has been overestimated by Fidelistas. Huberman and Sweezy apparently first gave the total of 20,000 deaths during the Cuban insurrection, a figure they attributed to Castro. This number quickly was converted—and this is a typical occurrence in the building of revolutionary mythology—into the killing of 20,000 *innocent civilians* by Batista.[3] These figures appear to have no factual basis, and there is good reason to lower the total number of deaths by a factor of ten. A list of the war dead published in Bohemia on 11 January 1959 (i.e., after Castro's victory) counted 898 dead, over half of whom were combatants. These figures exclude deaths of peasants, which probably numbered several hundred.[4] Estimates of hundreds or perhaps about a thousand deaths due to Batista's terror are also supported by comments made by Fidel Castro and other Batista critics during the war itself.[5] The 20,000 figure apparently is a gigantic balloon blown up by anti-Batista emotions.

Batista's terror was especially evidenced by the faithfully fulfilled "no prisoners" rule. Following the Moncada attack of 26 July 1953, Castro himself was only saved from summary execution by a lieutenant who knew him from the university. Later, an attempted landing of guerrilla reinforcements and a naval uprising at Cienfuegos (both in 1957) ended in the same fashion: all those who surrendered were shot on the spot.[6] Batista lacked the air power with which to inflict severe casualties upon the Sierra Maestra peasantry, but deaths did result from his bombing of the region. These, however, are unimportant relative to the number of deaths caused by direct troop attacks on peasants. Many of these attacks did not even have the pretext of seeking information, as army units whose commanders were afraid to go into the guerrilla zones would simply attack peasant villages on the outskirts of the zones, and then report the number of "guerrillas" killed. One particularly brutal officer in the Sierra Maestra region, Lieutenant Casillas, literally drove the peasantry from the village of Palma Mocha, and kept human ears in a box to show to visitors.[7] Taking a small page from Spanish general Weyler's book of strategy during Cuba's 1890s War for Independence, Batista also forced the evacuation of several hundred Sierra Maestra peasants (Weyler's program had aimed at 500,000 forced relocations).[8]

As in almost all of the cases under review, much government terror consisted of the torture of urban cadres, innocent victims, and peasants transported to town jails and prisons. Those who lived to tell such tales can relate grisly stories. Haydée Santamaría was shown the extracted eye of her brother in an attempt to make her inform on M-26 (Castro's 26th of July Movement) operations in Santiago de Cuba.[9] While we will usually restrict our examples to terror that takes place in rural settings, these broader aspects should be understood.

The Venezuelan case provides us with many, many examples of terror, but the sheer number should not overly impress the reader. Dead men indeed tell no tales, and the high survival rate of Venezuelan guerrillas has led to a fairly extensive literature of interviews and memoirs. The exceptional number of surviving guerrillas suggests that terror against guerrilla combatants themselves was considerably more muted than in Cuba, even though terror against the peasantry was still common during army sweeps through guerrilla zones.

As regards the number of peasant deaths due to such tactics, an author very unfriendly to the governments of Rómulo Betancourt (1959–64) and Raúl Leoni (1964–69) attributes to them "more than 200" peasant deaths, while another unfriendly source cites more than 1,000 persons overall killed under Betancourt alone, suggesting again a very strong imbalance in favor of urban terror. The vast bulk of peasant killings were in Falcón and Lara states, the number of which we may place at between 100 and 300, from a variety of sources.[10]

Guerrilla zones were bombed regularly in Venezuela, usually just before the army began sweeps or encirclement campaigns in the regions. While some peasants allegedly died in such bombings, evidence is fragmentary. The army would at times force the evacuation of peasants from villages and then bomb the area. These evacuations Luigi Valsalice described as "more or less voluntary."[11] An example of the latter is seen in the following talk given by an army officer in a village in Falcón:

> All the peasants have to leave the area because we're going to bomb these lands. Whoever remains will be burnt to death. So get ready to leave, you old bastards.

and later:

> You worthless, you're all guerrillas. Get out of here. We're going to burn it, to bomb it.

Valsalice also reports forced evacuations in Lara State.[12]

There is little doubt that torture took place during the sixties in Venezuelan prisons, especially that carried out by national police agents of DIGEPOL (General Directorate of Police), as occasional congressional investigations revealed. DIGEPOL's public reputation was so tarnished that President Rafael Caldera was forced to reorganize the agency after taking office in 1969.[13]

A torture session might begin with a warning speech such as the following delivered in a DIGEPOL jail cell in Falcón:

> You know who I am, don't you? To you I'm called Captain Vegas, you fucking commie. Look at me, you shitty commie. I am Captain Vegas, I'll be the terror of you faggots. Look at me well so you'll remember me your entire life.[14]

The tortures that followed, at least in a well-equipped Caracas DIGEPOL headquarters, might consist of suction devices applied to the fingers, electric shocks, steel rods placed with pressure between the fingers, a large paper clip–type device for pulling/pinching the skin, and other tortures: ice picks under fingernails, dunking the head in unflushed toilets, lemon juice in the eyes, standing with arms over head for hours, beatings with rubber tubing, and hot candle wax applied to the skin.[15] (In rural areas, techniques by army patrols were cruder, but these will be discussed below.) The routine goal of torture sessions was to obtain information on the FALN guerrillas. After the torture sessions or beatings, especially if a court appearance was required, the following advice might be given to the potentially talkative: "Careful what you say. No one has beaten you. And if you deny your written declarations, we'll take another, more serious jaunt to the camp."[16]

It is perhaps more important that the "hidden" terror in rural areas should be placed on the historical record. In spite of allowing a substantial discount for propaganda, the record of rural terror is a brutal one, as even a skeptic such as Valsalice admits. Occasional reports of abuse and torture even reached the orthodox press and the halls of Congress.[17]

In Falcón, FALN leader Elías Manuitt alleged that peasants had been publicly tortured in the Sierra del Coro, while his comrade Douglas Bravo described a raid on a village by thirty commandos in which every woman was raped, including one over forty whose violation was carried out before the eyes of her husband and children. He also alleged a gang rape of a sixteen-year-old peasant girl by twenty-five soldiers at Pueblo Nuevo in 1963.[18] As we shall see below, the common incidence of such assaults on female members of "heretic" populations in guerrilla war bears closer theoretical scrutiny.

In Lara, Angela Zago's hamlet was raided by army troops, from whom she was forced to hide, but the events related to her by the peasants who experienced the terror were grisly indeed. Peasants were tied to jeeps and dragged on the ground; others were beaten to death or had their hands cut off; women were raped; huts and grain stores were burnt. A small boy was allegedly shot for refusing to sell meat pies to a soldier. One woman (who had only grudgingly accepted the guerrillas in the area) was taken into the center of the hamlet, disrobed, and stomped by soldiers for thirty minutes. More than fifteen soldiers raped one pregnant woman. Another pregnant woman was also raped and miscarried as a result. Zago sums up the results: "What the government wanted it got: the peasants are terrified."[19]

More fragmentary reports are available from other areas, including Miranda, Portuguesa, Trujillo, and the *llanos* (plains states), where the residence of a guerrilla was blown to pieces with grenades without first attempting to see if it was occupied, and three women were raped by National Guard (Fuerzas Armadas de Cooperación—FAC) troops. When one of the victims lodged a complaint at the local FAC post, the captain replied, "No sir! Take these 100 bolívares and buy some new clothes; and take care what you say, because the next time we'll kil' them. And you're not to say anything about this."[20]

Even if one takes these reports with many grains of salt, the record is still one of agonizing human misery. This is not to say that this activity was official policy or that it always occurred, nor that the guerrillas did not employ it for propaganda purposes. Two illuminating comments were made by guerrilla leader "El Gavilán" (José Díaz) when he came down out of the Lara hills in August 1965. He indicated not only that he had been well treated by the soldiers who captured him, contrary to his expectations, but also that such a public statement might cost him his life.[21] Governments are apparently not alone in wishing to control information flows during guerrilla war, and guerrillas also obey the rules of propaganda control.

The contrast of Venezuelan government terror with that carried out in Guatemala is striking from a methodological point of view. There is far less specific information in the latter case, even though the terroristic executions of Guatemalan peasants ran into the thousands, as opposed to a few hundred in Venezuela. Indeed, the Guatemalan experience in 1966 and 1967 clearly stands out as the most brutal regime of terror imposed upon a peasantry in all the time period under review, dwarfing Batista's terror against the Cuban *guajiros*. The estimates of deaths in this terror run from 589 to as high as 6,000 for a one- or two-year period.[22] Furthermore, there is striking agreement between government and guerrillas on two items: the magnitude of the terror, and the fact that very few of those killed in the army campaign in Zacapa Department in 1966–67 were in fact guerrillas. The guerrillas in 1968 claimed that 3,000 civilians had died in the previous four years, while the army reported 2,000 dead—but only forty to fifty guerrillas killed—in the one-year Zacapa campaign.[23] This campaign was supervised by Colonel Arana Osorio, who later campaigned for the presidency in 1970, promising to turn all Guatemala into "another Zacapa." The FAR guerrillas *favored* his candidacy, apparently on the grounds that the worse the repression in the country became, the better would be their chances for success.[24] By 1972 Arana may well have been carrying out his campaign promises, as the Communists claimed 2,000 dead after one to two years of his government.[25]

Guatemala saw the first large-scale emergence of right-wing terror groups in Latin America. Such groups killed at least 100 persons in April 1967 alone, and may have killed up to 4,000 persons by 1974. As Aguilera has demonstrated, they were activated under extremely patriotic and virulently anti-Communist symbols, and were linked to certain landowners and businessmen, as well as to the police and the army. The elements of vigilantism in these groups—as opposed to those elements of official (though sub rosa) sponsorship—were summed up in a speech by a right-wing congressman: ''The regime shouldn't find it remarkable when the bourgeoisie organizes itself in order to take the law into its own hands.'' One other intriguing characteristic of these death squads was the presence of ''numerous ex-guerrillas'' in their ranks.[26]

A second aspect of terror in Guatemala was the bombing of guerrilla areas. At first the United States restricted the military's use of its eight B-26 bombers and fifteen F51D Mustangs to Zacapa, but by 1971 they were available wherever needed. The use of napalm was apparently quite liberal, and not only for the purpose of burning fields: the guerrillas reported that five peasants were found dead near Río Hondo, burnt beyond recognition by napalm.[27]

Terror appeared in army and police sweeps throughout Zacapa. One particular twist, also reported in Venezuela, was that local feuds or vendettas were grafted onto army terror. One peasant would point out a local ''enemy'' as a guerrilla collaborator whom the army would promptly execute. In the Guatemalan case, the heavy elements of distrust and suspicion were accentuated by the presence of local military outposts or *comisionados*, which apparently took on the aspects of a vast spy network after 1954, a feature accentuated during and after the Zacapa sweep of 1966–67.[28] In the Guatemalan case, then, the totalitarian elements of government and right-wing terror reached their highest peaks for the period prior to 1970. It should be no wonder, then, that the government succeeded in eliciting collaboration from peasants under such extraordinary conditions, especially when such terror was wedded to simultaneous civic action campaigns in the same regions. (The government's employment of both terror and civic action would escalate yet further from 1978 to 1984.)

The broad outlines of terror in Zacapa have been described by the FAR guerrillas and others. *Mano Blanca* (White Hand), the premier right-wing terrorist group, apparently was the cutting edge, or at least a major participant in the terror. In the prorevolutionary villages the army came in, gathered peasant leaders, and shot them in front of everyone, threatening to execute more if the villagers did not collaborate with the authorities. This kind of activity continued for more than half a year, and the peasant casualties numbered in the thousands. It was Walter's "regime of terror" at its most brutal.[29]

Yet army terror neither began nor ended with Zacapa, 1966–67. In February and March of 1964, army bombing of Izabal guerrilla areas allegedly resulted in seventeen peasant deaths, and army sweeps in the same area routinely employed torture of peasants for information. On the day following a guerrilla visit and talk ("armed propaganda") to the Kekchí Indian village of Panzós in Alta Verapaz, the army raided the town. One pregnant woman was gang-raped by thirty soldiers, and five peasants were executed at a nearby hacienda where the guerrillas had paid a similar call. (That same town would suffer a notorious massacre by the military in 1978.) The guerrillas worked more carefully following this tragedy, but government terror still occurred. In a similar sequence of events at the village of San Jorge, near the town of Zacapa, another pregnant woman was gang-raped and her womb cut open. After this the guerrillas returned to the village to execute the man who had pointed out guerrilla contacts to the army. The most brutal employment of terror up to 1966–67 was probably during Operation Falcón in Zacapa in September and October 1965, which was carried out much more quietly than the campaign a year later. The guerrillas reported that at least fifteen peasants innocent of guerrilla contacts were taken out to a quarry near San Lorenzo. There they were beaten and tortured for information. One man had his penis cut off and stuffed in his mouth. Among the techniques applied were a suffocating oil cloth hood placed over the head (*capucha*); being hoisted up by one's arms after they were tied behind one's back; beatings on head and testicles; breaking of arms; and outright shootings. To top off these grisly tales, an American missionary reports that the government employed Orwellian techniques "to cover the traces of bombings and massacres, [re-routing rivers] as well as razing forests and bulldozing villages."[30] Again, even giving a heavy discount to such stories—and the Guatemalan reports have high rates of confirmation by nonguerrillas—

one must conclude that rural Guatemalans experienced government terror in the most extreme forms we will encounter.

In Colombia, a full understanding of the extent of violence during the period of the guerrilla movements proper is only possible with knowledge of the awesome amount of violence that occurred during *La Violencia* from roughly 1948 to 1964. After fifteen years of careless or hyperbolic estimates of the dead—going as high as 500,000—Paul Oquist employed more careful techniques to arrive at the conclusion that more than 200,000 died during *La Violencia*.[31] Much violence occurred not only within the peasantry, but also in acts of the army, police, and *pájaros* against peasants, the victims almost all being of Liberal Party affiliation. (*Pájaros*, literally "birds," were vigilante groups informally created by the Conservative Party, and their attacks on Liberal peasants were ignored by the army and Conservative police.)

Many allegations of later army violence against the peasantry, particularly in guerrilla areas and former centers of *La Violencia,* were gathered in a work (unfortunately underdocumented) by a group of left-wing Colombians.[32] Official government figures also suggest that army terror may have continued. From 1 January 1966 to 31 March 1967—a period of heavy guerrilla activity—the army reported the following death totals in the counterguerrilla campaign: military, 154; guerrillas, 29; others, 384. Similar data appeared in the annual *Memorias* submitted by the Ministry of Defense to Congress. From these data it is very difficult to separate those peasants killed intentionally by bandits from those killed by soldiers or by guerrillas, or even from those caught in cross fires. One suspects that the army contributed more than its share of peasant deaths.[33] Still, the most persuasive *negative* evidence may come from the guerrillas themselves, for one of their members candidly admitted that the Colombian army had "changed completely. It no longer frightens, it wants to reassure." If he was right, then terror was not routinely applied in Colombia, and was instead largely replaced by civic action.[34]

Army terror against the peasantry in the guerrilla period was apparently most intense during the 1964–65 campaigns to bring quasi-autonomous "peasant republics" back under federal authority. There are reports of army troops cutting off the heads and hands of peasant dead, for identification purposes if not out of sheer barbarism. Standard army procedures were aerial attacks with napalm and other bombs followed by helicopter landings. At the same time, ground troops employed ever tightening cordons sanitaires around towns, gradually creating free-fire zones outside the circles. One guerrilla of this period alleges that hundreds of peasants died due to such indiscriminate military action.[35] Throughout this entire period the government continued to refer to the operation as an antibandit campaign, but this label is not persuasive. Guzmán and his collaborators listed violent events in Colombia by *municipio* for the 1958–63 period, and the core areas of the peasant republics were *not* prominent in degrees of banditry or violence; indeed, there is substantial evidence that they were created as havens *from* violence. For example, the *municipio* of Marquetalia, in Caldas, which gave its name to the most important peasant republic, only had one violent event in that period.[36]

Personal testimony providing particular examples of government torture, beatings, and killings was given before the Colombian Congress in November 1964 (i.e., at the beginning of the guerrilla movements proper). Among the techniques reported were the placement of a grenade in a prisoner's mouth and threatening to pull the pin; faked firing squads; punching, kicking, and walking on prisoners; electric current applied to the genitals, hands, and ears; burning with cigarettes; and outright execution.[37] It is hard to believe that such tortures—aimed at finding later–FARC commander Manuel Marulanda (a.k.a. *Tiro Fijo*, or "Sure Shot")—ended once the guerrillas went mobile.

Estimates of the scope of terror in Peru vary widely, and one suspects the presence of body-count inflation similar to that noted above for Cuba and Colombia. The highest number, probably taken from a MIR propaganda sheet and propagated further by Victor Villanueva, claimed the government was forced "to massacre 8,000 peasants" to suppress the guerrillas, while Petras suggested over a thousand such deaths. Yet a MIR radio broadcast spoke only of hundreds killed, and the MIR's newspaper "El Guerrillero" on 5 September 1965 spoke only of "dozens" killed in Junín, area of the heaviest fighting and bombing. Clearly most of the dead peasants were there and in Béjar's area of Ayacucho, where he lodged the inflationary charge of "genocide." Gall, our best chronicler of the Peruvian events, suggests hundreds of Campa Indians killed in Junín alone. Overall, an estimate of "only" 300 to 1,000 deaths from government terror is a best guess, and still bloody indeed for a scarce six-month military campaign.[38] Indirect evidence also indicates that hundreds of peasants died at the hands of the army. The guerrillas, including those in Piura who never fought a battle, only numbered 100–150 at best, yet by mid-August, before any serious guerrilla losses were ever incurred, the government was claiming to have killed 100 or even more guerrillas in the Satipo and Pucutá areas of Junín alone.[39]

Army bombing of guerrilla zones in Peru was the most intensive seen in Latin American guerrilla warfare until the Nicaraguan civil war of the late 1970s. Mercier even uses the phrase "saturation bombing" to describe the air force's attack style, which was certainly not precision bombing when applied through the dense fog covering the Mesa Pelada in Cuzco, an area shelled intensely from mid- to late September.[40] Guerrilla zones in Junín were bombed in mid-July, but then much more intensively between 5 and 15 August. This included the dropping of napalm in the areas of Pucutá, Ajospampa, and Rosario Pampa. Bombing in Junín was renewed in late September. Interestingly enough, there were no news reports of air force bombings of Béjar's ELN front in Ayacucho, which was apparently liquidated through the use of ground troops alone.

Finally, three major guerrilla leaders—Javier Héraud (Puerto Maldonado, 1963), Luis de la Puente Uceda (MIR-Cuzco), and Máximo Velando Gálvez (MIR-Junín)—were all apparently killed by the army after surrendering or trying to do so.[41] Similar fates overtook several Venezuelan guerrilla leaders (perhaps including Fabricio Ojeda), and Ché Guevara in Bolivia as well.

Our descriptions of terror in rural areas have largely come from all sources but the people who experienced it directly, the peasants themselves. In this case we are fortunate to have exceptional data: transcript summaries of the trials of peasants for alleged collaboration with or participation in the Túpac Amaru guerrilla front in Peru (Junín). What did these peasants say?

Pablo Torres Córdova reported being threatened with death by the Investigative Police (PIP) if he would not sign a deposition indicating his presence at the sites of various guerrilla raids (he had indeed joined the guerrilla band, but said he was tricked into doing so). Evaristo Pahuacho Valverde testified that he was beaten by the authorities; that his father had been beaten so that he died as a result; and that his two female cousins, thirteen and ten years old, were raped by the police before his very eyes. The judge asked Guillermo Loardo Avendaño why he had deserted the guerrillas, and he wryly replied, "Because I saw how the police burned houses in the village, the reprisals taken against the people," and decided to desist if government violence continued. In his deposition he claimed that guerrillas massacred people, but later repudiated the document. When asked, "You didn't think you would be attacked?" after joining the guerrillas, Loardo replied, "I didn't think at all. I didn't think that police burned houses, stole cattle, raped women." Moisés Suárez Mercado claimed he was tortured while in jail, and that the Civil Guard killed his farm animals. When asked, "Have the police injured your family?" he replied, "No, but my countrymen, yes." Miguel Matensio Torres also said that he was tortured in jail to force a confession to the charges against him. A somewhat more educated peasant (?) and MIR member, José Miranda Balbin, testified that he had served as a guerrilla contact only after a month of torture in which he was hung up and beaten into unconsciousness.[42]

These Peruvian peasants also had to worry, as in Venezuela, of the possible consequences of retracting torture- and threat-induced "confessions" once they entered public courtrooms, since they knew that they would not always be in the presence of legal protections. Nonetheless, some exchanges were remarkable, even injecting elements of macabre humor into the proceedings:

> Prosecutor: Have they [the jailers] mistreated you?
> Peasant: Only verbally.
> Defense lawyer: What did this verbal mistreatment consist of?
> Peasant: They hung me up and beat me.

Another peasant, after the prosecutor exposed inconsistencies in his testimony concerning a trip to Cuba, exculpated himself by suggesting, "I'm sick in the head, I forgot because they beat me a lot."[43]

We come now to the Bolivian experience. Despite Ché Guevara's comments recorded at the beginning of this article, the Bolivian guerrilla war was almost completely devoid of terror on either side, an issue to which we shall return in our theoretical discussion below. The government, for its part, felt assured of the support of the peasantry, while the guerrillas were too mobile, too weak, and too fragmented to be able to derive any practical advantages from terror. Allemann argues that reprisals against the peasants by the government occurred "only exceptionally" in Bolivia, but gives no examples.[44] Guevara's diaries did note the bombing of guerrilla areas (in a very sparsely populated zone) on 24 March, 28 March (napalm), and 3 September 1967. On 5 September he also noted that soldiers coerced nearby peasants into giving them information about the guerrillas.

Those guerrillas who deserted or surrendered were in some cases the victims of sadistic excess. Two deserters had silhouettes traced with bullets (wounding one), while a guerrilla who tried to surrender following the Vado del Yeso ambush (late August) had his arm literally shot to pieces after an exchange of invective with a soldier, and was killed shortly thereafter.[45] The most famous case is that of Guevara himself. After initial reports of a death in combat, various investigative reporters revealed that he had been shot in a schoolhouse in La Higuera on orders from the government in La Paz.

Guerrilla Terror

> *Kill just one and frighten ten thousand others.*
> —Chinese proverb

There is no doubt that the terror used by government troops was vastly greater than that used by guerrillas. This fact should not be confused with the position that terror is generally an unimportant element of guerrilla activity. This thesis emerged in its boldest outlines from the Vietnam War, when Viet Cong sympathizers argued that the NLF was successful simply because it won the "hearts and minds" of the populace. The Vietnamese case provides a most curious dais from which to propound such a thesis, for the Viet Cong unleashed a siege of terror upon the civilian populace the dimensions of which have not been approached by any other guerrilla movement. Perhaps 50,000 deaths were the direct result of Viet Cong terror in a decade and a half of civil war. Nor can one claim that those civilians killed were strictly government officials (not that such an argument would legitimate such killings). In the period after 1968, when data were finally kept on nonofficial deaths as well, 80 percent fell in the nonofficial category.[46]

A certain type of argument tries to legitimate insurgent terror against noncombatants on two grounds. First, it is argued that the insurgents must use terror in order to survive early regime assaults upon their insecure movement. Second, it is argued that such terror is highly selective, and used only against government officials, informers, deserters, and local criminal elements, including "social" criminals such as landlords.[47] Despite those assumptions, some guerrillas have succeeded virtually without terror (notably in Cuba), while those guerrilla movements that do employ terror can see the range of their victims broaden in scope (notably in Cambodia). Are the guerrillas not bound by the same combatant-noncombatant categories to which the army is expected to conform? Bond sums up the objection nicely: "Why an internal struggle for power should transform what is otherwise murder into a legitimate act of war, without the conditions that normally justify killing in war [i.e., fire-fight engagement], is not clear."[48]

The consistent reappearance of guerrilla terror against fellow countrymen in the most diverse settings is due directly to two factors: the guerrillas' claim to constitute legitimate authority, and the high degree of guerrilla vulnerability to "information leakage."[49] This second point means simply that many guerrillas can only survive as sub rosa organizations, and must control information flows about them if they are to survive. Yet survival, *pace* Eqbal Ahmad, provides insufficient moral grounds for guerrillas to kill noncombatants, just as "suppression of guerrillas," "regime survival," or "defense of the fatherland against communist subversion" do not provide such grounds for the military.[50] From such legitimations are "dirty wars" created.

In general, attempts to legitimate the killing of civilians contain elements of a moralized Whig history, that tendency to view certain present results, and some putative future ones, as providing historical and moral validation for past or present evils. History is indeed often written by the victors of such wars, yet the tales of the losers and the dead also have much to tell us.

Guerrilla terror is generally far more selective than government terror. For one thing, socialist guerrillas are often fundamentally motivated by a moral vision of a better world, which precludes terrorist actions as inconsistent with such a vision. There are, of course, always exceptional cases. One of the more interesting is Ché Guevara, who behaved in a highly principled fashion in Bolivia, while writing the quotation that began this article, as well as the following: "In fact, if Christ himself stood in my way, I, like Nietzsche, would not hesitate to squish him like a worm."[51] Yet such sentiments are rare and one should not underestimate the role of moral principles in restricting guerrilla terror.

Second, guerrilla terror is, death-for-death, far more effective than government terror in eliciting compliance from the peasantry. Students of criminal deterrence have argued that quick and sure punishment, more than severe punishment, maximizes deterrent effects. If we visualize guerrilla and government terror in these terms, we may understand why minimal terror can be so effective. A peasant may collaborate with the guerrillas, yet still have a good chance of escaping the indiscriminate combing of an area by army troops. Guerrillas, unlike the army, tend to establish a more or less permanent presence in an area, and will have the information necessary to sort out actual "offenders" (i.e., informers and spies for the government) from the faceless peasantry.[52] Thus a peasant informer to the government is more likely to be found out than one who collaborates with the guerrillas. Apologists for guerrilla violence who argue that insurgent terror is selective fail to recognize that terror doesn't have to be indiscriminate to be highly effective. In addition, the public nature of either government or guerrilla terror maximizes the empathic immediacy of the deterrent on the target population, the local villagers.

Third, guerrilla terror can be so effective because it is combined with a program to promote peasant interests. This wedding of power to beneficence is crucial to understanding the magnetic power of guerrilla movements.[53] Newby sums up this "deferential dialectic" nicely by noting that "The great benefactor could also be the great persecutor."[54] This fundamental element of guerrilla *power allied with benefactions* cannot be ignored in analysis of guerrilla relations with the peasantry.

Information on guerrilla terror is sketchy because guerrillas attempt to hide from the public actions incongruent with their professed values, a stance common to social movements in general. The Venezuelan guerrillas, in an internal memo, suggested a halt to the death penalty for traitors to the cause, since guerrillas should practice "justice not vengeance" to obtain the correct image among the people and gain their support.[55] The memo also proposed the quiet punishment of informers, again to avoid adverse effects on the cause. Rarely do guerrillas announce their executions, except when the victim is locally or nationally infamous. Hence, much of our information on guerrilla terror comes from former members, peasants willing to talk, and newspaper accounts supplied either by governments or local reporters.

The Colombian ELN provides our only case where an ex-member revealed the precise degree of guerrilla terror. He still considered himself a revolutionary when he was executed by the ELN in Bogotá for publishing the exposé. In *La guerrilla por dentro*, Jaime Arenas outlined the death tolls attributable to the ELN's "*ajusticiamientos*" of peasants. Over a period of more than four years, the ELN killed 44 soldiers or police and lost 44 of their own numbers in battle, but killed 57 others, including civilians and members of the guerrilla band itself.[56] Unlike the corporeal atrocities committed by bandits under *La Violencia*, however, guerrilla terror typically occurred as forthright executions.[57]

Arenas's report on the Colombian ELN is particularly rich and thorough, and we lack anything quite like it for other guerrilla movements. This fact raises some critical questions. Are his findings generalizable to other guerrilla movements, which simply lack a Khrushchev to reveal the hidden crimes of their Stalin? Have other guerrilla movements also killed a peasant for every enemy dead, merely being more successful in hiding the fact? I would offer as an answer a cautious "no," because the ELN exhibited some unusual characteristics. Sharp intellectual vs. peasant conflicts split the movement, and the latter group mostly followed the authoritarian personality and behavior of ELN chief Fabio Vásquez Castaño, who ordered the bulk of the killings.[58]

Fidel Castro and Raúl Castro (in their respective Cuban fronts) and Ché Guevara (in both Cuba and Bolivia) held degrees of power similar to that held by the ELN's Vásquez, yet there is little or no terror associated with these guerrilla movements. It is true that Fidel Castro tried and executed bandits, rapists, and criminals in the Sierra but, by all accounts, the "trial" procedures were carried out with care (probably more so than the [in-]famous stadium trials of 1959). An internal rebel death penalty for desertion, insubordination, and defeatism was apparently never used. Aside from this, an hacienda foreman from the Sierra was executed for arranging an *hacendado*'s grab of land from some peasants; Eutimio Guerra was executed for becoming a double agent for the army, that is, for espionage; and three peasants were executed as army informers in mid-1957 (the difference between the last two examples is the difference between legitimate application of the rules of war and ad hoc justifications). Barquín lists others executed by the rebels, and argues that some were simply noncooperative peasants falsely categorized as bandits, especially in Raúl Castro's front. There is evidence from Raúl's treatment of enemy soldiers and bandits that he had far fewer moral scruples about killing than did his brother Fidel.[59]

In Bolivia, guerrilla terror never went beyond the planning stages, as the sole references are the entries in Guevara's diary, such as the one at the end of April: "The peasant base has not yet been developed although it appears that through planned terror we can neutralize some of them; support will come later." Other than this, guerrilla responses to a distrustful civilian population never went beyond threats and occasional seizures of supplies or food, usually in response to some offense such as informing. Despite this, the peasants regularly received the guerrillas in fear or even "panic-stricken terror."[60]

The guerrillas used more terror against the peasantry in Peru. The Peruvian Ministry of War accused the guerrillas of having barbarously executed peasants who might have supplied information to the authorities, and also listed six civilians killed by guerrillas in the six-month guerrilla campaign, four of whom were peasants.[61] One charge particularly difficult to evaluate is that the guerrillas in Junín shot and killed two captured members of the Civil Guard after applying burning tortures to their bodies (the guerrillas denied this). Photos of two corpses with massive burns on various parts of the bodies were prominently displayed by the authorities and newspapers during the antiguerrilla campaign, and the army produced doctors who claimed the burns occurred prior to shooting.[62]

Several Peruvian peasants reported while on trial that the guerrillas had used threats to induce their cooperation with the insurgents. On 23 October 1965, the army asserted that the MIR guerrillas of Cuzco/Mesa Pelada, desperately fleeing the army's relentless pursuit, killed three peasants who refused to help them. The guerrillas, as might be expected, "reversed the charges" by blaming the deaths on the army. This same guerrilla group reportedly shot four deserters in the previous month, which is not inconsistent with its history of desertions and scattered reports that the *foco* was literally torn apart by internal dissension. Members of this same *foco* apparently executed Indians near the Apurímac River when they refused to help build rafts to cross the water. The man who brought news of the event also reported the torture of his two sons.[63] There was also a rather bizarre report that guerrillas in Concepción Province (Junín) beheaded six members of a peasant family, aged five to forty-two. At this time Guillermo Lobatón's guerrillas were desperately fleeing army pursuit, and Lobatón himself died fighting two weeks later.[64]

The Guatemalan guerrillas used still more terror than in Peru, but selected their targets more carefully: *hacendados* and their foremen, informers and *suspected* informers, and villagers whose collaboration with the armed forces led to the deaths of innocent peasants. Luis Turcios Lima of the FAR defended executions by arguing that "We only respond to violence with violence. We deal out revolutionary justice." Indeed, one account of the *ajusticiamiento* of a villager was quoted directly from a proguerrilla source by Munson. The guerrillas pounded on the offender's door with the command, "Open in the name of revolutionary justice." In general, however, there is little evidence, despite one critic's claim, that the guerrillas' use of terror paralleled the government atrocities we saw earlier.[65]

By far the best documentation on guerrilla terror is available for Venezuela. In this case, I do not believe the amount of documentation misleads us as to its extent. Venezuelan guerrillas were faced with the task of gaining support from a peasantry that was largely organized by and supportive of the *Acción Democrática* (Democratic Action, or AD) party, which held governmental power from 1959 to 1969. One might expect that terror in such a milieu would be directed especially against AD peasant leaders, just as most of the early Viet Cong terror was directed against local officials appointed by the Diem government of South Vietnam. Our expectations are largely borne out by reports on guerrilla executions. Norman Gall reports the guerrilla execution of a local AD peasant leader, Rodolfo Romero, in October 1964 in Falcón. "With his hands tied behind his back, the guerrillas hung him from a tree by his armpits and threw broken bottles in his face to make him bleed. They read an execution decree accusing Romero of betraying the cause of national liberation, then shot him as the whole community watched." In addition, Alexander reports that Romero was beaten, his teeth knocked out, and his fingers and toes broken before being shot, all before the eyes of his wife and small children. Gall also reported on the FALN's kidnap and killing of four peasants in Trujillo State.[66]

The number of civilian deaths—almost all peasants—attributable to rural guerrillas in the Venezuelan literature is at least twenty-nine and perhaps as high as fifty. The comment by a radical leftist that the victims of guerrillas can be "counted on one's fingers" therefore seems a bit of an understatement, especially in view of the FALN's record of massive urban terror.[67] At times the executions by guerrillas took on grisly aspects, as in the one already described. On one occasion two uncooperative peasant leaders were killed and their bodies hacked to pieces, and in another instance the guerrillas allegedly shot the victim, stabbed him seven times, and stuffed his mouth with propaganda leaflets. However, allegations by the government of the guerrillas' "brutal and insane" rape of many women report no details and are largely unpersuasive.[68]

Venezuelan guerrillas did not restrict terror to noncompliant peasants. On 27 November 1966, a school for U.S. children was machine-gunned; a former government social security official was kidnapped and killed in early 1967; many peasants were kidnapped and later released in addition to those simply executed; and at least two guerrillas—and probably many more—were executed for trying to desert the *focos*.[69] In urban areas, the FALN also killed 160 policemen from 1960 to 1966; these were not generally chosen for specific crimes, but rather as representatives of government. Critics, radical sympathizers, and ex-guerrillas agree that this tactic eventually generated revulsion toward the FALN among poor *barrio* residents, since most of the police came from these same *barrios*. Finally, and in reference to our previous discussion of DIGEPOL's use of torture, an instance of "sweet revenge" occurred in September 1964: a guerrilla deserter reported that three captured DIGEPOL agents had been tortured with hot irons and executed by his former guerrilla companions.[70]

Accounting for Terror

My approach to terror differs in fundamental ways from some trends in the literature. First, I reject as unscholarly those analytic attempts which, entering into collusion with the combatants, choose to describe the killing of human beings in euphemisms. Guerrillas commonly use euphemisms for their various actions. Bank robberies become "expropriations" and the shooting of peasants becomes "*ajusticiamiento*," or the application of revolutionary justice.[71] Yet the moral legerdemain hidden by such phrases pales beside the pernicious use of euphemism in military, state department, and think tank circles. In such circles the mass murder of Guatemalan peasants was described as the elimination of the FAR's "peasant infrastructure" and "population resource." In Vietnam the military referred to village bombings as depriving the enemy of its "population base." In Leites and Wolf's systems analysis of insurgency, killing guerrilla fighters becomes "destroying R's [the Rebellion's] outputs." Removal of a "population buffer" is the label they attach to massive village uprooting and relocation programs. The use of a cordon sanitaire, with strict control of all movement of people and supplies into and out of an area (hence martial law in extremis), becomes "raising R's input costs."[72] Robin Williams has shown how euphemism tends to be used to legitimate acts of violence that otherwise could not be legitimated, and it is inappropriate for a scholar to get caught up in the legitimizing terms used by the participants in the conflict.[73]

Further prefatory remarks about causal and ethical analysis are required. Among sociologists and the public alike, causal analysis of behavior is consistently confused with absolution of responsibility for such behavior. (A recent and striking example occurred in the public discussion of the vicious beating of a female New York jogger, apparently by a group of youths on a "wilding" spree. All the issues I raise here have been raised concerning that event.) Thus, where sociologists claim to explain patterns of behavior such as deviance or crime, they themselves and the general public are both apt to confuse such theories about the behavior of people in group settings with the ethical evaluation of such behavior. Such a mixture is invalid for two reasons. First, there are elements of the ecological fallacy in such an admixture, the error of identifying the properties of groups with the properties of individuals within those groups. Causal sociological analysis consists of *probabilistic* statements about the *incidence* of such behaviors, including statements about the incidence and intensity of such behaviors within different groups, neighborhoods, communities, or societies. "Poverty" can explain neither the stealing of food by a particular hungry child nor the theft of a television by a particular unemployed teenage looter, since theory must also explain cases of nonoccurrence, and most poor people do not steal or loot. In contrast, ethical analysis is concerned precisely with the evaluation of such individual behaviors. To conflate these two modes of analysis is a variant of the ecological fallacy.

The second objection, which applies just as well to terroristic acts committed during guerrilla war, was stated eloquently by John Dewey over half a century ago. Dewey argued that one should never try to lay total blame on society or the criminal (read: soldier/guerrilla) for crime (read: terror), because this implies an unreal separation of man from his surroundings, mind from the world. Causes for an act always exist, but causes are not excuses. Questions of causation are physical, not moral except when they concern future consequences. . . . Society excuses itself by laying blame on the criminal, he retorts by putting the blame on bad early surroundings, the temptation of others, lack of opportunities, and the persecutions of the officers of the law. Both are right, except in the wholesale character of their recriminations.

Dewey adds that good intentions alone do not merit per se the estimation of "good," for the consequences of an act also fix its moral quality.[74]

The purpose of this introductory preface is simple: the reader should not understand my following attempt to build a theory of terror as an attempt to exculpate those who commit atrocities in guerrilla war. Readers may make judgments based on the information presented here, but I cannot be Virgil to their Dante in this ethical realm, where we are in principle all equals and where claims to moral virtuosity inevitably smack of hubris.

The Commonality of Terror against the Peasantry

Element One: Support Systems in Guerrilla War

In modern conventional war, which has grown increasingly "capital intensive" over the past few centuries, combatants, civilian populations, and support systems are clearly defined. Support systems include arms, factories, transportation networks, and the supply lines that connect the sources of supplies with the combatants. The combatant-noncombatant distinction is perhaps the central issue. Under the laws of war, deriving primarily from the Geneva Convention, combatants are to be distinguished from noncombatants by standard uniforms with a distinctive insignia visible at a distance. Attempts are also made to keep the civilian population distinct from support systems, but the mere presence of a civilian population near an arms factory does not, under the Laws of War, always protect the factory from attack. Under "Rules for the Limitation of Dangers Incurred by the Civilian Population in Time of War" (1956), chapter 11, article 6, it is stated that attacks on the civilian population as such are prohibited, but "should members of the civilian population . . . be within or in close proximity to a military objective they must accept the risks resulting from an attack directed against that objective.'' Such attacks, however, are forbidden if the military gain is not proportional to the degree of destruction involved. Furthermore, the presence of "individual combatants" within the civilian population does not immediately render the latter subject to attack.[75]

In situations of guerrilla warfare—and Vietnam serves as the clearest case—the distinction between combatant and civilian is intentionally blurred by the guerrilla fighters, who accentuated this in Vietnam by actually locating themselves within villages, fortifying them, and then firing at army patrols from within the villages. This tactic often produced, as a response, village bombings and terroristic sweeps, with drastically reduced regard by U.S. soldiers for the combatant-noncombatant distinctions, which in an extreme case produced the My Lai massacre of 150–500 civilians.

In fact, that tripartite distinction between combatant, noncombatant, and support/supply system is *typically* blurred in guerrilla war, *unlike conventional war*. Does the villager who carries potatoes to the guerrilla camp, as in Peru, constitute a military target? What of the peasant who lodges a guerrilla for the night (a common occurrence)? Or the peasant who serves as lookout for the guerrillas? Or peasants who regularly provide tortillas and other food for guerrillas, as in Guazapa, El Salvador? Or those who, as in Guatemala and later in El Salvador, serve on sporadic or permanent peasant militias? In El Salvador's guerrilla war, for example, evidence strongly indicates that the peasantry has often mixed with the guerrillas in ways that make them very hard indeed to distinguish.[76] Those features only accentuate in high relief the features found in bas-relief in those nations where the peasants supported the guerrilla movements discussed here: Cuba, Venezuela, Guatemala, and Colombia. (Even in El Salvador, however, a distinction continued to be made between those who supported the insurgency and those who decided to *incorporarse*—become full-fledged soldiers.)

Terror against civilians is apparently a far more regular, even "natural," concomitant of modern guerrilla warfare than of modern conventional warfare. Highly suggestive evidence along these lines comes from different behavior of U.S. combat troops in Europe (including Germany) during World War II, versus their behavior in some areas of

Vietnam, as Susan Brownmiller's sequential accounts of the two wars suggests, despite her own (rather different) intent and conclusions. Other suggestive evidence comes from the Vietnam War itself, where the United States' military forces seemed to employ terror more commonly in insurgent areas of *South* Vietnam, than in the enemy's homeland, *North* Vietnam.[77] I submit that such different behavior of American combat troops—in degree, not in absolutes—derived from the different types of army/civilian/supply-network complexes that they faced: lesser degrees of terror where they faced a state-controlled, -supplied, and -directed conventional army, with a civilian population still residing at home far from the fronts; greater levels of terror, at times quite intense, where they instead faced a guerrilla army intimately tied into the civilian peasant population, especially in the Mekong Delta and (perhaps) in certain coastal areas.[78]

Terror is particularly common in guerrilla warfare because there is an aggregation and mixture of combatant, noncombatant, and support system into a very small social and geographical space. The nature of the support system is fascinating, for it consists in large part—not completely—of the peasantry itself. Whether the peasantry acts willingly or not, in guerrilla warfare there is often a very deep social and geographical overlap between the support system (the source of military intelligence, food, supplies, and recruits) and the civilian population, and a large overlap between the civilian population and the combatants as well, often in the form of peasant militias. The contrast with conventional war may be illustrated with Venn Diagrams. (See Figures 3.1 and 3.2.)

The shaded areas in Figure 3.2 can be understood to represent not just support, but also areas of potential reprisals against the civilian population. That is, the deeper and more thorough the overlap between the guerrilla combatants and the civilian population, the more likely that the government will engage in terror against the civilian population in guerrilla zones.

Two types of comparative evidence strongly suggest that the depth of "system overlap" within guerrilla zones is correlated with the intensity of government terror. From the period covered in this essay, we can clearly detect two areas in which the local peasants were not subjected to terror by the military: La Convención, Peru (although the nearby, isolated *foco* site was certainly bombed); and Bolivia during Guevara's insurgency. In both cases, the peasantry had given clear

Figure 3.1 **Social Forces in Conventional Warfare**

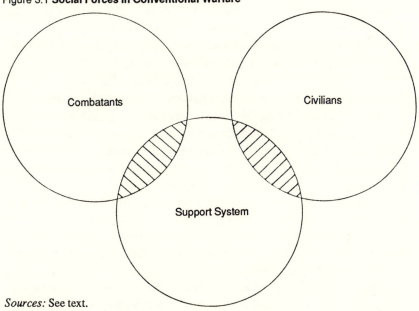

Sources: See text.

Figure 3.2 **Social Forces in Guerrilla Warfare**

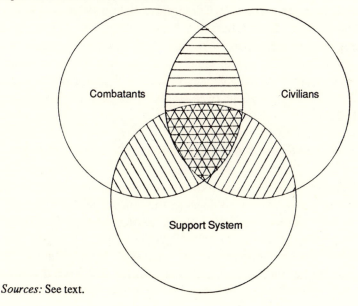

Sources: See text.

indications that they were indifferent to the insurgency, if not actively hostile to it. In one Peruvian case (Cuzco), several local peasant leaders abandoned the insurgency after a brief period of membership, and later guided the army to the destruction of the campsites on the Mesa Pelada. In Bolivia, the nation's peasantry, especially in the Cochabamba Valley, were very strong backers of and voters for the Barrientos government; their national confederation declared support for him in mid-1967; and the leader of the peasant union in Guevara's locale was also a pro-Barrientos man.[79] In contrast, we encountered terror almost everywhere else in our other four cases, and in all those cases we have clear evidence of strong peasant support for the guerrilla movements in certain areas of each nation.

The second type of comparative evidence comes from the "second wave" of insurgencies in Latin America, after about 1975. Every one of these movements, except perhaps in Nicaragua, established bases of peasant support in the countryside far stronger than the pre-1970 movements had done. Hence the number of guerrilla combatants was routinely in the thousands, not the hundreds seen in the early period: perhaps 10,000 in El Salvador, 7,000 in Colombia, 6,000 in Guatemala, and at least 5,000 for Peru's *Sendero Luminoso*, when each peaked in the early 1980s.[80] Those numbers are sure signs that peasant support for the insurgency—and hence the overlap of our three systems—has been greater since 1975 than it was before 1970. The correlate of that greater support has also been obvious: in nations with major rural insurgencies since 1975 (including Nicaragua), the central government, and often the death squads linked thereto, have responded with levels of terror that have taken up to 10,000 civilian lives (perhaps less in Colombia), and perhaps over 50,000 lives each in El Salvador and Guatemala.

Element Two: Legitimate Authority and "Heresy"

This correlation strongly suggests the second necessary element in understanding terror against civilians in the context of guerrilla warfare. As I have argued earlier, drawing particularly on Barrington Moore's *Injustice*, governments and the underlying civilian populace typically iron out an "implicit social contract," uniting rulers and ruled in a system of interlocking rights and duties. The main duties of the populace are obedience to appropriate directives and the rendering of surplus to support their governors; the duties of the rulers are to defend the region, to provide police and conflict resolution, and to provide for the material security of the populace. Where those rights and duties are perceived as fulfilled and intact by both parties, we may speak of legitimate authority. However, the peasant populace in many regions of Latin America has clearly transferred its loyalty to guerrilla "governments" in many instances, precisely because the central governments (or informal landlord "governments") do *not* protect, defend, and benefit the locals; indeed, they may do just the reverse.[81]

Notwithstanding such a peasant viewpoint, the authorities view the peasants' allegiance to and support of guerrilla governments—and the consequent existence of dual power or a counter-state in the nation as a whole—as tantamount to denial of the central goverment's "contractual" claim to the obedience of the populace, i.e., as traitorous activity. They have become heretics, not from the church militant, but from the body politic. The sheer numbers of guerrillas, and the depth of peasant support for them in certain regions of these nations, have made them something more: a cancer in the body politic, something to be rooted out and destroyed through surgical terror.

The right-wing nature of the regimes that the guerrillas faced, or at least the right-wing sentiments in the officer corps of the military, might well contribute here to the intensity of the terror that the peasantry has suffered. "Right-wing" radicalism has ideological features which in part distinguish it from leftist radicalism, and the most distinctive of those features, it seems, are (1) the exaltation of violence per se (rather than the grudging acceptance of violence as a painful but necessary means, so common on the left); and (2) the emphasis on *purity*—cultural and biological—whose best-known outcropping has been, of course, the Nazi and Japanese emphases on such issues in World War II.[82]

If terror is the response of a government to a decline of, and open challenge to, its authority in the body politic, then we would expect to find *guerrilla* terror against the peasantry in similar circumstances: where the claims by guerrilla movements that they constitute legitimate counter-states, new governments in microcosm, are being most sharply challenged, usually through the populace's unwillingness to cooperate with *their* "legitimate directives." The evidence from both Peru and Venezuela on the timing of guerrilla terror is consistent with the view that terror is a response of any "government" when its very authority to give orders is deeply challenged.

In Peru, guerrillas are alleged to have killed uncooperative peasants only at the end of the brief insurgency, as the insurgents were fleeing from the armed forces and most in need of succor, with their "counter-state" clearly in disarray. In Venezuela, the evidence is rather clearer. In the countryside, the government alleged virtually no guerrilla "terror" against the peasantry during the years 1962 and 1963, as the insurgents began to build up strong support in certain rural areas. However, the government charged the guerrillas with twenty-nine to fifty peasant killings in the period from May 1964 to November 1965—the very period in which the guerrillas were being flushed from their rural strongholds and when, especially in Lara State, there were clear signs of declining support and cooperation from the peasantry. In urban areas, the link of guerrilla terror to challenged "authority" was even clearer. The guerrillas called on the Venezuelan populace not to participate in the December 1963 elections, which constituted the first opportunity for a consecutive electoral transfer of power in national history, and which were a severe challenge to the FALN guerrillas' claims that they were a legitimate counter-state. (In their offices in Havana, the FALN was issuing memos on stationery with the masthead: "República de Venezuela. Fuerzas Armadas de Liberación.") The revolutionaries did more than exhort: in their pre-election wave of terror twenty-two to thirty-four persons were killed and over one hundred were wounded.[83] One might draw latter-day parallels to the Salvadoran FMLN's antielectoral "campaigns" as well. Shortly prior to the 1989 elections, for example, they threatened forty more mayors into forced resignations, a choice the officials found preferable to the lethal alternative. *Sendero Luminoso* has consistently done similar things in the Peruvian Sierra.

These mutually exclusive claims to authority may help us better understand why guerrilla war is not fought like conventional war, and why terror, especially by incumbent governments, is so common and often so massive. In conventional war one expects to defeat the enemy's soldiery and to make the enemy's citizenry acquiesce in, not hail, that conquest. In guerrilla war the enemy is not just a military foe, but a renegade and heretic who rejects such claims to exclusive authority.

To summarize: government terror against the civilian population in guerrilla war is common because of the conflation of guerrilla, non-combatant, and support systems, and because of the lack of information on the part of government soldiers necessary to sort out these categories. An additional element explaining the intensity of the "regime of terror" is that the guerrillas and all who assist them are viewed as renegades rejecting an authority self-defined as legitimate.[84]

The Incidence of Rape by Government Troops

One of the most common features we encounter in our descriptions of government terror in guerrilla warfare is rape. (In contrast, in a decade of research, I have encountered but one or two such persuasive allegations against leftist guerrillas.) How can we understand the intensity and regularity of rape, and often gang rape, of female civilians under conditions of guerrilla warfare? We can quickly dismiss the "horny soldier" view which attributes to soldiers some form of pent-up sexuality that demands release at any opportunity. Decades of systematic sociological study of rape have increasingly demonstrated that rape is a political act rather than a sexual one, and there is no reason to challenge that interpretation here, as we shall see.[85] While some scholars have indeed tracked down some distinctive pyschological profiles differentiating rapists and men prone to rape from the general populace, such psychological differences are ill-suited to explain the recurrence of rape in particular, well-defined *social* situations, including the situation under consideration here: counterinsurgency operations in rural areas and rural villages. Moreover, Susan Brownmiller has made a strong, although not completely convincing, argument about the essentially "ordinary" character of the rapist. Just as Hannah Arendt pointed to the "banality of evil" when considering the Nuremberg defendants, Brownmiller has suggested that one doesn't have to be a psychological monster to do monstrous deeds.[86]

Confronted with the near ubiquity of rape in counterinsurgency operations, one can take two theoretical paths. One can argue, as Gerda Lerner and Brownmiller do, that the rape of conquered females is as old as systematic warfare itself, dating back to the second millennium B.C. in Lerner's estimation. If this were true, then our analysis could stop here. Yet I am not convinced. For one thing, the ancient evidence is extremely weak on that central question, which is essentially a statistical one: the *variations* in the frequency of rape. Indeed, that evidence is incapable of addressing the issue at all, or of explaining the absence of rape by guerrilla soldiers. Furthermore, while Brownmiller clearly supports the general thesis that rape is natural to male warfare, her own rather more nuanced analyses of rape in warfare during this century suggest a great deal of variation, as she herself comes close to conceding, if uncomfortably so. The Germans and Japanese and North Africans (the last while participating in the European reconquest) seem to have been more rape-prone than other armies. Certain American soldiers in Vietnam, in particular those fighting in Viet Cong–dominated areas of the coast and Mekong Delta, were apparently more rape-prone than other G.I.'s in Vietnam, or those in World War II.[87]

For those seeking to understand variations in rape-prone cultures, Peggy Sanday and Rodney Stark have turned up some highly instructive findings. Stark has demonstrated statistically for the fifty United States and for the Canadian Provinces that higher rates of rape occur in those states/provinces where there are relatively more men living in households with no women present. Roughly similar results show up in the city of Seattle, where districts with higher ratios of unmarried men to unmarried women have more rapes. (He also shows that a substantial, positive, zero-order correlation between rape rates in the U.S. and pornographic exposure—indexed by *Playboy* circulation—*disappears* when controlling for the relative number of male-only households.) Paralleling this finding in her earlier cross-cultural study, Sanday found three clear correlates of societies that were more rape-prone: (1) a heavy stress on interpersonal violence; (2) an ideology of male dominance and toughness (which she appropriately code-named "Macho"); and (3) the presence of male-segregated social institutions (the last prefiguring Stark's later study). She found no significant correlation between rape and "sexually repressive" societies. Summarizing those findings, Sanday argued that rape will be more common where there is clear social disruption of the harmony between men and their natural environments, which, her argument suggests, should naturally entail closeness to a variety of women.[88]

Those "disruptive" elements of separateness and social distance from women dovetail with another increasingly consensual finding among sociologists who study rape: rape is likely to be more prevalent where women are "objectified," including the proverbial treatment as naught but sex objects. Men who live in sex-segregated environments, and those who stress sharp masculine-feminine differences, are precisely those lacking in the nuanced and intimate contacts with women—including mothers, sisters, friends, and sociosexual intimates—which would lead them to treat women in nuanced ways, not as objects. Such men seem to be the prime candidates for rape.

To speak the obvious yet heretofore unspoken: the barracks life of soldiers heavily emphasizes all three of the elements that Sanday found to be present in rape-prone cultures. Hence we would expect soldiers in general to be particularly prone to rape when they come into contact with the civilian population in a context of war (i.e., "interpersonal violence"). The aggravating feature of *guerrilla* warfare with regard to the incidence of rape lies in the extraordinarily intense "objectification" of the civilian populace that takes place. To reiterate my earlier point, the civilian supporters of the guerrillas have placed themselves, from the regime's perspective, outside the body politic, as its "enemies"; worse than that, they have declared themselves heretics and renegades. The recurring use of official language that utterly dehumanizes and categorizes all civilians in guerrilla zones—who become naught but "communists," "reds," and "subversives," to use the three foremost phrases—is an indication of the symbolic political excommunication that has taken place, for they are no longer viewed as one's fellow Cubans, Guatemalans, Peruvians, and so forth. Those who have moved "beyond the pale" of the body politic therefore suffer the double objectification of being traitors, and not simply the citizens of a conquered enemy province.

In contrast to the behavior of government troops, there is very little evidence that left-wing guerrillas have committed rape against civilian women, even in areas that have not provided support for the insurgency. Two contributory elements here are of an ideological nature: (1) left-wing radicalism, unlike right-wing radicalism, has not generally glorified violence per se (although the writings of Frantz Fanon give us pause here); (2) the strong egalitarian elements in all socialist ideologies, including the stress on comradeship, also militate against rape. Both of these left-wing ideological elements are the *opposites* of Sanday's first two findings about rape-prone cultures (i.e., they are the opposite of emphases on interpersonal violence and on male dominance). The last of Sanday's elements is relevant to the soldier-guerrilla distinction as well: guerrillas typically live cheek-by-jowl in cooperation with the local peasantry, including peasant women, and hence do not have the utterly sex-segregated life of barracks soldiers. Moreover, and perhaps sociologically most important to the rape-prone differentiation of the two armies, guerrilla armies were *partially* sex-integrated in the 1950s and 1960s, but by the late 1970s and afterwards, anywhere between 20 and 40 percent of the rebel armies of Nicaragua, El Salvador, and Peru were women.[89] If any social structural feature of guerrilla armies, as opposed to an ideological one, should limit the rape-proneness of *guerrilleros*, it would be close cooperation with fellow *guerrilleras*.

The Consequences of Terror

Peasants typically find themselves caught between pressures exerted by both contenders for power, and there is little doubt that they react with fear and terror at the prospect and reality of fire-fights, bombings, and military roundups. Where possible, flight from the area is a logical course of action. Such a step involves an enormous sacrifice in lost crops and changed lives, yet still occurs often. Indeed, massive flight and emigration from the war zones of Nicaragua, Guatemala, and El Salvador since 1975 serve only to confirm that flight is a prime option for the war-torn. On a clearly lesser scale, we have already observed similar flight in Venezuela, while Peru's Campa Indians fled en masse from their villages following bombing attacks, and Cuban squatters of the Sierra Maestra similarly fled Batista's terror early on.[90]

Yet peasants subject to terror might instead stand and fight. Moore suggests that one of the prerequisites of revolutionary action by the lower classes is that the prospect of flight or escape must seem impossible.[91] Various guerrilla groups agreed, at times indicating that peasants fought because there was no other way out. Peasant resistance is also fueled by moral indignation in the face of government terror, for terror violates fundamental norms supposedly governing the relationships between rulers and ruled.[92]

Most observers now recognize that government terror leads to new waves of recruits for guerrilla bands. When the Bolivians requested extensive U.S. material assistance in 1967 to fight Ché's guerrillas, a U.S. official said, "We are certainly not going to supply the means for the Bolivian army hotheads to start bombing and napalming villages or even suspected guerrilla hideaways. Civilians would inevitably be killed and we have a long experience that this inevitably produces a stream of recruits for the guerrillas."[93]

Government terror did indeed produce new recruits for guerrilla movements in Latin America, and they may have been extremely zealous fighters. Batista's terror especially drove the people of Santiago and the Sierras into Castro's fold, as even Castro's critics have confirmed. Barquín wrote that Batista's campaign of terror "sealed the alliance" between the guerrillas and the squatters of the Sierra Maestra, and Draper refers to the "universal revulsion" loosed by Batista's wave of violence.[94] In Venezuela a guerrilla suggested there was probably a new recruit for every woman raped by soldiers. After a particularly brutal raid on a village in Lara State (described previously), the guerrillas received a whole new wave of recruits; similar events occurred in Colombia.[95]

How could such recruits be used? The outrage that created such peasant warriors (in Moore's terms, the injection of "iron in the soul") was difficult indeed to contain within the guerrillas' organizational boundaries. One Venezuelan insurgent argued that "The *campesinos* want us to fight to mitigate repression against them, but we cannot because it would disrupt our plans for organizational consolidation."[96] In Guatemala such cases were especially frequent (unsurprisingly, given the levels of terror there). One peasant proudly related his recruitment after the army had raided his town and burned down his hut. Another summed up his own battle morale: "I fight well because I hate well." One fighter, Rocael, had seen his uncle tortured and his penis cut off and stuffed in his mouth. Luis Turcios Lima summarized the attitudes of such recruits: "It was also significant to see with what rage those *campesinos* fought whose families had been assassinated." As in Venezuela, the guerrilla leaders tried to mold the peasants' battle lust to the guerrillas' perceived organizational, military, and political needs. Peasant attitudes were ones of "desperate anger wanting to kill and be killed killing," but "they have to be calmed down" and the "spirit of classical peasant revolt has to be channeled into the painstaking and scientific strategy of the conscious revolutionary."[97]

One variation on this theme occurs when terror produces a temporary contraction of guerrilla-peasant cooperation, yet portends a longer-term cooperation with the insurgents and alienation from the authorities. Hence Béjar claimed that Peru's 1965 terror wave in Ayacucho produced "an unbridgeable abyss" between peasants and government authorities. While the evidence is thin for Peru, Japan's 1941 "Three-All" policy in rural China ("Kill all! Burn all! Destroy all!") did indeed produce that temporary guerrilla contraction followed later by prolonged peasant support and movement expansion.[98]

When terror, however, is combined with civic action or other benefits, the results may be to break the back of the insurgency. The guerrilla movement, as a counter-state in formation, is obliged to protect the peasantry from such violence, and lack of protection may lead peasants to withdraw their support. We now have recorded instances of such "peasant withdrawal," on a greater or lesser scale, from the Chinese Communists in the 1930s and 1940s, and from certain areas of Guatemala, Colombia, and Peru, the latter in both 1965 and the 1980s during the *Sendero* period. Under such conditions of withdrawal, it would not be surprising to see the emergence of an attitude such as "A plague on both your houses."[99]

In Lieu of an Epilogue

The preceding descriptions and explanations of terror could clearly be extended past this period to encompass the far more widespread terror in post-1970 guerrilla warfare in Latin America. Tens of thousands of innocent civilians have perished under such terror; indeed, that many were killed by governments and death squads in both El Salvador and Guatemala since 1975. The documentation of this second, more violent wave of terror is far superior to that of the earlier period, in good part due to the efforts of Amnesty International and other independent monitors of human rights violations.[100] Moreover, in at least two cases—El Salvador and Peru—the guerrillas themselves have also stepped up the degree of terror, taking the lives of well over a thousand, perhaps many thousand, civilians in their own terror waves.[101] I lack the space to pursue these latter-day comparisons in greater detail. Instead I simply note in conclusion that, as if to confirm (tragically) this perspective down to the goriest details, guerrilla warfare has once again given rise not only to even more widespread terror, but also to arguments and excuses on behalf of terror that exactly parallel those so regularly offered by governments and insurgents in the preceding two decades.[102] *Plus ça change, plus c'est la même chose.*

Notes

1. See James E. Bond, *The Rules of Riot: Internal Conflict and the Laws of War* (Princeton, N.J.: Princeton University Press, 1974), for a full discussion of the rules of war and possible applicability to guerrilla warfare.

2. Eugene Victor Walter, *Terror and Resistance* (New York: Oxford, 1969), chapters 1, 2. For some less formal observations about the social functions of terror, see Rogger Mercado, *Las guerrillas del Perú* (Lima: Fondo de Cultura Popular, 1967), pp. 160–61, and Héctor Béjar, "Ne pas surestimer ses forces" *Partisans* (Paris) 38 (July–September 1967), p. 111.

3. Leo Huberman and Paul Sweezy, "Cuba: Anatomy of a Revolution," *Monthly Review* 12 (July–August 1960), p. 29.

4. Hugh Thomas, *Cuba: The Pursuit of Freedom* (New York: Harper and Row, 1971), p. 1044; Boris Goldenberg, *The Cuban Revolution and Latin America* (New York: Praeger, 1965), p. 144.

5. Fidel Castro Ruz, *Revolutionary Struggle: Vol. 1 of The Selected Works of Fidel Castro*, ed. and with introduction by Rolando E. Bonachea and Nelson P. Valdés (Cambridge, Mass.: MIT Press, 1972), pp. 375, 399; Thomas, *Cuba*, pp. 972, 999.

6. Ramón L. Bonachea and Marta San Martín, *The Cuban Insurrection, 1952–1959* (New Brunswick, N.J.: Transaction, 1974), pp. 134–37, 151–52.

7. Bonachea and San Martín, *The Cuban Insurrection*, pp. 270, 192, 276; Günter Maschke, *Kritik des Guerillero* (Frankfurt, Germany: S. Fischer, 1973), p. 85; Thomas, *Cuba*, p. 920.

8. Thomas, *Cuba*, p. 335; Ramón Barquín López, *Las luchas guerrilleras en Cuba*, 2 volumes (Madrid: Plaza Mayor, 1975), vol. 1, pp. 14–15; *Newsweek*, 17 June 1957, p. 60.

9. Such tales can be told only where there are survivors. This and other stories can be found in Carlos Franqui, *The Twelve* (New York: Lyle Stuart, 1968).

10. Luigi Valsalice, *Guerriglia e Politica: L'esempio del Venezuela* (Florence, Italy: Valmartina Editore, 1973), p. 135 n. 12; Efraín Labana Cordero, *TO–3: Campo Antiguerrillero.* (Caracas: Ediciones Bárbara, 1969), p. 110; Angel Raúl Guevara, *Los cachorros del Pentágono* (Caracas: Salvador de la Plaza, 1973), p. 8 (1000s dead); François Maspero, ed., *Avec Douglas Bravo dans les maquis vénézuéliens* (Paris: François Maspero, 1968), p. 52 (the interlocutor with Bravo here could well be Régis Debray); Jean Lartéguy, *The Guerrillas* (New York: World Press, 1970), p. 195; Teodoro Petkoff, "Pre-Election Climate in Venezuela (An Interview with Comrade Teodoro Petkov [*sic*])," *World Marxist Review* (England) 11 (April 1968), p. 30. Betancourt stated once (cf. *Daily Journal* [Caracas, 21 June 1963]), that according to "certain delirious, cheap literature" the government was staging "mass murders" of peasants, and rejected such allegations. One should be open-minded on such matters and not accept these data uncritically, since the guerrillas are the usual source. This need for a critical eye is a point forcefully driven home by the name of the original publisher of Cabieses's work (see note 13)—"FALN publications"; cf. Klaus Lindenberg, "Zur Krise der revolutionären Linken in Lateinamerika: Das Beispiel Venezuela," *Vierteljahresberichte—Forschungsinstitut der Friedrich Ebert Stiftung (FFES)* 33 (September 1968), p. 288.

11. For bombing reports in the news see *El Nacional* (Caracas) 3 February 1963, 4 April 1963 (both Falcón), 30 October 1964 (Trujillo), 17 November 1964 (Falcón), 9 June 1965 (Lara). Bombing clearly frightened nearby peasants even when not striking their villages, e.g., *El Nacional*, 6 April 1963,

and Valsalice, *Guerriglia e Politica*, p. 126. Also see Timothy F. Harding and Saul Landau, "Terrorism, Guerrilla Warfare and the Democratic Left in Venezuela," *Studies on the Left* 4 (Fall 1964), p. 125.

12. Guevara, *Los cachorros del Pentagono*, pp. 164, 166; Valsalice, *Guerriglia e Politica*, p. 135.

13. Examples abound in Manuel Cabieses Donoso, *¡Venezuela, okey!* (Santiago, Chile: Ediciones del Litoral, 1963). One DIGEPOL torture-killing of a Communist was revealed by the Judicial and Technical Police (PTJ); cf. J. Carrera "The Murderers of Alberto Lovera Will Be Punished," *World Marxist Review* (England) 9 (June 1966), pp. 46–47.

14. Guevara, *Los cachorros del Pentagono*, p. 32. The translation attempts to capture flavor rather than exact denotation. Lists of killing and torture victims of government—whatever their accuracy—can be found in Cabieses, *¡Venezuela, okey!* pp. 269–76, and Eduardo Vicente, "On the FALN," *Studies on the Left* 5 (Winter 1965), p. 99.

15. Cabieses, *¡Venezuela, okey!* p. 203; Walter H. Slote, "Case Analysis of a Revolutionary," in Frank Bonilla and José A. Silva Michelena, *A Strategy for Research on Social Policy* (Cambridge, Mass.: MIT Press, 1967), p. 30.

16. Guevara, *Los cachorros del Pentagono*, pp. 118–20.

17. *Daily Journal* (Caracas) 4 February 1966, 9 March 1966, 3 June 1966; *El Nacional* (Caracas) 4 May 1962, 13 August 1965.

18. James D. Cockcroft and Eduardo Vicente, "Venezuela and the FALN since Leoni," *Monthly Review* 17 (November 1965), p. 36; Maspero, *Avec Douglas Bravo*, p. 53.

19. Angela Zago, *Aquí no ha pasado nada* (Caracas: El Sobre, 1972), pp. 111–46, 149–50, 156–57, 170.

20. Maspero, *Avec Douglas Bravo*, p. 53; Cabieses, *¡Venezuela okey!* pp. 204–5; Norman Gall, "Teodoro Petkoff: The Crisis of the Professional Revolutionary—Part II: A New Party," *American Universities Field Staff Reports—East Coast South America Series (AUFSR-ECSA)* 17, no. 9 (August 1973), p. 6. On the *llanos* events, see the memoir by Antonio Zamora, *Memoria(s) de la guerrilla venezolana* (Caracas: Síntesis Dosmil, 1974), pp. 88, 99, 125 (quotation).

21. *El Nacional* (Caracas), 27 August 1965.

22. Several estimates are gathered by Gabriel Aguilera Peralta, *La violencia en Guatemala como fenómeno político* (Cuernavaca, México: CIDOC, 1971), p. 4/18. Also see Robert F. Lamberg, *Die castristiche guerilla in Lateinamerika: Theorie und Praxis eines revolutionären Modells* (Hannover, Germany: Verlag für Literatur und Zeitgeschehen, 1971), p. 65.

23. Luis Mercier Vega, *Guerrillas in Latin America: The Technique of the Counter-State* (New York: Praeger, 1969), p. 129; Norman Gall, "The Legacy of Che Guevara" *Commentary* 44 (December 1967), p. 42.

24. Fritz René Allemann, *Macht und Ohnmacht der Guerilla* (Munich: R. Piper, 1974), pp. 359–60.

25. Francisco J. Prieto, "The Communist Role in Guatemala," *World Marxist Review* (England) 15 (September 1972), p. 27.

26. Allemann, *Macht und Ohnmacht*, pp. 184–86; Aguilera, *La violencia en Guatemala*, pp. 4/21 to 4/25.

27. Susanne Bodenheimer, "Inside a State of Siege: Legalized Murder in

Guatemala," *Ramparts* 9 (June 1971), p. 52; Eduardo Galeano, "With the Guerrillas in Guatemala," in James Petras and Maurice Zeitlin, eds., *Latin America: Reform or Revolution?* (Greenwich, Conn.: Fawcett, 1968).

28. Georgie Anne Geyer, "Guatemala and the Guerrillas," *New Republic* 163 (4 July 1970), p. 18; Richard N. Adams, *Crucifixion by Power* (Austin: University of Texas Press, 1970), pp. 271–72; Camilo Castaño, "Avec les guérillas du Guatemala" *Partisans* 38 (July–September 1967), p. 152.

29. Castaño, "Avec les guérillas du Guatemala," p. 152.

30. C. Tzul, "Reaction Rampant in Guatemala," *World Marxist Review* (England) 7 (September 1964), p. 87; Donn Munson, *Zacapa* (Canoga, Calif.: Challenge, 1967), pp. 160–64, 172–73, 194–95, 64–65; Norman Diamond, "Why They Shoot Americans," *The Nation* 206 (5 February 1968), p. 167.

31. For a range of earlier, ever-higher estimates, see Germán Guzmán Campos, Orlando Fals Borda, and Eduardo Umaña Luna, *La violencia en Colombia*, 2 volumes (Bogotá: Tercer Mundo, 1962–64), vol. 1, pp. 287–93; Richard Gott, *Rural Guerrillas in Latin America* (Harmondsworth, Middlesex, England: Penguin, 1973), p. 272; James Petras, "Revolution and Guerrilla Movements in Latin America: Venezuela, Colombia, Guatemala, and Peru," in Petras and Zeitlin, *Latin America*, p. 334; Régis Debray, "Problems of Revolutionary Strategy in Latin America," *New Left Review* 45 (September–October 1967), p. 40; Walter Schump, *Las guerrillas en América Latina: El principio y el fin* (Buenos Aires: Punto Crítico, 1971), p. 16. Russell W. Ramsey, "Critical Bibliography on La Violencia in Colombia," *Latin American Research Review* 8 (Spring 1973), p. 10, entry no. 32, notes a stern critique of early, high estimates. Paul Oquist, *Violence, Conflict and Politics in Colombia* (New York: Academic, 1980).

32. Comité de Solidaridad con los Presos Políticos, *Libro negro de la represión: Frente Nacional 1958–1974* (Bogotá: Editorial Gráficas Mundo Nuevo, 1974). This work is a good example of political blinders in moral evaluation; no guerrilla violence against peasants is reported, except for one peasant who was *ajusticiado* ("judged," the euphemism for executed). The two verbs employed to describe killings by government are consistently different from those used in describing killings by guerrillas.

33. Mercier, *Guerrillas in Latin America*, pp. 236–37.

34. Lartéguy, *The Guerrillas*, p. 69.

35. Specific allegations of violence against peasants in guerrilla zones appear in Comité de Solidaridad, *Libro negro*, on pp. 69, 70, 83, 87, 88, 90, 119, 151; Jacobo Arenas, *Diario de la resistencia de Marquetalia* (Bogotá?: Abejón Mono, 1972), pp. 27–28, 70–72, 89. See also Jaime Velásquez García, *Contrainsurgencia y guerra revolucionaria* (Bogotá: Tinta Roja, 1975), pp. 20–23.

36. Guzmán et al., *La violencia en Colombia*, II, pp. 301–26.

37. *Colombia: An Embattled Land* (Prague: Peace and Socialism, 1970), pp. 19–28.

38. For a reproduction of the pamphlet see Rogger Mercado, *Las guerrillas del Perú: De la prédica ideológica a la acción armada* (Lima: Fondo de Cultura Popular, 1967), pp. 230–32. For Villanueva's use of the figure see Sara Beatriz Guardia, *Proceso a campesinos de la guerrilla 'Túpac Amaru'* (Lima: Compañía de Impresiones y Publicidad, 1972), p. 15; Petras, "Revolution and Guerrilla Movements," p. 349; Lamberg, *Die castristiche Guerilla*, p. 118; "Perú: En-

trevista a dos guerrilleros," *Pensamiento Crítico* (26 July 1967), p. 192; Gall, "The Legacy of Che Guevara," p. 39.

39. Lamberg, *Die castristiche Guerilla*, p. 117; *La Prensa* (Lima) 14 August 1965. Notably, by late September the government only claimed fifty guerrillas killed in the area in the previous two months, cf., *La Prensa,* 28 September 1965.

40. See *La Prensa*, various issues, especially 7 August 1965; Guardia, *Proceso a campesinos*, p. 20; Mercier, *Guerrillas in Latin America*, p. 84; Norman Gall, "Peru's Misfired Guerrilla Campaign," *The Reporter* 36 (26 January 1967), p. 38.

41. Mercado, *Las guerrillas del Perú*, pp. 55–60; Gall, "Peru's Misfired Guerrilla Campaign," p. 38; Guardia, *Proceso a campesinos*, p. 21.

42. Guardia, *Proceso a campesinos*, pp. 41–66. Similar reports of peasants killed by troops appear in a private letter from Guillermo Lobatón to Luis de la Puente on 20 June 1965, cf. Mercado, *Las guerrillas del Perú*, pp. 154–55; or Gott, *Rural Guerrillas*, pp. 421–23.

43. Guardia, *Proceso a campesinos*, pp. 44–45, 66–70.

44. Allemann, *Macht und Ohnmacht*, p. 238.

45. Luis J. González and Gustavo Sánchez Salazar, *The Great Rebel: Che Guevara in Bolivia* (New York: Grove, 1969), pp. 167, 171–72.

46. On Viet Cong terror see Guenther Lewy, *America in Vietnam* (New York: Oxford, 1978), pp. 272–79, and Douglas Pike, *Viet Cong: The Organization and Techniques of the National Liberation Front of South Vietnam* (Cambridge, Mass.: MIT Press, 1966), esp. pp. 238–51. Deaths from U.S. terror, mostly aerial, were probably about 150,000; cf. Neil Sheehan, "Should We Have War Crimes Trials?" *The New York Times Book Review*, 28 March 1971, pp. 1–3. Peter Berger has also rejected the "hearts and minds" view of the Vietnam War; cf. his "Indochina and the American Conscience," *Commentary* 69 (February 1980), p. 33.

47. For a debate focused on my second point, in this case concerning El Salvador's recent killings, see Phillip Berryman, "Another View of El Salvador," *Dissent* (Summer 1982), p. 356 and, in the same issue, "Gabriel Zaid Replies," p. 359.

48. Bond, *The Rules of Riot*, p. 89.

49. Among the more unlikely outcroppings: the Vendée revolt in eighteenth-century France and a twelfth-century revolt of an English earl. See Walter Laqueur, *Guerrilla: A Historical and Critical Study* (Boston: Little, Brown, and Co., 1976), p. 27, and John Beeler, "XIIth Century Guerrilla Campaign," *Military Review* 42 (August 1962), pp. 44–45.

50. Eqbal Ahmad, "Revolutionary Warfare and Counterinsurgency," in Norman Miller and Roderick Aya, eds., *National Liberation: Revolution in the Third World* (New York: The Free Press, 1971), pp. 159–62.

51. Dolores Moyano Martín, "A Memoir of the Young Guevara," *The New York Times Magazine* (18 August 1968), p. 62.

52. Daniel Glaser, *Social Deviance* (Chicago: Markham, 1971), p. 58, cites a study by Tittle which shows that certainty but not severity of punishment is inversely related to crime rates. See as well the discussion and accompanying references in Marshall B. Clinard, *Sociology of Deviant Behavior* (New York: Holt, Rinehart and Winston, 1974), pp. 346–50. One Eurasian officer noted of

earlier Indochina that "the French destroy at random because they don't have the necessary information"; cf. Nathan Leites and Charles Wolf, Jr., *Rebellion and Authority: An Analytic Essay on Insurgent Conflicts* (Chicago: Markham, 1970), p. 109.

53. See the preceding chapter for more detailed arguments and evidence.

54. Howard Newby, "The Deferential Dialectic," *Comparative Studies in Society and History* 17 (April 1975), p. 164.

55. Ralph H. Turner and Lewis M. Killian, *Collective Behavior* (Englewood Cliffs, N.J.: Prentice-Hall, 1957), p. 337; *El Nacional* (Caracas) 29 August 1965; *Daily Journal* (Caracas) 29 August 1965.

56. Jaime Arenas, *La guerrilla por dentro* (Bogotá: Tercer Mundo, 1970), pp. 199–204.

57. The atrocities of *La Violencia* are now legend both for their number and for their grisly and creative character; for an account of one hacienda raid, punctuated by rape and dismemberment, see Evelio Buitrago Salazar, *Zarpazo the Bandit: Memoirs of an Undercover Agent of the Colombian Army* (Tuscaloosa, Ala.: University of Alabama Press), p. 61.

58. Arenas, *La guerrilla por dentro*, passim. For more information on Vásquez's importance in the ELN, see Mario Menéndez Rodríguez, "Colombia: ¡Al ataque!" *Sucesos* (Mexico City) 1777 (24 June 1967), pp. 21–22. This was the first of a series of four or five weekly articles where the journalist reported on his visit to the ELN's *foco*. The reports are very informative, if uncritically laudatory, especially of Vásquez.

59. Ernesto "Ché" Guevara, *Reminiscences of the Cuban Revolutionary War* (New York: Monthly Review Press, 1968), p. 65; Bonachea and San Martín, *The Cuban Insurrection*, pp. 100–101, 190, 197, 368 n. 80; Barquín, *Las luchas guerrilleras*, vol. 1, p. 364.

60. Ernesto "Ché" Guevara, *The Complete Bolivian Diaries of Ché Guevara and Other Captured Documents*, edited and with an introduction by Daniel James (New York: Stein and Day, 1968), pp. 151–52, 170–71, 178–79. (Entries: Analysis of the Month for April, 20 June, 3–7 July, all in 1967.)

61. Peru, Ministerio de Guerra, *Las guerrillas en el Perú y su represión* (Lima?: Ministerio de Guerra, 1966), p. 386.

62. Armando Artola Azcarate, *¡Subversión!* (Lima: Editorial Jurídica, 1976), pp. 64–65; Guardia, *Proceso a campesinos*, p. 14; *La Prensa* (Lima) 3 August 1965.

63. Guardia, *Proceso a campesinos*, pp. 38–63; Ministerio de Guerra, *Las guerrillas en el Perú*, p. 67; Mercier, *Guerrillas in Latin America*, p. 185; Mercado, *Las guerrillas del Perú*, pp. 199–201; *La Prensa* (Lima) 25 September 1965, 14 October 1965.

64. *The New York Times*, 24 December 1965; Manuel Castillo, "Las guerrillas en el Perú," *Estudios* (Buenos Aires) 581 (April 1967), p. 165.

65. Munson, *Zacapa*, pp. 111, 115; Georgie Anne Geyer, "Guatemala and the Guerrillas," *The New Republic* 163 (4 July 1970), p. 18. For some references to executions, see Lartéguy, *The Guerrillas*, p. 88; Robert Rogers and Ted Yates, "The Undeclared War in Guatemala," *Saturday Evening Post* 239 (18 June 1966), p. 33; Adolfo Gilly, "The Guerrilla Movement in Guatemala II," *Monthly Review* 17 (June 1965), p. 11.

66. Gall, "The Continental Revolution," pp. 4–5; Robert J. Alexander, *The Communist Party of Venezuela* (Stanford, Calif.: Hoover Institution Press, 1965), pp. 94–95. Two elements of further interest in this case: (1) Romero was accused by some of "fingering" local enemies to the army as guerrilla collaborators, and (2) thirty families abandoned their farm plots in the area in the next few days. On "official" targets, see Valsalice, *Guerriglia e Politica*, p. 221; *El Nacional* (Caracas) 14 January 1965, reported that an ex-guerrilla directed the army to the graves of the four peasants.

67. Venezuela, Oficina Central de Información (OCI), *Six Years of Aggression* (Caracas: Imprenta Nacional, 1967?), pp. 36–49; Valsalice, *Guerriglia e Politica*, pp. 141, 216 n. 23, 221; *Daily Journal* (Caracas) 19 August 1964, 18 November 1965; *El Nacional* (Caracas), 28 March 1962, 18 August 1964, 14 September 1964. Guevara, *Los cachorros del Pentagono*, p. 8 (quotation).

68. Venezuela, OCI, *Six Years of Agggression*, pp. 42–43, 48–49; *Daily Journal* (Caracas), 18 November 1965.

69. Venezuela, OCI, *Six Years of Aggression*, p. 64; Alphonse Max, *Guerrillas in Latin America* (The Hague: Interdoc, 1971), p. 33; *El Nacional* (Caracas), 7 July 1964.

70. Valsalice, *Guerriglia e Politica*, p. 169; Talton F. Ray, *The Politics of the Barrios in Venezuela* (Berkeley: University of California Press, 1969), pp. 130–36; Norman Gall, "Teodoro Petkoff: The Crisis of the Professsional Revolutionary—Part I: Years of Insurrection," *AUFSR—ECSA* vol. 16, no. 1 (January 1972), p. 15; *Daily Journal* (Caracas), 13 September 1964. More evidence on Venezuela appears in the following section.

71. Lamberg, *Die castristiche Guerilla*, p. 40; Bonachea and San Martín, *The Cuban Insurrection*, p. 91.

72. Victor Perera, "Guatemala: Always *La Violencia*," *The New York Times Magazine* (13 June 1971), p. 71; Sheehan, "Should We Have War Crimes Trials?" pp. 1–3; Leites and Wolf, *Rebellion and Authority*, pp. 36–37.

73. Robin M. Williams, Jr., "Legitimate and Illegitimate Uses of Violence: A Review of Ideas and Evidence," paper prepared for the Behavioral Studies Research Group of the Hastings Center, May 1979, pp. 9–18.

74. John Dewey, *Human Nature and Conduct* (New York: Carlton House, 1922), pp. 18, 44–45.

75. Bond, *The Rules of Riot*, pp. 201, 214.

76. See the comments by Joaquín Villalobos in Marta Harnecker's collection of interviews with Central American revolutionaries, *Pueblos en Armas* (México, D.F.: Ediciones Era, 1984), pp. 173–232; the report of a brief visit by Philippe Bourgois, "What U.S. Foreign Policy Faces in Rural El Salvador: An Eyewitness Account," *Monthly Review* 34, no. 1 (May 1982), pp. 14–32; and an M.D.'s report of a longer period administering medical care in the Guazapa region, Charles Clements, *Witness to War: An American Doctor in El Salvador* (Toronto: Bantam, 1984).

77. Susan Brownmiller, *Against Our Will: Men, Women and Rape* (New York: Simon and Schuster, 1975), chapter 3. For more on the selectivity of American terror in Vietnam, see Lewy, *American in Vietnam*, ch. 11, and Tom Wolfe, "The Truest Sport: Jousting with Sam and Charlie," *Mauve Gloves and Madmen, Clutter and Vine* (New York: Bantam, 1977), pp. 24–58.

78. Brownmiller, *Against Our Will*, pp. 73–78, 86–113.

79. See chapter 2 above, and my "Winners, Losers, and Also-Rans: Toward a Comparative Sociology of Latin American Guerrilla Movements" in Susan Eckstein, ed., *Power and Popular Protest: Latin American Social Movements* (Berkeley: University of California Press, 1989), p. 157. Some excellent detail on Barrientos's support among the Bolivian peasantry, including 1966 electoral tallies, can be found in Jean-Pierre Bernard et al., *Guide to the Political Parties of South America* (Harmondsworth, Middlesex, England: Penguin, 1973), pp. 135–46.

80. The 10,000 figure for El Salvador has been widely disseminated; for the 7,000 Colombian guerrillas, see *Latin America Weekly Report*, 31 August 1984; for the 6,000 Guatemalan guerrillas, see James Dunkerley, *Power in the Isthmus* (London: Verso, 1988), p. 483; for *Sendero Luminoso* of Peru, I am indebted to private conversations with Michael Smith, and also to Cynthia McClintock, "Peru's Sendero Luminoso Rebellion: Origins and Trajectory," in Eckstein, *Power and Popular Protest*, p. 63.

81. See chapter 2 above, and Barrington Moore, Jr., *Injustice: The Social Bases of Obedience and Revolt* (White Plains, N.Y.: M. E. Sharpe, 1978), ch. 1, esp. pp. 20–22.

82. Barrington Moore clearly asserts the first principle, and the Nazi diaries that he quotes from strongly suggest the second; cf. *Injustice*, pp. 413–34.

83. Colonel Edward F. Callanan, "Terror in Venezuela," *Military Review* 49 (February 1969), pp. 49–56; *The New York Times*, 23 November 1963 and 2 December 1963; Gall, "Teodoro Petkoff I," p. 16; Gott, *Rural Guerrillas*, p. 210.

84. For more thoughts on renegades, see Robert K. Merton, *Social Theory and Social Structure*, 3d ed. (New York: The Free Press, 1968), pp. 209–11, 323; Charles Tilly, *From Mobilization to Revolution* (Reading, Mass.: Wesley-Addison, 1978), pp. 106–14, deals analytically with the way in which the acceptability of an acting group, rather than just the quality of its actions, affects the way repressive forces treat it.

85. Edwin M. Schur, *Labeling Women Deviant: Gender, Stigma, and Social Control* (New York: Random House, 1984), pp. 145–56.

86. Brownmiller, *Against Our Will*.

87. Gerda Lerner, *The Creation of Patriarchy* (New York: Oxford, 1986), pp. 80–81; Brownmiller, *Against Our Will*, ch. 3.

88. Rodney Stark, *Instructor's Resource Book with Demonstrations and Activities to Accompany Sociology*, 2d ed. (Belmont, Calif.: Wadsworth, 1987), pp. 46–47, 51–53, 109–13; Peggy Reeves Sanday, "The Socio-Cultural Context of Rape: A Cross-Cultural Study," *Journal of Social Issues* 37, no. 4 (Fall 1981), pp. 5–27, especially the results on pp. 23–24.

89. On leftist radicalism, again see Moore, *Injustice*, pp. 420–33; on the sex breakdown of the guerrillas, see George Black, *Triumph of the People: The Sandinista Revolution in Nicaragua* (London: Zed, 1981), pp. 323–24; for El Salvador and Nicaragua both, see Stanford Central America Action Network (SCAAN), ed., *Revolution in Central America* (Boulder, Colo.: Westview, 1983), pp. 383, 416–17; for Peru, McClintock, "Peru's Sendero Luminoso Rebellion," original ms., and a private communication from Michael Smith.

90. Gall, "The Continental Revolution," p. 5; Minsterio de Guerra, *Las guer-*

rillas en el Perú, p. 60; *La Prensa* (Lima) 23 June 1965; Guevara, *Reminiscences*, p. 94. In the Peruvian case the army reported that the mass exodus was due to guerrilla-caused "excitement."

91. Moore, *Injustice*, p. 125.

92. Again, see chapter 2 above. Also see Peter A. Lupsha, "Explanation of Political Violence: Some Psychological Theories versus Indignation," *Politics and Society* 2 (Fall 1971), pp. 89–104.

93. Gall, "The Legacy of Che Guevara," p. 32 (quotation); similar thoughts are also expressed in Lt. Colonel Harold R. Aaron, "Why Batista Lost," *Army* 15 (September 1965), p. 71; Lt. Colonel Neal G. Grumland, "The Formidable Guerrilla," *Army* 12 (February 1962), p. 65; and Chalmers Johnson, "Civilian Loyalties and Guerrilla Conflict," *World Politics* 14 (July 1962), p. 652. Benedict Kerkvliet has also argued that government repression transforms mere protests into political rebellion, cf., *The Huk Rebellion: A Study of Peasant Revolt in the Philippines* (Berkeley: University of California Press, 1977), pp. 260–62.

94. Daniel Friedenberg, "Notes on the Cuban Revolution," *New Republic* 138 (17 February 1958), p. 15; Barquín, *Las luchas guerrilleras*, vol. 1, p. 319; Theodore Draper, *Castro's Revolution: Myths and Realities* (New York: Praeger, 1962), p. 126.

95. Zago, *Aquí no ha pasado nada*, pp. 173–74; Régis Debray, *Strategy for Revolution*, edited by Robin Blackburn (London: Jonathan Cape, 1970), p. 103.

96. *El Nacional* (Caracas), 31 August 1962.

97. Adolfo Gilly, "The Guerrilla Movement in Guatemala I," *Monthly Review* 17 (May 1965), pp. 24–25; Munson, *Zacapa*, pp. 194–95; Schump, *Las guerrillas en América Latina*, p. 55; A. P. Short, "Conversations with the Guatemalan Delegates in Cuba," *Monthly Review* 18 (February 1967), p. 37.

98. Guevara, *Reminiscences*, pp. 192–94; Héctor Béjar, "Bilan d'une guérilla au Pérou," *Partisans* 37 (April–June 1967), p. 98; Béjar, "Ne pas surestimer ses forces," p. 111; Lt. Colonel John W. Woodmansee, Jr., "Mao's Protracted War: Theory and Practice," *Parameters* 3, no. 1 (1973), pp. 40–41.

99. See chapter 2 above for detail on all but the final case; for some evidence that *Sendero Luminoso*'s support in the Andes has fallen because they failed to protect the peasantry, see McClintock, "Peru's Sendero Luminoso Rebellion," p. 90.

100. For Amnesty International (A.I.) information on a variety of cases, see their *The Republic of Nicaragua* (Nottingham, England: The Russell Press, 1977); a capsule summary, "Guatemala: A Government Program of Political Murder," in Jonathan L. Fried, Marvin E. Gettleman, Deborah T. Levenson, and Nancy Peckenham, eds., *Guatemala in Rebellion: Unfinished History* (New York: Grove, 1983), pp. 139–45, and a summary of their findings for the early period under General Efraín Ríos Montt, in *Latin America Weekly Report* (London), 15 October 1982, p. 11; for Guatemala in 1983, see as well the summary of the Americas Watch findings, in "Extermination in Guatemala," *The New York Review of Books*, vol. 30, no. 9 (2 June 1983), pp. 13–16; two summaries of A.I.'s reports on Peru and El Salvador appear in, repectively, *Latin America Weekly Report*, 23 September 1983, p. 10, and *Latin America Political Report* (London; same periodical), 21 March 1980, p. 12. Independent church authorities also criticized and documented government terror as well, especially in Nicaragua and

El Salvador. For more detail on government terror, mostly from left-wing sources, see, for Nicaragua: Doris Tijerino, *Inside the Nicaraguan Revolution, As Told to Margaret Randall* (Vancouver: New Star, 1978), pp. 165–75; *Latin America Political Report*, 29 June 1979, pp. 194–96; *The New York Times*, 2 March 1977, section 2, p. 1. For Guatemala: George Black et al., *Garrison Guatemala* (New York: Monthly Review, 1984), pp. 94–97; Concerned Guatemala Scholars, *Guatemala: Dare to Struggle, Dare to Win* (San Francisco, Calif.: Solidarity, 1982), pp. 67–72; and *Proceso* (Mexico City) no. 412 (24 September 1984), pp. 40–43, for an extensive list of massacres and body counts. For El Salvador, see Vicente Navarro, "Genocide in El Salvador," *Monthly Review* 32, no. 11 (April 1981), pp. 1–16; Allan Nairn, "Behind the Death Squads," *The Progressive* 48, no. 5 (May 1984), pp. 20–29, on reports of U.S. government backing for terror; and Shirley Christian, "El Salvador's Divided Military," *Atlantic Monthly* 251, no. 6 (June 1983), pp. 50–60 on military-civilian links to terror. For Peru, see Cynthia McClintock, "Sendero Luminoso: Peru's Maoist Guerrillas," *Problems of Communism* 32, no. 5 (September–October 1983), pp. 30–32.

101. Guerrilla terror also has expanded in scope, with insurgents using far more kidnapping, extortion, bank robbery, attacks on economic and utility targets, and interdictions of road traffic than in the past; all have occurred in El Salvador, at least a few in other locales. On *Sendero*'s terror in Peru, with estimated civilian deaths well into the thousands, see McClintock, "Sendero Luminoso," pp. 19, 32; Mario Vargas Llosa, "Inquest in the Andes," *The New York Times Magazine* (31 July 1983), pp. 18–23ff. (which also documents government terror); *(Latin America) Weekly Report*, 18 January 1985, p. 10, and 13 January 1984, pp. 10–11. The kind of widespread agreement on *Sendero*'s wave of terror is not shared in the literature on El Salvador, where left-wing scholars routinely deny such features; for suggestive evidence, including references to the guerrillas' self-recorded killings of thousands of civilians, see Penn Kemble, "The Liberal Test in El Salvador," *The New Republic*, 14 March 1981, pp. 18–19; R. Bruce McColm, *El Salvador: Peaceful Revolution or Armed Struggle?* (New York: Freedom House, 1982), pp. 23–24, 43; Mark Falcoff and Robert Royal, eds., *Crisis and Opportunity: U.S. Policy in Central America and the Caribbean* (Washington, D.C.: Ethics and Public Policy Center, 1984), pp. 199–200, 269; Michel G. Englebert (Interviewer), "Flight: Six Salvadorans Who Took Leave of the War," *The Progressive* 47, no. 3 (March 1983), pp. 38–43, including victims of both sides; and *(Latin America) Weekly Report*, 16 March 1984, p. 1; for a more general view, see Gabriel Zaid, "Enemy Colleagues: A Reading of the Salvadoran Tragedy," *Dissent* (Winter 1982), pp. 13–40.

102. This is clearest in Guatemala and El Salvador; in the former, the government under General Efraín Ríos Montt (1982–83) legitimated army (not death squad) terror against civilians as justifiable attacks on "subversives"; for a typical defense (that is, by minimization and justification) of the guerrillas' terror in El Salvador, see Berryman, "Another View of El Salvador," and Zaid's critique in "Gabriel Zaid Replies."

4

Ideology and Revolution?
The Limitations of Consciousness
Raising in Revolutionary Struggles

Consciousness Raising and Revolutionary Movements

In the early 1960s a Brazilian educator named Paulo Freire and his
collaborators developed a technique in the Brazilian backlands through
which they could teach adults to read and write in the space of three to
four weeks. This technique centered the literacy training process on
"generative" words, that is, themes involved in peasants' day-to-day
lives, from which the process of learning to read and write flowed
readily. Part and parcel of Freire's project was his attempt to move the
peasants toward a critical view of the oppressive reality of their lives,
this view to be elicited through a dialogue between educator and student. Freire named this entire process *concientização*, which translates
literally as "bringing to consciousness," "making conscious," or,
most commonly in English, "consciousness raising."[1]

In his early work, Freire did more than simply elaborate a new
theory and practice, for he also provided a scathing critique of the
practices of others. While his most contemptuous words were directed
at liberal reformers of the social-worker ilk, he also strongly criticized
those revolutionaries who attempted to impose their definitions of the
world on the masses, arguing that they merely mirrored the techniques
of the dominant classes. He insisted rather that there occur a genuine
dialogue between educator and learner, and he contrasted such an
(egalitarian?) relationship with what he called the "cultural invasion"
of oppressed peoples by dominant groups (and some revolutionaries).[2]

Through such dialogues, Freire hoped to get the peasants to view their situations not fatalistically, but as socially created, and hence mutable, structures of oppression.

In criticizing some revolutionaries, Freire was implicitly acknowledging certain developments in Marxist theory and practice over the preceding century. In Marx's theory proletarians were to arrive at revolutionary consciousness, revolutionary solidarity, and finally revolutionary action through the collective experience of oppression in their everyday lives. That consciousness is precisely specified: the recognition by the working class of its own existence and interests as a class (the oft-cited *klasse für sich*) and of its pivotal role in the overthrow of capitalism and the subsequent birth of socialism. Yet what if the proletarians do not view themselves in such terms? In such a case they are the victims of cultural manipulation by the ruling class—first and foremost by the priests and theologians who serve that class—and hence have a *false consciousness* concerning their own lives and situations (Freire does occasionally employ this idea).[3]

Lenin's later revision of Marx is also crucial to this issue, for Lenin rejected the idea that revolutionary (i.e., true) consciousness would arise solely from the life conditions of the proletariat, insisting rather that it must be brought to them (and out of them) by the agitation of a revolutionary vanguard. Without the actions of said vanguard, Lenin argued, the working class could only arrive at "economism," a sorry reformist substitute for the proper proletarian ideological destiny. The vanguard, in the form of a revolutionary party, thus will speak and act on behalf of the working class.

Thus, if for Marx the proletariat is the acting subject of revolution, in Lenin's revision the workers become rather more like the acted-upon objects of revolutionary exertions. Moreover, there is a good vanguardist parallel to Lenin's model in the latter-day actions of revolutionaries in Latin America since the 1950s, as the protoguerrilla forces retire to the countryside to rouse to a revolutionary pitch the peasants who are not apparently becoming a revolutionary force under their own steam.[4] Moreover, the 1960s guerrillas did not simply assume or create this implicit model, for it had the imprimatur of none other than Fidel Castro. Lenin's "vanguardist" model therefore seems to provide *exactly* the kind of "cultural invasion" of the lower classes that Freire criticized so sharply.

Nonetheless, the apparent incongruities between Freirean and Leninist approaches to "revolution" should not blind us to some deeper similarities. Indeed, so deep are these similarities in thought and action between Freirean educators and Leninist agitators that we can perhaps be forgiven if we suspect that Freire's educational project might be hoist on its own petard.

We might begin with the most basic similarity: both perspectives view the people as being "awakened" by the ministrations—presumably selfless, as Peter Berger has noted—of selected higher-class political activists. Indeed, this image of a dormant lower-class population is a recurrent one in revolutionary groups, appeals, and cultural artifacts throughout Latin America.[5] Perhaps the most apt of the myriad examples is a film concerning popular mobilization in Chile two decades ago, entitled "*Cuando despierta el pueblo*" ("When the People Awake"). Therefore we should not be surprised that a Venezuelan guerrilla spokesman could discuss the FALN's plans of "convincing them [the peasants] and awakening them politically," while Régis Debray more optimistically saw them already "waking up in their own turn." In an unfortunate turn of phrase, whose intent is nonetheless clear, Richard Adams described peasant mobilization in 1950s Guatemala as a "sociological awakening." Similar accounts and quotations prevailed throughout the 1960s in guerrilla movements, leading Richard Gott finally to compare the guerrillas to the Russian *narodniki*, who sought "to *stir up* the passive peasantry to understand the nature of the wrongs they are obliged to suffer. With the people aware and mobilized revolution would then be on the agenda." The same themes recur over and over: dormancy, passivity, and awakening. Clearly Freire's project is not so distinct from the Leninist one as he thought.[6]

Revival of the *Instrumentum Vocale*?

In the ancient world, the Romans distinguished three types of "tools" to be used in the course of economic exertions. First were the *instrumenta muta*, tools used for working the land, wood, pottery, and so forth. Second was the *instrumentum semi-vocale*, a reference to the ability of cattle to utter guttural noises. Finally they referred to the *instrumentum vocale*, or the agricultural slave commonly used for work on the great latifundia of the Roman Empire.[7] The distinguishing feature, it seems, of any "instrument" is that its proper purpose is to serve the commands and directives of others, rather than to seek its own ends. It is beyond question that such an attitude toward servile labor persisted among landed upper classes in certain areas well into the twentieth century; the most famous modern example concerns U.S. judicial debates over the rights of southern slave-owners to their "chattel." Most striking for our purposes here, however, is the degree to which residues, and sometimes more than residues, of this ideology pervade the thinking of professed consciousness-raising "revolutionaries" when they initiate relationships with peasant and working-class populations. While we will concentrate here mostly upon the peasantry, this debunking procedure could be applied with little alteration to mobilizers "working" upon working-class groups, or to feminists attempting to raise the consciousness of their "prefeminist" female counterparts.

We can tender the theoretical assumptions of the consciousness raisers as a series of propositions:

1. There exist higher and lower levels of consciousness.

2. Peasants are ordinarily at a relatively low level of consciousness.

3. Peasants do not understand the reality of their own social world. *Corollary:* Peasants are controlled by and have internalized the ideology of the dominant group or ruling class.

4. The world view internalized by peasants inhibits their radical action. *Corollary:* Acquisition of a different world view through consciousness raising will lead to radical action.[8]

5. Peasants can attain a higher level of consciousness only through interaction with other groups, specifically revolutionary intellectuals.[9]

Each of these propositions is simply false or subject to serious challenge.

Proposition 1

Peter Berger has mounted a decisive phenomenological assault on the notion that human beings possess "higher" or "lower" levels of consciousness. From his perspective, each human being inhabits a social, meaning-providing world, one partially "given" and partially (and socially) constructed; each such world is unique, although shared in varying degrees with other humans. As opposed to Freire, Berger posits the equality of all empirically available social worlds. While an individual from one social world may certainly transfer information both useful and welcome to an individual inhabiting a very different social world, this process is in principle an exchange between equals. Although Freire, at least in his earlier writings, emphasizes the necessity of a meeting of minds between the consciousness-raising educator and the learner from the target group, even there the educator is learning just enough about the learner to make the process of *concientização* more effective. The learner-peasant is to learn from the educator-revolutionary, not the other way around. (As Berger succinctly puts it, the sociologist should always concretize such matters by asking *whose* consciousness is to be raised and *who* is doing the raising.)

Therefore whenever revolutionaries begin from a thesis that peasants and workers suffer from false or lowered levels of consciousness, there will be elements of arrogance in their attempts to effect change. As Berger again observes, therein prevails that curious missionary blend of arrogance ("We know the truth") and benevolence ("We want to save you").[10]

If this procedure is not, and phenomenologically cannot be, a process of "raising" the consciousness of others, then what is it? It may most accurately be termed, in Berger's view, a process of *conversion*, in which the target individual's social world is (at least in part) swallowed up by the *weltanschauung* of the revolutionary "consciousness raiser." How should the outside observer treat this newly acquired consciousness? With the same respect one reserves for any cultural system that provides meaning to its carriers, but *not* as an epistemologically privileged one. The enthusiasms of converts are now legend—no matter whether the converts suddenly become Roman Catholics, evangelical Christians, Jehovah's Witnesses, feminists, members of the Unification Church ("Moonies"), Nazis, Communists or ex-Communists, or for that matter, sociologists—but the critical sociologist does not need to grant epistemological carte blanche to any of these world views; indeed, such a sociologist should actively question all such claims.

Proposition 2

If the first proposition is false, then it follows that peasants are just as conscious of their social worlds as intellectuals are of theirs. Freire instead argues that the illiterate peasant is literally dehumanized by this pre-elevated state of consciousness (unlike the "obviously" more human educator). Revolutionaries and their admirers have responded to the situations of various peasantries with very similar observations. Miguel Sobrado distinguishes a certain Costa Rican peasant as having a "much more advanced point of view" than most of his peers; two Venezuelan leftist intellectuals proposed that the university should form a national culture "which raises substantially the ideological and political level of the people;" former Colombian ELN (Army of National Liberation) member Jaime Arenas wanted political instruction among the guerrillas to seek "combatants at an acceptable political level which should be permanently growing"; and revolutionary Héctor Béjar observed that the "Peruvian peasant is extremely backward and subject to ancient beliefs and prejudices."[11]

One might even agree with the goals of revolutionaries in all these instances, yet still be able to observe that, in all these cases, the perceived acceptability of the "level" of peasant consciousness appears to hinge on how closely it approaches that of the (revolutionary) writer. That alone should alert our critical faculties. In fact, by implicitly adopting a consciousness-raising model for revolutionaries' interactions with peasants, the former have often done more than simply adopt an ill-named synonym for "conversion." Instead they have at times arrived, albeit via a different intellectual route, at a perspective that dovetails with the world view of their most despised enemies, as the following five quotations may make clear:

1. "We don't know what to do with the Indians. They are animals. These Indians are good for nothing, not even for eating."

2. "The inhabitants have to be hunted down to be able to speak with them for they are like little animals."

3. "The Indian is the animal that most resembles man."

4. "This level of consciousness . . . for men, means living like animals. It is often impossible for such men to recognize the differences between themselves and, say, horses."

5. "[Indians are just] animals, like deer or iguanas."

The first and third quotations above are, respectively, by a Peruvian landlord and from an old racist adage repeated by Peruvian *mestizos*. The fifth quotation, similarly, was the defense used by Colombian cowboys after they massacred fifteen Cuiva Indians whose jungle lands were in the path of a ranch expansion. (In that same nation a few years previously, similar murderers were absolved by a judge of their crimes when he accepted the defense that they didn't know Indians were human beings.) The second quotation above, however, is from the pages of Ché Guevara's Bolivian diaries, where he also occasionally compared the inhabitants of his operations area to "stones." The fourth quotation, where peasants apparently cannot distinguish themselves from horses, is from none other than Paulo Freire himself.[12] We might infer a rule from this striking juxtaposition of saddening words: you do not know who your bedfellows will be once you begin discerning levels of "consciousness."

At times, guerrillas (or their proponents) may not go quite so far as to attribute animalistic qualities to human beings, preferring instead to describe them in terms appropriate to children or savages. Peasants in such writings are portrayed as "brutalized" and "ignorant"; as being unaware of the meaning of land ownership; as withholding support from Ché's revolutionaries in Bolivia due to their "lack of understanding"; or simply as "innocent and ignorant of the moment in which they lived."[13]

Proposition 3

Some decades ago, many well-intentioned scholars adhered to the third proposition, that peasants were either the ideological thralls of agrarian elites or, in a related view, had irrational resistances to developmental improvements in rural areas. The latter view of peasant irrationality is far less widely held nowadays, as development "experts" encountered a dismal series of failures when projects ignored the locals' definition and understanding of their own agricultural and rural conditions. The same problems attended their attempts to impose "rational" birth control in those areas where having many children could provide "old-age insurance" for the peasantry.[14] The former view, however, showed a more persistent stubbornness for some time, but is now seen for the naked emperor it always was. Eric Wolf, Theda Skocpol, Joel Migdal, Jeffery Paige, Samuel Popkin, and James Scott have—all in different manners—made it abundantly clear that social and political constraints, rather than "false consciousness," inhibit the collective, radical action of the peasantry;[15] to paraphrase Mae West, consciousness has nothing to do with it.

Rather than merely circumventing the whole "vexed issue of rationality," as the late George Homans once put it, certain scholars have tackled the question of peasant consciousness head-on. Employing the modish argot of the social sciences, they have asked whether elites do indeed exercise "ideological hegemony" over the lower classes, which might account for the masses' lack of revolutionism. The most careful theoretical and empirical explorations of this "dominant ideology thesis" have found the whole perspective to be remarkably barren for understanding the true ideological stances of the working class and the peasantry, not to mention their actions.[16] The persistence of that pernicious postulate—that the masses are brainwashed and do not know their "real" interests—can be seen in the widespread publicity and attention given to recurrent works of pseudo-sociology which peddle that thesis in slightly altered form, apparently for each new decade of readers. Hence the intellectually unpotable "old wine" of Marcuse's *One-Dimensional Man* can be found in new bottles; one of the latest such vintages is by Noam Chomsky.[17] One of the remarkable features about such recurring works is how little the arguments rely on empirical research in the social sciences. *Careful* investigations into the effects of advertising on consumer choice in the "most capitalist" society of them all, the United States, have also turned up precious little real evidence that "consciousnesses" can be successfully manipulated through such devices. Barrington Moore, despite being a stern critic of his own society, reviewed and summarized the evidence thusly:

> The main impression that such studies convey is that the American population is neither dominated nor brainwashed by the media. By and large, most people pay no attention to what the media have to say if they are not interested in the subject to begin with, as is very frequently the case. The research findings [suggest that] ordinary people form their ideas from their immediate experiences, not from mass media, or not to any great extent. Similar data on the lack of "political" attitudes also indicate that people have *no* ideas, or very random ones, on areas remote from their immediate day-to-day concerns.[18]

The lack of a coherent ideology—conservative or radical—among the American masses has been confirmed by careful survey research into the political and economic concerns of the American population. That professional intellectuals and ideologues (e.g., Chomsky) still decry the ideological incoherence of most citizens says far more about the former group's psychological need for ideological consistency and purity than it does about the "consciousness" of the masses.[19]

Proposition 3, Corollary

Returning to the case of peasantries, Scott's work especially demonstrates that peasants have well-defined normative and rational definitions of their life situations, which by no means correspond to those of landlords or other elites. If we accept Scott's definition of false consciousness ("symbolic alignment of elite values and peasant values . . . a group's belief in the social ideology that justifies its exploitation"),[20] then Freire's scattered examples thereof are hardly persuasive in the light of the mass of counterevidence. Furthermore, recurring attempts to dichotomize peasant consciousness into the opposites of false and elite-aligned versus true and revolutionary ignore the real possibility that peasants may define their own situations in very different ways, rejecting the world views of all urban and upper-class groups.

Some theorists may supplement Scott's analysis, and yet others reject his assumptions and conclusions (e.g., Popkin and Paige), but virtually all contemporary theorists of peasant behavior now assume that peasants are quite capable of understanding their own interests, and acting upon those interests if conditions allow.

Proposition 4

Even if the third proposition *were* true, it would not lead inevitably to the fourth proposition above, i.e., that peasants are inhibited from radical action by their internalized ideology of submission. Events from Peru in the 1950s and 1960s give us serious reason to doubt even that "obvious" conclusion. The sierran peasants of Peru had been observed by virtually all visitors to show extraordinary levels of deference, not only to their *hacendados*, but also to all white men who came up to the Sierra (as Cornell University's reformer-organizers in the Vicos project found out to their dismay). Yet in 1962 and 1963 a series of land invasions unprecedented in Peruvian history rocked the Sierra. Some 350 to 400 peasant communities, and some 300,000 persons, participated in the invasions. The key factors in this extraordinary outburst were the anticipation of land reform by the newly elected government of Fernando Belaúnde Terry (who had promised agrarian reform), high preexisting levels of community solidarity, and the relaxation of repression in certain areas (particularly La Convención Valley in the department of Cuzco). The greatest single set of invasions occurred on 28 July 1963, the very day Belaúnde took the sash of office. Yet this entire wave of invasions took place without the leadership of the Communists or any other left-wing party.[21]

That curious sequence of events, widespread deference followed by widespread land invasions, suggests that deference may be a peasant ploy for easing through the difficulties of submission to powerful authority. Black slaves in the United States were also noted for their submissiveness (the "Sambo" personality), yet recently some black and white scholars have argued that such a persona was but a façade over a personality that in no way accepted the ideology of the oppressor.[22]

Despite this critique, the corollary proposal that the conversion of the peasantry to the guerrillas' world view will lead to radical action strikes me as plausible, if somewhat trivial. The real concern is to establish precisely under which conditions such transformations are more (or less) likely to occur.

Proposition 5

To assume that peasants can only attain higher levels of consciousness through interaction with revolutionaries is, at best, badly phrased. To term that newfound consciousness "higher" than the previous one is merely hubris. Scholars as different as William Foote Whyte, E. J. Hobsbawm, and Theda Skocpol all agree that social explosions by peasants can take place without any prompting from outside agitators. Nonetheless, they also agree that such persons may serve as catalysts, agitators, accelerators, or redefiners of such collective behavior.[23] Rather than calling such a contribution consciousness raising, we might follow one Marxist's unorthodox advice, and suggest that such "intruders" are introducing new values, norms, and reference groups into the rural social order, which conflict violently with some of those already present. Oddly enough, a pair of U.S. military analysts have suggested a roughly similar analysis.[24] What occurs then, really, is a value shift, not a raising of consciousness and, once again, we need to know under what circumstances such shifts are more and less likely to occur.

Along these lines, we must observe that such peasant value shifts toward the ideological views of revolutionary intellectuals came rather more rarely than the latter group sought. This should not surprise us. The social and phenomenological distance between an impoverished and illiterate farmer and a café Marxist (to borrow Béjar's term) is enormous, and not easily bridged by an act of will, nor by the revolutionary's redefinition of his or her own middle-class self as "oppressed." One Venezuelan newspaper noted acerbically that the guerrillas "have as much in common with the peasants as a ballet dancer with a coal miner"; it also noted that the soldiers who fought the guerrillas often *were* of peasant stock. Carlos Rangel suggested that a Boy Scout would have been better prepared for guerrilla activity than the typical bourgeois *guerrillero* of the 1960s. What peasant guerrilla would have written the following in his diary (or indeed kept a diary at all)?: "I must write letters to Sartre and B. Russell requesting them to organize an international fund in support of the Bolivian Liberation Movement."[25]

One could, once again, agree with the political aims of the revolutionaries yet still observe how steep were the phenomenological barriers between the intellectuals and the peasants they sought to mobilize to revolutionary ends. Such barriers have a deep and long history, in Latin America and elsewhere, which is reflected not just in action, but also in fiction about the lower classes. Hence Solzhenitsyn argues that literature created by the upper classes about the lives of the poor is always marred by "the incapacity genuinely to understand. . . . They simply could not climb into the *pelts* of the members of the lower stratum." In a surprising convergence with that apostle of Russian religious conservatism, Peruvian revolutionary Héctor Béjar argued that the "revolutionary or café Marxist" is very far from the reality of the Peruvian peasant, and also agreed with Solzhenitsyn that only through pain and suffering can the upper- or middle-class revolutionary (or writer) come to touch (or understand) the lower classes. Perhaps Allemann sums up the barriers to interchange most aptly, in noting that only exceptionally do intellectuals have "a practical grasp of the thought patterns [*Denkweise*] of the 'underprivileged' or even personal contact with the masses of the people," and adds elsewhere that "[a]n intellectual can perceive himself theoretically as the advocate and helper of the oppressed and exploited campesinos; yet this still does not guarantee that he can meet man-to-man with an Indian peón, tenant, or small peasant and understand their mentality."[26]

Again and again in the descriptive literature on guerrilla movements we encounter this image of a social and mental barrier between urban, university-educated guerrillas and the peasant "target" population. To the Cuban guerrillas the *guajiros* of the Sierra Maestra were at first "utterly alien." In Venezuela, Valsalice reports of the "mutual incomprehension" of the two groups, and intellectuals being able to "comprehend neither the spirit nor the political interests of the peasants." In Peru, another critic suggested that the "pure products of the intelligentsia of San Marcos University and the *enfants terribles* of the urban middle class could not surmount the barrier between themselves and the little Quechua-speaking men."[27]

To dwell overlong on these barriers to cooperation, however, would falsify the revolutionary record. Latin American revolutionaries *have* succeeded in enlisting substantial peasant cooperation with their revolutionary ends in many instances over the last third of a century: Cuba in the 1950s; Venezuela, Colombia, and Guatemala in the 1960s; and truly impressive numbers of peasant participants in post-1970 guerrilla activity in Nicaragua, El Salvador, Colombia, Guatemala, and Peru. Evidence suggests that such peasant cooperation came when the structure and history of the *peasant* experience in the countryside served to create a partial convergence of peasants' radicalism and intellectuals' revolutionism, particularly focusing on their common enemies—landlords and the state.[28] Furthermore, guerrillas actively promoted and enlisted peasant cooperation through a series of government-like activities that I have already reviewed in chapter 2 above.

I do not doubt that some peasants, somewhere, do eventually come to view their world and situations through the lenses of the Marxist sociology typical of revolutionary cadres. Yet when we hear of revolutionaries actually communicating with peasants, especially in the early encounters, there is virtually none of the ideological Marxism that the intellectual leaders themselves have learned. Instead, when addressing the peasantry during village *tomas* (seizures) and sessions of "armed propaganda"—militarily taking over a town and addressing the gathered citizenry in the town square—the guerrillas emphasize more immediate issues: hunger, tiny coffins, the loss of land to rapacious elites, and the commonality of violence against any peasants who demand better treatment. Exploitation, death, land theft, and violence are the guerrillas' recurring negative themes about the prevailing social order, while the peasants, for their part, often wish to be released from such ills, to get their lands back, and to get schools built and medical care provided. Generally absent from the guerrillas' themes are abolition of private property in the means of production; collectivization of agriculture; the suppression of middlemen and of independent market activity not controlled by government; imposition of central control over the purchase of most or all agricultural commodities; and nationalization of industry and finance. That is, guerrillas typically are *not* promoting the very institutions—historically embedded in socialist economies dominated by Marxist-inspired political parties—that they seek to emulate after the revolution.

Peasant Guerrillas: Did They "Convert" before They Joined?

The pure conversion model of guerrilla-peasant interaction is so indelibly stamped in Marxist thinking—what Alvin Gouldner would have termed a "domain assumption" of their approach—that affirmations of the need to raise peasant consciousness routinely fill the literature. The first real theorist of the guerrilla sums up the typical sequence of events: "The group formed initially in its totality by city-bred individuals is converted, in time, into a predominantly *campesino* organization, yet one still regulated by essentially (but not exclusively) urban cultural patterns."[29]

An implicit model lies behind the guerrillas' attempts to convert the peasantry. Imposed conversion is to take place through military occupation of a town or area; *tomas* and armed propaganda, or long-term indoctrination;[30] and gradual conversion of some members of the locality to the guerrillas' moral stance vis-à-vis the existing social order, with the accompanying commitment to revolutionary change through guerrilla action. The only guerrilla movements for which such a model seems clearly inappropriate are the MR-13 (November 13th Revolutionary Movement) in Guatemala during its Trotskyist phase, and Ché's Bolivian guerrilla movement, which never managed sustained peasant contact.

The Cuban case is distinctive because Fidel Castro's "revolutionary" goals were defined in terms that all but the most conservative elements of the society could embrace. Furthermore, Castro's 26th of July Movement (M-26) never had to deal with the problem of winning the sierran peasants away from strong commitment to an existing social order. The squatters' hostility to government authorities, the rural guard, and local eviction-happy landlords was of ancient vintage, and Castro's guerrillas were welcome allies to the heretofore overmatched *precaristas* (a term which suggests the precariousness of their tenures). Despite this serendipitously available ally, the guerrillas evinced no sustained attempts to ascertain their particular demands. Rather, Castro established a guerrilla military and legal presence, executed bandits, and rigorously enforced his own imposed authority throughout the Sierra, as did his brother Raúl in his front further north. The latter showed some movement toward rapprochement with the peasants through the organization of peasant councils, but there was never any question that Raúl would ''define the situation'' and exercise power in the area of his purview. Raúl showed some degree of trust in allowing peasants into positions of real power in the guerrilla forces. In contrast, Ché Guevara, who commanded yet another front, has been described as ''kind and extremely patient, though he never showed them [peasants] deep trust.'' He also referred to one guerrilla task as the ''indoctrination of the peasant masses,'' a task to be extended to the working class if located nearby. In the *Directorio Revolucionario*'s (DR, or Revolutionary Directorate) own guerrilla front in the hills of Las Villas Province, the insurgents attempted two feats of conversion which failed: formation of agrarian cooperatives and male consciousness-raising sessions. When Castro finally did bring land reform to Cuba after the revolution, the socialist land reform he put into place did not correspond to the values of the Sierran peasant of the pre-1959 period, whom Guevara had described as petty-bourgeois and land-loving.[31] To summarize the Cuban experience, peasant conversion to the professed values of the revolutionaries was not really something to be explained, since virtually the entire society by 1958 agreed with that series of reformist, more than revolutionary, social programs.

Cuba's contrast with Venezuela is striking, for in the latter nation the revolutionaries had to work and sweat to recruit peasants in certain areas, who had long been largely committed to the guerrillas' hated enemy, the governing *Acción Democrática* party. FALN guerrilla leader Douglas Bravo candidly described the insurgents' modus operandi, clearly a model of conversion: ''The struggle was first born within the middle classes, in the petty bourgeoisie, among intellectuals and students: these are the ones who communicate these ideas to the rest of the population.''[32]

Bravo also admitted that many peasant members of the FALN guerrillas did not share the leadership's ideology and philosophy, but rather joined to combat government atrocities.[33] Likewise, a Venezuelan guerrilla in the state of Portuguesa describes recruitment to the guerrilla movement in words that appeal more to poverty and inequality than to any notion of consciousness raising:

> They took us to their homes and spoke with us, we explained to them why we had come, that we were not there as thieves, but rather to liberate the people, to liberate the peasants. That it was a struggle to liberate the poor, and they told us how they lived, that some of them had gone to the city to see how the rich live and how the poor live. How they live in these little huts, that look just like Indian huts, and that moved them to sorrow. They had nothing but a little donkey to transport their crops with. They understood very well these necessities, really, of what it was like and how they were exploited. Then the *campesinos* began to collaborate with us.[34]

This tale is a prototype for guerrilla tales of the *actual* process of peasant recruitment: initial contacts; hospitality; tales and experiences of the rich and the poor; interpretation of that in very simple terms of exploitation; implicit or explicit promises of a new, nonexploitative social order; and commitment to a social movement that promises to bring about such a new society. A great advantage of such discourses stems from what Alvin Gouldner called the "metaphoricality of Marxism": behind the dense theory is a compellingly simple clarion call for an end to the exploitation of human beings, and an end to the poverty that such exploitation (presumably) creates. That "metaphorical" and eschatological appeal of revolution exists irrespective of any more thoroughgoing "Communist" project professed by the revolutionary leadership. As Peter Berger pointed out some time ago, regardless of the comparative realities of capitalist and socialist societies, there is no question that socialism has by far the better "myths" concerning the society it wishes to create.[35]

In Guatemala the FAR employed armed propaganda in order to gain recruits to their movement. As in Cuba, their words fell on fertile soil, for many of the listeners had experienced the revolutionary promise and reality of the Jacobo Arbenz government, and had had those hopes dashed by the 1954 coup and subsequent counterrevolution. The guerrillas, during one journalist's visit, spoke compellingly to peasant villagers of large tracts of land lying idle, while peasants could not feed their families adequately; of the personal abuses the peasants suffered at the hands of local elites; and of the small coffins that villagers carried so regularly to the cemetery because of their poverty. To each statement the assembled peasants responded, *"Sí, es cierto"* (Yes, it's true), and as the litany of abuses continued their voices moved into "the unmistakeable register of defiance."[36]

Evidence for the effectiveness of such armed propaganda in generating recruits is sketchy, but there is evidence that the socialist revolutionaries of Guatemala fully intended, if victorious, to follow in the footsteps of Stalin, Ho Chi Minh, and Mao Zedong on the issue of collectivization. Luis Turcios Lima told a reporter that "agrarian reform is the first requisite. It must be a radical reform.... Then, gradually, we will change the conscience of the men of this country until there are better forms of work. By that I mean cooperation and socialism."[37] This account again exemplifies the pure "conversion" model of guerrilla-peasant relations, and suggests as well a point made by Tom Wolfe—in considering the horrors inflicted during the construction of Soviet society—that terror may arise from the very attempt to reorganize morality on an a priori basis.[38] Turcios's words evoke this same kind of image: the peasantry will be molded to fit *our* image of what a society should be like. In considering such attempts to "remake" the social order via "consciousness raising," proponents of change might consider Charles Issawi's comments on carpentry and metallurgy: "Revolutionaries [et al.] ... believe they are handling steel beams and bars, whose dimensions and tensile strength they know to the millimeter and milligram, and which they can bend to any conceivable shape and weld in any desired combination. If the materials diverge from the prescribed norms—as they often do—they can be scrapped and liquidated."[39] The pure conversion approach of the committed consciousness raiser *always* contains a germ of this possibility, which is precisely why Berger suggests "cognitive respect" as a fundamental ethical principle for development.[40]

In Peru's Junín Department, an interesting sequence of events ensued in which the Campa Indians were recruited into assisting the guerrilla cause—based on a promise, it appears, to return to them their ancestral tribal lands—and later were "deprogrammed" and "converted" to become assistants and guides for government troops.[41] It is not easy to sort out any value-based elements in these shifts because offers of land (by the guerrillas) and terror and civic action (by the government) were important elements in the processes of recruitment. However, one story, reported by the military, suggests that the Campa may have had real practical grievances with their short-term guerrilla allies. The Campa sought the division of one hacienda that Guillermo Lobatón and the MIR (Movement of the Revolutionary Left) took over during the 1965 insurgency, yet Lobatón instead "partied" with the landlord's wife all night, pronounced the estate's records "in order" in the morning, and left the estate intact with his grumbling allies in tow.[42]

Even before heading into the hills, the leader of the MIR, Luis de la Puente Uceda, employed a levels-of-consciousness approach to the masses, stating the main goals of the revolution:

> There is a need to avoid letting our people fall once again into the hands of some adventurer and again suffer the ensuing deceptions. The people must be made to see the fraud of which they are the victims, to abandon those whom they hoist on their shoulders who then serve only to exploit them; to avoid their falling into new traps, to avoid their easily believing in something alien to their destiny; to make them understand that they still are the victims of the deception of closely controlled and catch-all parties, which must be always explained to them. Ideas are our basic weapon in this joint task with the masses. Let us make of our politics a vocational mission and a pedagogy. Let us raise the revolutionary consciousness of our people with example and with illuminating preaching.[43]

The missionary tones, the dubious assumptions of the consciousness raiser, the certainty of truth—all are present in this speech. In no other movement was the sectarianism, the sense of possession of absolute right, and the social distance from the peasantry so concentrated as among the Peruvian guerrillas. One may be forgiven, then, for suspecting some association between such traits and the abysmal failure of the Peruvian insurgency. The guerrillas' claims that their consciousness-raising efforts ("*tareas de conciencialización*") bore fruit in gaining widespread peasant commitment to the armed struggle are simply not borne out by any other kind of evidence—most certainly not from any massive recruitment success.[44]

Somewhat different attempts by guerrillas to meet the peasants half-way, through rapprochement of situational definitions and a true system of *mutual* education, were relatively uncommon during the 1960s. Héctor Béjar of the Peruvian ELN (Army of National Liberation) has written the most along these lines, and many of his writings give the impression that he is ruefully discussing the ideal patterns his movement failed to achieve. Béjar insists, first, that guerrillas cannot speak to peasants "from the heights of a professorial chair" but must engage in real work among the masses. Second, he argues that the guerrilla program must be geared to the concrete, local demands of a particular group of peasants, "making their worries and desires our own in order to carry the peasants on toward higher objectives." This is a very clear expression of rapprochement rather than conversion. Still, Béjar's suggestions—which, again, were not necessarily his ELN's practices in 1965—truly embody the spirit of the *narodnichestvo* practiced by Russia's agrarian populists during the 1800s: go out to the people, share their lives, and raise them up. Third, Béjar even argues for a rapprochement of psychology and experience between the guerrillas and the peasantry:[45]

> Many say that the conditions of the struggle are not present, because the peasant does not have political consciousness, and the first task is to give him a revolutionary political consciousness. To them we answer that they do not know the peasants. Our tactic must be to adapt ourselves to the psychology of the Peruvian peasant. . . . For the peasant to develop politically one lives alongside him, not as a simple propagandist or a union organizer, or even as a chance visitor who comes, presents an unintelligible discourse and departs with nothing more or less, in order to make his report to the party in the urban leadership. . . . Above all, however, [in addition to being armed] he must endure enemy repression. To endure is the obligation of the guerrilla because, to the degree we survive, we demonstrate to the people that revolution is not only necessary, but possible.

That theoretical procedure had been put into practice earlier by Hugo Blanco, who began his organizing campaign by working as a humble agricultural subtenant in La Convención Valley. However, in contrast to Blanco's and Béjar's movements, which gained real (if fleeting) support among the peasantry, perhaps through their sharing of the peasants' existence, the MIR *foco* in Cuzco was torn apart by internal ideological dissent and by the desertion of three members—all of them peasant leaders—who claimed that de la Puente was only using peasants to forward his own goals, and that the peasants' material existence made them susceptible to the MIR's "bribes and promises."[46]

Outside of Peru there are scattered claims of real guerrilla identification with peasant interests, albeit allied with the further desire to raise peasant consciousness. Sartre argued that the Cuban revolution became possible when the peasants became rebels, which could only happen when the rebels became peasants. (Such statements say more about Sartre's propensity for dialectical exercises than about any realities of social change among the Cuban rebels, who most certainly did not "become peasants" during the revolution. Indeed, many became government bureaucrats after the revolution.) Jaime Arenas of the Colombian ELN quoted Béjar's program approvingly—"to flow toward the peasantry, join ourselves to their worries and longings in order to carry them to higher goals"—but added that the ELN failed to advance the peasantry toward those goals (i.e., they failed to convert them to revolutionary Marxism.) In Guatemala, César Montes said that the FAR's basic program was "the land for those who work it," but added the qualifier "in one or another form," suggesting that the victorious guerrilla movement would decide the particular form.[47]

None of these three fragments really suggests a serious attempt at rapprochement with peasant world views, save in the case of the standard call for a land to the tiller reform. Socialist revolutionaries have consistently demonstrated after victory that such an agrarian system is incongruent with their view of socialism. Therefore, calls for "the land for those who work it" should not be considered rapprochement with peasant interests unless the revolutionaries evince a serious commitment to a type of land reform congruent with peasant desires, which clearly rules out collectivization: no peasantry, *pace* Communist Chinese claims, has voluntarily collectivized itself in modern history.[48]

There is a third "model" for guerrilla-peasant interaction that goes beyond conversion ("consciousness raising"), and even beyond a rapprochement of interests between the two groups. The *self-submission* model of guerrilla-peasant interaction derives from the Trotskyist revolutionary stance. Trotskyists are distinguished from other Marxists by their categorical rejection of the growth of a centralized, bureaucratic state apparatus which becomes an organ for repressing the masses who made the revolution. They therefore reject the Stalinist model. Hence Trotskyists seek to develop a revolution through the growth of "soviet power." This means the increasing concentration of worker self-control in the factory and peasant self-defense in the countryside, both to be enforced by lower-class militias ruled over by decentralized councils. Those councils are themselves to be *organized* by the revolutionary vanguard but *ruled* by workers and peasants. The fundamental Trotskyist dream is to carry out a revolution without the heretofore inevitable confrontations of will between the newly formed revolutionary state and the revolutionary masses. (As Berger put it, "What begins as a liberating community ends up as the all-embracing state.") Power is to remain in the hands of the masses, as in the Bolshevik revolutionary cry of 1917: "All power to the Soviets!" Trotskyists thus share to some extent Berger's skepticism about revolutionary vanguards who claim to speak on behalf of the masses (and who, Berger notes archly, presumably have a great deal of trouble in speaking for themselves).[49]

This is the model of guerrilla-peasant interaction avowed by the Guatemalan MR-13 guerrilla movement for several years in the mid-1960s. It was reported then that "[t]he function of the guerrillas is seen as that of organizing the peasants and becoming their revolutionary instrument." Marco Antonio Yon Sosa, chieftain of the MR-13, constantly referred to his guerrillas as being the "instruments" of peasant will, of peasant power and authority. The emphasis in their day-to-day activities among the peasantry was on the formation of peasant self-defense groups and a network of village organizations, and on the anticipation of a "spontaneous" agrarian reform. This model provides a stark contrast with the "Cuban model," in which the revolutionaries impose law and policy upon the peasantry, even though application of that law may be far more benevolent than previous government law enforcement. One should add that the Trotskyist program for revolutionary change elicits a vehement reaction from every non-Trotskyist revolutionary. Soviet- and Chinese-line Communist parties, Fidel Castro, and Régis Debray, despite their own mutual squabbles, all issued barbed denunciations of the Trotskyist leanings of the MR-13.[50]

There is one fragmentary report of rapprochement or self-submission in Venezuela. Suggestively, perhaps, the guerrilla involved was a long-time member of the *non*-Marxist Venezuelan left, and was about fifty-six years old when he came down out of the hills in 1965—both of these quite atypical of the young, Marxist revolutionaries of Venezuela and other nations. José "El Gavilán" Díaz reported the impending internal disintegration of the Lara guerrilla front at that time, and contrasted its fate with his earlier goals:

> Our first goal when we went to the mountains in 1962 was to educate the *campesinos* and then to reap the harvest we had sown. . . . But we were too eager to reap the harvest. . . . When I first joined the guerrillas there were few of us and we went there to educate the *campesinos*, to prepare them for our long-range war. If we had had *campesino* support, I wouldn't be here now. Our original plans were to go there, to become *campesinos* and, as we educated them, we would have found supplies available to us. We would have become *campesinos*.[51]

The reader will note the tension between consciousness raising and self-submission embodied in this poignant account.

By the early 1980s peasant recruitment was remarkably successful in the combined guerrilla organizations of El Salvador (ten to twelve thousand combatants) and Guatemala (as many as six thousand). In both of those nations, assaults on the security of peasant cultivators were ongoing processes prior to the formation of guerrilla movements. While the sheer threat to subsistence may not have been as great as in the *Sendero*-dominated areas of Peru, in Central America such threats could be much more directly traceable to human agency, especially by the state, the military, and domestic and foreign business elites.[52] Hence there was a strong "interest element" in peasants joining any kind of movement that opposed such processes and promised to protect and benefit the peasantry. The numbers certainly indicate high levels of recruitment success.

There is less evidence, however, that the peasants became ideological converts in guerrilla-dominated regions. Peasants apparently joined before receiving political indoctrination in both nations, and the guerrillas' schools sought to transmit literacy first, politics second. In El Salvador in the early 1980s political indoctrination was "voluntary, by all accounts, and received with mixed reviews" and "some people say they have trouble understanding the students or city-types that come to the villages to talk about imperialism or socialism and democracy."[53] Where peasants recount the biographical events that preceded their joining the armed struggle or fleeing to guerrilla-controlled zones, the most common experience is that of terror, where they or their kin suffer attacks by government forces.

In the postrecruitment phase—with remarkable similarity in both nations—guerrillas made persuasive claims that they and/or the peasants had taken steps toward cooperative forms of agriculture, perhaps even collective agriculture (although the term may be misused by observers). It seems that peasants in El Salvador split their time between private plots and collective ones; such dual forms, interestingly, also prevailed under the colonial tribute system that Spanish conquerors had imposed on Spanish American Indian communities. Such "dual" forms of agriculture are also suggested for Guatemala, to provide guerrillas with food sources without cutting into peasant subsistence. In fact, cooperative agriculture among new colonizers predated guerrilla activity in northern Guatemala. The Salvadoran insurgents also argued, less persuasively, that *machismo* among male peasants was declining under the guerrillas' feminist influence and egalitarian role-behavior.[54] However, in neither case do we see the level of ideological fanaticism and commitment found in our next case.

There is only *one* clear case in the Latin American guerrilla record of overwhelming peasant conversion to a radically "other" world view: the members of *Sendero Luminoso*, Peru's Maoist "Shining Path" guerrilla movement. The ideological fervor of *Sendero*'s rank-and-file has been remarked upon by all chroniclers. Some of the best evidence appears in their behavior in prisons once they are captured. They keep very much to themselves; maintain exceptionally high levels of order, discipline, and cleanliness; refer to the movement's leader, former philosophy professor Abimael Guzmán, as "President Gonzalo," and study his "guiding thoughts" while imprisoned; and, finally, have engineered one massive and other minor prison uprisings, with the authorities ruthlessly killing inmates after the largest such event in the mid-1980s.[55] Here is the one clear case in which the guerrilla rank-and-file has been converted to "Marxism-Leninism–Mao Zedong Thought," as the Chinese used to term it during the Cultural Revolution. Here, then, we would expect to find an unusual set of social conditions for integrating the peasantry into the guerrilla movement. And that is just what we shall encounter below, after we have first examined some general principles in network analysis.

Mobilizing the Peasantry through Social and Religious Networks

If the preceding events from three decades of insurgency are represen-
tative of the patterns of guerrilla-peasant interaction, then it is most
unlikely (1) that consciousness raising (as opposed to material benefits
or promises) brought peasants into revolutionary guerrilla movements,
although (2) such ideological transformations may take place after the
peasant recruits have been politically indoctrinated by their new comrades in arms. In contrast to that explanatory barrenness, I have elsewhere clearly outlined three ''ecological'' correlates of radical
peasantries, that is, *regional* characteristics that have been associated
with rebellious peasantries throughout Latin America.[56] However,
such analyses leave a large gap in our understanding, for they cannot—
given the regional analytical level at which they are directed—help us
to understand how peasants of certain *communities*, or selected peasants *within* communities, came to join or support guerrilla organizations. The answers promised by the literature on consciousness raising,
we have seen, put their attention solely on the *psychologies* of individuals, and have proven themselves mostly empty for understanding, in
particular, the cultivators' decisions to join or to stand apart. What we
need, therefore, is an analytical level *in between* the studies of regions
and of individuals. A promising candidate to fill that lacuna comes
from network theory.

Disappointed with more high-blown, and necessarily abstract, analyses of ''social structure'' at the macrolevel of entire societies, sociologists over the last decade or two have turned increasingly to the
analysis of actual *networks of interaction* in order to understand the
true manner in which social structures operate on those who ''people''
the social structure. In one of the earliest studies employing the concept of networks, Elizabeth Bott studied 1950s London working-class
networks of both husbands and wives, and used the notion of separate-
yet-intersecting networks to understand variations in the domestic,
emotional, and sexual closeness of couples.[57] Since the publication and
''ingestion'' of Bott's pathbreaking work, sociologists have turned, bit
by bit, ever more in the direction of network analysis to provide accurate *descriptions* of social structures; one important contribution has
come via exchange theory, where theorists try to build up to larger
social structures from elementary exchange networks between individuals.[58] In some such cases, the descriptions of networks are important

per se, for example when researchers uncover "corporate interlocks" showing how corporations are linked by individuals who sit simultaneously on the boards of directors of two or more corporations.[59] In other, rather different ventures, researchers have advanced the study of social networks to a quite advanced level of mathematical and statistical sophistication. In such ventures, the sociological challenge has been to achieve substantive or theoretical breakthroughs worthy of the fancy methodological tools. One of the latest contributions to the field suggests that sociologists have tried to get the methods linked to crucial substantive issues, although the merger is still, evidently, not a completely digested one.[60]

Networks and Attachments: Theoretical Principles

Barry Wellman has suggested a series of theoretical approaches to, or propositions underlying, network-oriented approaches to social structure and social change, and some of them are particularly relevant to the problem we face here, that of discerning under what specific local conditions peasants will "flow into" guerrilla movements. Most useful are the following:[61]

1. "Structured social relationships are a more powerful source of sociological explanation than personal attributes of system members." *Application:* Therefore we would expect social structural features, more than religious-type conversion, to be a recurring prelude to the guerrillas' successful mobilization of the peasantry.

2. "Norms emerge from location in structured systems of social relationships." *Application:* Since we have found little evidence that peasants ever "convert" to Marxism prior to joining revolutionary movements, such cases as exist probably occur during the course of "political education" once they are *already* members of guerrilla movements, that is, embedded in a social network where such beliefs are normal rather than deviant. In a similar fashion, the Marxist intellectuals who lead guerrilla movements typically emerge as such either from left-wing family backgrounds (occasionally) or through a process of political socialization that takes place on certain university campuses—and some *liceos*, or high schools—in Latin America, where Marxist ideology is deeply imbedded in large portions of the studentry. Such campuses provide dense interaction networks favorable to such conversion processes, just as do the guerrilla movements themselves.[62]

3. "Ties link network members indirectly as well as directly. Hence they must be defined within the context of larger network structures." *Application:* Since networks concatenate and join to other networks, this viewpoint suggests that we look for ways in which peasants might be imbedded in larger networks of national or even international scope. More than any other application, leftist scholars have been concerned with the "exploitative" economic networks that link peasants into national and international market systems. Rightist scholars, however, have been highly concerned with guerrillas' ties to international military networks, especially via arms shipments from the socialist nations. Here we are rather more concerned with peasants' positions within political networks and, to a lesser degree, religious networks that might influence peasants' political choices vis-à-vis revolutionary movements and the opportunities they offer.

4. "Networks structure collaborative and competitive activities to secure scarce resources." *Application:* Loosely translated into plain English, this means that networks create both allies and "enemies" in one's quests. Hence the adage "any friend of yours is a friend of mine," while in the opposite direction, "the enemy of my enemy is my friend." Moreover, this proposition also entails the observation that peasants deeply imbedded in certain types of social structures— those which "push" them toward cooperation with guerrilla movements—are more likely, in fact, to become involved in such resistance movements. In contrast, peasants and other persons lying, in a sense, "outside of" such (dense) networks of social organization become unlikely candidates for any kind of mobilization.

Rodney Stark has explored the social psychological aspects of social networks in a very accessible way in his unusually pointed introduction to sociology. Drawing especially on "balance" and "cognitive dissonance" theories from social psychology, Stark consistently employs the concept of *interpersonal attachments* to account for the kinds of religious and political choices that people make within society. Such attachments are the social psychological "face" of social networks themselves, and clarify the psychological mechanisms underlying the manner in which networks structure the behavior of their "occupants."[63]

Finally, Kenneth Wilson and Anthony Orum have pulled together a variety of analytical levels in a brief theoretical gem. They link together (1) social bonds at the interpersonal level, corresponding to

Stark's concept of attachments; (2) the social ties linking individuals to *organizations*, including variations in the intensity of such ties; (3) the nature of organizational *infrastructures*, especially the linkages between organizations; and (4) the manner in which social structural effects (for example, class interests) operate mainly via these organizational networks, rather than in a free-floating manner within society.[64] In brief compass, then, the authors have spelled out the structures through which interpersonal attachments-cum-organizational memberships might be "shifted upward" out of the local social structure to mobilize people into national systems of collective action.

Networks and Attachments: Some Illuminating Applications

Stark's most intriguing applications of the concept of attachment networks appear in his book's treatment of the Unification Church (the "Moonies") and the Nazi Party. In their own research, Stark and Jon Lofland found that Sun Myung Moon's principal disciple was remarkably unsuccessful in her early attempts to convert strangers, despite public speeches to women's clubs, and so forth. However, after a longer period of residence in an area, and the building up of friendships (i.e., attachments), conversions began to come rapidly as people were brought to the Unification Church via the friendship networks she had established. Conversion *never* came unless attachments to current church members were stronger than the convert's attachments to nonmembers. Indeed, in some cases, individuals joined the church while expressing complete disbelief in Moon's teachings (read: ideology). Stark concludes that "the primary basis of conversion was attachment. Rather than being drawn to the group mainly because of the appeal of its doctrines, people were drawn to the doctrines because of their ties to the group." He adds that replications on other groups have consistently reported the same finding.[65]

In the case of the Nazis, we know that the sales of Hitler's ideological treatise, *Mein Kampf* ("My Struggle"), rose in Germany *after* membership in the Nazi Party had increased, not before; apparently possession of that dense work was a badge of loyalty more than a tool for conversion. William Sims Bainbridge argues, further, that a key contribution to Nazi growth—apart from its "natural constituency" among economically prostrate ordinary Germans shocked by Weimar inflation and unemployment—lay in its "vigorous internal society."

The Nazi party created and then concatenated its internal network, forming a dense set of social ties that drew non-Nazis into the movement, where they could become real Nazis.

> The Nazi Party was an independent social structure made of hundreds of thousands of personal relationships. When the party set up soup kitchens to feed hungry Germans, it was not only providing a needed service that the government had failed to provide but also offering the needy the possibility of developing new human relationships. Newcomers would make friends among the party members and then become members themselves.

Nazism, in Bainbridge's view, worked "passively" to bring newcomers into the fold, mainly by promoting an ideology that promised to answer the needs of all Germans, rather than a class-based or class-conflictual program.[66]

Evidence from Latin American Guerrilla Movements

In this section we will examine the guerrilla experience mostly in a reverse chronological order, while also generally looking first at those movements with the most successful levels of peasant mobilization. Given the logics just outlined above, we would expect to find peasant recruitment into guerrilla movements to take place largely through the operations of social networks, with the "tightest" network patterns present where we see the most peasant recruitment. We might outline a few general principles to guide our search: (1) recruitment of peasants into guerrilla movements will be more successful where preexisting social networks exist linking together the "target" peasantry and the guerrilla leadership; (2) where those networks additionally include elements of protoguerrilla power and/or authority over peasants, such recruitment should be even more successful; (3) the most intense and successful recruitment to guerrilla movements will come where peasants and guerrillas meet in the context of "total institutions" set apart from the rest of society, or in an emotionally intense setting, such as the family; (4) where peasants live in a relatively "atomized" state in the countryside, recruitment can be successful, but only with a substantial additional investment of more arduous work on the part of the revolutionaries; the one advantage to such a situation is that peasants are *not* imbedded in competing or hostile social networks; (5) where peasants interact regularly with landlords or nonrevolutionary political parties in a relatively "balanced" exchange relationship—see my discussion in chapter 2 above—revolutionaries will be far less successful in recruiting new guerrillas from the peasantry, because such cultivators are, ipso facto, already imbedded in competitive or even hostile social networks, and hence unavailable for revolutionary mobilization.

Sendero Luminoso in Peru represents the most impressive combination of intense commitment and large numbers of peasant followers; the movement came to have perhaps 6,000 armed members and at least twenty supporters for every soldier.[67] It also has two features about it that might account for the extraordinary levels of peasant "conversion" that I noted above. First, the children and grandchildren of Quechua-speaking peasants began to attend the University of Huamanga in large numbers after that provincial institution was reopened around 1960. That pattern has *no* remote parallel in any other guerrilla movement, and served to bring bilingual peasants into the very quasi-total institutional setting that has been so productive of guerrilla leaders throughout Latin America; yet at Huamanga *peasants*, and not just the middle classes, were subject to that radicalizing experience. Second, as the 1960s progressed, *Sendero* in its earlier guise came to dominate the university's education department, and was even associated in the local town with a variety of welfare and outreach programs that the university sponsored. As the university graduated its closet *senderistas*, they were dispersed throughout the Sierra as teachers and educational (and sometimes agricultural) extension workers; those teachers then often intermarried into the communities that they served.[68] Hence the peasantry that later became militantly Maoist *senderistas* had been subjected to a near-maximum of intense exposure to such ideologies, from university professors and local teachers, and even from family members. Furthermore, given Guzmán's purported charisma in recruiting new members, plus the multiple benefits proto-*Sendero* bestowed upon the regional population, *Sendero*'s achievements should not surprise us in the least. *Sendero*'s extraordinary successes in combining large numbers with mass "conversions" are perfectly in accord with a network-oriented analysis: the new ideology followed from peasants being placed within exceptionally intense social networks (university and family), rather than ideological conversion leading to a wave of new *senderista* recruits.

In both El Salvador and Guatemala, as we saw above, guerrilla organizations secured thousands of peasant recruits under rural conditions that threatened peasant subsistence. However, those conditions provided only the structure of (threatened) peasant interests, not an organizational framework through which actual resistance could be expressed. There were, again in both cases, two *other* organizations, apart from the guerrillas, that (1) in part predated the guerrilla movement; (2) in part overlapped with the guerrilla organizations, that is, they shared members; and (3) in part overlapped with each other as well. In El Salvador, evidence suggests that the Federation of Christian Peasants (FECCAS) later contributed substantial membership to the guerrilla movements, including a leader of both organizations, Facundo Guardado. The former head of a national peasant organization of day laborers also later emerged as the head of all civilian operations in the Guazapa guerrilla zone. In addition, there is also substantial evidence that CEBs (*Comunidades Eclesiales de Base*) or religious base communities of the 1970s were also strongest in regions that later provided guerrilla havens; for example, at least some of the CEB followers of Father Rutilio Grande entered the Guazapa guerrilla organization following his assassination. Finally, there is also an apparent connection between FECCAS and the CEBs. The overall pattern produces a substantial overlap (but not an identity)—and hence a fairly dense network of common cause and common contacts—among the three organizations.[69]

In Guatemala the CEBs were also of similar, but lesser, importance nationally, with the greatest effects in the EGP guerrilla stronghold of El Quiché Department. Also important was the formerly conservative religious organization, Catholic Action, whose presence was later correlated with peasant proletarianization and with successful guerrilla recruiting. The Guatemalan counterpart to FECCAS was the Committee for Peasant Unity (CUC—*Comité de Unidad Campesina*), which organized large numbers of peasants from the highlands, whether in their roles as migrant workers on plantations or as subsistence farmers at home in the western highlands (that is, those were often the same persons). This organization was in part created by the EGP (Guerrilla Army of the Poor), and served to channel radicalized peasants into the guerrillas' ranks. The overlap among, and the overall importance of, the two "feeder" organizations was substantially less in Guatemala than in El Salvador, which may in part account for the lesser growth of the guerrilla movement there: the revolutionaries' (pre-)organizational infrastructure was simply less developed.

The Guatemalan guerrillas were helped in part by the strong solidarity of Indian communities in the western highlands; once Indians decided to "join" the revolution, they often did so as villages, not as individuals, and both ORPA (the Organization of the People in Arms) and the EGP recruited through Indian mediators and in the Indian tongues, while committing their organizations to racial equality as well as socialist revolution.[70] The Salvadoran guerrillas, by contrast, recruited best in the least attractive, northern agricultural regions of El Salvador, where cash crop agriculture and landlord political dominance did not prevail to the same degree as elsewhere.

In Nicaragua, the guerrillas certainly secured peasant support in the countryside—the memoirs of Henry Ruiz and Omar Cabezas confirm this—but that support was much more fragmented and the recruits less numerous than in El Salvador or Guatemala. One important barrier to the guerrillas' mobilization of the peasantry in the peripheral regions to the north and east of the capital was the prevalence throughout those regions of squatter agriculture (see chapter 7 below). Squatters tend to develop the most atomized, unstructured forms of rural settlements— that is, they have the weakest network system—and hence should be quite difficult to mobilize. In addition, the Somoza regime had informants ("ears") and the rural constabulary (*jueces de mesta*) scattered through such areas; those persons provided to the *regime* a certain fragmentary network to control the countryside. Hence the process of organization came more arduously, with many setbacks, some due to the sheer difficulty of organizing a dispersed farming population, some due to informing and consequent military disasters. By the mid-1970s, however, Ruiz had developed a basic series of family-network ties, which he called *en cadena*, utilizing fictive kinship and godparenthood, as well as the family ties of the supporters themselves. The FSLN (Sandinista National Liberation Front) would later employ identical uses of kinship ties to gain recruits in the suburban Subtiavan Indian community in León, the seat of both spontaneous and planned uprisings against the Somoza regime. In eastern Matagalpa, the FSLN in 1966–68 would build upon the earlier contacts Rigoberto Cruz had established as physician-cum-*curandero* (folk healer) in that region from 1963 to 1966. There and in the northern-most areas of FSLN rural development, in Jinotega and Nueva Segovia, the Sandinistas also consistently built upon the remnants of Augusto Sandino's 1930s guerrilla forces, which continued as a shadow network of personal and family contacts, and as a culture of resistance to Somoza and his national guard. Such Sandino veterans were present in the formation and middle leadership of the bulk of the early guerrilla ventures. Finally, CEBs were at work earliest of all in Nicaragua, and led to the highest levels of revolutionary activity where they were strongest; one such area was the department of Zelaya where, as it happens, the rural guerrillas put down substantial roots, and from which the Eastern Front was launched during the final offensive.[71]

Fidel Castro mobilized part of the Cuban peasant population, who became both fighters and supporters; they were also, like their Nicaraguan counterparts, largely a squatter population from the Sierras of eastern Cuba. They differed from the Nicaraguan squatters in two important respects, however. The Batista regime had virtually no presence in that area, and treated it like the national backwater that it was; and the squatters were *not* as atomized as their Nicaraguan counterparts, but instead had organized themselves, during the 1940s and 1950s, into armed bands that sought to resist the attempts at eviction then rampant in that region. The leader of the largest single squatter group was Crescencio Pérez, who led perhaps as many as 50,000 of the *guajiros*, and exercised authority through an impressive kinship and patronage web throughout the area. Fidel Castro "tapped into" this preexisting social network when he signed an accord with Pérez in mid-1956, which would give protection and land to the squatter population if it helped Castro to seize power. Pérez's dense network of family ties—including several cousins and sons by several different wives—were instrumental in rescuing Castro's group after their disastrous landing in December 1956. The squatters thereafter provided the initial source of new recruits in late December, as well as constant support throughout the two-year guerrilla campaign.[72]

In Guatemala, Colombia, Venezuela, and Peru during the 1960s guerrilla campaigns, guerrilla movements secured new recruits, at least in part, by tapping into preexisting social networks where they could benefit from local "authorities"—including peasant leaders in some cases—who committed themselves to the guerrilla movement and brought a substantial "following" with them. In some cases that authority was not personified but institutionalized in political parties.

In Venezuela, where such networks were most impressive, the sons (in one case, a nephew) of *hacendados* in the states of Lara and Falcón became Communists and guerrilla leaders, and used preexisting patron-client relationships with the peasantry, and ties to their own kinship webs, to secure substantial peasant support for the insurgency. More-over, the guerrillas secured their greatest peasant backing in two *municipios* where the Communist Party won over half the vote in the 1958 national elections (versus about 5 percent nationwide). The party used that preexisting support network to provide automatic backing for its revolutionary creation, the FALN guerrilla forces.[73]

In Guatemala, the 1960s guerrillas secured substantial support in both Izabal and, to a lesser degree, Alta Verapaz; in both cases they tapped into local peasant leaders. In Izabal, guerrillas gained much support and some recruits through the efforts of the head of the local banana workers' union, Estanislao de León, who was also a member of the Communist Party, with which the guerrillas were allied against the military regime. In Alta Verapaz, the guerrillas formed a column of Kekchí Indian guerrillas through the efforts of the former mayor of Rabinal, "Pascual Ixtapá" (born Emilio Román López), a Kekchí Indian leader who also spoke Spanish and joined the guerrilla forces in 1962. With regard to the entire guerrilla operations area in those two departments and Zacapa, guerrilla leader Pablo Monsanto (who fought guerrilla wars against the regime in both the 1960s and the 1970s–1980s) argued that "the guerrilla movement could not have formed this social base of support by itself."[74]

The Colombian guerrilla movement which "officially" began around 1965 can be summarized simply: the guerrilla movements emerged *from* the peasantry, rather than coming *to* the countryside, and thus the whole "mobilizational" model is largely irrelevant to the Colombian experience, as is the consciousness-raising approach. Yet the guerrilla movements from the 1960s to today nonetheless had clear organizational-mobilizational predecessors on which they built. (I will only discuss the FARC [Colombian Revolutionary Armed Forces] here, by far the largest group over the entire quarter-century of insurgency.) Areas of peasant quasi independence—Sumapaz, Viotá, and Tequendama—clearly existed already by 1948, with roots decades older. Those same areas fell under the influence of the Colombian Communist Party (PCC) very early on, and later became the bases of true "peasant republics," which formed as self-governing, self-defense areas during *La Violencia* of the 1950s. By that time, the convergence between the PCC and future FARC guerrillas was already firmly in place; among the leaders of all three groups would be Jacobo Arenas, Isauro Yosa, Ciro Trujillo, and Manuel Marulanda. Speaking as a FARC leader in the early 1980s, Arenas summarized events of the 1950s succinctly: "The independent republics were the agrarian and self-defense movements that we directed." When the military "conquered" those areas in the mid-1960s, the FARC was born in those selfsame regions as a mobile guerrilla army, clearly allied in its early years with the Communist Party.[75]

Finally, for the case of Peru, we have only modest evidence of peasant support for any of the guerrilla movements of the 1960s. The MIR (Movement of the Revolutionary Left) *foco* in Junín Department provides the clearest such example, and also the clearest example of the use of a preexisting authority network to mobilize such support. Second-in-command of the Junín wing of the MIR was Máximo Velando Gálvez, who had spent the years preceding the 1965 insurgency working in the area as a peasant organizer. More than that, he had been elected to head the local peasant federation several years before his *foco* exploded in the Sierra in mid-1965.[76]

Conclusions

The cases I have just reviewed range from instances in which thousands of peasants streamed in to swell the ranks of guerrilla forces, to the final and more modest case of Peru in 1965. In almost every instance we can trace the success in mobilizing the peasantry to the exploitation of, or, less commonly, the formation of networks to achieve such ends. Beyond that simple distinction, we can identify one peculiarity of those regions where the guerrillas did *not* find such networks already available: such regions had not been the object of mobilization by any previous groups. Peru's *Sendero* developed in an area that otherwise had been bypassed by all the political organizers who had streamed into the highlands beginning in the 1950s.[77] Nicaragua's Sandinistas were mobilizing a scattered and largely atomized peasantry who, like the populace more generally, had been subjected to demobilizing pressures during almost a half a century of Somoza family rule, including attacks on all political parties, labor unions, and even business organizations. Somoza was far more interested in controlling his National Guard, his own Liberal Party, and his

Conservative opposition with various corrupt rewards than he was in mobilizing the kind of mass movement seen under fascist regimes (see chapter 7 below). Hence even the exceptional cases conform to the hypotheses that I put forth above.

There remains the suspicion among certain analysts of revolution, however, that these network features I have analyzed are epiphenomenal in character rather than basic to the revolutionary process. Indeed, one critic has suggested that such network analysis really adds little to the regional sources of peasant rebellion I alluded to above, and hence may be theoretically dispensable.[78] Perhaps, the critique continues, the only concept we need to understand peasant support for revolution is the presence of violated peasant class interests, which provide them with the "will" to rebel, whereupon the "way" to revolution is created through one mechanism or another.

I do not believe that the study of organizational networks can be so easily banished from the analysis of revolution, and here I join forces with one of our best theorists thereof. Charles Tilly has argued very cogently that the structure of class interests does not by itself lead to the intense social conflicts characteristic of revolutionary struggles. Instead, interests must be channeled into, and resources mobilized by, organizations seeking to further the class interests of either incumbent groups or challenging groups. His analysis implies an aphorism: no organizational mobilization of resources, no revolutionary contention. Disembodied hostility does not create a revolutionary movement.[79] As Trotsky noted some time ago, if sheer exploitation were enough to generate an uprising, then the masses would always be up in arms.

Furthermore, there is some substantial evidence that the collapse of supportive organizational networks actually does damage the guerrillas' capacity to fight. The clearest case is from Venezuela, where two events in the years 1964–65 led to a sharp decline, almost a collapse, in the strongest *foco* in Venezuela. At the time, the guerrilla front in Lara State began to disintegrate under the impact of two otherwise unrelated events: (1) the Communist Party's backing away from the armed struggle, and hence the guerrillas' loss of its deep infrastructural network in certain areas of that state, not to mention its urban cadres and resources; (2) the accidental death of guerrilla chief Argimiro Gabaldón, whose social position as the son of a regionally famous *patrón*—one who led a massive peasant rebellion in the region in the 1920s—was supplemented by his own efforts in organizing the peasants into unions during the 1950s. Gabaldón was beloved by all in the region, and the loss of his contribution to the armed struggle led to a sharp decline in guerrilla fortunes in the following year.[80] In a similar fashion, when the Guatemalan and Colombian Communist parties withdrew, at least partially, from the armed struggle during the late 1960s, there was a downturn in guerrilla fortunes in both nations. In Bolivia, the failure of the Bolivian Communist Party to commit itself to Ché's guerrilla movement crippled the insurgents from the start.[81]

Much more generally, we should note that violated peasant interests—except in Colombia—never themselves produced peasant insurrection during this thirty-year period, but always had to be funneled through the guerrillas' own organizational apparatus in order to come to life. When the guerrillas were militarily defeated, as happened in a number of instances, the peasant component of the insurrection also subsided. Therefore, the concatenation of both the guerrilla network and the peasant network served to strengthen the insurgency both militarily and socially, and the disruption of either or both could lead to a sharp decline in guerrilla fortunes.

I shall end here by pointing to the potentially disastrous consequences for an insurgency should either or both of those networks be disrupted. In Venezuela in the 1960s, and in both El Salvador and Guatemala during the 1970s–1980s, incumbent regimes ''invaded'' and occupied university grounds, or they were simply the targets of massive death squad activity. In each of those cases the effect was to reduce the resources flowing to the rural insurgency or the effectiveness of the urban organization with which it was linked. In contrast, the failure of the Somoza regime to do something similar at the Autonomous University of León may have helped to preserve León and the surrounding countryside as a haven for Sandinista resistance up until the end.[82] Finally, if a guerrilla organization—like any effective subterranean resistance group—lives by its networks, then it can also die by them. While there are several instances that fit that portrait, the most telling experience was that of ORPA in Guatemala. Its urban network was largely shattered early in the 1980s when the government applied its *own* brand of ''network analysis'' to counterinsurgency: it did a computer review of telephone calls, electric bills, and so forth in the capital, leading, among other things, to the unearthing of a ''safe house'' used to manufacture land mines. It is unlikely that ORPA's urban organization has ever recovered from that loss.[83]

Notes

1. This discussion draws on Paulo Freire, *Pedagogy of the Oppressed* (New York: Herder and Herder, 1971), and on two articles in the *Harvard Educational Review* (*HER*): "The Adult Literacy Process as Cultural Action for Freedom," *HER* 40 (May 1970), pp. 205–25, and "Cultural Action and Conscientization," *HER* 40 (August 1970), pp. 452–77. The latter essays also appear in Portuguese in *Ação cultural para a liberdade e outros escritos* (Rio de Janeiro: Paz e Terra, 1978). As I hope I make clear, I also owe an invaluable intellectual debt to Peter Berger's "unmasking" of Freire's assumptions, performed in the former's *Pyramids of Sacrifice* (New York: Basic Books, 1974), chapter 4; without Berger's critique this essay could not have been written.

2. Freire, *Pedagogy*, pp. 150–86.

3. Freire, *Pedagogy*, p. 125, and "Cultural Action and Conscientization," p. 471.

4. Richard Kiessler, *Guerilla und Revolution: Parteikommunismus und Partisanenstrategie in Lateinamerika* (Bonn-Bad Godesberg: Verlag Neue Gesellschaft, GmbH., 1975), p. 33; Boris Goldenberg, "The Strategy of Castroism," *Military Review* 50 (April 1970), pp. 39–40. This affirmation, that guerrillas are a vanguard necessary to the revolutionary mobilization of the heretofore ignorant and isolated peasantry, is stated baldly in the "Second Declaration of Havana," Castro's major statement on guerrilla ideology and policy; see A. P. Short, "Conversations with the Guatemalan Delegates in Cuba," *Monthly Review* 18 (February 1967), p. 37.

5. Karl Mannheim also once noted that one of the peculiar self-appointed missions of intellectuals was that of awakening "class-type" consciousness in other groups; see *Ideology and Utopia* (New York: Harcourt, Brace and Co., 1936), pp. 142–43.

6. Malcolm Deas, "Guerrillas in Latin America: A Perspective" *World Today* 24 (February 1968), p. 76; Régis Debray, *Strategy for Revolution*, ed. Robin Blackburn (London: Jonathan Cape, 1970), p. 96; Alberto Domingo, "Guerrilla in Venezuela" *Monthly Review* 15 (February 1964), p. 543; Richard N. Adams, *Crucifixion by Power: Essays on Guatemalan National Social Structure, 1944–1966* (Austin, Texas: University of Texas Press, 1970), p. 205; Richard Gott, *Rural Guerrillas in Latin America* (Harmondsworth, Middlesex, England: Penguin, 1973), pp. 566–67.

7. Perry Anderson, *Passages from Antiquity to Feudalism* (London: Verso, 1978 [1974]), pp. 24–25.

8. For Propositions 3 and 4, see Freire, *Ação cultural*, pp. 53–54, and *Pedagogy of the Oppressed*, pp. 54–56. Examples where guerrilla leaders shared such perceptions of peasants appear in Manuel Cabieses Donoso, *¡Venezuela, okey!* (Santiago, Chile: Ediciones del Litoral, 1963), p. 98; Jacobo Arenas, *Diario de la resistencia de Marquetalia* (Bogotá?: Abejón Mono, 1972), pp. 66–67; Luis J. González and Gustavo Sánchez Salazar, *The Great Rebel: Che Guevara in Bolivia* (New York: Grove Press, 1969), p. 229.

9. In contrast to these simpler views, Eric Wolf, while agreeing that only in making cross-class alliances will peasant revolts have revolutionary consequences, insists that the peasant perspective imbedded in peasant revolts, while

antiexploitative, is backward-looking and obviously not Marxist; see his *Peasant Wars of the Twentieth Century* (New York: Harper and Row, 1969), chapter 7, where both issues are discussed.

10. Berger, *Pyramids of Sacrifice*, pp. 111–20.

11. Freire, *Ação cultural*, p. 69; Z. Martin Kowaleski and Miguel Sobrado, *Antropología de la guerrilla* (Caracas: Nueva Izquierda, 1971), p. 87; Orlando Albornoz, *Ideología y política en la universidad latinoamericana* (Caracas: Instituto Societas, 1972), p. 243; Cabieses, *¡Venezuela, okey!* p. 181; Jaime Arenas, *La guerrilla por dentro* (Bogotá: Tercer Mundo, 1970), pp. 138–39; Héctor Béjar, *Peru 1965: Notes on a Guerrilla Experience* (New York: Monthly Review Press, 1970), p. 66.

12. In order, the five quotations come from: (1) Norman Gall, "Letter from Peru," *Commentary* 37 (June 1964), p. 65; (2) Ernesto "Ché" Guevara, *The Complete Bolivian Diaries of Ché Guevara and Other Captured Documents*, edited and with an introduction by Daniel James (New York: Stein and Day, 1968), p. 170 (Diary entry: 19 June 1967); (3) Julio Cotler, "The Mechanics of Internal Domination and Social Change in Peru," in *Peruvian Nationalism: A Corporatist Revolution*, ed. David Chaplin (New Brunswick, N.J.: Transaction, 1976), pp. 43–44; (4) Berger, *Pyramids of Sacrifice*, p. 114; (5) Fund-raising letter from Cultural Survival, Inc., January 1990.

13. John and Barbara Ehrenreich, "A Favorable View of the FAR," *Monthly Review* 18 (February 1967), pp. 26–27; Theodore Draper, *Castro's Revolution: Myths and Realities* (New York: Frederick A. Praeger, 1962), pp. 33–34, citing Huberman and Sweezy; Pombo, one of the survivors of Ché's Bolivian *foco*, quoted in *El Siglo* (Santiago, Chile), 24 February 1968, as recorded by Klaus Esser, "Guevaras Guerilla in Bolivien," *Vierteljahresberichte—Forschungsinstitut der Friedrich Ebert Stiftung* (henceforth *VJB-FFES*) 37 (September 1969), p. 332; Rogger Mercado, *Las guerrillas del Perú: De la prédica ideológica a la acción armada* (Lima: Fondo de Cultura Popular, 1967), pp. 230–32.

14. See, respectively, Edgar Owens and Robert Shaw, *Development Reconsidered: Bridging the Gap between Government and People* (Lexington, Mass.: Lexington Books, 1972), and Mahmood Mamdami, *The Myth of Population Control* (New York: Monthly Review Press, 1972).

15. I review their respective theories in the following two chapters.

16. On the working class, see Nicholas Abercrombie, Stephen Hill, and Bryan S. Turner, *The Dominant Ideology Thesis* (London: Allen and Unwin, 1980), or for a more summary argument, Abercrombie and Turner's "The Dominant Ideology Thesis," *British Journal of Sociology* 29, no. 2 (June 1978), pp. 149–70; on the peasantry, James C. Scott has done the main intellectual demolition of this view: see *The Moral Economy of the Peasant* (New Haven, Conn.: Yale University Press, 1976), esp. ch. 7; *Weapons of the Weak: Everyday Forms of Peasant Resistance* (New Haven, Conn.: Yale University Press, 1985); and most clearly "Hegemony and the Peasantry" *Politics and Society* 7, no. 3 (1977), pp. 267–96. Oddly, Scott wrote the piece "Hegemony" while in part accepting the theses concerning "ideological domination" of the urban working class, which Abercrombie et al. were to demolish in the following few years.

17. Herbert Marcuse, *One-Dimensional Man: Studies in the Ideology of Ad-*

vanced Industrial Society (Boston: Beacon, 1964); Noam Chomsky, *Necessary Illusions: Thought Control in Democratic Societies* (Boston: South End Press, 1989).

18. See Michael Schudson, *Advertising, The Uneasy Persuasion: Its Dubious Impact on American Society* (New York: Basic Books, 1984), for a review of the evidence; Barrington Moore, Jr., *Injustice: The Social Bases of Obedience and Revolt* (White Plains, N.Y.: M. E. Sharpe, 1978), pp. 100–101 (quotation).

19. The observations concerning ideological inconsistency are now sufficiently elementary to be included in introductory textbooks, with which writers like Chomsky could stand to familiarize themselves; see Rodney Stark, *Sociology*, 3d ed. (Belmont, Calif.: Wadsworth, 1989), pp. 455–61, including many references to original research. In an interesting convergence of independent analyses, Axel van den Berg has come to remarkably parallel conclusions in a work I encountered after coming to these conclusions several years ago; see his *The Immanent Utopia: From Marxism on the State to the State of Marxism* (Princeton, N.J.: Princeton University Press, 1988), pp. 509–13. Concerning the basically economic concerns (and usually economic satisfactions) of the American masses, there is now little doubt, given the publication of Richard F. Hamilton and James D. Wright, *The State of the Masses* (New York: Aldine, 1986).

20. Scott, *Moral Economy of the Peasant*, p. 231.

21. Chaplin, *Peruvian Nationalism*, pp. 297, 285; Jeffery M. Paige, *Agrarian Revolution: Social Movements and Export Agriculture in the Underdeveloped World* (New York: The Free Press, 1975), ch. 3, also deals with these events, and argues forcefully that the structure of peasant communities explained the virtual absence of atomized "serfs" from the land invasion process.

22. See, for an early summary of the historians' debate, David Hackett Fischer, *Historians' Fallacies* (New York: Harper and Row, 1970), pp. 205–6; see also Charles R. Silberman, *Criminal Violence, Criminal Justice* (New York: Vintage, 1980), pp. 189–205, for a discussion of black culture under slavery and Jim Crow, and the hidden messages of resistance in the "trickster" stories; also see Moore, *Injustice*, ch. 14, where he discusses both "Sambo" personalities and the conditions for the emergence of resistance, as he does more generally in that book.

23. William Foote Whyte, "Rural Peru: Peasants as Activists," in *Peruvian Nationalism*, ed. Chaplin, p. 42; E. J. Hobsbawm, "Economic Fluctuations and Some Social Movements" *Economic History Review*, 2d series, vol. 5, no. 1 (1952), pp. 23–24; Theda Skocpol, *States and Social Revolutions* (Cambridge, England: Cambridge University Press, 1979), ch. 3, and pp. 252–62.

24. Kowaleski and Sobrado, *Antropología de la guerrilla*, pp. 37–38; Lt. Colonel William J. Buchanan and Lt. Colonel Robert A. Hyatt, "Capitalizing on Guerrilla Vulnerabilities" *Military Review* 48 (August 1968), pp. 38–39.

25. *Daily Journal* (Caracas), 4 April 1966; Carlos Rangel Guevara, *The Latin Americans: Their Love-Hate Relationship with the United States* (New York and London: Harcourt Brace Jovanovich, 1977), pp. 133–34; Guevara, *Complete Bolivian Diaries*, p. 127 (entry for 21 March 1967).

26. Aleksandr I. Solzhenitsyn, *The Gulag Archipelago, 1918–1956*, volume 2 (New York: Harper and Row, 1975), pp. 490–91; Fritz René Allemann, *Macht und Ohnmacht der Guerilla* (Munich: R. Piper, 1974), pp. 209, 416.

27. Draper, *Castro's Revolution*, p. 11; Luigi Valsalice, *Guerriglia e Politica: L'esempio del Venezuela* (Florence, Italy: Valmartina Editore, 1973), pp. 216–17; Luis Mercier Vega, *Guerrillas in Latin America: The Technique of the Counter-State* (New York: Praeger, 1969), p. 149.

28. For a survey of these events, and the various fortunes of the guerrilla groups, see Timothy P. Wickham-Crowley, "Winners, Losers, and Also-Rans: Toward a Comparative Sociology of Latin American Guerrilla Movements," pp. 132–81 in *Power and Popular Protest*, ed. Susan Eckstein (Berkeley: University of California Press, 1989).

29. Alvin W. Gouldner, *The Coming Crisis in Western Sociology* (New York: Basic Books, 1970), pp. 29–35 and passim; Kowaleski and Sobrado, *Antropología de la guerrilla*, p. 44.

30. This should not be understood to imply that the guerrillas lie to the peasantry to convert them. There are generally sufficient damning data (re: exploitation, poverty) from the peasants' everyday existence to obviate the need for guerrilla creativity.

31. Ramón L. Bonachea and Marta San Martín, *The Cuban Insurrection, 1952–1959* (New Brunswick, N.J.: Transaction Books, 1974), pp. 182–84, 195–96, 283–84; Mercier, *Guerrillas in Latin America*, pp. 78–79; Boris Goldenberg, *The Cuban Revolution and Latin America* (New York: Praeger, 1965), pp. 145–46.

32. François Maspero, ed., *Avec Douglas Bravo dans les maquis vénézuéliens* (Paris: François Maspero, 1968), p. 54.

33. Maspero, *Avec Douglas Bravo*, p. 53.

34. Antonio Zamora, *Memoria(s) de la guerrilla venezolana* (Caracas: Síntesis Dosmil, 1974), p. 33.

35. For Gouldner's notion of "metaphoricality," I am indebted to a brief but illuminating conversation with Frank Heard some years ago; Berger, *Pyramids of Sacrifice*, chapter 1. Berger also compares capitalist and socialist realities in that book, as he does in more detail in *The Capitalist Revolution* (New York: Basic Books, 1986).

36. Alan Howard, "With the Guerrillas in Guatemala," *The New York Times Magazine*, 26 June 1966, p. 25.

37. Donn Munson, *Zacapa* (Canoga, Calif.: Challenge, 1967), p. 118.

38. Tom Wolfe, *Mauve Gloves and Madmen, Clutter and Vine* (New York: Farrar, Straus and Giroux, 1976), p. 108. There is a special, and grisly, prophetic significance in these words if we note that they were apparently written before the Cambodian holocaust.

39. Charles Issawi, *Issawi's Laws of Social Motion* (New York: Hawthorn Books, 1973), pp. 54–55.

40. Berger, *Pyramids of Sacrifice*, pp. 223–24.

41. Mercier, *Guerrillas in Latin America*, p. 85.

42. General Armando Artola Azcarate, *¡Subversión!* (Lima: Editorial Jurídica, 1976), pp. 71–78.

43. Speech by Luis de la Puente in Lima in 1964, making his call for revolution, as recorded in Mercado, *Las guerrillas del Perú*, p. 85. This almost exact translation does capture somewhat the oratorical flavor common in Hispanic cultural discourse.

44. De la Puente, quoted in Mercado, *Las guerrillas del Perú*, p. 215.

45. Héctor Béjar, "Ne pas surestimer ses forces," *Partisans* 38 (July–September 1967), pp. 111, 113–14, and idem, *Peru, 1965*, p. 116; on the Russian *narodniki* see Leonard Schapiro, *The Communist Party of the Soviet Union* (New York: Vintage, 1971), pp. 1–5.

46. Allemann, *Macht und Ohnmacht*, pp. 196–97; *La Prensa* (Lima) 12 September 1965, p. 1.

47. Gil Carl Alroy, "The Meaning of Peasant Revolution: The Cuban Case," *International Review of History and Political Science* 2 (December 1965), pp. 90–91; Arenas, *La guerrilla por dentro*, p. 165; Walter Schump, *Las guerrillas en América Latina: El principio y el fin* (Buenos Aires: Punto Crítico, 1971), p. 56.

48. Moore, *Injustice*, p. 475.

49. Berger, *Pyramids of Sacrifice*, pp. 90–91.

50. Adolfo Gilly, "The Guerrilla Movement in Guatemala I," *Monthly Review* 17 (May 1965), pp. 6–7, and "The Guerrilla Movement in Guatemala II," *Monthly Review* 17 (June 1965), pp. 38–40; Allemann, *Macht und Ohnmacht*, p. 176; Robert F. Lamberg, *Die castristiche Guerilla in Lateinamerika* (Hannover, Germany: Verlag für Literatur und Zeitgeschehen, 1971), p. 58.

51. *Daily Journal*, (Caracas), 28 August 1965.

52. See Cynthia McClintock, "Peru's Sendero Luminoso Rebellion: Origins and Trajectory," in Eckstein, *Power and Popular Protest*, pp. 67–70; for Central America, the best single discussion is Robert G. Williams, *Export Agriculture and the Crisis in Central America* (Chapel Hill: University of North Carolina Press, 1986).

53. For El Salvador, see Robert Armstrong and Janet Shenk, *El Salvador: The Face of Revolution* (London: Pluto, 1982), pp. 204–8 (quotations on last page); Don North, Director, *Guazapa* (Washington, D.C.: Northstar Productions, 1984); "Life with the Salvadorean Rebels," *Latin America Weekly Report*, 19 November 1982, p. 9. For Guatemala, see ORPA, "Eight Years of Silent Organizing," in *Guatemala in Rebellion: Unfinished History*, ed. Jonathan L. Fried, Marvin E. Gettleman, Deborah T. Levenson, and Nancy Peckenham (New York: Grove, 1983), pp. 270–71; Eduardo Galeano, José González, and Antonio Campos, *Guatemala: Un pueblo en lucha* (Madrid: Editorial Revolución, 1983), pp. 178–79 (on quick, early recruitment by ORPA).

54. On cooperative forms in agriculture, see Don North's *Guazapa*, where he refers to collectivization; but also see the discussion of individual vs. collective plots near that Salvadoran volcano, in "Life with the Salvadorean Rebels," p. 9.; for Guatemala, see George Black, with Milton Jamail and Norma Stoltz Chinchilla, *Garrison Guatemala* (New York: Monthly Review Press, 1984), p. 104; and EGP, "The People Become Guerrillas," p. 277 in Fried et al. *Guatemala in Rebellion*; on cooperative agriculture in northern Guatemala, see Concerned Guatemala Scholars, *Guatemala: Dare to Struggle, Dare to Win* (San Francisco: Solidarity, 1982), pp. 39–40, 44. On attempts to root out *machismo*, see the optimistic assessments by Armstrong and Shenk, *El Salvador*, pp. 204–6, and North's *Guazapa*; in contrast, Charles Clements, who lived for a long period near Guazapa, said that, even among the guerrillas themselves, women held "few illusions" about the disappearance of the pervasive *macho* mentality; see his *Witness to War: An American Doctor in El Salvador* (Toronto: Bantam, 1984),

p. 189. For one Guatemalan revolutionary's account of, and one passing reference to, challenges to *machismo* in Guatemala, see, respectively, Luz Alicia Herrera, "Testimonies of Guatemalan Women," in *Revolution in Central America*, edited by Stanford Central America Action Network (SCAAN) (Boulder, Colo.: Westview, 1983), p. 399, and María Lupe, "Up in the Mountains Everything is Different," in Fried et al., *Guatemala in Rebellion*, pp. 275–76. In neither case, however, do the writers claim that *machismo* in the peasantry has been seriously undermined.

55. For *Sendero*'s behavior in prison, see *The New York Times*, 7 September 1984.

56. Wickham-Crowley, "Winners, Losers, and Also-Rans."

57. Elizabeth Bott, *Family and Social Network* (London: Tavistock, 1957).

58. See the review of the ongoing work by Richard Emerson in Jonathan H. Turner, *The Structure of Sociological Theory*, 4th ed. (Chicago, Ill.: The Dorsey Press, 1986), ch. 13.

59. For examples, see Beth Mintz and Michael Schwartz, "The Structure of Intercorporate Unity in American Business," *Social Problems* 29 (1981), pp. 87–103; William G. Roy, "The Unfolding of the Interlocking Directorate Structure of the United States" *American Sociological Review* 48, no. 2 (April 1983), pp. 248–57; or Donald Palmer, Roger Friedland, and Jitendra V. Singh, "The Ties That Bind: Organizational and Class Bases of Stability in a Corporate Interlock Network" *American Sociological Review* 51, no. 6 (December 1986), pp. 781–96.

60. See the grab-bag of contributions to Barry Wellman and S. D. Berkowitz, eds., *Social Structures: A Network Approach* (Cambridge, England: Cambridge University Press, 1988). For one such highly sophisticated approach to networks, power, and exchange, which looks solely at some experimental data rather than "the real world," see Barry Markovsky, David Willer, and Travis Patton, "Power Relations in Exchange Networks" *American Sociological Review* 53, no. 2 (April 1988), pp. 220–36.

61. Barry Wellman, "Structural Analysis: From Method and Metaphor to Theory and Substance," in Wellman and Berkowitz, *Social Structures*, pp. 31–35, 41–42, 46–47.

62. For a discussion of the connection between university students and guerrilla activity, see Timothy P. Wickham-Crowley, *Guerrillas and Revolution in Latin America* (Princeton, N.J.: Princeton University Press, forthcoming 1991), chapters 2, 3, and 9; for the observation that university student movements socialize incoming students into Marxist ideology, see Aldo Solari, *Estudiantes y política en América Latina* (Caracas: Monte Avila, 1968), p. 62. For the argument that university campuses provide conditions similar to those of total institutions, and hence favor the proliferation of counter-ideologies, see Gláucio Ary Dillon Soares and Loreto Hoecker, "El mundo de la ideología: La función de las ideas y la legitimidad de la política estudiantil," in Solari, *Estudiantes y política*, pp. 338–41.

63. Stark, *Sociology*, passim, esp. chs. 1, 3, and 4.

64. Kenneth L. Wilson and Anthony M. Orum, "Mobilizing People for Collective Political Action," in *Political Sociology: Readings in Research and Theory*, ed. George A. Kourvetaris and Betty A. Dobratz (New Brunswick, N.J.: Transaction Books, 1980), pp. 275–90.

65. Stark, *Sociology*, pp. 84–88 (quotations: 86–87).

66. Stark, *Sociology*, pp. 623–32 (quotations: 624, 628). Bainbridge contributed the chapter on collective behavior and social movements to Stark's work.

67. For these observations on *Sendero*, I am indebted to private conversations and one public presentation by Michael Smith.

68. Once again, I am indebted here to Michael Smith. See as well David Scott Palmer, "Rebellion in Rural Peru: The Origins and Evolution of Sendero Luminoso," *Comparative Politics* 18, no. 2 (January 1986), esp. pp. 127–28, 135–38.

69. On FECCAS and the CEBs, see Tommie Sue Montgomery, "Liberation and Revolution: Christianity as Subversive Activity in Central America," in *Trouble in Our Backyard*, ed. Martin Diskin (New York: Pantheon, 1983), p. 93; Armstrong and Shenk, *El Salvador*, pp. 78–83; Clements, *Witness to War*, pp. 93, 99–101, 169–70, 200; Robert S. Leiken, "The Salvadoran Left," in *Central America: Anatomy of Conflict*, ed. Robert S. Leiken (New York: Pergamon, 1984), p. 115; on Guardado, see *[Latin America] Weekly Report* (London), 26 October 1984, p. 6.

70. On CEBs, Catholic Action, and the CUC in Guatemala, see Montgomery, "Liberation and Revolution," pp. 87, 92; Shelton H. Davis, "State Violence and Agrarian Crisis in Guatemala: The Roots of the Indian-Peasant Rebellion," in Diskin, *Trouble in Our Backyard*, pp. 164–67; Lars Schöultz, "Guatemala: Social Change and Political Conflict," pp. 194–97, in the same volume; the report of EGP leader Rolando Morán, "El éxodo campesino," *Proceso* (Mexico City) 413, 1 October 1984, pp. 43–44; Black et al., *Garrison Guatemala*, p. 98; Concerned Guatemala Scholars, *Guatemala*, pp. 37, 39–41; Robert M. Carmack, "Estratificación y cambio social en las tierras altas occidentales de Guatemala: El caso de Tecpanaco" *América Indígena* 36, no. 2 (April–June 1976), pp. 291–93, 301, on Catholic Action; EGP, "The People Become Guerrillas," p. 277; Galeano et al., *Guatemala*, pp. 154–55, 224–25; Mario Payeras, "Days of the Jungle: The Testimony of a Guatemalan *Guerrillero*, 1972–1976" *Monthly Review* 35, no. 3 (July–August 1983), passim, esp. pp. 64–71.

71. Henry Ruiz, "La montaña era como un crisol donde se forjaban los mejores cuadros," *Nicaráuac: Revista Bimestral del Ministerio de Cultura* 1, no. 1 (May–June 1980), pp. 8–24; Omar Cabezas, *Fire from the Mountain*, translated by Kathleen Weaver (New York: Crown, 1985 [1982]), esp. pp. 36–38, 40–41, 168–71, 216–20; David Nolan, *The Ideology of the Sandinistas and the Nicaraguan Revolution* (Coral Gables, Fla.: Institute of Interamerican Studies, University of Miami, 1984), pp. 24–26; Manlio Tirado, *La revolución sandinista* (México, D.F.: Nuestro Tiempo, 1983), p. 39; Montgomery, "Liberation and Revolution," pp. 90–91, 93.

72. On the role of Crescencio Pérez, see Ramón Barquín López, *Las luchas guerrilleras en Cuba*, 2 volumes (Madrid: Plaza Mayor, 1975), vol. 1, pp. 272f., 309, 313, 327–30; Carlos Franqui, *The Twelve* (New York: Lyle Stuart, 1968), p. 67; Enrique Meneses, *Fidel Castro* (New York: Taplinger, 1966), p. 46 and passim; Günter Maschke, *Kritik des Guerillero* (Frankfurt, Germany: S. Fischer, 1973), p. 76; Ernesto "Ché" Guevara, *Reminiscences of the Cuban Revolutionary War* (New York: Monthly Review, 1968), pp. 50–53; Hugh Thomas, *Cuba: The Pursuit of Freedom* (New York: Harper and Row, 1971), pp. 902, 906, 920.

73. For details on these Venezuelan events, see my *Guerrillas and Revolution in Latin America*, chapter 7, part 2. For sources, see Valsalice, *Guerriglia e Politica*, pp. 123, 131–33, 195–98; Zágo, *Aquí no ha pasado nada*, esp. pp. 13–15, 46, 73, 85; Norman Gall, "Teodoro Petkoff: The Crisis of the Professional Revolutionary," parts 1 and 2 in, respectively, *American Universities Field Staff Reports—East Coast South America Series* 16, no. 1 (January 1972), pp. 1–19 (esp. p. 13), and 17, no. 9 (August 1973), pp. 3–20 (esp. p. 6); Allemann, *Macht und Ohnmacht*, pp. 139–40, 395; Debray, *Strategy for Revolution*, p. 92; Norman Gall, "A Cheerleader's Report," *The New York Times Book Review*, 28 March 1971, p. 6; idem "The Continental Revolution," *The New Leader* 48 (12 April 1965), p. 7; Benedict Cross (pseud.), "Marxism in Venezuela," *Problems of Communism* 22 (November–December 1973), p. 68; V. L., "Venezuelan National Hero," *World Marxist Review* (England) 8 (May 1965), pp. 58–59; and *El Nacional* (Caracas), 7 April 1963, 26 and 27 August 1965.

74. On León, see very similar comments by politically diverse observers: guerrilla leader Marco Antonio Yon Sosa, "Breves apuntes históricos del Movimiento Revolucionario 13 de Noviembre," *Pensamiento Crítico* 15 (1968), p. 137; and two conservative-to-moderate chroniclers: Carlos Sáiz Cidoncha, *Guerrillas en Cuba y otros países de Iberoamérica* (Madrid: Editora Nacional, 1974), p. 184; and Lamberg, *Die castristiche Guerilla*, p. 55; also see Información Documental de América Latina (INDAL), *Movimientos revolucionarios de América Latina I: Documentación propia*, 2d ed. (Caracas: INDAL, 1972), pp. 104–7 for another printing of Yon Sosa's piece. On Ixtapá, see Sáiz, *Guerrillas en Cuba*, p. 184; Julio del Valle, "Guatemala bajo el signo de la guerra," *Pensamiento Crítico* 15 (1968), p. 63, and, in the same issue, Aura Marina Arriola, "Secuencia de la cultura indígena guatemalteca," p. 99. For Pablo Monsanto's look back, see his comments to interviewer Marta Harnecker in her *Pueblos en armas* (México, D.F.: Era, 1984), p. 241.

75. The best discussions of the Communist/peasant republics/FARC links are in Lamberg, *Die castristiche Guerilla*, pp. 89–91; Jean Lartéguy, *The Guerrillas* (New York: World Press, 1970), pp. 151, 158–59; and Boris Goldenberg, "Kommunismus in Lateinamerika: Die Kommunistiche Partei Kolumbiens," *Der Ostblock und die Entwicklungsländer (VJB-FFES)* 21 (September 1965), pp. 246–48, 256–58; for Arenas's interview and quotation, see Manuel Arango Z., *FARC: Veinte años—De Marquetalia a la Uribe* (Bogotá: Aurora, 1984), pp. 30, 112.

76. Allemann, *Macht und Ohnmacht*, pp. 196–97, 205; *La Prensa* (Lima), 23 June 1965; Artola, *¡Subversión!*, pp. 44–45; Peru, Ministerio de Guerra, *Las guerrillas en el Perú y su represión* (Lima?: Ministerio de Guerra, 1966), p. 16.

77. McClintock, "Peru's Sendero Luminoso Rebellion," pp. 70–76.

78. The critic is an anonymous reviewer of another of my works, where I outline an argument similar to the detailed one found here.

79. Charles Tilly, *From Mobilization to Revolution* (Reading, Mass.: Addison-Wesley, 1978).

80. Valsalice, *Guerriglia e Politica*, p. 131; Gall, "Teodoro Petkoff II," p. 6; Lamberg, *Die castristiche Guerilla*, pp. 79–80; V. L., "Venezuelan National Hero." For an insider's report on the decline in Lara, see José Díaz's story, reported above, as found in *El Nacional* (Caracas), 26 and 27 August 1965.

81. See Lamberg, *Die castristiche Guerilla*, passim, for discussions of the shifting positions of Communist Parties in each of those nations.

82. On Venezuela, see Lamberg, *Die castristiche Guerilla*, pp. 77, 82; Armstrong and Shenk, *El Salvador*, pp. 164–65; Black et al., *Garrison Guatemala*, pp. 91–92; for recurring references to the role of the university in León, see Cabezas, *Fire from the Mountain*, passim.

83. *Latin America Weekly Report*, 6 November 1981, pp. 1–2, and *Latin America Regional Reports: Mexico and Central America*, 24 September 1982, pp. 6–7.

Part Two

WHERE THEORY CONTEMPLATES PRACTICE: EXPLORING THE OUTCOMES OF THEORETICAL AND REVOLUTIONARY CONFLICTS

5

Revolutionary Outcomes and Theories of Revolution

Among the many topics engendering strong, even passionate debate among macrosociologists is the study of social revolutions. Nowadays, little of that ongoing debate concerns itself with the thankless question of whether or not revolutions are "good" things, although narrower issues of welfare and coercion can be addressed.[1] Instead, many sociologists and other social scientists have tended to treat social revolutions simply as historical givens, and have tried objectively to understand the social conditions under which they occur. A few such social scientists have made the sensible decision to compare revolutionary instances to nonrevolutionary ones, in order to make sounder the theoretical conclusions they reach concerning the genesis and impact of revolutions.[2] In the current state of debate, the most important unresolved issues in the study of revolution seem to be the following.

1. Are revolutions *made* by the conscious actions of the revolutionaries themselves, or are they rather the *unplanned outcome* of an unusual pattern (or patterns) of intergroup relations?

By "intergroup" I refer to all interactions among collectivities of actors: e.g., states, social classes, and formal organizations such as the military or guerrilla forces. Theda Skocpol has been the strongest, and apparently a quite lonely, advocate of the latter viewpoint among social scientists, in insisting with Wendell Phillips that "Revolutions are not made; they come."[3] Among the more common "purposive" views of revolution, endorsing (sometimes implicitly) the theoretical position that revolutions occur because of the revolutionary intent of revolutionary actors, are those of Marx himself; the organization-cum-mobilization, class-conflict theory of Charles Tilly; and Jeffery Paige's class-based theory of Third World peasant movements, among whose variety are numbered socialist and nationalist revolutionary movements.[4]

In contrast, Theda Skocpol has made a very strong theoretical and evidentiary case that the conscious actions of revolutionary groups did *not* lead to the collapse of the old regimes of France (1789), Russia (1917), or China (1911).[5] Those consciously revolutionary groups did not even exist in France when the Estates General were assembled in 1789, for it was out of part of that gathering that the National Assembly would be formed, later to split into several contending revolutionary groups, notably the Girondins and the Montagnards. The Russian state clearly collapsed largely due to its disastrous military defeat at the hands of the Germans in World War I, with the final push over the brink administered by bread-line rioters in Petrograd.[6] At that moment, Lenin was in Switzerland and the Bolsheviks were underground. The Manchu Dynasty in China, after a long period of decay and the siphoning away of its imperial powers into the hands of provincial elites, finally fell in 1911. Mao Zedong was but a teenager then, and the Chinese Communist Party was not formed until 1921.

Skocpol does not, however, define revolution solely in terms of such regime collapses. Rather, she defines social revolutions as "rapid, basic transformations of a society's state and class structures; and they are accompanied and in part carried through by class-based revolts from below."[7] That definition is a good and sensible one, with perhaps one necessary qualification: the word "class-based" should perhaps be changed to "mass-based," to allow for cross-class, populist insurrections *or* insurrections rooted in ethnic conflict rather than class relations. For Skocpol, then, the collapse of the old regime is not the revolution per se, but is one of two key contributions that, in a sense, are the proximate causes of a revolutionary transformation. The second key feature that contributes to a revolutionary outcome, in her view, is widespread peasant insurrection that destroys the property basis of the old regime's landed elite. And once again, for the cases of France and Russia, Skocpol shows—and mostly persuasively, I think—that peasant insurrection did not depend on the conscious actions of the revolutionary leaders or cadres. For her Chinese case, however, she clearly shows that peasant mobilization depended upon the intrusion of outside forces, Mao's rural Communists.

Skocpol therefore has made a very strong case, at least for the three great revolutions, that the actions of revolutionary groups become decisive in the overall process of revolution mainly in the *aftermath* of the decisive struggles over the state and the land. In a sense, they step in *après le déluge*, and proceed to reconstitute a new, stronger, more centralized regime out of the rubble of the old order, to whose downfall they had contributed very little.

The main problem with Skocpol's interpretation is not in her reading of the three cases, but in whether it enables one to generalize beyond them. There are other social revolutions, unlike the pattern she (mostly) found, in which the sequence she observed has not been replicated. To wit: (1) There are regimes that have clearly fallen (in large part) because of the conscious actions of the revolutionaries themselves. Bolivia (1952) and Iran (1979) clearly qualify and, if we allow for revolutionaries to be allied with more moderate forces, often in a populist alliance, we can also include the Mexicans' overthrow of Porfirio Díaz (1910), and the Cuban (1959) and Nicaraguan (1979) revolutions as well. (2) In many revolutions, like Skocpol's Chinese case, it is clear that outsiders have mobilized the peasantry, typically into guerrilla armies, rather than the peasants mobilizing themselves into land-invading, landlord-destroying insurrectionary forces. While the Mexican peasantry's self-mobilization behind Emiliano Zapata fits the French-Russian "model," and while the Bolivian peasantry showed a mix of self-mobilization and intrusion by outsiders,[8] many other "revolutionary" peasantries (in both failed and successful revolutions) have instead been mobilized by outsiders: the Cuban squatters of the Sierra Maestra; the Nicaraguan marginal peasantries of the north-central mountains, as well as the ex-peasants of the northwestern cities; the Salvadoran peasantry of the marginal, northern regions of that nation, especially in Chalatenango and Morazán; the Guatemalan Indian communities lying in the northwestern departments and in the area around Lake Atitlán; and so forth.[9]

Skocpol is too good a scholar to have missed these variants. Indeed, in two subsequent articles, she addressed both of these objections. She recognized that mass-mobilizing revolutionaries could indeed bring about the collapse of an unweakened state (Iran), and implied elsewhere that mobilization of the peasantry by guerrilla forces was clearly a "functional alternative" (as Robert Merton might term it) to the peasants' autonomous collective action, in contributing to revolutionary outcomes.[10]

We are therefore left with the task of specifying the historical conditions under which revolutionaries bring down old regimes versus those in which regimes collapse without such intervention. We are also posed with a similar dichotomy for the peasantry: in what circumstances do they rise up on their own versus being mobilized by outsiders? Skocpol has in fact gone a long way toward addressing these issues as well, especially the latter,[11] so I can content myself below in trying to specify such conditions more concretely and with greater conceptual clarity. Serendipitously, my attempt to specify which conditions make peasants "revolutionary" dovetails with question (2) immediately below, while my attempt to specify which regimes collapse with, and which without, the oppositional shoves of revolutionaries, dovetails with questions (3) and (4) below, where we consider the relevance of dual power and regime strength to revolutionary outcomes.

2. Which social groups, whether by action or inaction, provide the decisive forces in producing the revolutionary outcome?

I have not begged question (1) here; this manner of framing the question allows actors to produce social revolutionary outcomes in purposive ways or in unplanned ways; it even allows for ironies of history, in which the actions of social groups can produce revolutions despite their express and vehement opposition to social change. That is, it allows for the "unanticipated consequences of purposive social action" of which Robert Merton wrote a half-century ago. Precisely such unplanned social outcomes are what make sociology interesting, and emphases on such social phenomena are crucial, I think, if one wishes to understand fully the sociologies of Karl Marx and Max Weber.[12]

The Working Class

Most analysts of revolution have long since abandoned the idea that the working class is the decisive agent of revolution, even of socialist revolution. Indeed, it is almost a sure sign of what C. Wright Mills once termed "canned Marxism" to continue to embrace that hoary interpretation. Among prominent systematic theorists of revolution, only James Petras continues to hold to the increasingly isolated Marxist position viewing the working class as the decisive force in revolution, and even he sees that role only as a partial one, happening in alliance with other social classes.[13] The utter lack of influence such interpretations have had in the study of revolutions, even on Marxisant, class conflict–oriented theorists like Paige, Tilly, and Skocpol, is perhaps an index of how weak Petras's case seems to be for the crucial— literally, at the crux—role of the working class. We might especially note his strained attempt to treat the working class as the "revolutionary subject" in China and Cuba (not to mention Vietnam).[14]

On my reading of the historical evidence, one can only make a strong case for *decisive* working-class participation—that is, the proletariat as the sine qua non of revolution—in two instances: Russia (1917) and Bolivia (1952).

Furthermore, even the case for a "proletarian revolution" in Russia has been partially undermined by the work of Victoria Bonnell. Her exquisite research into Russian primary sources (a model for *historical* sociologists who wish to take their adjective seriously) has demonstrated the critical contributions to mobilization, radicalization, and ultimately, revolution made by craft-type *artisanal* workers, those in "small, dispersed, and unmechanized work environments," the virtual opposite of proletarian labor for big capital. She concludes that "the most consistently active unionized groups proceeded from small or medium-sized firms or from small shops within a larger enterprise," and further that "the groups relegated by Marx and Soviet historians to the so-called backward ranks of the labor force, because they belonged to the preindustrial economic order, thus stood in the forefront of the movement to form collective organizations in tsarist Russia."

She continues:

> The partially artisanal printers, the sales-clerks, and various artisanal groups provided enthusiastic support for the first class-based organization—the Soviet—and subsequently promoted regional and national consolidation of the union movement. Thus if industrial workers have a special disposition to adopt a class perspective, as Marx and others have assumed, they were certainly not the only ones to do so.

And, finally and carefully,

> To be sure, factory workers in major industries such as metalworking occupied a position of exceptional importance and influence in the labor movement, often setting the pace for others. But artisans, sales-clerical groups, and even service workers took an active part in virtually all types of voluntary association and collective activity.[15]

Such systematic contributions of artisanal, as opposed to proletarian, manual workers to the long-term process leading to the Russian revolutionary upsurge of 1917 are most interesting, not only because of the limitations they suggest for orthodox Marxist theory, but also because they do not stand alone. The French Revolution of 1789 and the German "revolution" of 1848 both also involved the systematic participation of artisanal workers (rather than social dregs or proletarians), while the German near-revolution of 1918–20 similarly—not identically—involved a new working class whose radical consciousness and ideology derived from an earlier artisanal background.[16]

The Bolivian case thus remains our best, clear case of a decisive contribution of the working class to a successful revolution. In 1952, the middle-class–led Nationalist Revolutionary Movement (MNR) waged a successful uprising against an increasingly moribund Bolivian state. The decisive battle was fought by workers, largely tin miners, against the remnants of the army in La Paz. The revolution thus ushered into power a party led by the radicalized middle classes and supported by a revolutionary working class.[17] By any standards, the outcome was certainly revolutionary, given the conjuncture there of (1) rapid political change, witnessing the destruction of the state and the military; (2) class-based upheavals from below, for in addition to the tin-miners' revolt, there were peasant upheavals, especially following the collapse of the old regime; and (3) massive transformations of property relations. The last included nationalization of the tin mines, thus destroying *la rosca*, the mining-based trio of capitalists who had so dominated Bolivia; but it also included the destruction of the giant holdings of the landed elite through rent and labor strikes, land invasions, and official postrevolutionary agrarian reforms.

Notwithstanding its clear claims to be a working-class–based social revolution, the Bolivian case creates more theoretical problems than it solves. For one thing, no one considers the Bolivian case to constitute a socialist revolution, despite its proletarian credentials; indeed, Marxist references to its "bourgeois" character are now commonplace. Along similar "rejectionist" lines most specialists, Marxist and non-Marxist alike, consider the Bolivian revolution, even more strikingly than its Mexican counterpart, to be the prime exemplar of a "failed" revolution.[18] Perhaps such widespread perceptions of "failure" explain Bolivia's nigh-universal omission from systematic theorizing about revolutionary cases.[19]

The Peasantry

Unlike the proletariat, there now exists near-universal agreement that the peasantry has been the decisive "mass" in effecting the majority of social revolutions to date. An emphasis on the actions of the peasantry can be found in the analytical and hortatory writings of Mao Zedong and Ché Guevara, and in the social scientific analyses of revolution found in the works of Barrington Moore, Eric Wolf, Jeffery Paige, Joel Migdal, James Scott (perhaps), Theda Skocpol, and Samuel Popkin.[20]

Such happy consensus falls apart, however, when we press these theorists further: *which* peasants are likely to be revolutionary? For it is obviously true that peasants are not always and everywhere revolutionary in intent or in the consequences of their actions, even if we include many cases of failed revolutionary movements backed by the peasantry.[21] The answer to that question can focus on historical issues, and ask whether or not the peasantry is embroiled in certain enabling, angering, or liberating processes that make revolution more likely. Or the answer could instead focus on a given peasant social structure, and ask which stratum of peasants therein is likely to be revolutionary. Or it could focus on comparative social structures, and give Durkheimian answers, suggesting that different levels of social solidarity and collective consciousness affect the peasants' capacity to act collectively for revolutionary ends. Or, still looking at comparative social structures, the theorist could give Marxian answers about the different forms of rural class conflict, and argue that only certain types of peasant-centered class conflict give rise to revolutionary peasantries. All such answers have in fact been tendered by different scholars, and we must blend together their answers—after first clarifying our concepts—if we are to arrive at a synthetic theory of revolutionary peasantries, one which also allows us to detect *un*-revolutionary peasants. But such detailed issues I will have to attend to in the next chapter.

The Military and the Intellectuals

I have grouped these two social actors together for several reasons. First, both groups lie "outside" the class structure of society; indeed, if we consider intellectuals the residents primarily of university communities, then both groups are not just outsiders to the class system, but are inhabitants of *total institutions*, or quasi-total ones: formal organizations where the worlds of residence, work, and sometimes leisure are all rolled into one life-encompassing whole.[22] Such institutions, due to their (quasi-)hermetic structures, are partially impervious to class-based forces, and provide to their members the possibility of developing cultural orientations that, in a sense, belie their class backgrounds; perhaps this is due to their "recruitment" into them at an impressionable age. A second reason to pair this odd couple is that comparative analysts of revolution have argued well that the "transfer of allegiance" (of the intellectuals), or the "disloyalty" (of the armed forces), vis-à-vis old regimes have been crucial historical contributors to revolutionary outcomes.[23] Third, the main organizers of the military battles that have constituted "revolutionary struggles," especially in this century, have come from these two antagonistic groups.

The sheer regularity of their antagonistic struggles strongly suggests that they are central to the revolutionary process. The intellectuals are particularly important in mobilizing the peasantry in those circumstances where the latter group has not done so autonomously. In particular, it is easy to make a very strong case that these two groups have made more crucial contributions than the proletariat to revolutionary outcomes, albeit clearly in opposing ways. Proportionately, it would appear that intellectuals have been far more likely to fly revolutionary colors than any other social group, with the possible exception of the peasantry (and the attendant limitations, already noted, on the definition of "revolutionary" in their case). None other than Fidel Castro said, "To be quite honest, we must admit that, often before now, when it came to crucial issues, to imperialist aggression and crime, it was the intellectual workers who showed the greatest militancy, who reacted with the greatest determination, and not those political organizations whom one might in all conscience, have expected to give the lead."[24]

Marxist naiveté regarding the military, a naiveté more generally shared by sociologists ignorant of the nature of military life, had led until recently to a systematic depreciation of the military's role in revolution. In particular, prorevolutionary theorists—but not the practitioners, Barrington Moore noted—have always argued (or implied, by ignoring it) that the military would become irrelevant in the face of popular, solidary uprisings against upper-class rule. From the mid-1970s onward, however, theorists of revolution—chiefly Russell, Moore, Tilly, and Skocpol—have finally started giving military matters their due. In that vein, especially concerning armed confrontations with the citizenry, Moore has argued strongly that competing armies rather than working-class struggles have decided this century's revolutions. Tilly has made a similar point in stressing the historical efficacy of full-scale repression against popular uprisings throughout early modern Europe.

The respective roles of intellectuals and the military in revolution, however, still remain "undertheorized" (to employ, but only briefly and pointedly, the inept diction currently so fashionable among graceless writers), although some advances have been made. The late Alvin Gouldner probably contributed the most to understanding why intellectuals are found in the forefront of revolutionary struggles, when their typically privileged class origins and rosy class futures should predict just the opposite. For Gouldner, the key idea is that intellectuals emphasize their own mastery of "cultural capital" (roughly, learning), and oppose themselves to the claims of the existing "ruling class" derived from industrial or financial capital. They thus tender cultural claims to legitimate political leadership in society. The (perceived) stark mismatch between their positions as the "barons" of cultural capital, and their blocked political (and economic) ascendancy, tends to induce them toward revolutionary opposition to the existing system. Their ultimate political model is that of the Platonic philosopher-king, as Gouldner nicely observed.[25]

Katharine Chorley and Diana Russell have made the greatest contributions to understanding the fact that disloyalty in the armed forces, or their weakening in external military struggles, has been a crucial correlate of revolutionary success.[26] But those facts only take us part of the way, for they do not get "inside" the military, in a way that helps us to understand why a force nowadays composed largely of men from lower middle-class backgrounds should be, oddly, so regularly a defender of social orders that often serve (and often serve little more than) upper-class interests.[27] If we wish to get inside the military, we will have to look at the processes of political socialization that take place within this total institution, especially on teenage officer-trainees, such as to generate within it "independent morale."[28] Alfred Stepan's superb case study of the Brazilian military helps us to understand why they seized power (conservatively) in 1964, and provides a model for this type of "inside job," as do his and others' studies of the Peruvian military, whose strikingly different "revolution from above" began with a coup in 1968. Furthermore, Richard Millett has given us a painstaking historical study of a very different type of army—this one dependent upon patrimonial control by a family dynasty—in his portrait of the Somozas' National Guard in Nicaragua.[29] Perhaps sociologists have to start looking at a series of such studies in order to understand why and how the military will act in the face of revolution, but few have essayed the attempt. (My intuitive sense is that when sociologists study the military carefully and analytically, their colleagues tend to view them as closet militarists. Such a perception, to put it mildly, would not win them popularity contests in university atmospheres, for reasons that should already have become clear.)

I have tried to deal with both of these groups already, although the answers remain only partial. In my *Guerrillas and Revolution in Latin America*, I have tried to search for some of the social and cultural sources of intellectual revolutionism and of the military's counterrevolutionary strengths or weaknesses in different societies.[30] My comments on the former were detailed, but the military analysis could be extended here. I concluded, echoing Russell's findings, that a decisive element contributing to the defeat of revolutionaries was the military's own *solidarity* in the face of revolution—that is, its willingness to stick together and to continue defending the incumbent regime. Furthermore, there and in chapter 7 below, I have tried to develop some rough guidelines for understanding why military disloyalty to the regime, and military internal disintegration, are more likely to occur under *certain types* of political systems than others. As we shall see, if the military is to continue defending an existing government and/or state—and by extension the people and nation whom the polity purportedly serves, that is, the *patria* or fatherland—then the regime it defends must plausibly look like an "extension" of the populace. The weakness of certain types of *personalistic states* is precisely that such an image of the polity becomes, and *clearly* so, downright implausible, and hence makes the army vulnerable to decay, factionalism, and/or disloyalty. That is, where the armed forces can no longer tender the reasonable claim that in fighting revolutionaries they are defending the *patria*, and not just a tyrannical despot, their internal solidarity *and* their willingness to fight are both likely to decay. That image is a reasonable picture of the events that transpired in Cuba, Nicaragua, and Iran, and probably in Mexico and China (during the latter's 1927–49 period of civil war) as well.

The Upper Class

Based on the comparative analysis of a number of revolutions, the upper class can play a role, perhaps decisive, in the revolutionary process, but not at all in the usual Marxist sense, where they are viewed simply as failing to repress a widespread worker insurrection, with some members, including ideologists, perhaps deserting to the revolutionaries at the very end of the old regime.[31] Instead, comparative analyses of revolution suggest that the conscious actions of the upper class *in opposition to the state* have contributed to a number of revolutions to date, and they have done so in two rather different ways. There is no need to detail those ways here, for I will cover them in chapter 7. Suffice it to say that the upper class could contribute to a revolution by using its existing strengths *within* the state to block fiscal reforms, thus paralyzing the state and precipitating its (near-)collapse. Such is Skocpol's analysis of France and China. In the second variant, an upper class completely excluded from, and hence *outside* a personalistic (and corrupt) political system, could enter into a cross-class, populist alliance with other more radical social forces in order to force such a regime out—in order to effect a shift toward a more participatory, constitutional polity; yet the actual shift could be far more revolutionary than the upper class desired, both in the polity and in the economy. Such is my portrait of Cuba and Nicaragua in chapter 7, and a rougher image of events in Mexico and Iran.

Other States

Theda Skocpol has made the strongest theoretical argument that the continued, and sometimes intensified, pressure from other states has been a recurrent condition leading to revolution in the modern world.

As her analysis of Iran makes clear, however, it is by no means a necessary concomitant of revolution. Other states can, in her argument, inadvertently produce revolutionary situations in their rivals in one of two fashions. First, they can exert continuous military and/or economic pressure upon a state, thus forcing it to increase the size and effectiveness of its own military forces if it is to maintain or expand its geopolitical position. Since such expansions require revenues, states are therefore forced to try to improve their tax-collecting abilities; yet such attempts may engender systematic and successful opposition to fiscal reforms, perhaps from elite interests lodged in the organizational apparatus of the state itself. This is Skocpol's "model" for the collapse of the old regimes of France and China. Under such circumstances, the paralysis, even the collapse of the state, is a probable outcome, which would then allow revolutionary upsurges to occur in an unimpeded fashion. A second form of state collapse must be thought of as more historical and contingent, and less sociological and structural: the destruction of the army and the collapse of the state due to defeat in a war (Russia in World War I is the epitome). In the wake of such a state collapse, uprisings can once again take place without repression effectively derailing them.

We might add a third possible form of "international intervention" that could also contribute positively to a revolutionary outcome. Given that the international realm consists of multiple states that are not only in conflict but also in alliance with one another, we must concede the possibility that international alliances might help to sustain states in the face of internal "revolutionary" pressures, while the absence or collapse of such alliances might crucially weaken such states. Barrington Moore has argued that if we are to understand the politics of small states, we also have to pay close attention to the politics of their larger neighbors, for the former are in part dependent upon the latter.[32] For example, many small states in the world arena rely, more or less heavily, on military aid from the superpowers to sustain or expand their armed and police forces. Therefore one clearly plausible revolutionary scenario for a small, dependent state—and several such states have experienced revolutions—is the withdrawal of military support by a larger state whose aid sustained its junior partner's firepower and the morale of its ruler and military. That scenario is quite a good description of the nature and the effects of the withdrawal of U.S. support from the Batista regime in Cuba (beginning in late 1957), and from the Somoza regime in Nicaragua (especially from 1977 onward).

3. Is dual power a necessary precursor to, or concomitant of, social revolutions?

In his general theory of mobilization, Charles Tilly has argued system-atically that the presence of dual power is an integral part of the "revo-lutionary situation" and thus of the revolutionary transformation itself. The concept of dual power derives from Leon Trotsky's analysis of the events of 1917 during the Russian Revolution when, following the collapse of the tsarist regime in February, the Bolsheviks developed a structure of authority parallel to and competing with the Provisional Government headed by the socialist Alexander Kerensky. Opposing themselves to Kerensky's right to the obedience of the populace, Lenin and the Bolsheviks—after securing decisive influence within these or-ganizations—proclaimed "All power to the Soviets!" (that is, to the workers' political committees that began to spring up early in the century, then blossoming dramatically in 1917). Tilly has taken this idea and run with it, sociologically speaking. He has generalized the idea to one of "multiple sovereignty," which he argues is virtually identical to the "revolutionary situation" itself. Multiple sovereignty exists when the unique claims to central authority made routinely by central governments no longer go unchallenged; instead, one or more—hence multiple, not dual—challenging groups also give direc-tives to the populace and a "substantial portion" of the populace ac-knowledges those directives by obeying them and by providing resources to the challengers, despite contrary directives from the gov-ernment. The revolutionary situation will be resolved, he argues, once unitary sovereignty is reestablished; we may speak of a revolution if the resulting power wielders are now the revolutionary challengers, not the original incumbents.[33]

Oddly enough, despite his impressive credentials as both historian and sociologist, Tilly does not develop these ideas inductively through a comparative study of revolutions; instead, they are developed to accord with his more general model of conflictual political mobiliza-tion. If we examine the assumptions behind his theoretical model we can note that it is a *purposive* model of revolution in which some actors clearly seek a revolutionary outcome, and act to secure it. It is also a *mobilizational* model of revolution, where part of the populace becomes members of, or minimally obeys the directives of, the group(s) of revolutionary challengers, thus helping them to victory through the sheer size of the challenging group's efforts and resources. Finally, and as the corpus of Tilly's writings and the rest of that particular work demonstrate, his is largely a *class-conflict* model of revolution, but one where class conflict only has such consequences if it coalesces into effective organizational forms. We should also note that Tilly definitely treats the balance of military forces as a crucial contributor to resolving the revolutionary situation.[34]

Skocpol has made note of, and strongly criticized, various assumptions imbedded in Tilly's model, as well as his failure to take the state seriously as an autonomous organizational actor pursuing its own interests.[35] For our purposes, though, a further assumption Tilly makes is yet more intriguing, and opens the door to a critique of his model as a *generalizable* account of revolutionary processes. While Tilly does distinguish analytically the revolutionary situation from the revolutionary outcome, he seems to assume that the latter does not come unless preceded by the former: no dual power, no revolution. That is, unless there are revolutionary challengers banging at the gates of power, revolutionary situations will not arise, and revolutionary outcomes cannot ensue. Oddly enough, Tilly's assumption, in this respect, precisely parallels Thomas Kuhn's analysis of *scientific* revolutions, which can occur only when a competitor claiming superior explanatory powers is present to supplant an older theory. Further in parallel, both theorists carefully distinguish a crisis in the old system (a revolutionary situation for Tilly, a crisis in normal science for Kuhn) from a revolutionary outcome (Tilly's regime shift, Kuhn's paradigm shift).[36]

While it is difficult to locate a revolution in which dual power did not emerge at *some* stage in the revolutionary process, it is even more difficult to argue that dual power always antedates the revolutionary transformation (i.e., state collapse, mass uprisings, widespread property shifts). For example, in Crane Brinton's half-century–old classic, *The Anatomy of Revolution*, we already can encounter a Trotsky-inspired empirical generalization about "dual sovereignty," drawn from the American, French, and Russian revolutions and the English Civil Wars of the mid-1600s. Yet strikingly in contrast to Tilly's model, some of Brinton's cases involve competition *among* the revolutionary groups themselves, *after* the old regime has fallen: in the French case, the National Assembly vs. the Jacobin clubs; in the Russian case, the Provisional Government vs. the Soviets; and in the English case, Cromwell's New Model Army vs. Parliament. Tilly, like Brinton, sees multiple sovereignty as a competition between contending political organizations for the obedience of the populace; yet for Tilly one of those organizations is always, it seems, the prerevolutionary government itself.

Ironically, Tilly's central revolutionary concept, dual power, was originally produced to understand a revolution whose central defining events do not clearly include dual power. Russia's old regime collapsed in February 1917 *in the absence* of any clear alternative; bereft of any obvious group whose alternative commands they were already obeying, the Petrograd crowds and soldiers marched in search of directives to the seat of the Duma, the Tauride Palace.[37] The ongoing peasant insurrections in the countryside even more clearly did not involve obedience to central authorities, and the Bolsheviks had few ties to the peasantry (a feature which Skocpol has theoretically linked to their later policy of terroristic collectivization of the peasantry).[38] Before any claims to dual power were being effectively acknowledged in Russia of 1917, therefore, all the events that serve to define a revolution had already happened or begun: the fall of the old regime, popular upheavals, and ongoing transformations of property rights. (One might make a roughly similar, although weaker, argument for the French Revolution, given the existence of the National Assembly.) The one revolutionary element that had *not* occurred in Russia of early 1917 was a more purely political event: the consolidation in power of a new, revolutionary regime, which would not be firmly set in place until after the period of civil war and "War Communism" (1918–21). There Tilly's analysis and the concept of multiple sovereignty can do us good service.

Therefore, not only is dual power *not* a necessary precursor to revolutionary transformations, but an undue emphasis on that concept also directs (and distracts) our attention to purely political processes that are not necessarily tied to the social upheavals that define these events as revolutionary. If I am right, and this theory does indeed too strongly partake of the purely political elements of authority, directives, and obedience, then we would expect it to apply all too readily to political shifts that are not revolutionary ones. For example, let us imagine a political confrontation over the "rights" to state power between two different party factions of the upper class (common in early nineteenth-century Nicaragua); or between two different factions of the military during an attempted coup against a military government (a Latin

American commonplace, e.g., Bolivia since 1969); or between an opposition calling for a general strike and a military regime (Cuba in April 1958; Panama in 1988); or between a military government and a joint civilian-military opposition (Venezuela, 1957–58; El Salvador, 1979). In each scenario, as one contender seeks to secure support for its claims, it gives directives to the populace. Sectors of the populace may indeed obey the challengers' orders rather than those of the incumbents at an early stage in the transition. The populace may indeed adhere to a general strike. Different military bases, or sectors of the armed forces (e.g., the navy) may join with or oppose the challengers. And the conclusion, as happened in those last two instances in Venezuela and El Salvador, could be a transition in power from the incumbents to a new civil-military regime, which might even pass some reforms.[39] All of Tilly's elements are there, except that the outcome is not a "revolutionary" one by almost anyone's definition of revolution. By defining the entire revolutionary process in terms of political shifts, he seems to have misplaced the socioeconomic shifts that lead us to deem certain events revolutionary, and other events "only" as coups, usurpations, *pronunciamientos* by regional *caudillos*, political uprisings, barracks revolts, and so forth.

What can we now conclude about dual power and the genesis of revolutions? First, dual power is not a necessary precursor to that joint change of both polity and society that we call revolution. Clearly in both Russia and China (the 1911 Manchu Dynasty collapse), and probably in France, one can make a strong case that the old regime collapsed without a clear alternative authority already existing. However, in yet other cases of revolution, it is just as clear that Tilly's concept of multiple sovereignty points our noses quite properly in the direction of challengers, often guerrilla forces, who oppose existing authorities and through political and military strategies sap their strengths away, securing a transfer of allegiance and obedience to commands of the revolutionaries: thus it happened with Madero and with Zapata, and later with Huerta, with Villa, and with Carranza during the Mexican Revolution (where that word "multiple" is really necessary); thus, too, with the challenge of the MNR in Bolivia in 1952, that of Castro's 26th of July movement in Cuba, and that of the Sandinistas in Nicaragua.

Second, dual power can emerge before the revolutionary collapse of the old regime, after the collapse, or both. Since we have just noted cases where the two polar situations occurred, we can content our-selves with specifying "dual" cases of dual power. In the English Civil Wars of the mid-1600s, the first emergence of dual power was prior to the onset of military hostilities, in the confrontations between and mutually exclusive claims tendered by the Long Parliament and King Charles I, ultimately leading to civil war, Parliament's victory, and the beheading of the king. After the abolition of the monarchy, however, political contention emerged anew between Cromwell, espe-cially as the head of the New Model Army, and the more moderate parliamentary forces, a conflict eventually resolved when he dissolved the chamber. In the case of the Iranian Revolution, while the Shah was still alive, exhortations from *mullahs* living in the cities of Teheran, Qum, and elsewhere (including taped messages from Ayatollah Khomeini living in Iraqi and Parisian exile) consistently urged the faithful to ignore the orders of the monarch and instead to obey Islamic law, as the clerics interpreted it. After the 1979 departure of the Shah in the face of mass uprisings, and hence the "revolutionary" transi-tion, dual power emerged once again between civilian president Abolhassan Bani Sadr and the clerics of Qum, with the latter eventu-ally prevailing and forcing Bani Sadr, also and ironically, into Parisian exile.

Third, we can do more than simply assert that dual power can occur at any time in the course of revolution. The construction of dual power prior to revolution *must* be linked to those cases in which the masses are being *mobilized* to revolutionary activity, since it is the challengers for power who *are* the mobilizers. If this is true, then we might also postulate that where dual power exists prior to a revolution, one is likely to find a state that has *not* collapsed due to its own internal and international pressures, but in good part has fallen because of pressures and demands placed upon it from within civil society. This postulate leads us to our next, and final, unresolved question in the study of revolutions.

4. Which types of political regime are highly vulnerable to revolutions, and which are relatively impervious?

In *States and Social Revolutions*, Skocpol argues that a particular type of state or political regime is highly vulnerable to revolution, so vul-nerable indeed that the state can collapse even without massive military pressure from foreign wars. That type of state we may term an agrarian protobureaucracy, ''proto'' because the professionalization of office-holding has not yet been firmly established. These regimes are *agrarian* bureaucracies because the bulk of tax revenues is derived from the peasantry, and certain elites are commonly tax-exempt (e.g., the aristocracy and clergy of premodern Europe). Agrarian bureaucracies are particularly susceptible to peasant revolts, at least in certain cases, because state taxation of the peasantry is compounded with the exactions made by the landed elite (land rents, feudal dues, labor services, sharecropping, etc.), thus placing especially heavy burdens upon the peasantry. (Sometimes church tithes and fees doubly compound such burdens.) The very centralization of such systems—although Skocpol does not seem to make this point—also makes them more vulnerable to *revolutionary* consequences (i.e., the dissolution of the central polity) than were feudal systems of exploitation, where the claimants to peasant resources would be singular and local, not multiple and centrally placed.[40] It is hard to imagine a revolution taking place without the presence of a cohesive central state.

Yet not all agrarian bureaucracies are *highly* vulnerable to such collapses. Such stark weaknesses occur where there is a *partial overlap* in personnel and powers between the landed elite and the apparatus of the state. That occurred in France, where the aristocracy controlled key judicial and military positions, and in China, where the core of the imperial bureaucracy was composed of landed gentry. The gentry's powers in their home provinces increased sharply in the 1800s when the emperor had to recruit local forces to suppress the Taiping and Nien rebellions; prior to that time imperial service in one's home province had been discouraged, if not forbidden. The partial overlap between state and elite, Skocpol argues, enabled the strategically lodged elites to pursue their class interests and block state reforms—including proposals to tax landed elites—thus leading to the collapse of the French monarchy in 1789 and of the Manchu Dynasty in 1911.[41]

Where the upper class has largely been absorbed into the state apparatus and made economically dependent, as in Russia after Peter the Great, the state remains vulnerable to revolutionary collapse, but not nearly so much as in the French and Chinese cases. Here the pattern is one of *complete absorption*, with the upper class the dependent partner. (There is some resemblance here to Wittfogel's ''Oriental Despotism,'' and Wittfogel does consider Russia a partial exemplar of the type.)[42] Russian society still remained subject to peasant revolts, but since the (former) landed elite had insufficient resources outside the state to act independently against tsarist authority, they could form no effective paralytic force within the state. Instead, massive military defeat in World War I directly led to the collapse of the old regime, thus liberating the peasantry from state forces that could have repressed them (which had happened in 1905); the result was widespread peasant insurrection throughout the "Black Earth" regions of Russia.

The third interesting variant of revolution, which I will not explore in detail here, is the very opposite of the "Russian pattern." This can occur when the state and landed elite are *relatively separate* groups, rather than partially or completely overlapping ones. Ellen Kay Trimberger has argued—on the basis of study of Meiji Japan, Ataturk's Turkey, Nasser's Egypt, and Peru of the "revolutionary" generals (1968–75)—that the independence of the state from the landed elite can, in certain unusual circumstances, allow part of the state to break off, mobilize some popular support, and carry out a state-led "revolution from above" that is very different from the usual pattern of social revolutions we have analyzed here (and indeed, does not fit our definition, since it involves no mass-based upheavals).[43]

Unlike these three variants of agrarian protobureaucracies, Skocpol believes that modern industrial bureaucratic states are virtually invulnerable to revolutions, perhaps because they utterly lack the elite-linked vulnerabilities of the French and Chinese cases.[44] One might add the coda to this theme that, with the rise of the welfare state in industrial societies, the state no longer is making those "nonreciprocal claims" upon the lower classes that were the traditional feature of agrarian bureaucracies.[45] Instead, welfare states funnel monies and other resources (such as free education and health care) back into civil society, binding the two in a complex of heavy taxation and government transfer payments. Perhaps that complex is why Skocpol argues further that "it seems highly unlikely that modern states could disintegrate . . . without destroying societies at the same time. . . ."[46] In such societies, military spending absorbs only a fraction of total government expenditures, typically far less than one-fourth. (In earlier times, the bulk of government resources went to war, and war-making was a key driving force behind state expansion through taxation.)[47] This complex, welfare-state pattern applies to Communist and advanced capitalist societies both, even though the pattern of taxation is hidden in

Communist societies due to centralized price setting.[48] The overall pattern of industrial bureaucracies suggests that Skocpol may have hit a keystone in noting the intense interdependence between state and society typical of such systems, and hence the difficulties such a system poses for modern revolutionaries. As infuriating as her conclusions have been to orthodox Marxists, they may be correct. As Max Weber noted, a bureaucratic system when firmly set into place is among the most difficult of all social systems to destroy, precisely because it becomes indispensable for those whom it governs.[49]

Skocpol's analysis of Iran, however, leads us to believe that there is another type of regime that, like tsarist Russia, was *partially* vulnerable to revolution, but would not fall without an appreciable push. If, in the Russian case, the shove came from war, the Iranian Revolution clearly came about in part due to the popular mobilization of the masses against the incumbent regime.[50] In chapter 7 I will describe in more detail the curiously parallel features of the Cuban and Nicaraguan regimes that also made them societies remarkably ripe for mass-mobilizing revolution against partially vulnerable regimes.

The Iran-Cuba-Nicaragua model of regime weakness that I shall develop in chapter 7 helps us to unite this analysis of regime vulnerabilities with the previous discussion of dual power. First, dual power, secured through an elite-mobilized mass opposition to an incumbent regime, has been a crucial contributor to successful revolution (only?) in those instances where the regimes already exhibited *partial* vulnerabilities to revolution. Second, where regimes were, instead, *highly* vulnerable to revolution—or suddenly became that way through a military defeat—prerevolutionary dual power was *not* a necessary contributor to a revolutionary outcome (France, Russia, China). Third, and here I predict rather than retrodict, where regimes are, to the contrary, highly *impervious* to revolution—and I will describe those impervious types in chapter 7—the development of dual power will be sharply restricted in scope, usually only to limited areas of the countryside, where the "guerrilla governments" I described in chapter 2 are likely to emerge.

Notes

1. On the issues of coercion and welfare, we can find informative treatments in two books by Peter L. Berger, *Pyramids of Sacrifice: Political Ethics and Social Change* (New York: Basic Books, 1974), and *The Capitalist Revolution*

(New York: Basic Books, 1986). In those books, like many other such discussions, the issue of the effects of revolution per se tends to be mixed up with the relative merits of capitalism and socialism as systems, which is an analytically separate issue. The best comparative study of the welfare effects of revolution remains the careful one by Susan Eckstein, "The Impact of Revolution on Social Welfare in Latin America," *Theory and Society* 11, no. 1 (1982), pp. 43–94.

2. Eckstein, "The Impact of Revolution"; Theda Skocpol, *States and Social Revolutions: A Comparative Analysis of France, Russia, and China* (Cambridge, England: Cambridge University Press, 1979). A recent piece on Latin America also pursues such systematic comparison, but unfortunately focuses on but *one* difference between the two cases treated (that of inequality of land ownership), when there are in fact many such differences; cf. Manus I. Midlarsky and Kenneth Roberts, "Class, State, and Revolution in Central America: Nicaragua and El Salvador Compared," *Journal of Conflict Resolution* 29, no. 2 (June 1985), pp. 163–93. Such contrasts are, I think, crucial to good theorizing about revolutions. For example, James Petras's failure to examine any contrasting, nonrevolutionary cases in his theory of socialist revolutions (discussed below) sharply weakens our faith in the conclusions that he draws.

3. Skocpol, *States and Social Revolutions*, pp. 14–18, quotation on p. 16.

4. Charles Tilly, *From Mobilization to Revolution* (Reading, Mass.: Addison-Wesley, 1978); Jeffery M. Paige, *Agrarian Revolution: Social Movements and Export Agriculture in the Underdeveloped World* (New York: The Free Press, 1975).

5. Skocpol, *States and Social Revolutions*, chapter 2. See also, on the Chinese case, Eric R. Wolf, *Peasant Wars of the Twentieth Century* (New York: Harper and Row, 1969), ch. 3, where he also notes the loss of imperial authority at the center, especially following the emperor's forced reliance on provincial military forces to suppress the mid-1800s Taiping and Nien rebellions.

6. On the final days in Petrograd, and the circumstances leading up to the February revolution there, see the expert analysis by Barrington Moore, Jr., *Injustice: The Social Bases of Obedience and Revolt* (White Plains, N.Y.: M. E. Sharpe, 1978), ch. 10.

7. Skocpol, *States and Social Revolutions*, p. 4.

8. This is perhaps most clearly shown in the intensively researched anthropology thesis by Jorge E. Dandler-Hanhart, "Politics of Leadership, Brokerage and Patronage in the Campesino Movement of Cochabamba, Bolivia (1935–1954)," (Ph.D. dissertation, University of Wisconsin, 1971). For a roughly similar "balanced" view, one emphasizing somewhat more the actions of outside mobilizers, including the postrevolutionary state, see Dwight B. Heath, Charles Erasmus, and Hans C. Buechler, *Land Reform and Social Revolution in Bolivia* (New York: Praeger, 1969), pp. 37–49.

9. For details see Timothy P. Wickham-Crowley, *Guerrillas and Revolution in Latin America* (Princeton, N.J.: Princeton University Press, forthcoming 1991), chs. 4, 6, 7, and 10, or "Winners, Losers, and Also-Rans: Toward a Comparative Sociology of Latin American Guerrilla Movements," chapter 4 of *Power and Popular Protest: Latin American Social Movements*, ed. Susan Eckstein (Berkeley: University of California Press, 1989).

10. Theda Skocpol, "Rentier State and Shi'a Islam in the Iranian Revolution," *Theory and Society* 11, no. 2 (May 1982), pp. 265–83; "What Makes

Peasants Revolutionary?" *Comparative Politics* 14 (April 1982), pp. 351–75, esp. 361–67.

11. "What Makes Peasants Revolutionary?" passim.

12. Robert K. Merton, "The Unanticipated Consequences of Purposive Social Action," *American Sociological Review* 1, (December 1936), pp. 894–904; for an interpretation of Weber emphasizing historical ironies, see Bryan S. Turner, *For Weber: Essays on the Sociology of Fate* (Boston: Routledge and Kegan Paul, 1981). In Marx's general theory of revolutionary change, it is clear that the upper class in each social system, especially capitalism, acts in the pursuit of self-interest in ways that are ultimately system-dissolving; in particular, the capitalist class, through ever-expanding production, produces an ever-larger proletariat that will one day overthrow its rule.

13. James Petras, "Toward a Theory of Twentieth Century Socialist Revolutions," *Journal of Contemporary Asia* 8, no. 2 (1978), pp. 167–95, and "Socialist Revolutions and Their Class Components," *New Left Review* 111 (September 1978), pp. 37–64.

14. Even China experts view the Chinese Revolution as one in which the victors secured their decisive military resources and manpower from the peasantry; Petras, a Latin Americanist, hardly provides us with sufficient grounds for rejecting that view. For nonspecialists' views of the interaction between Communists and peasants, by scholars who nonetheless devoted considerable time to the study of Chinese history *and* revolutions, see Barrington Moore, Jr., *Social Origins of Dictatorship and Democracy: Lord and Peasant in the Making of the Modern World* (Boston: Beacon, 1966), ch. 4; Skocpol, *States and Social Revolutions*, pp. xii–xiii, 147–54, 252–62; and Eric Wolf, *Peasant Wars,* ch. 3. One very suggestive study of the nature, importance, and limitations of Communist-peasant alliances can be found in Roy Hofheinz, Jr., "The Ecology of Chinese Communist Success: Rural Influence Patterns, 1923–1945," pp. 3–77 in *Chinese Communist Politics in Action*, edited by A. Doak Barnett (Seattle: University of Washington Press, 1969). Petras's views on Cuba should be treated with great respect, for he has studied that nation closely and published widely from his studies; for a strong critique of his thesis that a *revolutionary* Cuban working class was decisive to the *genesis* of the Cuban Revolution—whatever its role in the aftermath—see the closely-argued case by a writer who also lived in 1950s Cuba, Samuel Farber, *Revolution and Reaction in Cuba, 1933–1960* (Middletown, Conn.: Wesleyan University Press, 1976), pp. 130–44. The working class *did* make some contributions to the *populist,* cross-class upheaval that ousted Batista, and they are best recounted in the superb study by Ramón L. Bonachea and Marta San Martín, *The Cuban Insurrection, 1952–1959* (New Brunswick, N.J.: Transaction, 1974), passim. A similar cross-class constellation of forces also ended the old regimes of Mexico, Bolivia, Iran, and Nicaragua, and thus clearly could end in other than *socialist* revolutions.

15. Victoria E. Bonnell, *Roots of Revolt: Workers' Politics and Organizations in St. Petersburg and Moscow, 1900–1914* (Berkeley: University of California Press, 1983), first quotation on p. 11; also see her "Conclusions," esp. pp. 442–46; the grouped quotations are from 445–46.

16. On France, see George Rudé, *The Crowd in History: A Study of Popular*

Disturbances in France and England, 1730–1848, rev. ed. (London: Lawrence and Wishart, 1981), ch. 13; and Alfred Cobban, *The Social Interpretation of the French Revolution* (Cambridge, England: Cambridge University Press, 1964), ch. 11. On Germany, see the close analysis by Barrington Moore in *Injustice*, esp. ch. 9.

17. For Bolivia's history just preceding the revolution, along with a brief account of the central events thereof, see Herbert S. Klein, *Bolivia: The Evolution of a Multi-Ethnic Society* (New York: Oxford University Press, 1982), ch. 7; on the background, historical ideology, and postrevolutionary experience of the MNR as a governing party, a good, brief overview is in Jean-Pierre Bernard et al., *Guide to the Political Parties of South America* (Harmondsworth, England: Penguin, 1973), pp. 107–49.

18. One early collection of entries on Mexico was Stanley Ross, ed., *Is the Mexican Revolution Dead?* (New York: Alfred E. Knopf, 1966), published a scant quarter-century after the widespread transformations effected under the government of Lázaro Cárdenas (1934–40). For one study of Bolivia emphasizing the unachieved, yet written even before the economic and political debacles of the last two decades, see James M. Malloy, *Bolivia: The Uncompleted Revolution* (Pittsburgh: University of Pittsburgh Press, 1970).

19. Perhaps symptomatic of this tendency either to ignore Bolivia, or to resist calling it revolutionary, is one study that *does* deal systematically with the Bolivian revolution, but chooses to term it a "successful rebellion;" cf. D. E. H. (Diana) Russell, *Rebellion, Revolution, and Armed Force* (New York: Academic, 1974), pp. 100–103.

20. Moore, *Social Origins*; Wolf, *Peasant Wars*; Paige, *Agrarian Revolution*; Joel S. Migdal, *Peasants, Politics, and Revolution: Pressures toward Political and Social Change in the Third World* (Princeton, N.J.: Princeton University Press, 1974); James C. Scott, *The Moral Economy of the Peasant: Rebellion and Subsistence in Southeast Asia* (New Haven, Conn.: Yale University Press, 1976); Skocpol, *States and Social Revolutions*; Samuel Popkin, *The Rational Peasant: The Political Economy of Rural Society in Vietnam* (Berkeley: University of California Press, 1979). The "perhaps" for Scott recognizes his denial that he is trying to create a theory of "peasant revolution;" cf. *Moral Economy*, p. 4.

21. I clearly distinguish the issue of peasant support for revolutionaries from the revolutionary outcome, in "Winners, Losers, and Also-Rans."

22. Erving Goffman, "On the Characteristics of Total Institutions" in his *Asylums* (Garden City, N.Y.: Anchor Books, 1961), pp. 1–124.

23. See, respectively, Crane Brinton, *The Anatomy of Revolution*, revised and enlarged edition (New York: Vintage Books, 1965), pp. 39–49, and Russell, *Rebellion, Revolution, and Armed Force*.

24. Alvin Gouldner, *The Future of Intellectuals and the Rise of the New Class* (New York: Continuum, 1979), pp. 53–57, quotation on p. 53.

25. Gouldner, *The Future of Intellectuals*, passim, esp. pp. 57–73.

26. Katharine Chorley, *Armies and the Art of Revolution* (Boston: Beacon, 1973 [1943]); Russell, *Rebellion, Revolution, and Armed Force*.

27. On Latin America, see John J. Johnson, *The Military and Society in Latin America* (Stanford, Calif.: Stanford University Press, 1964), pp. 51–52, 78, 105–10. For the United States, where a high proportion of elite officers came from

upper-middle- as well as lower-middle-class families in mid-century, see Suzanne Keller, *Beyond the Ruling Class: Strategic Elites in Modern Society* (New York: Random House, 1963), pp. 294–95; for the earlier upper-class origins of American elite officers in the year 1900 and before, see C. Wright Mills, *The Power Elite* (New York: Oxford, 1956), p. 180. Such a pattern would apply to Latin America as well; a strong guide is José Nun, "A Latin American Phenomenon: The Middle-Class Military Coup" in *Latin America: Reform or Revolution?*, ed. James Petras and Maurice Zeitlin (Greenwich, Conn.: Fawcett, 1968), pp. 145–85.

28. Mills, *The Power Elite*, pp. 192–97 gives us a fine, if brief, portrait of such processes for the American military, and also suggests the impermeability of the military institution to the class influences of its officer-recruits.

29. Alfred Stepan, *The Military in Politics: Changing Patterns in Brazil* (Princeton, N.J.: Princeton University Press, 1971), and idem, *State and Society: Peru in Comparative Perspective* (Princeton, N.J.: Princeton University Press, 1978), ch. 4; both works focus on the shifting trends of education experienced by different "cohorts" of officers in the "war colleges" of Brazil (the *Escola Superior de Guerra*) and Peru (the *Centro de Altos Estudios Militares*). Richard Millett, *Guardians of the Dynasty* (Maryknoll, N.Y.: Orbis, 1978). For a close-up view of an army with somewhat similar features, see Louis A. Pérez, Jr., *Army Politics in Cuba, 1898–1958* (Pittsburgh, Penn.: Pittsburgh University Press, 1976).

30. See chapters 5, 8, and 11 of that work.

31. The desertion of part of the ruling class to the revolutionary forces appears in the "model" of revolution suggested by the Communist Manifesto, near the end of Part I of that work; see Robert C. Tucker, *The Marx-Engels Reader*, 2d ed. (New York: W. W. Norton, 1978), p. 481.

32. Moore, *Social Origins*, pp. xii–xiii.

33. Tilly, *From Mobilization to Revolution*, ch. 7, esp. 190–94, 200–11.

34. Tilly, *From Mobilization to Revolution*, pp. 211–16.

35. Skocpol, *States and Social Revolutions*, ch. 1, esp. pp. 10–11, 26–27.

36. Thomas S. Kuhn, *The Structure of Scientific Revolutions*, 2d ed., enlarged (Chicago: University of Chicago Press, 1970), pp. 77, 92–94.

37. Moore, *Injustice*, pp. 364–68; Adam B. Ulam, *The Bolsheviks* (New York: Collier, 1968), pp. 314–18.

38. Theda Skocpol, "Old Regime Legacies and Communist Revolutions in Russia and China" *Social Forces* 55, part 1, no. 2 (December 1976), pp. 284–315.

39. On the Venezuelan reforms under 1958 interim president Wolfgang Larrazabal, see Talton F. Ray, *The Politics of the Barrios in Venezuela* (Berkeley: University of California Press, 1969), pp. 87–88; on El Salvador's transition juntas (four different ones from 1979 to 1982), which combined violent repression with some unprecedented reforms, see the convenient schedule of events and laws in Enrique Baloyra, *El Salvador in Transition* (Chapel Hill: University of North Carolina Press, 1982), pp. 78–81.

40. Perry Anderson refers to this central feudal trait as "parcellized sovereignty"; cf. *Passages from Antiquity to Feudalism* (London: Verso, 1978 [1974]), pp. 147–53.

41. In addition to Skocpol's book, see Wolf, *Peasant Wars*, ch. 3.

42. Karl Wittfogel, *Oriental Despotism: A Comparative Study of Total Power* (New York: Vintage, 1981 [1957]), pp. 219–25, 427–29.

43. See her *Revolution From Above: Military Bureaucrats and Development in Japan, Turkey, Egypt and Peru* (New Brunswick, N.J.: Transaction, 1978).

44. Skocpol, *States and Social Revolutions*, pp. 289–93.

45. Skocpol, *States and Social Revolutions*, p. 115.

46. Skocpol, *States and Social Revolutions*, p. 293.

47. This idea has been progressively developed over the years by Charles Tilly; see, for example, *Big Structures, Large Processes, Huge Comparisons* (New York: Russell Sage, 1984), pp. 9–10, 141–43.

48. On the pattern of "hidden" taxation and the implicit transfer of resources from the populace to the state that ensues therefrom, a good guide for Poland (briefly) and the Soviet Union is Michael Voslensky, *Nomenklatura: The Soviet Ruling Class*, translated by Eric Mosbacher (Garden City, N.Y.: Doubleday, 1984), pp. 164–69. Voslensky estimates that, in the Soviet case, only 10 percent of such resources come from the relatively modest overt taxes, while 90 percent of such transferred surplus comes hidden in the cost of goods, in particular. Some Communist societies, like North Korea, have no open state taxation whatsoever.

49. Hans H. Gerth and C. Wright Mills, eds., *From Max Weber: Essays in Sociology* (New York: Oxford, 1958), pp. 228–30; Reinhard Bendix, *Max Weber: An Intellectual Portrait* (Garden City, N.Y.: Doubleday, 1962), p. 430.

50. Skocpol, "Rentier State and Shi'a Islam," pp. 265–83.

6

What Makes Peasants Insurrectionary?

We turn now to the realm of the "revolutionary" peasantry, where I will fly a few theoretical kites which, nonetheless, still have some earthbound moorings in social scientific and historical research. Nonetheless, this chapter should be understood as more speculative than those preceding, with the attendant needs for critique and possible reformulation. In the discussion that follows, I will eschew the usual procedure of discussing each author's theory sequentially, a task done by several other scholars to date (and once again I stress that Theda Skocpol has already touched on and prefigured my themes in her own discussion of this very topic; I acknowledge her precedence by paraphrasing her title for my use here).[1] My own exegeses would only serve to bore the reader, so I choose here instead to extract *recurring themes* from the various theorists, and indicate at the end how we can put them all together. One of the services I hope to render here is to indicate as well the social conditions under which peasants are *not* likely to be insurrectionary nor likely to act in revolution-promoting ways.

First we need to define our terms. Peasant *autonomy* exists when, in day-to-day cultivating practices and in harvest times, peasant actions are not subject to close scrutiny and control by representatives of economic (estate foremen, majordomos, etc.) or political (e.g., state overseers of corvée labor) elites. Such autonomy seems to exist in two polar instances: (1) where tightly knit village communities operate independently of direct landlord controls, while still perhaps paying taxes or dues at appropriate times; and (2) where independent smallholding farmers, whether owners, pioneers, or squatters, farm far apart from all political controls. The first type is more likely to be found in tightly nucleated village settlements, the second on dispersed farm-steads, but residence alone does not determine autonomy.

Peasant *solidarity* exists when the day-to-day lives of cultivators provide recurring, often compelling, situations for collective decisions and collective actions governing each others' lives. Especially impor-tant in this regard are two common activities: (re-)allocating village lands to members of the community, including seasonal decisions about when to open up land to common pasture; and the payment of taxes and tributes (including labor services) when they are assessed on the entire community, rather than on individuals. In such cases, indi-vidualism is reduced both as a value and as an everyday reality. In a sense, such solidarity becomes embedded in tradition and behavior, and provides a ready resource that can be drawn upon should villagers find themselves in a sudden crisis where they must all hang together lest they all hang separately, as Benjamin Franklin observed in another revolutionary context. Marxist theorists have always, and quite prop-erly, emphasized that in solidary, unified action the lower classes can attain strength that far belies their meager economic resources. Clearly, the tightly knit village that I mentioned in the preceding paragraph can often provide solidarity in addition to autonomy. In a second variant, Jeffery Paige has applied Marxian ideas to rural areas, and has argued that, where cultivators survive, not from the possession of a plot of land, but from wages—in sharecropping and in estate or plantation labor—their cooperative lives will also create, ipso facto, solidarity in their actions.[2]

We may speak of *mobilization* as the process whereby peasants (for our purposes) come to commit their resources (land, food, time, en-ergy, even their lives) to revolutionary organizations. As we shall see—and as Skocpol clearly argues—mobilization by revolutionaries functions as an alternative path to peasant insurrection, when other conditions do not provide sufficient social resources for the peasantry to achieve those same ends on their own. Since I have already explored this concept in chapters 1 and 4 above, the reader should by now be thoroughly disabused of any illusion that the *attempt* by revolutionary leaders to mobilize the peasantry always results in the real thing. Thus, even if outside mobilization *can*, indeed, sometimes rouse a peasantry to act with regime-destroying consequences, there are various barriers to (and some facilitators of) that process that simply cannot be taken for granted. Ché Guevara learned that lesson to his misfortune in Bolivia.

Finally, despite Skocpol's argument that peasants are always exploited, always subject to "nonreciprocal claims" upon their resources—and hence always discontented, we must assume—we need to introduce some notion of *"damage"* if we are to comprehend and distinguish *fully* those situations in which peasants rise up against their enemies, and those rather different situations where cultivators are content just to continue tilling the soil.[3] We may speak of "damage" therefore (1) when peasants themselves perceive that their access to basic subsistence needs is fundamentally threatened; or, more cautiously, (2) when suggestive "macroeconomic" evidence strongly indicates similar types of damage to subsistence possibilities (crop yields, falling crop prices, loss of land to plantations, etc.). Clearly the former type of information is superior to the latter, since only the participants know their own situations best, yet information on peasants' perspectives on their material lives is generally very scarce.

As we have already seen in chapter 2, not all peasants share the same sense of being "damaged" in their everyday relations with political and economic elites, and some actually feel that they derive security and sometimes even prosperity from those relationships. Theorists who wish to dismiss any concept of "damage" from the study of revolution should do something very simple: look at some of the literature on peasants who have received secure access to land and the fruits thereof immediately *following* revolutions, such as those in Bolivia, Cuba, and Nicaragua over the last half-century. Even a cursory perusal would disabuse such theorists of the notion that *all* peasants are candidates for revolution if only the right *structural* conditions somehow are created.

All of the above conditions can be contributors to a revolutionary peasantry—once again, in consequences, not in intent. To support that statement we should first look at the range and mix of positions on this issue that have been taken by theorists on this topic who have gone before us, presented in the chronological order in which they saw the light of day (see Table 6.1).

I will not give a detailed exegesis of each theorist's position, for those familiar with the literature will understand my decisions, but a few brief summary comments are in order. If classical Marxism saw the proletariat eventually becoming revolutionary under advanced capitalism (and its own correspondingly advanced pauperism), the Leninist revision was to argue that, under its own auspices, the proletariat

Table 6.1

Locating the Insurrectionary Peasantry:
Recurring Themes in Modern Theories of Revolution
(X = major theme; * = stress; 0 = denial of its role)

	Theories involving:			
	Solidarity	Autonomy	Mobilization	Damage
Marxism: Proletariat ("Communist Manifesto")	X	X	0	X
Leninist "Vanguardism" (Lenin; Guerrillas)	X?	0	X*	X?
Barrington Moore *Social Origins; Injustice*	X?	X*	0?	X
Eric Wolf *Peasant Wars*		X		X
Joel Migdal *Peasants, Politics*			X	X
Jeffery Paige *Agrarian Revolution*	X*	0	0	X?
James Scott *Moral Economy of the Peasant*	X	X	0	X*
Samuel Popkin *Rational Peasant*	0*	X*	X?	0*
Charles Tilly *From Mobilization*, etc.	X?		X*	X
Theda Skocpol *States & Social Revolutions*; "What Makes Peasants Revolutionary?"	X*	X*	(X) (China)	0
Major Conceptual Focus:	Social structures		Contingent historical events, processes	

would only achieve economism (that is, economic demands), and would not seek social revolution. The proletariat hence needed a Leninist vanguard to prompt it to its "proper" revolutionary state of mind and action. Guerrillas have done quite analogous things in the countryside with the peasantry. Barrington Moore argued, in a recurrently cited passage, that Communist revolution came to Russia and China when a "damaged but intact" peasantry rose up in rebellion. Eric Wolf's peasants are revolutionary when damaged by commercialization and population growth, and where they further have "tactical mobility" (i.e., autonomy) due to their social or geographical location. Joel Migdal also emphasizes the damage done to peasants by world-expanding capitalist relations, but emphasizes selective benefits as the key lure in recruiting dislocated cultivators into revolutionary organizations. Jeffery Paige, like Wolf and Migdal, also finds revolution in the context of world commercial capitalism, but only among solidary, wage-earning cultivators facing zero-sum conflicts with landed elites. More than anyone else, James Scott emphasizes the damage done to traditionally autonomous and solidary peasant villages by the spread of world capitalism, with the concomitant growth of state taxation and elite extractive demands. In his detailed critique of Scott, Samuel Popkin denies that rebellions in Vietnam were correlated with deep subsistence crises, challenges the very notion of a solidary village peasantry, and proffers, in its place, a utilitarian model of individual peasants pursuing self-interests, even in the context of revolutionary organizations. Charles Tilly has for decades emphasized that the rhythms of popular rebellions have corresponded to damage caused by state expansion (e.g., taxation, the draft) and the spread of capitalism; later he wedded these class-conflict themes to his mobilization theory of revolution. Finally, Theda Skocpol rejects any "psychological" or "discontent" theories of peasant rebellion, further rejects the whole "damage-via-commercialization" argument, and focuses instead on whether or not peasantries have had the sociopolitical resources, deriving from autonomy and solidarity, to wage successful rebellions, especially against weakened states and landlords. Autonomy could be provided, as in China, by outside mobilizers (the Red Army) who act as a buffer against repression and hence supply protected opportunities for agrarian revolt against the landed elite.[4]

We are now in a position to integrate these four variables affecting the revolutionary actions of peasants, by uniting them into a series of three-vector influences. Out of the following highly simplified tables, we will be able to derive, I hope, a series of propositions about the conditions promoting (or not) peasant-based revolution. However, we should always remember that in no case will the actions of the peasantry, self-united or in alliance with elite-mobilizers, be sufficient to explain a successful revolutionary outcome, without considering at least some of the other issues raised earlier in chapter 5.

We will promptly put aside the concept of mobilization from our tabular analysis to follow. This suggests strongly the first proposition about revolutionary peasantries.

Proposition 1: When a solidary and autonomous peasantry is "damaged" by ongoing economic processes, peasant revolts are more likely than in any other rural social system. Even so, the actual appearance of such revolts hinges greatly on the likelihood and efficacy of repressive action from elites and the state. If either solidarity or autonomy is attenuated, peasant insurrection will be less likely, ceteris paribus.

Proposition 2: Outsider mobilization will be the key to the creation of an insurrectionary peasantry only under a combination of specific circumstances: (a) the absence of solidarity and/or autonomy within the peasantry; and (b) a peasantry damaged by traditional or recently intensified economic exactions; and (usually) (c) some form of structured access giving mobilizers channels to peasants (see chapter 4 above).

Note that my restrictive conditions for its "success" have taken mobilization out of the realm of the purely historical and contingent, and into the realm of the sociological and patterned. If Proposition 2 is accurate, then outsider mobilization has become, as Skocpol suggested, a functional alternative to the peasants' own solidarity and autonomy, in promoting insurrection. Yet there may be more than simply "alternatives" at work here, there may be exclusive processes operating: the very existence of peasant autonomy implies that there will be relatively few structured opportunities for mobilizers to come into contact with the peasantry, thus making yet more arduous their revolutionary tasks. If mobilization is, however unlikely, wedded to autonomous and solidary insurrectionary activity, it should be understood as accentuating features already present in social structure, rather than breathing life into revolutionary movements. Our clearest illustration of that principle comes from revisionist work on the Civil Rights Movement in the United States. Such research now deemphasizes the mobilizing role of freedom riders from northern states, and correspondingly stresses the role played by autonomous black southern churches and colleges, in contributing to the organization of protest in the South.[5]

Yet even if all three elements are present, I would still insist that peasantries only rarely will be moved to insurrection unless they have suffered, or are suffering, economic *damage* in their ongoing relationships with other social groups. Therefore, in the next two tables, I will look first at "damaged" peasantries, and explore how damage affects

Table 6.2

Will Peasants Be Insurrectionary?
The Impact of Autonomy and Solidarity on a Damaged Peasantry

	Autonomy?	
	Yes	**No**
Solidarity? **Yes**	** Independently Insurrectionary *Pattern:* Elite extraction from villages now onerous, but without supervision, control over process. *Examples:* Black Earth Russia after 1861; Seine and Loire Valleys of France, 1789; south-central Mexico, 1910– (Zapata); some rural Bolivia, 1930s–1950s; sharecropping.	(+) Only Sporadic Revolts? *Pattern:* Elite supervision over peasant "villages," with intense extraction. *Examples:* Yucatán, Mexico in 1910; barracks or gang slavery; plantation labor; colonial Indo-America; "Oriental Despotism" in decline; Central Mexican Plateau, 1910–17 (estate residents)
No	* Mobilizable for Insurrection *Pattern:* Peripheral peasantries with minimal/insecure access to land; e.g., squatters, bandit-peasants. Dispersed farmsteads, no villages. *Examples:* Chinese north, 1930s; Oriente, Cuba, 1950s; north-central Nicaragua, 1970s; northern El Salvador, 1970s– .	* Mobilizable for Insurrection *Pattern:* Increasingly exploitative patron-client system *or* elite-peasant socioeconomic linkages. Damaged "triangle without a base." *Examples:* Philippines, 1930s; China, 1930s; Andean Peru, 1950s.

their actions when they display high or low levels of solidarity and autonomy; then I will look at a second fourfold table with the same categorical divisions, but instead focusing on undamaged or "healthy" peasantries. In both instances I will therefore be looking at polar opposites, roughly speaking, rather than middling cases. I will subdivide each of the eight cells of the following two tables, indicating the general pattern in the upper part, and one or more examples in the lower part. In table 6.2 an asterisk (*) in the upper-left corner of a cell will indicate a peasantry "prone" to insurrection; two asterisks (**) will indicate a peasantry able to "rise" without the benefit of direct outsider intervention.

The Damaged Peasantry and Revolution

Solidarity plus Autonomy: The Independent Insurrectionaries

Whether or not a damaged peasantry turns to widespread insurrectionary activity depends on its own capabilities or on the historically contingent actions of outside mobilizers. In the upper left-hand cell of table 6.2 we see a peasant "type" that historically has underlain social revolutions in France, Russia, Mexico, and, more modestly, in Bolivia, while also contributing greatly to the strength of rural revolutionary movements in contemporary Guatemala (1975–).

Skocpol has explored the autonomy and solidarity of peasantries in both France and Russia in her comparative work.[6] In Russia, both of the elements were especially accentuated because many of the landed elite had little presence in the countryside (thus increasing peasant autonomy) while the intensely communal activity of the Russian village *obshchina* (or *mir*), in both land and tax-burden allocations, established a long-term basis for solidarity. In minor contrast, there were greater social divisions among the French peasants than their Russian counterparts, and landlords were likely to have a more permanent presence in rural zones. In both instances, "damage" to the peasantry had been accentuated in the half-century prior to revolution. Russian peasants groaned under the weight of the "redemption payments," which were the cost they bore for emancipation from serfdom (1861), while the French peasantry experienced not only a series of damaging harvests just prior to 1789, but also greater seigniorial demands since the landed aristocracy had tried to revive and intensify older, sometimes defunct, feudal burdens. In both instances, notwithstanding their minor differences (given our concerns), the peasantries rose up in the year of revolution, with the French cultivators especially invading manors and burning manorial records, and their Russian counterparts later, and often led by returning peasant-soldiers, ousting landlords and redistributing newly acquired lands through the mechanism of the *obshchina*.

Skocpol herself has clearly shown the focus of Russian events in the "Black Earth" regions of Russia. However, Arthur Stinchcombe has argued that Skocpol's discussion of the French peasant insurrections misses the fact that they were heavily concentrated in the Seine and Loire valleys, and rather less so in the *massifs* of Brittany and Central

France. He in turn traces those differences to ecological, settlement, farming, and agrarian institutional differences that nonetheless still support Skocpol's main point: insurrections were most likely in areas of peasant solidarity and autonomy, and less likely, for example, where dispersed and isolated farmsteads prevailed. Ironically, that latter type was quite common in the area that saw the counterrevolution a few years later: the Vendée. In those areas, the church tended to provide a sense and a reality of community where residential farming patterns did not, and the counterrevolution was strongly, perhaps decisively, influenced by those proreligious, anti-anticlerical aspects, as Tilly showed.[7]

In Mexico, as Womack (focusing on southern Mexico and Emiliano Zapata) and later comparative work can confirm, strong Indian village communities were under systematic assault by, and many had indeed been lost to, the expansion of modern commercial agriculture, especially sugar plantations in Zapata's home state of Morelos. More generally, the region south of Mexico City, west of the Yucatán, and northeast of Oaxaca had probably harbored the densest pre-Columbian populations in the entire hemisphere, and many Indian villages had survived the centuries of conquest, epidemic, and exploitation by the Spanish elites, and continued to speak their aboriginal tongues and orient themselves to communal ways. Many communities, unlike Zapata's village of Anenecuilco, had already fallen to the forces imposed by domestic elites, state power, and often foreign capital, especially since the beginning of the long regime of Porfirio Díaz (1876–1910).

Frank Tannenbaum, and later Eric Wolf and Walter Goldfrank, all pointed to peculiar features of those areas, mostly south of Mexico City, that "rose up" in rebellion in the second decade of the century under the leadership of Zapata. Peasants in the south professed allegiance to his "Plan de Ayala," a program for radical agrarian reforms. Those areas were the sole remaining areas of Mexico in which a substantial proportion of peasants still retained control over community lands, that is, they did *not* live on the grounds of the great estates, which would have severely limited their autonomy. Concerning damage, the one state of this group that was clearly *not* involved in the peasant insurrection, Oaxaca, contained a peasantry that had escaped damage from the commercially expanding estates. The solidarity of villages in these regions, while strengthened by Indian tongues (especially Nahuatl) and other forms of ethnic separateness, had been attenuated by partial loss of lands to upper-class encroachments; peasants therefore often had to look for sources of additional income in occasional work on nearby haciendas.

In addition, historian Alan Knight, following his predecessors' lead, has carefully discussed a second set of regions that also were loci of rebellion, that of Pancho Villa being the best known among them. These *serrano* areas, as Knight terms them, were generally undesirable lands in marginal areas—sierras or jungles—often with mestizo or racially mixed populations. Unsuitable for plantation agriculture, such regions did not attract the attention of expanding plantations or commercial haciendas, and hence the autonomy of these marginal cultivators was substantial, while their "fragmented" social life and ethnic diversity probably reduced levels of community solidarity. Thus the Mexican Revolution saw two loci of rebellion in the 1910s: the core areas of Zapata's revolt displayed substantial levels of solidarity with attenuated autonomy, and the *serrano* areas had high levels of autonomy due to the marginal conditions that characterized them. Yet both areas rose up in rebellion in response either to the expansion of the great estates (Zapata's south) or to the tax encroachments of the state (the *serrano* areas).[8]

The contribution of the Bolivian peasantry to that nation's revolutionary upheaval differed from Mexico in two respects. First, evidence suggests a greater element of external mobilization in bringing the Bolivian peasantry to insurrection. Second, much of the upheaval followed rather than preceded the fall of the old regime in April 1952. Despite those peculiar features of Bolivia, which reduce the peasantry's revolutionary role relative to other groups, our concepts can still clarify Bolivian events.

First, the Bolivian peasantry had experienced widespread and ongoing damage throughout the century preceding the revolution. Indian communities had lost large tracts of land to haciendas; independent community farmers were being transformed into *colonos* (usufructuaries) resident on the large estates; and peasants in the densely peopled Cochabamba Valley were forced onto the market to make ends meet, by providing a series of artisan crafts for sale.[9] From 1846 to 1950, Indian community members fell from 60 percent of all Bolivian peasants to less than 15 percent.[10] Community-oriented agriculture remained strongest in the altiplano areas of La Paz, Oruro, and Potosí and, as June Nash has shown, undoubtedly contributed to the well-known solidarity, and even to the militancy, of Bolivian mining communities nearby.[11] Weaker but partial community organization prevailed on those particular estates of the Cochabamba Valley where *rancherías* were the prevailing form of settlement, rather than more dispersed patterns. Oddly enough, such preservation of *some* community structures also characterized the estates of the altiplano.[12] In both regions, moreover, the Indian language produced sharp (Aymara in the altiplano) or substantial (Quechua in the Cochabamba Valley) social divisions between peasants and town dwellers, including the absentee landlords (the typical pattern). Therefore substantial solidarities remained in these areas despite the loss of communal lands to haciendas, while autonomy was limited due to the sheer loss of community lands, and due further to peasants' residence on the great estates.

The Cochabamba Valley "rose" earliest for reasons that bear some resemblance to Skocpol's analysis of Chinese events.[13] The valley's Quechua-speaking peasantry came into close social and cultural contact with the mestizos and the *gente decente* (the Hispanic upper class) in the market towns, where the peasantry sold their goods, including crafts and textiles. This quite unusual (for Bolivia) market orientation thus intensified intergroup contacts. The unusual results were widespread peasant bilingualism, the "mobilization" of the peasantry through local schools that increased their literacy, and the later politicization of that mobilizing process, through the joint actions of a nascent cooperative movement and a new peasant union (*sindicato*).

Discontent and politicization were triggered in this particular structural context, but not elsewhere in rural Bolivia, by peasant soldiers returning after defeat in the Chaco War with Paraguay (1932–35). The organization of the first *sindicato* occurred soon after, in 1936, but was driven underground by repression in 1939. Nonetheless, the delegitimizing effects of the Chaco War persisted, and led to the election of an unprecedented reformist government in 1943, headed by Gualberto Villarroel.[14] Whereas the state had previously *suppressed* peasant collective action, it now *sponsored* it, organizing a National Indian Congress on 10–15 May 1945. The delegates to that Congress were invited by the government to submit a list of the grievances and petitions of their respective communities. (The parallels to the French crown's solicitation of the communities' *cahiers des doleances* in 1789, and subsequent revolutionary upheavals, is remarkable.[15]) The delegates were also met by members of the cabinet and the governing MNR party, and greeted by President Villarroel himself as *"mis hermanos campesinos"* (my peasant brothers).[16] Villarroel then announced sweeping reforms in agriculture, which were never in fact implemented.

From this point on, the fate of Bolivia's old regime was probably sealed. The elite's response to Villarroel's reform proposals and to the national mobilization of the peasantry was a violent one, resulting in the demobilization of peasant organizations and the lynching of Villarroel in mid-1946. This holding pattern was not permanent, and military repression could only barely sustain the regime in power over the next six years (known as the *sexenio* in Bolivian historiography), for neither the peasants nor the miners could be returned to their pre-Chaco "quiescence." The final, decisive revolt of 9 April 1952 pitted the MNR, armed workers (especially tin miners), and the national police force against the army's remnants in La Paz; the army lost.[17]

Soon after the fall of the old regime—and echoing post-collapse events in both France of 1789 and Russia of 1917—peasant land invasions, rent and sit-down strikes, and other armed actions began first in the Cochabamba Valley, just as collective action had begun there in 1936: "Sporadically at first, than almost daily, reports reached La Paz of peasant uprisings and land seizures in the Cochabamba Valley. By December, the uprisings had spread to the departments of La Paz, Oruro, and Sucre." Collective actions were usually less violent and less radical in the altiplano than in Cochabamba, while the remaining regions of Bolivia, the east and the far north, were mostly silent.[18]

The government would later abet and expand such activities, leading to a long scholarly debate as to whether the peasants had acted autonomously or had been mobilized by the state and political parties. Apparently both processes were at work, but in different proportions in different Bolivian regions.[19] Yet those just-cited events of 1952 suggest that the peasantries of the Cochabamba Valley and of the altiplano had finally been given a real opportunity to rebel—presented to them by a collapsing state previously weakened by war—and they had used their (however attenuated) autonomy and language-related solidarity to rise up against and destroy the Bolivian landlord class.

Finally, apart from specific national case studies we have Jeffery Paige's theory of agrarian revolution, where he predicts revolutionary activity from sharecroppers (socialist revolution) and from migratory

estate laborers (nationalist revolution); indeed, he does more than predict such activity, he statistically demonstrates his correlations for
world events and regions between 1948 and 1970. He also has demonstrated a connection between such patterns and the Guatemalan insurgency since 1975, which has taken place near and been rooted in
solidary Indian communities of the western Guatemala highlands. My
own Latin American research has confirmed that regions characterized
by disproportionately high levels of sharecropping or migratory estate
labor were, in fact, havens for revolutionary guerrilla movements in
Venezuela, Guatemala, and Colombia during the 1960s, and in El Salvador and Guatemala during the 1970s and 1980s.[20] According to
Paige, both groups exhibit solidarity ipso facto because they are paid in
wages; this, he argues, creates solidarity among wage-earners (including the urban proletariat), whereas individualized land-holding instead
leads to a more atomized peasantry (Marx's "sack of potatoes" or
Banfield's "amoral familism"). Migratory estate laborers, in addition, typically dwell in their ethnically distinct villages for most of the
year, a situation yielding them some measure of autonomy to add to
their solidarity. Paige's sharecroppers, however, do not clearly fall
into the autonomous category, although his description of their life
circumstances does suggest considerable independence in the cultivation process itself, until the harvest comes and the crop sale revenues
are divided.[21]

Solidarity without Autonomy: Sporadic Revolts

In the upper right-hand cell of table 6.2 we find a peasantry that retains
strong, internal, lateral, cooperative ties while still being subject to the
close control of elites, typically from the landlord class. This pattern is
perhaps best exemplified by closely supervised gang-slavery and near-
slavery. The former, of course, prevailed for a century or more in
many circum-Caribbean regions, plus the United States South. While
collective, large-scale slave revolts did occur sporadically in those regions—and were clearly rather less common in the United States South
than elsewhere, *pace* Herbert Aptheker—a more common event was
the formation of maroon communities of runaway slaves, typically in
the hinterlands of Brazil, the larger Caribbean islands, and elsewhere.[22]
Furthermore, when one compares, very roughly, the incidence of slave
revolts with that of peasant uprisings in the histories of Russia, China,

or Bolivia, one again sees the greater vulnerability of slaves than of peasants to repressive action. The only successful slave revolt in the entire modern era occurred in Haiti, in an extended sequence of events from roughly 1791 to 1804 and the final declaration of Haitian independence. However, even there the mulatto-led uprising—on an island where 90 percent of the population were African slaves—can still be traced mainly to the weakening of the French imperial state due to the revolutionary events of 1789–93. The result was the ideological as well as military inability of a new republic committed to *egalité* to reimpose control over a slave colony; even Napoleon failed in that quest.[23]

The concept of near-slavery is perhaps best exemplified by plantation labor in the Yucatán. The Yaqui Indians of the Mexican northwest proved so unruly, despite repeated attempts to subdue them and seize their lands for commercial use, that the Porfirian government in the late 1800s finally entered into open warfare against them, and the survivors were shifted en masse hundreds of miles across the nation—Mexico's version of the "trail of tears"—to become near-slave labor in the henequen plantations of the Yucatán peninsula.[24] While the Mayan peoples of that region had historically engaged in occasional sporadic revolts, the newly imported Yaqui (and some Mayo) Indians were not important participants in the rural uprisings of the Mexican Revolution.[25] We must surely trace their sudden shift in rebelliousness—from open warfare against a solidly entrenched Porfirian regime to quiescence when the rest of the nation was up in arms—to their structural shift from independent and solidary Indian communities to plantation labor deprived of any vestige of autonomy.

Finally, there are some similarities here to Wittfogel's rendering of the operations of "oriental despotism" in "hydraulic societies." The village communities in such societies seemed to retain high degrees of solidarity—Marx termed them the "foundation" of oriental despotism—but were subject to the close control of a highly bureaucratic state apparatus, which Wittfogel likens to, and sees as a precursor to, totalitarian regimes of the twentieth century. Such systems may be especially prone to revolts when irrigation systems silt up, dikes fall into disrepair, and subsistence crises arise for the peasantry; thus a "damaged but intact" peasantry could confront a state apparatus in crisis. (Such political unrest, one should add, could easily take the form of dynastic upheavals or barbarian invasions, rather than peasant uprisings.)[26] One such massive peasant upheaval, as a prominent theory holds, may have caused the destruction of classic Mayan civilization in the ninth century A.D.[27]

Autonomy without Solidarity: The Agrarian Periphery

Peasantries typically have damaged lives but some autonomy when living in, or forced into, agriculturally undesirable frontier areas as squatters or even as bandits. These lands are often marginal ones, thus allowing only minimal subsistence opportunities. Conflicts with landed elites may recur over access to frontier plots, and over the very definitions of and perceived rights to landed property. Eric Wolf, more than anyone else, has analyzed the "tactical mobility" such peripheral peasantries have enjoyed, and their contributions to "peasant wars" throughout the world: in northern China, eastern Cuba, and elsewhere.[28] In chapter 7 I make my own contribution to this perspective by showing that the rural revolutionaries of Cuba and Nicaragua settled into areas with strikingly high percentages of squatters. In addition, my own and others' ongoing researches have demonstrated that the most marginal, least populated, and least cash-crop–conducive areas of El Salvador, especially Chalatenango and northern Morazán, have provided the strongest havens for the Salvadoran insurgency since 1975.[29]

However high may be their tactical mobility, low levels of solidarity are common in such frontier areas. One contributing feature to such patterns is the weak presence of strongly nucleated village communities and often the total lack of community institutions. Instead, one common pattern is that of dispersed farmsteads. This pattern was the norm in rural Cuba prior to the revolution, and village solidarity was also noticeably absent in rural El Salvador and (apparently) in much of mountainous interior of Nicaragua as well.[30] In each of those areas, guerrilla movements mobilized part or most of the peasantry for revolutionary ends, thus providing from without substantial organizational resources mostly lacking from within. Such events bear a close resemblance to the mobilization of the Chinese peasantry carried out by Mao's Red Army in the 1930s.[31]

Peasants Lacking Solidarity and Autonomy

When patron-client systems lose their reciprocal elements, as I argued above in chapter 2, peasants are likely to resent strongly the transformation of a reciprocal exchange relationship into a predatory system of exploitation. But resentment and rebellion are not the same thing, and one does *not* translate readily into the other, for a whole series of reasons, some of which James C. Scott has carefully explored.[32]

The damaged patron-client relationship, distinctively, produces discontented peasants completely lacking in both autonomy *and* solidarity, and provides the structurally opposite form to the peasant communities given such prominence in Skocpol's work. Patron-client relations are often described in the literature as a "triangle without a base,"[33] which visually captures both the lack of lateral ties within the peasantry and the subjection to elite authority. Given that image, the solidary and autonomous communities of prerevolutionary France and Russia may be described, complementarily, as "bases without triangles."[34] The portrait of a damaged, indeed a moribund, patron-client system fits the case of the Filipino peasantry who saw their subsistence rights and security decay with increasingly commercial landlordism, and who responded in the 1950s with the "Huk Rebellion." Interestingly in this case, nonviolent forms of protest had prevailed in the 1930s and early 1940s. Violent rebellion came after World War II. During the war the peasants had mobilized into an anti-Japanese (i.e., politically acceptable) resistance called the Hukbalahap; postwar attempts to demobilize this group without meeting their grievances produced the Huks. Thus, as in China, mobilization of peripheral peasant rebellion was made easier by the invasion of a foreign power, the weakening or destruction of the incumbent state, and the nationalist elements (rather than class conflict) involved in the mobilization process.[35]

Paige also treats peasants lacking in both autonomy and solidarity, in his category of "serfs": peasants who get the rights to work a plot of land for their own subsistence, in exchange for regular labor on the estate of the landlord. While Paige's serfs are meant to echo the experience of manorial agriculture in medieval Europe, his serfs differ in that they are imbedded in systems of commercial, export-oriented agriculture; that systemic location, Paige argues, should be especially productive of "damage" to peasants subject to the vagaries of world market forces. Despite the intense levels of exploitation, subordination, and humiliation that serfs often experience—the Peruvian Sierra provides a wealth of such tales—Paige predicts mostly quiescence from such groups, but expects land invasions or rent strikes to occur if conditions become exceptionally favorable; that is precisely what he finds in his statistical analyses. Such favorable conditions do *not* emerge from the peasants themselves, but instead from the "field of power" surrounding them, to use Wolf's apt phrase. Promising conditions for such "agrarian revolts," as Paige terms them, arise when there is (1) a sudden power "drop-off" within the landlord class that has controlled the peasantry; (2) a sudden increase in the power of the serfs, typically when they acquire powerful outside allies, such as guerrilla organizations or established political parties; or (3) both of these circumstances simultaneously. To put these conditions in our terms: either the elites must be demobilized or the peasantry effectively mobilized, or revolts will not occur. By themselves, therefore, serfs will rarely be able to transmute high levels of discontent into effective action.[36]

The "Healthy" Peasantry and the Absence of Insurrection

Since the cultivators under discussion here are notable for their lack of insurrectionary activity, we do not have to dwell as long on the differing structural characteristics of the various groups. Indeed, one could make a strong argument, in many of these cases, that the term "peasant" is completely inappropriate to certain rural cultivators, and "farmer" should be used instead. Cultural contacts between English-speakers and others highlight this distinction; "peasant" and its European counterparts—German *Bauer*, Italian *contadino*, French *paysan*, Spanish *campesino*, and Portuguese *camponês*— always sound foreign to the ear of the average American. Correspondingly, "farm" and "farmer" have no good counterparts in Spanish usage, as Francisco Miranda noticed two centuries ago while visiting the United States.[37]

There are a number of weighty treatments of the conceptual status of the term "peasant," which insist that it is a category to be distinguished sharply from what Americans would casually call a farmer. In general, despite the impressive credentials and conceptual fine-tuning of many such theorists, I am unpersuaded by the sharpness of such distinctions.[38] Not all peasants, for example, are subject to the whims or the controls of landed elites, as such discussions occasionally make clear. Moreover, as we shall see, both groups may be subject to the economic demands and interventions of the state. While there is some agreement that peasants are subject to market forces beyond their controls, that portrait fits as well virtually any American family farmer since the eighteenth century. Finally, the suggestion, typically made, that peasants are producing essentially for their own subsistence, whereas farmers are more commercially oriented, tries to convert a continuum into a dichotomy. Ours is not the sort of world, as one observer noted, in which middles can be excluded unambiguously, and the world of the colonial American farmer certainly could fall onto many places in such a continuum. Both "peasants" and "farmers" vary greatly in their "imbeddedness" in systems of commercial transactions, and therefore such commercial involvements can hardly succeed in separating out the two groups. There seems to be no good conceptual reason, therefore, for continuing long tradition and speaking in one breath of the American or English "farmer" (sometimes "yeoman" farmer in the latter case), while somehow speaking in another of Irish or French "peasants." As Paige's work, more than any other, makes clear, *all* types of cultivators, and all types of property-cum-class structures, can be imbedded (or not) in systems of commercial transaction.

Since we cannot establish a clear conceptual divide between the farmer and the peasant on the basis of class relations or commercial transactions, cultivators typically called by the former term can now enter our analysis. In Table 6.3, I have built up hypotheses concerning the social conditions *not* supportive of peasant insurrection, from various secondary sources. Before discussing these four cell entries very briefly, we can note several general features. First, there is very little evidence, when we look at these undamaged or "healthy" peasantries—when we can find them—that they have ever been involved in the kind of recurring insurrections that have proven fatal to old regimes. Second, I have encountered very little historical evidence for revolutionary or insurrectionary activity on the part of (1) secure family farmers; (2) cowboys, sheepherders, and pastoralists (Pancho Villa's followers in Mexico are the main exception to this "cowboy" exemption); (3) the peasant-clients in reciprocally functioning patron-client relationships. In all of those situations, the nature of the social relationships, and/or the very nature of the agricultural/property situation itself seems to lend itself to highly individualized responses to damage, when it occurs. This leads us to our third general proposition about the peasants and insurrection.

Proposition 3: An intact and undamaged peasantry, or agrarian social systems characterized by dispersed family farms, cattle-ranching, and/or pastoralism, or intact patron-client relationships, will not provide centers of rural insurrection.

Table 6.3

Will Peasants Be Insurrectionary?
The Impact of Autonomy and Solidarity on a "Healthy" Peasantry

	Autonomy?	
	Yes	**No**
	Conservative small-holder villages	Conservative, interdependent system
Yes	*Pattern:* Peasant villages have secured landholdings, or do so at expense of weaker landed elite. Solidarity probably weakening, due to individualized land-holding.	*Pattern:* "Model" serfdom, with paternalistic cross-class relations or seamless stratification "ladder" from elite downwards, bound by kinship, economic ties.
	Examples: Villages of France, western Germany, c. 1400–1550; early New England villages; Oaxaca, Mexico in 1910; postrevolutionary villages of France, Bolivia, Mexico (*ejidos*).	*Examples:* Medieval, open-field (*champion*) manor-bound villages, in northwest Europe.
Solidarity?		
	Conservative homesteaders, cowboys resent external interference	Cross-class ties protect but also conservatize peasants
No	*Pattern:* Dispersed homestead, small-holder agriculture and cattle-ranching, sheepherding regions.	*Pattern:* Reciprocally functioning patron-client agriculture. Intact "triangle without a base."
	Examples: U.S.: Mid-Atlantic States, Midwest, and Great Plains, later New England; France in 1789: *massif* areas of Brittany, center. Cowboys/gauchos/vaqueros/vaqueiros/sheepherders of U.S., Argentina, Uruguay, Brazil, etc.	*Examples:* Some Philippines, pre-1930; scattered "precapitalist" rural areas around the world.

Finally, we can look at peasants from a geographical-historical perspective, rather than looking at "damage" or social types. Taking just such a broad comparative view, Barrington Moore has noted the relative infrequency of peasant revolts in medieval and early modern Europe, as compared to the frequency and intensity of such events in the history of Russia and China. India provides the limiting case here, with revolts being quite infrequent.[39] To the list of nations with few or no peasant uprisings we can readily add the history of the United States and Canada as well.

Autonomous and Solidary Village Farmers: No Damage, No Insurrections

In the upper left-hand cell of Table 6.3, we encounter peasants/farmers dwelling in solidary villages, with few or no threats to their subsistence possibilities from landlord-elites or from state taxation. Indeed, where landlord-elites are absent from the social structure and/or the state makes no or only meager attempts to tax production, these villages could display exceptionally high levels of autonomy to abet their solidarity.

Even where there is a clear and arguably exploitative landlord element, the peasantry may retain sufficient collective organization and resources to resist landlord encroachments in manners short of outright revolt. Robert Brenner has argued that the peasant villages of late medieval France and western Germany generally succeeded in defending and extending villagers' holds on the land, against the "manorial reaction" that followed the Black Death of the fourteenth century. Such villages thus secured the subsistence of their communities against most (but not all) landlord claims, especially concerning the possession of land itself. Through the ensuing centuries, however, a long-term pattern of population growth and parcelization of plots tended to erode peasant living standards. Perhaps Barrington Moore intended us to think of such areas when he noted that peasant rebellion, while clearly less severe than in Russia or China, "was frequently beneath the surface in medieval Europe."[40]

The initial Puritan settlements of colonial New England certainly displayed high levels of solidarity in their community-oriented patterns of everyday life, and functioned as such in the absence of a landlord class. That social structural lacuna leads us to expect virtually no evidence of peasant revolts. John Winthrop's famous vision—"Wee shall be as a Citty upon a hill"—was not merely cant in the first century of New World occupation.[41] These settlers did allocate lands *somewhat* unequally, to be sure, but in proportion to perceived "station," and in so doing created no class of vagrants or landless workers (although they did appear later). The result was highly egalitarian when viewed in any comparative perspective. To a lesser degree such solidarity and landed equality also prevailed in the later Quaker settlement areas in the Delaware Valley. Puritan or Quaker peasant revolts in America apparently did not happen; the very notion seems oxymoronic. Even when we encounter an historian predisposed to find (not to mention endorse) radicalism and rebellion among ordinary colonial Americans, the cases (still clearly exceptional) occurred in areas with landlord-tenant or proprietor-tenant conflicts over quitrents, notable in certain parts of New Jersey ("East Jersey") and New York, which were atypical of the (proto-)nation as a whole.[42]

Both Bolivia and Mexico have been mostly immune from peasant revolts since the massive land distribution that followed the consolidation of each nation's revolution: in Mexico beginning with the presidency of Lázaro Cárdenas (1934–40), in Bolivia beginning with the land invasions and rent strikes that followed the 1952 revolution. Interestingly in Mexico, some peasant land invasions have occurred, especially in the north, where legal subterfuge and political corruption have permitted the survival and expansion of large estates, worked often by landless laborers producing export crops like cotton. The post-revolutionary agrarian reforms systematically improved the "health" of the peasantry, albeit more so in Mexico than in Bolivia. In Mexico, solidary villages, although under ever-greater economic stress due mainly to population growth and limited credit, were created and persist in the *ejidos* (communal villages) common in the south, whose inalienable lands belong in common to the villagers. In Bolivia, Indian languages, more than village community life, help to retain some levels of solidarity, for the individualized distribution of lands since 1952 has probably set in motion a process of population growth-cum-parcelization similar to events in France, Germany, and Mexico.[43]

Solidary Cultivators without Autonomy from Elites

The upper right-hand cell of Table 6.3 instead points to a "healthy" village peasantry still subject to the control of landed elites and/or the state, and hence lacking in autonomy. In the medieval European context, solidarity in such villages derived in good part from the *champion* or open-field system of agriculture—which did not prevail everywhere in Europe[44]—where villages allocated to their members scattered strips of land, whose seasonal rhythms of cultivation the village determined communally.

The "model" for a healthy, solidary, yet nonautonomous peasantry comes from the corresponding "model" of medieval European serfdom, in which an implicit exchange presumably took place between the lord of the manor and the local villages (or parts thereof) that comprised his fiefdom: he protected those villages and even contributed to their welfare in exchange for exactions of surplus, especially labor on the *demesne* land belonging to the manor. Marc Bloch even suggests that the dependent cultivators' obligations in the manorial system became stabilized and institutionalized in the later Middle Ages ("custom of the manor" is one common phrase). One should never forget, moreover, that serf-worked estates were created from the earliest to the latest Middle Ages by making land grants *to* peasant cultivators in exchange for servile work on the *demesne*. The common term for such voluntary subordination from Carolingian Europe was "commendation," and in such relationships the elements of mutual benefit are most apparent.[45] It is often all too easy, given the present state of academic discourse, to laugh off the notion of such a protective exchange with a "Marxist guffaw" (as one author put it in another context). *All* writers on this topic, not just Marxists, therefore clearly discuss as well the realities and possibilities for landed elites to employ pure coercion in these relations; I am certainly not denying such features, just qualifying them.[46]

The "mutual benefit" model surely retains some accuracy in some regions for some periods of the European millennium we call the Middle Ages. One very plausible period for which the historian can suggest strong exchange elements in lord-peasant relations is the late Roman Empire and the early Middle Ages, when a dissolving empire, multiple barbarian invasions, and rural anarchy combined to create a set of conditions under which cultivators could indeed benefit greatly from the protection of armed military elites. Postan in particular resists the suggestion that manorialism only appears magically in the later Middle Ages, and insists on tracing its origins back to the end of the Roman Empire.[47] In the following centuries recurrent invasions by Saracens, Scandinavians (especially), and Hungarians from about 700 to 1000 A.D. created roughly parallel conditions for ordinary people— an intense need for protection.[48]

Thus an exchange of agricultural surplus—in kind or in labor—for rural peace, order, and protection from bandits could certainly be a highly "rational" exchange for all parties concerned, especially during the first half-millennium of the Middle Ages. In such quasi-anarchic conditions, bandits could survive and exact ransoms and tolls even for decades without serious hindrance, while those peasants who managed to organize themselves and take up arms against invading armies were inevitably massacred.[49]

As it happens, there are only the most fragmentary references to "peasant revolts" in Carolingian Europe (ca. 800–900 A.D.), according to Pierre Riché. Reviewing such references, he concludes that, in fact, "these movements appear primarily to have been manifestations of self-defense against bandits and invaders," which certainly places them outside our realm of interest, peasant insurrections.[50]

Autonomy without Solidarity on the Frontier

A peasantry living on dispersed farmsteads, especially in frontier areas, has been the typical pattern throughout most of American history. That history has been mostly bereft of anything resembling the peasant insurrections that litter the rural histories of Bolivia, Mexico, China, and Russia. Even a work devoted to finding "farmers' movements" in that sweep of three centuries comes up with relatively few exceptional cases, such as the antilandlord movements of New York and New Jersey that I mentioned above. Beyond those exceptional, and only occasionally riotous, confrontations between landlords and tenants, most of the farmers' movements of American history fall into two categories. First, there were a number of backwoods rebellions that occurred in the agrarian interiors of the eastern coastal states. These uprisings inevitably centered around the damaging actions of governments, rather than landlords, and had as their typical grievance unfair or corrupt taxation of subsistence farmers' incomes. Here I would included Shays's Rebellion (Massachusetts), the Whiskey Rebellion (Pennsylvania), Bacon's Rebellion (Virginia), and the North Carolina Regulators' Movement.[51]

The second type of farmers' movement that has commonly arisen in American history, and that increasingly has come to prevail as *the* form of rural unrest since the late 1800s, involves farmers' opposition to the operations of unfettered commodity and credit markets. In these latter cases, farmers are not engaged in "peasant insurrections" against landlord and state, but instead are especially seeking what Norbert Wiley has termed "commodity socialism" and "credit socialism": government regulation over (1) the prices they pay for inputs, (2) interest rates on their farmlands and loans, and (3) the prices they receive for their crops. That is, they are engaged in what Jeffery Paige terms a "reform commodity movement" which, as his discussion makes clear, is structurally and culturally worlds apart from the agrarian revolutionaries or outraged serfs he discusses elsewhere in his work. Paige also clarifies conceptually loose discussions of "agrarian socialism" in the history of the United States and Canada, by noting that the socialism in question was only of the very limited form Wiley outlined, and had nothing to do with radical redistribution of land or income.[52]

Similar to the case of family farmers, the rural horsemen called variously cowboys, *vaqueros* (Mexico), *vaqueiros* (Brazil), *gauchos* (Argentina, Uruguay, and Brazil), and *llaneros* (Venezuela) in the New World have rarely provided the basis of a true peasant insurrection. The sheer independence from central authority that such groups have consistently displayed is not insurrection, nor is their participation in various range-wars and other rural conflicts, whether collective or individual. They have, however, consistently been involved in various kinds of elite-led social movements in Latin America that (1) seek to consolidate regional autonomy from central government controls, or (2) seek to place those regional elites in the seats of power, brought there by their horse-borne supporters. In certain cases, like that of Argentina's nineteenth-century dictator Juan Manuel de Rosas, the *caudillo*—"regional warlord with a personal following" is a rough meaning—could proclaim the first aim while in fact achieving the second.[53] Finally, I have seen no evidence that pastoralism in the form of sheepherding—whether in Britain, the United States, Argentina, or Australia—has ever been associated with insurrection.

When considering cultivators or herders who have migrated to agrarian frontiers, evidence strongly suggests that they enjoy high degrees of autonomy from the demands of central governments (and often from the demands of landlords as well). Such autonomy in everyday life seems to generate high levels of independence and individualism, and a great deal of resentment against any exactions that might impinge on such virtues. In the American case, that initial independence often came when farmers settled as squatters in unsurveyed frontier areas. Afterwards, they would commonly secure titles to the lands they tilled and hence secure their subsistence.[54] Such an experience seems the very antithesis of "damage."

The insurrectionary frontier cultivators in China, Cuba, and Nicaragua, by contrast, commonly had gone through a rather different sequence of events. In those contrasting cases one can often find a prior history in which they were forced onto such frontiers by earlier subsistence pressures, land seizures, plantation expansions, and so forth, yet did not attain landed security even on the frontier. Thus the Chinese north, where banditry was more common, was one such haven for those who had been squeezed out of Chinese village life by population-induced subsistence pressures or landlord demands; the mountainous Cuban east housed a squatter population in one of the few areas of the island where King Sugar could not seize yet more land; and the north-central mountains of Nicaragua had become a haven (yet still a vulnerable one) for those who fled the sequential twentieth-century advances of coffee, cotton, and beef into lands previously controlled by peasant subsistence farmers.[55] Hence, unlike their frontier counterparts in American history, these insurrectionary peasants probably had been and still were experiencing damage in the conditions under which they lived.

Undamaged Peasants Lacking Solidarity and Autonomy: Clients and Their Patrons

The final pattern, found in the lower right-hand cell of Table 6.3, concerns those peasants who are both subject to the direct supervision of elites and lacking in intragroup solidarity with one another. I have briefly alluded to such types in the section above where I discussed symbiotic systems in medieval agriculture: those serfs who entered into individualized relations with landlords, and exchanged land grants for servile labor, fall naturally into this category as well. Yet this individualized pattern seems to have been atypical of medieval Europe, where the granting of fiefs often meant one or more villages, not individual cultivators, taken under manorial rule.

However, we now have a wealth of gathered information on precisely this individualized form of social relationship: the intact patron-client relation, where an upper-class individual establishes a series of personal, individualized, exchange relationships with lower-class individuals. These relations typically imply that the lower-class individuals will render political support, and often material resources, to the higher-class individuals who, in turn, use power, influence, material resources, or brokerage capabilities not only to advance their own interests, but also to provide protection, security, and benefits to their followers. James Scott has provided the most careful conceptual dissection of this special type of asymmetrical exchange relation, while he and a host of others have examined a variety of examples of political clientelism throughout the world, especially in Asia, the Middle East, southern Europe, Africa, and Latin America.[56]

Even a cursory perusal of the great number and variety of contributions to patron-client theory makes very clear to the reader that, under certain sets of rural conditions, typically in precapitalist societies where there is little or no effective central government activity, patron-client relationships are the typical form of relationship, rather than an extraordinary excrescence on rural social structure. As Scott and Kerkvliet make clear in a number of important contributions, we can also analyze the breakdown of such reciprocal relationships, which typically occur with the expansion of the state, the spread of capitalistic market relationships, population pressures, or all three changes at once. Under such conditions patron-client relations can decay, and such decaying relations can generate massive discontent within the rural populace which, under the appropriate conditions, can generate peasant insurrections.[57] But this is to stress the atypical over the typical, for the common form of patron-client relationships in premodern societies is one in which such cross-class relations between patrons and clients serve the interests of both parties, protect the peasant-clients from economic damage, and, in effect, serve as a "protective wall" against revolution. The strong implication of the literature on political clientelism is that such relations provide very unpromising materials for rural rebellion.[58]

Considering Exceptions to the Rule

Even in Europe, despite the prevalence of solidary and often exploited peasant villages, large-scale peasant revolts were few and far between in most nations from the later Middle Ages onward. Often the major national episodes of collective revolt were cross-class movements, uniting peasants and others against common enemies, rather than events clearly pitting peasants against landlords or the state: early revolts among the Catalans (1400s) and later of the *comuneros* or *comunidades*, (1521–23) in Spain, and the virtually simultaneous English Civil Wars, the French *Fronde*, and the (second) Revolt of the Catalans in Spain, all in the 1640s.[59]

Certain rural revolts, clearly dominated and led by rural cultivators, did occur at times even in those nations with virtually no history of "peasant revolts." They are instructive because they still tend to show in indirect ways that the theoretical principles tend to hold true. The single most pronounced instance in English history is Wat Tyler's Rebellion, also known as the Peasants' Rising of 1381. In the United States, four famous incidents of rural rebellion are Shays's Rebellion, the Whiskey Rebellion, Bacon's Rebellion, and the North Carolina Regulators, all in the late 1700s. In three of those uprisings (excepting the Regulators) there had been recent changes in government, and in all but one the main animus was against the government, rather than landlords—Wat Tyler's Rebellion focused on both—with the main issue one of taxation.

Each rebellion had a clear regional focus in an area with a somewhat unusual social and cultural pattern. In none of them was predatory landlordism an issue, for small, and often dispersed, family farms were the modal pattern. Wat Tyler's Rebellion was heavily concentrated in East Anglia, an area with a long history of cultural difference from the rest of England; Shays's Rebellion pitted rural debtors against urban creditors, with taxes and loss of farms a central issue; the Whiskey Rebellion was located in the hilly back country of Pennsylvania where taxes on liquor ate into the subsistence minimum; and the Carolina Regulators began in a back-country region geographically cut off from the coastal zones by natural barriers, where locals rose against corrupt and unfair tax collections by sheriffs. In all four cases, a region with strong elements of "separateness" was struck hard by damaging tax claims, and farmers overcame their structured lack of solidarity—given highly individualized farming in all locales—to rebel against the central government.[60]

The best clear case of a true major peasant revolt in early modern Europe is the German *Bauernkrieg* ("Peasant War") of the 1520s. This particular case, as well as the regional social history preceding the war, have been closely analyzed by Robert Brenner and Barrington

Moore. As Brenner and Moore both note, despite substantially higher levels of exploitation inflicted on peasants further east (roughly eastern Germany today) as landlords imposed "the second serfdom," the *Bauernkrieg* occurred in the western parts of Germany. In those western lands, solidary peasant communities had previously succeeded in holding onto their lands despite concerted efforts by landlords to seize lands and render the peasantry unfree. Those same areas were largely the sites of the peasant war in the following century, and the one major area east of the Elbe River that did "rise" along with the west had social traits making it more similar to the western German peasant communities than to east German serfdom. Hence the single greatest peasant rising in European history prior to the French Revolution occurred in regions where a "damaged but intact" peasantry employed its solidary resources and autonomy from landlords to rise up in revolt.[61]

Envoy

A former teacher of mine, who will go unnamed, once prefaced a book review by noting that it would be a special act of arrogance, even for him, to review the book in question, since he was unlettered in the discipline in question. This essay has also been, in effect, a special act of arrogance, nay *hubris*, on my part, in attempting to survey over a thousand years of modern history, at least in Eurasia and the Americas. That hubris is made yet more profound by my attempt to draw relatively simple theoretical lessons from the historical complexities of those varied places and eras. Still, this essay should be understood literally as just that, an essay or an attempt, and not the final word on the subject. I write this in the spirit that ambitious yet possibly wrongheaded conclusions will be more fruitful for our theoretical and empirical maturation than safe yet uninteresting certainties. My former colleague David Gray once noted that sociology is too often cursed by articles of the latter sort, and lacks the ambitious works of the former variety. I am pleased if I have in fact contributed an essay of overarching ambition, even though it may soon lie in ruins due to critical responses. Let them come.

Notes

1. Jeffery M. Paige, "Social Theory and Peasant Revolution in Vietnam and Guatemala," *Theory and Society* 12, no. 2 (November 1983), pp. 699–737, discusses his own work, and that of Scott and Popkin; Theda Skocpol, "What Makes Peasants Revolutionary," *Comparative Politics* 14 (April 1982), pp. 351–75, dis-

cusses her own work, and that of Paige, Wolf, and Joel Migdal, with scattered references to other theorists.

2. Jeffery M. Paige, *Agrarian Revolution: Social Movements and Export Agriculture in the Underdeveloped World* (New York: Free Press, 1975), chapter 1, esp. pp. 25–40.

3. Theda Skocpol, *States and Social Revolutions* (Cambridge, England: Cambridge University Press, 1979), pp. 114–16.

4. Apart from authors already cited, see James C. Scott, *The Moral Economy of the Peasant* (New Haven, Conn.: Yale University Press, 1976); Eric R. Wolf, *Peasant Wars of the Twentieth Century* (New York: Harper and Row, 1969); Joel Migdal, *Peasants, Politics, and Revolution: Pressures toward Political and Social Change in the Third World* (Princeton, N.J.: Princeton University Press, 1974); Barrington Moore, Jr., *Social Origins of Dictatorship and Democracy* (Boston: Beacon, 1966), ch. 9 (quotation: p. 460); Samuel Popkin, *The Rational Peasant: The Political Economy of Rural Society in Vietnam* (Berkeley: University of California Press, 1979); Charles Tilly, *From Mobilization to Revolution* (Reading, Mass: Addison-Wesley, 1978), and *Big Structures, Large Processes, Huge Comparisons* (New York: Russell Sage Foundation, 1984). For detailed consideration of Paige and Skocpol, in particular, see the following chapter.

5. Doug McAdam, *Political Process and the Development of Black Insurgency, 1930–1970* (Chicago: University of Chicago Press, 1982); idem, "Tactical Innovation and the Pace of Insurgency," *American Sociological Review* 48, no. 6 (December 1983), pp. 735–54; and especially J. Craig Jenkins and Craig M. Eckert, "Channeling Black Insurgency," *American Sociological Review* 51, no. 6 (December 1986), pp. 812–29.

6. Skocpol, *States and Social Revolutions*, pp. 85–90, 118–21, 128–33.

7. On the lengthy history of the Russian village community, with some of its communal institutions extending back a thousand years, see Jerome Blum, *Lord and Peasant in Russia from the Ninth to the Nineteenth Century* (Princeton, N.J.: Princeton University Press, 1961), pp. 23–26. For France, see: Arthur L. Stinchombe, *Economic Sociology* (New York: Academic, 1983), pp. 12–14, 54–64, 153–57; Charles Tilly, *The Vendée* (Cambridge, Mass.: Harvard University Press, 1964), pp. 26–29, 83 for references to the settlement patterns of the *bocage/mauges* areas of southern Anjou; on the importance of the church in the counterrevolutionary areas, see pp. 101–4.

8. For Mexico, see John Womack, Jr., *Zapata and the Mexican Revolution* (New York: Vintage, 1968), esp. ch. 2; Frank Tannenbaum, *Peace by Revolution: An Interpretation of Mexico* (Freeport, N.Y.: Books for Libraries Press, 1971 [1933]), ch. 16, esp. pp. 192–93; Wolf, *Peasant Wars*, ch. 1, esp. pp. 16–19, 32–35; Walter Goldfrank, "The Mexican Revolution" in *Revolutions: Theoretical, Comparative, and Historical Studies*, ed. Jack A. Goldstone (San Diego: Harcourt Brace Jovanovich, 1986), pp. 104–17; Ronald Waterbury, "Non-Revolutionary Peasants: Oaxaca Compared to Morelos in the Mexican Revolution" *Comparative Studies in Society and History* 17 (October 1975), pp. 410–42; Alan Knight, *The Mexican Revolution: Volume 1—Porfirians, Liberals and Peasants* (Cambridge, England: Cambridge University Press, 1986), pp. 78–127 (esp. 96–101, 115–117), 188–201. Knight's magisterial history is probably

now our best historical *and* theoretical survey of the events in Mexico.

9. Peter DeShazo, "The Colonato System on the Bolivian Altiplano from Colonial Times to 1952" (Madison: University of Wisconsin Land Tenure Center, Pub. no. 83, n.d.), pp. 18–23.

10. DeShazo, "Colonato System," p. 16.

11. Dwight B. Heath, Charles J. Erasmus, and Hans C. Buechler, *Land Reform and Social Revolution in Bolivia* (New York: Frederick A. Praeger, 1969), p. 169; June Nash, "Cultural Resistance and Class Consciousness in Bolivian Tin-Mining Communities," ch. 5 in *Power and Popular Protest: Latin American Social Movements*, ed. Susan Eckstein (Berkeley: University of California Press, 1989).

12. Jorge E. Dandler-Hanhart, "Politics of Leadership, Brokerage and Patronage in the Campesino Movement of Cochabamba, Bolivia (1935–1954)" Ph.D. diss., University of Wisconsin at Madison, 1971, pp. 37–38; Heath et al., *Land Reform and Social Revolution*, p. 180.

13. Skocpol, *States and Social Revolutions*, pp. 252–62.

14. For accounts of this period, including the impact of the *sindicato*, see Gerrit Huizer, *The Revolutionary Potential of Peasants in Latin America* (Lexington, Mass.: Lexington Books, 1972), pp. 88–91; Huizer here draws heavily from Richard Patch, "Bolivia: U.S. Assistance in a Revolutionary Setting," in *Social Change in Latin America Today*, ed. Richard N. Adams et al. (New York: Vintage, 1960), esp. pp. 119–20.

15. Skocpol, *States and Social Revolutions*, pp. 123–26.

16. Dandler-Hanhart, "Politics of Leadership," pp. 111–14; a less detailed account is in Huizer, *Revolutionary Potential*, pp. 88–93.

17. Dandler-Hanhart, "Politics of Leadership," pp. 118–20, 130–33; Huizer, *Revolutionary Potential*, pp. 91–93.

18. James Malloy, "Revolution and Development in Bolivia," in *Constructive Change in Latin America*, ed. Cole Blasier (Pittsburgh: University of Pittsburgh Press, 1968), p. 201 (quotation); on the relative moderation of events in the altiplano, see Heath et al., *Land Reform and Social Revolution*, pp. 46–47.

19. This is the conclusion of Heath et al., *Land Reform and Social Revolution*, passim, esp. p. 49.

20. See Timothy P. Wickham-Crowley, "Winners, Losers, and Also-Rans: Toward a Comparative Sociology of Latin American Guerrilla Movements," ch. 4 in Eckstein, *Power and Popular Protest*, and my more detailed treatment of those issues in *Guerrillas and Revolution in Latin America* (Princeton, N.J.: Princeton University Press, forthcoming 1991), chs. 6, 10.

21. Paige, *Agrarian Revolution*, chs. 1, 2, and "Social Theory and Peasant Revolution," passim.

22. See the brief but devastating summation of Aptheker's *American Negro Slave Revolts* by David Hackett Fischer, *Historians' Fallacies* (New York: Harper and Row, 1970), pp. 274–75.

23. For a brief account, see Franklin W. Knight, *The Caribbean: The Genesis of a Fragmented Nationalism* (New York: Oxford, 1978), pp. 150–57; see also James G. Leyburn, *The Haitian People* (New Haven, Conn.: Yale University Press, 1966 [1941]), ch. 2. Several years later a similar sequence—imperial disarray leading to insurrection—would occur in Spanish America when the colonists rejected Napoleon's attempt to place a French puppet on the Spanish throne. Yet

that second insurrection would be far more conservative than the Haitian one, as the elites of the highlands of Mesoamerica and the Andean regions proceeded with the memories of that Haitian race-and-class war still etched firmly in their minds.

24. Lesley Byrd Simpson, *Many Mexicos*, revised and enlarged ed. (Berkeley: University of California Press, 1964), pp. 262–63.

25. Goldfrank, "The Mexican Revolution," pp. 110–12; Knight, *The Mexican Revolution*, pp. 153–54, discusses the history of intermittent revolts in such areas.

26. Karl Wittfogel, *Oriental Despotism* (New York: Vintage, 1981 [1957]), esp. pp. 171–73; Marvin Harris, *Cannibals and Kings* (New York: Vintage, 1978), ch. 13.

27. T. Patrick Culbert, *The Lost Civilization: The Story of the Classic Maya* (New York: Harper and Row, 1974), ch. 9, discusses that and other explanations for the collapse.

28. Wolf, *Peasant Wars*, passim.

29. The clearest discussion is in my *Guerrillas and Revolution in Latin America*, ch. 10, but also see the pioneering work by Robert G. Williams, *Export Agriculture and the Crisis in Central America* (Chapel Hill: University of North Carolina Press, 1986), pp. 63, 218 n. 39. See my "Winners, Losers, and Also-Rans," pp. 150, 152, for comments on other Salvadoran traits conducive to a revolutionary peasantry.

30. Lowry Nelson, *Rural Cuba* (Minneapolis: University of Minnesota Press, 1950), p. 60; Alastair White, *El Salvador* (New York: Praeger, 1973), p. 139.

31. On China, see Skocpol, *States and Social Revolutions*, pp. 252–62; on the partial self-mobilization of the Cuban squatter population, see my "Winners, Losers, and Also-Rans," p. 156.

32. Scott, *Moral Economy of the Peasant*, ch. 7; also see Moore, *Social Origins*, ch. 9 for a similar and clear discussion of this distinction.

33. See, for one clear discussion, F. LaMond Tullis, *Lord and Peasant in Peru: A Paradigm of Political and Social Change* (Cambridge, Mass.: Harvard University Press, 1970), pp. 42–45.

34. For the observation that Skocpol's autonomous and solidary peasant communities are the structural opposites of patron-client relationships, I am indebted to my former student Katia Song.

35. Benedict J. Kerkvliet, *The Huk Rebellion: A Study of Peasant Revolt in the Philippines* (Berkeley: University of California Press, 1977), pp. 250–67.

36. Paige, *Agrarian Revolution*, pp. 40–45, ch. 2, and ch. 3; Wolf, *Peasant Wars*, p. 290.

37. See the quote from Miranda in Lawrence E. Harrison, *Underdevelopment is a State of Mind* (Lanham, Maryland: Madison Books, 1985), p. 156.

38. For one classic treatment, highly informative apart from the sharpness of this distinction I criticize, see Eric R. Wolf, *Peasants* (Englewood Cliffs, N.J.: Prentice-Hall, 1966), esp. p. 2.

39. Moore, *Social Origins*, p. 459.

40. Robert Brenner, "Agrarian Class Structure and Economic Development in Pre-Industrial Europe," *Past and Present* (February 1976), pp. 68–71, and "The Origins of Capitalist Development: A Critique of Neo-Smithian Marxism" *New Left Review* 104 (July–August 1977), pp. 67–77; Moore, *Social Origins*, p. 459.

41. Quoted in Fischer, *Historians' Fallacies*, p. 59.

42. For detail on the lives, land distribution, and community institutions of Puritan and Quaker areas of America, see David Hackett Fischer, *Albion's Seed: Four English Folkways in America* (New York: Oxford, 1989), pp. 166–205, 566–84. For that radical, quasi-Marxist, social history of America, see Howard Zinn, *A People's History of the United States* (New York: Harper and Row, 1980), pp. 62–63; for more information on those movements, see Fred A. Shannon, *American Farmers' Movements* (Princeton, N.J.: D. C. Van Nostrand, 1957), pp. 19–20, 39–43. In a retrospective on his earlier study of Dutchess County, New York and constitutional opposition, for example, radical historian Staughton Lynd commented on his implicit hunch that class conflicts between landlords and tenants would coincide with conflicts over approval of the Constitution. He conceded that, while not inaccurate, his work was probably not generalizable to other areas of the newborn nation; see the discussion in Fischer, *Historians' Fallacies*, pp. 83–85. Zinn's work is almost utterly lacking in such self-reflective nuance. For a critique of Zinn's work and that of similar chroniclers of American history—where the author notes the irony of Zinn and his peers finding so much popular rebelliousness yet so few concrete accomplishments to show for it—see James Nuechterlein, "Radical Historians," *Commentary* 70 (October 1980), pp. 56–64.

43. A convenient guide to the Mexican peasantry since the revolution, including land invasions in certain areas, is Philip Russell, *Mexico in Transition* (Austin, Tex.: Colorado River Press, 1977), ch. 17; a useful later supplement is Alan Riding, *Distant Neighbors: A Portrait of the Mexicans* (New York: Alfred A. Knopf, 1985), ch. 9.

44. For a discussion of areas where the *champion* system did and did not prevail, particularly in England, see George Caspar Homans, *Sentiments and Activities* (London: Routledge and Kegan Paul, 1962), chs. 9, 11, and even more clearly in his *Certainties and Doubts* (New Brunswick, N.J.: Transaction Books, 1982), chs. 11 and 12. Although Homans is best known for his work in sociological theory, he was also an expert on English medieval agriculture, and his *English Villagers of the Thirteenth Century* (New York: Russell and Russell, 1960 [1941]) is still a basic work after fifty years. See also Max Weber, *General Economic History*, translated by Frank H. Knight (New Brunswick, N.J.: Transaction Books, 1981), pp. 3–25.

45. Two traditional medieval surveys in which this "mutual-benefit" approach is taken are Henri Pirenne, *Economic and Social History of Medieval Europe* (New York: Harcourt, Brace & World, 1937 [1933]), pp. 62–63, and R. W. Southern, *The Making of the Middle Ages* (New Haven, Conn.: Yale University Press, 1953), pp. 102–3. On the balance between servitude and freedom among different groups; the practice of commendation; the origins of serfdom in late Roman labor forms; and rural social patterns in France, Germany, and England, see Marc Bloch, *Feudal Society*, translated by L. A. Manyon, 2 volumes (Chicago: University of Chicago Press, 1961), vol. 1, pp. 241–74; for the stabilization of obligations, see pp. 275–79.

46. For a general discussion of the origins of the manor in Europe, with special reference to England, see M. M. Postan, *The Medieval Economy and Society: An Economic History of Britain in the Middle Ages* (Harmondsworth, Middlesex, England: Penguin, 1975), ch. 5.

47. Postan, *Medieval Economy and Society*, pp. 88–92.

48. See Bloch, *Feudal Society*, vol. 1, pp. 3–56.

49. On the last two observations, see Bloch, *Feudal Society*, vol. 1, pp. 52, 40.

50. Pierre Riché, *Daily Life in the World of Charlemagne*, trans. Jo Ann McNamara (Philadelphia: University of Pennsylvania Press, 1978), p. 111.

51. Shannon, *American Farmers' Movements*, chs. 3, 4.

52. Shannon, *American Farmers' Movements*, chs. 5, 6; Norbert Wiley, "America's Unique Class Politics: The Interplay of the Labor, Credit, and Commodity Markets" *American Sociological Review* 32, no. 4 (August 1967), pp. 529–41; Paige, *Agrarian Revolution*, pp. 45–48.

53. For two accessible treatments of the political roles of regional caudillos and their followers, see James R. Scobie, *Argentina: A City and a Nation*, 2d ed. (New York: Oxford, 1971), pp. 88–93; and Robert L. Gilmore, *Caudillism and Militarism in Venezuela, 1810–1910* (Athens, Ohio: Ohio University Press, 1964), esp. chs. 3, 5.

54. Shannon, *American Farmers' Movements*, pp. 8–10.

55. On China, see the appropriate sections of Skocpol, *States and Social Revolutions*; Wolf, *Peasant Wars*; and Moore, *Social Origins*. For a rough idea of how completely sugar plantations and mills covered the lowlands of Cuba—as they still do—see República de Cuba, Ministerio de Agricultura, *Memoria del censo agrícola nacional 1946* (Havana, 1951), pp. 99–102 (these unnumbered pages give the distributions of *"Precaristas"* and *"Caña de Azúcar,"* respectively). This pair of maps shows that sugar was located except where the land was mountainous, where, as it happens, the bulk of Cuban squatters lived; one can hardly consider such complementarity an historical accident. On the consecutive disruption of the lives of the Nicaraguan peasantry by coffee, cotton, and beef, our best guides are, respectively, Jaime Wheelock Román, *Imperialismo y dictadura: Crisis de una formación social* (México, D.F.: Siglo Veintiuno, 1975), chs. 2, 3; Jeffery M. Paige, "Cotton and Revolution in Nicaragua" in *States versus Markets in the World Economy*, ed. Peter Evans, Dietrich Rueschemeyer, and Evelyne Huber Stephens (Beverly Hills, Calif.: Sage, 1985), pp. 99–114; and Williams, *Export Agriculture and the Crisis in Central America*, part 2.

56. Steffen W. Schmidt, Laura Guasti, Carl H. Landé, and James C. Scott, *Friends, Followers, and Factions: A Reader in Political Clientelism* (Berkeley: University of California Press, 1977); Scott's conceptual clarification appears on pp. 123–32.

57. Scott, *Moral Economy of the Peasant*; Kerkvliet, *The Huk Rebellion*; and their very clear theoretical contribution, Scott and Kerkvliet, "How Traditional Rural Patrons Lose Legitimacy: A Theory with Special Reference to Southeast Asia," in Schmidt et al., *Friends, Followers, and Factions*, pp. 439–58. Also see chapter 2 above.

58. Schmidt et al., *Friends, Followers, and Factions*, passim; for the "protective wall" metaphor, see Fritz René Allemann, *Macht und Ohnmacht der Guerilla* (Munich: R. Piper, 1974), pp. 393–94.

59. For the earlier events in Catalonia, see Jaime Vicens Vives, *Approaches to the History of Spain*, trans. Joan Connelly Ullman (Berkeley: University of California Press, 1972), pp. 76–81; on later Spanish events, see J. H. Elliott, *Imperial Spain, 1469–1716* (New York: Mentor, 1963), pp. 142–56, 337–45; on England,

see Crane Brinton, *Anatomy of Revolution* (New York: Vintage, 1965), and Jack A. Goldstone, "The English Revolution: A Structural-Demographic Approach," pp. 88–104 in his *Revolutions*; for the *Fronde*, see Charles Tilly, *The Contentious French* (Cambridge, Mass.: The Belknap Press of Harvard University Press, 1986), pp. 91–100, 140–45; for analyses of several of these cross-class uprisings, see Robert Forster and Jack P. Greene, eds., *Preconditions of Revolution in Early Modern Europe* (Baltimore: Johns Hopkins University Press, 1970).

60. On Wat Tyler's Rebellion, see R. H. Hilton and T. H. Ashton, eds., *The English Rising of 1381* (Cambridge: Cambridge University Press, 1984), ch. 1, and Kenneth O. Morgan, *The Oxford Illustrated History of Britain* (New York: Oxford University Press, 1984), p. 180; for its focus in East Anglia and that region's curious features, also see Fischer, *Albion's Seed*, pp. 42–46; for the earliest evidence of East Anglia's cultural divergence from the rest of England, see George Homans, "The Frisians in East Anglia," ch. 11 of his *Sentiments and Activities*. On all the American uprisings, see Shannon, *American Farmers' Movements*, pp. 28–39; for more on Shays's Rebellion and its social origins, see James A. Henretta, *The Evolution of American Society, 1700–1815: An Interdisciplinary Analysis* (Lexington, Mass.: D. C. Heath, 1973), pp. 162–65, and, on the Whiskey Rebellion, see Fischer, *Albion's Seed*, pp. 839–41.

61. Moore, *Social Origins*, pp. 461–66; Brenner, "Agrarian Class Structure and Economic Development," pp. 58–60; he deepens and defends his argument in "The Agrarian Roots of European Capitalism" *Past and Present* 97 (November 1982), pp. 71–76, especially given his comments on the unusual revolt in the Samland east of the Elbe, the exception that proves his rule.

Of Peasant-based Rebellions and Weak Regimes: Adapting Revolutionary Theories to Latin American Realities

Paige and Skocpol on Revolution

Today in sociology, we have several notable examples of solid theorizing about revolution. The most important contributions to date have been those of Jeffery Paige and Theda Skocpol. These two works take sharply differing approaches to their subject matters. Paige's theory is part of a more general and highly formal theory of social movements in underdeveloped nations, employing newspaper accounts and government information to generate a statistical test of his model, which relates different types of agrarian class structures to different types of resistance movements in the Third World, and which comes to the conclusion that only specific kinds of rural class structures are associated with revolutionary movements—those in which the cultivators are sharecroppers or migratory estate laborers. Other kinds of rural class structures, he argues, do *not* generate revolutionary social movements, and he backs his argument with both world-embracing statistical analyses and more finely grained contextual-cum-statistical analyses of peasant movements in Peru, Angola, and Vietnam. Most strikingly, Paige finds the latter two to embody revolutionary cases, and he almost displays prescience in predicting revolution in Vietnam and Angola.[1]

Skocpol, in marked contrast to Paige, is not looking at social movements at all, but at the "Great Revolutions" in France, Russia, and China. Indeed, Skocpol denies that movements in any sense "create" revolutions. She quotes Wendell Phillips approvingly to this end:

"Revolutions are not made; they come."[2] Instead, she argues that the great revolutions came about through a coincidence of similar structural features, despite the apparently sharp distinctiveness of her three cases, dispersed as they were by time, space, revolutionary ideologies, and cultural variations. Through the fog of such variation, however, Skocpol zeroes in on distinctive structural features of the three prerevolutionary regimes. Each was an *agrarian bureaucracy* (more properly, a protobureaucracy), in which the state financed its activities through taxation of the peasantry. Each regime also retained a landed upper class—although somewhat toothless in the Russian case—which also lived off the peasantry, while having a foothold within the state bureaucracy. Revolutions came to these three nations, she argues, because of a coincidence of two structural features: the collapse or weakening of the state, on the one hand, and widespread peasant insurrection, on the other. Why did the states collapse? For one of two reasons: either massive external pressure led almost directly to the state's collapse (Russia in World War I), or the entrenched landed elite used its foothold in the bureaucracy to derail necessary fiscal reforms under more moderate external pressure, leading to the state's collapse in the face of overwhelming needs that could not be met without reforms.

Where did Skocpol's peasant insurrections occur? Where peasants had a long tradition of village solidarity against landlords, which provided the collective resources for mass resistance, and where peasant villages also were relatively free from direct landlord control. Once the state was weakened, such peasant villages were in a sense "free" to rebel. Skocpol not only makes her argument on the basis of the similarities of these three cases, but strengthens it by contrasting the social and political structures of three nonrevolutionary cases: Prussia/Germany, Japan, and England.

Can such different theories of revolution somehow be joined to illuminate the "little revolutions" of Cuba and Nicaragua? At first glance, the prospects are far from promising. For example, Skocpol argues that other revolutions are probably *not* explicable in her theoretical terms.[3] Furthermore, in her interpretation of the Iranian Revolution, she makes it clear that that case requires a different kind of interpretation than the three great revolutions, and she instead focuses on the nature of the Shah's *rentier state* and its unanticipated contribution to revolution there. She also concedes that the Iranian Revolution was in fact "made" by a movement, but only under conducive structural conditions.[4] Paige's model has a rather clearer application: we should expect to find revolutionary movements rooted in areas where sharecropping or migratory estate labor are the typical labor forms, and not where we find cultivators such as "serfs," small-holders, or rural proletarians working for capital-intensive agriculture (like sugar or sisal plantations).[5]

I wish to argue that a *modified* form of each of these theories, and a joining of the two results, in fact illuminates greatly the common features that led to the success of guerrilla-based revolutionary movements in Cuba and Nicaragua. The modification of Paige's theory involves paying special attention to the case of *squatters*, who are not considered in his original work. The modification of Skocpol's model involves some special attention to another kind of structurally vulnerable sociopolitical regime, which is certainly not like her agrarian bureaucracies, but rather like her rentier state. For want of a better term, we can call the Cuban and Nicaraguan regimes *mafiacracies*. These mafiacracies showed themselves to be especially vulnerable to a guerrilla resistance which converted itself into a mass revolution against an eventually isolated dictatorship. And like the Shah's rentier state, which had isolated itself from Iranian civil society and therefore made itself vulnerable to a mass movement, the Cuban and Nicaraguan regimes eventually fell to conscious revolutionary movements organized from below.

My disagreements with each theorist will become clear along the way, but let me briefly highlight them. Unlike Skocpol's structural model, but in accord with her Iranian analysis, conscious social movements of resistance *were* instrumental in bringing down the Cuban and Nicaraguan regimes. Second, in contrast with Skocpol's structural model of peasant insurrection, I would stress that types and levels of peasant discontent do matter, and stress again that the conscious actions of outside mobilizing agents were critical in allowing mass peasant resistance to appear. In this sense, these Latin American cases dovetail with Skocpol's analysis of the Chinese case, in which Mao's resistance forces were a crucial mobilizing force behind the peasant insurrections there.[6] Paige's model has one unnecessary assumption and one missing link. Peasant movements do not have to be based in an agricultural export sector (Paige's domain assumption), for exports were not, in fact, typical of the rural loci of the Cuban and Nicaraguan revolutions. Second, Paige's model predicts only revolutionary senti-ment and revolutionary activity, not revolutionary success. Hence it must be wedded to some *other* type of theory if we are to understand why some revolutionary movements succeed while others fail. Perhaps Skocpol's theory (modified) can be paired with Paige's theory to pro-vide that missing link.

Squatters and Revolution in Rural Cuba and Nicaragua

If we use Paige's original theory, we do in fact find it useful in predict-ing peasant support for guerrilla movements throughout Latin America since 1956. Guerrillas rooted themselves in areas with relatively high rates of sharecropping/tenancy in Colombia, Venezuela, and Guatemala in the 1960s, and where migratory estate laborers lived in Guatemala and El Salvador in the 1970s and 1980s.[7] Paige's theory is also useful for locating decidedly nonrevolutionary areas, most notably the Bolivian area graced by Ché Guevara's *foco* in 1967.

I have argued elsewhere that squatters should be responsive to revo-lutionary appeals as well, for they share with Paige's revolutionary cultivators a *zero-sum* form of conflict with landed elites.[8] Threatened squatters only seem to need opportunities to rebel. In a sense, squatters fit closely to Skocpol's logic as well, for they are outside the direct control of the landed elite. They also fit Eric Wolf's profile of revolu-tionary peasantries, for their location on the periphery of the power of landlords and the nation-state yields greater opportunities for resis-tance. Indeed, Wolf himself explored the rural portions of the Cuban Revolution more carefully than any other analyst.[9] Therefore, on the basis of three different theoretical approaches we expect squatters to be especially prone to revolutionary appeals.

This expectation is amply supported by an ecological analysis of peasant support for both the Cuban and Nicaraguan revolutionary movements. In Cuba, Fidel Castro's 26th of July Movement (M-26) grew and flourished in an area that housed most of the Cuban squatter population: the highlands of Oriente Province, including the famous Sierra Maestra. Not only did Oriente have a disproportionately high prevalence of squatters, compared to other provinces, but within Ori-ente itself the prevalence of squatting was twenty percentage points higher in the guerrilla strongholds than in the rest of the province. (See Table 7.1.) However, when the guerrillas descended from the moun-

Table 7.1

Distribution of Landholdings in Cuba, by Type of Tenancy, 1946
(percentage of units)

	Average Landholding (hectares)	Units Taken in Rent			Squatter Held
		All	Fixed	Share	
Cuba	57	54%	33%	21%	9%
Oriente*	51	33	17	15	22
Las Villas*	51	64	46	18	2
Camagüey	117	37	27	11	5
Havana	46	68	54	14	1
Matanzas	52	68	55	13	1
Pinar del Río	42	81	26	55	2

	All Landholdings (No.)	Held by Squatters	
		(No.)	Percent
Oriente Province			
Guerrilla Zones	33,479	9,872	29.5
Rest of Province	17,968	1,575	8.8
Las Villas Province			
Guerrilla Zone	15,373	197	1.3
Rest of Province	28,409	439	1.8

*Province with guerrilla movement

Source: Cuba, Ministerio de Agricultura, *Memoria del censo agrícola nacional 1946* (Havana, 1951), table 7, pp. 387–93, and pp. 408–19.

tains during the summer of 1958, the support they received down on the plains was considerably less forthcoming, as Ché Guevara's memoirs attest. In addition to ecological analyses, the historiography of the Cuban Revolution supports the contention that squatters provided the core of peasant support in the Sierra. In particular, squatter leader Crescencio Pérez threw his wide and deep network of squatter relatives and supporters behind Castro's movement even before the guerrillas actually landed in Cuba.[10]

In Nicaragua as well, the guerrilla movement that grew in the north-central mountains from 1971 to 1977 rooted itself in an area where squatters were the prevailing type of cultivator. According to Booth's maps of the guerrilla zones during that period, the departments in which the movement took deepest roots included Matagalpa, Jinotega, Nueva Segovia, and Zelaya. Taken together, 35.8 percent of the cultivators in those states were squatters; yet only 7.5 percent of the cultivators in the rest of Nicaragua were squatters. As in the Cuban case, if we look within each of these guerrilla departments, our conclusions are reinforced. In each department, the guerrilla zones had a far higher proportion of squatters than did the remaining areas of each department; in the above order: 45 vs. 6 percent; 36 vs. 6 percent; 52 vs. 12 percent; and 51 vs. 41 percent. (See table 7.2.) Indeed, even in Zelaya, where there were many squatters outside the department's guerrilla development zone (1971–77), the remaining squatter-dominated zone (Rama) became the center of the Sandinistas' Eastern Front during the remaining two years of the war.[11]

By accepting and extending Paige's logic, therefore, we have indeed thrown some new light upon the social structural conditions under which revolutionary movements take root (or not) in rural areas. In addition, by focusing on squatters, we encounter a group whose rebellious proclivities conform to the expectations of three rather different revolutionary theorists: Paige, Skocpol, and Wolf. Therefore the purpose of theoretical integration appears to be served as well.

Revolution and the Structural Weaknesses of Mafiacracies

Before discussing the special structural weaknesses of the Cuban and Nicaraguan regimes I wish first to sketch Skocpol's view of the weaknesses of agrarian bureaucracies. Agrarian bureaucracies existed mainly on the basis of taxes extracted from the lower classes, which in places competed with direct extractions by the landed elite. Taxation, then, tied the state and the lower classes together in a form of asymmetrical dependence. In class terms, Skocpol sees the state as an organization with its own interests, not reducible to a mere instrument of ruling-class domination. Nonetheless, in two of the cases Skocpol analyzes, members of the landed upper class have a foothold, if not a stranglehold, upon positions in that state bureaucracy, and therefore can at times pursue their class interests—no taxation of the privileged—against their interests as state office-holders (e.g., more tax revenues for the state, especially to sustain it against foreign pressure). The fatal weakness of each of these states, then, is its structural inability to reform finances—that is, to strengthen the

Table 7.2

Nicaragua: Proportion of Squatters in Guerrilla Zones and Other Areas

	Number of Units		
	Total	Squatter	% Squatter-held
1. Across Departments			
Nicaragua	88,223	16,049	18.2
Guerrilla Departments	33,309	11,929	35.8
1. Matagalpa	14,620	4,927	
2. Jinotega	6,772	2,116	
3. Nueva Segovia	4,003	1,296	
4. Zelaya	7,914	3,590	
Other Departments	54,914	4,120	7.5
2. Within Departments, by *Municipio*			
1. Matagalpa	14,620	4,927	33.7
Guerrilla Zones	10,422	4,652	44.6
Matagalpa	4,516	1,721	
Esquipulas	416	37	
Matiguás	2,754	1,811	
Muy Muy	417	8	
San Dionisio	345	165	
San Ramón	1,974	910	
Other Areas	4,198	275	6.6
2. Jinotega	6,772	2,116	31.2
Guerrilla Zones	5,759	2,058	35.7
Jinotega	5,267	2,030	
San Rafael del Norte	492	28	
Other Areas	1,013	58	5.7
3. Nueva Segovia	4,003	1,296	32.4
Guerrilla Zones	2,040	1,066	52.3
Jalapa	795	236	
Murra	599	503	
Quilalí	646	327	
Other Areas	1,963	230	11.7
4. Zelaya	7,914	3,590	45.4
Guerrilla Zones	3,373	1,733	51.4
La Cruz de Río Grande	994	852	
Prinzapolka	1,274	602	
Waspám	1,105	279	
Other Areas	4,541	1,857	40.9
Rama	1,948	1,414	76.1

Table 7.2 *(continued)*

| | Number of Units | | |
	Total	Squatter	% Squatter-held
5. Madriz[a]	4,870	458	9.4
Guerrilla Zone	1,308	229	17.5
Telpaneca	1,308	229	
Other Areas	3,652	229	6.4

3. Guerrilla *Municipios* vs. Rest of Nation

Guerrilla Zones (municipios)	23,428	9,757	41.6
Rest of Nicaragua	64,795	6,292	9.7

[a]Madriz is excluded from the "Guerrilla Departments" in Section 1 because only one of its nine *municipios* was involved.

Sources: For maps of FSLN rural zones, see Booth, *The End and the Beginning*, pp. 117 (1971–77 period), 149 (1977–79 period, "Eastern Front" in Rama); for corresponding departments and *municipios*, see one of the following: H. Nuhn, P. Krieg, and W. Schlick, *Zentralamerika: Karten zur Bevölkerungs- und Wirtschaftsstruktur* (Hamburg, Germany: Universität Hamburg, 1975), maps and lists in back pocket of volume; or Nicaragua, Dirección General de Estadística y Censos, *Censos nacionales, 1963: Volume 3(?)—Agropecuario* (Managua, 1966), pp. i–ix for maps; in same volume, see Table 3, pp. 9–19, for the land tenure data used above.

state—in the face of external pressures by (more) powerful rivals (France vs. England; Russia vs. Germany and Japan; China vs. Japan and the Western powers).

The Question of Taxation

The sociopolitical structures of the Cuban and Nicaraguan mafiacracies were utterly different. First, following a centuries-long pattern, Latin American states did not survive fundamentally on the basis of peasant taxation. In a way, they resemble a less extreme form of Skocpol's model of the (Iranian) rentier state. Latin American states often financed themselves largely through the taxation of foreign trade and through a series of relatively small consumption taxes. Head taxes and the direct income tax remain weak there, in comparison to Western Europe. There was no real parallel to the hated *taille* of prerevolutionary France. This pattern continued well into this century. In the last decade before the Cuban Revolution, 40 to 50 percent of Cuban federal government receipts still came from customs duties, rather than from direct taxation of the populace.[12] That pattern of relatively little direct taxation also prevailed in Nicaragua in the 1970s, where only one-fifth of government revenues came from direct taxation. Throughout Latin America, income taxes remain relatively unimportant as income generators, save in those countries where the incomes (i.e., profits) of foreign mineral companies and oil producers are highly taxed.[13]

Given such circumstances, central governments in Latin America tended not to appear as direct exploiters of the rural or even the urban populace. Instead, given the "organic statist" or "centralist" traditions of Latin American governance, the state might instead typically appear as a subsidizer of popular consumption, by holding down the prices of basic food staples and of mass transit in urban areas.[14] Given this state-society relation, the problem of tax-related discontent was minimal in Latin America, but fundamental in France, Russia, and China.

Historical Precursors of Mafiacracy

These are features common to most or all Latin American societies. What made the Cuban and Nicaraguan regimes different? In each case, a telescoped history of U.S. intervention in the nation's political affairs fundamentally weakened domestic party politics, which were already rather weak in Cuba and Nicaragua. The *recurrent* pattern of direct, extended, politico-military intervention in the first three decades of this century occurred in only four Latin American nations: Cuba, Nicaragua, Haiti, and the Dominican Republic. In each of these cases, party politics were (before as well as) afterwards very weakly institutionalized, especially in contrast with national politics in countries such as Argentina, Chile, Colombia, and Uruguay. In each of those first four cases, a personalistic dictator later consolidated power for an extended period of time: Somoza and his sons in Nicaragua; Batista in Cuba; Duvalier and his son in Haiti; and Trujillo in the Dominican Republic.

The result was eventually the rise of a mafiacracy in Cuba and Nicaragua, and also in Trujillo's Dominican Republic and Duvalier's Haiti. The distinguishing features of mafiacracy are as follows: (1) the weakening or obliteration of party politics and loyalties, and their replacement by a quite unveiled form of individual patronage politics, embodied in extreme degrees of corruption, spoils systems, and protection rackets; (2) the easing out of the "ruling class" from decisive control of the government apparatus, and often direct attacks by members of the government apparatus upon upper-class property; (3) an increasing disjunction between the state and society which, however, weakens the state apparatus while consolidating the power of government office-holders.

The Weakening of Party Politics

Ideological party politics was never consolidated in Cuba following the island's late and violent independence in 1898. The Conservative and Liberal parties of the 1910s and 1920s would give way to the Auténticos and Ortodoxos of the 1940s and 1950s. This pattern was reinforced by the routine tendency for political "losers" to request U.S. intervention at the drop of a hat, and the U.S. government's willingness to intercede, especially given the legacy of the Spanish-Cuban-American War and the Platt Amendment. Analysts as diverse as Domínguez, Blackburn, and Farber have agreed on the unusual weakness of ideological party politics in Cuba. The words "venality" and "opportunistic" appear again and again in accounts of Cuban politics and political actors, and Domínguez has documented the hemorrhage of party-switching occasioned by political gains and losses.[15]

In Nicaragua, politics had strong regional roots going back to the nineteenth century rivalries between León and Granada, and Liberal and Conservative parties did exist when Anastasio Somoza Garciá came to power. Prolonged U.S. occupation and repeated intervention weakened party politics there as well, especially in the years 1910 to 1930. Somoza transformed the Liberal Party into his personal machine, however, and thereafter he and his son Anastosio Somoza Debayle retained and at times co-opted the Conservative Party opposition in order to legitimate their democratic claims.[16]

Easing Out the Upper Class

The resultant weakness of party politics, under veiled dictatorial rule, also limited the abilities of the upper class to secure control over government and the state. Since parties tend to mediate between group interests in society and the control of government, the loss of such mediators weakened the ability of the old upper class to retain state power. Certainly in other Latin American nations one possible response was conservative, upper-class authoritarian rule with military support. And whether authoritarian or not, many political analysts have written of the "fourteen families" who ruled El Salvador, the "twenty-four families" who ruled Colombia, or the "oligarchy" who ruled Peru in the first half of this century.

That pattern of party-based or dictatorial upper-class "hegemony" did *not* consolidate itself in Nicaragua or Cuba. In each of these societies the upper class was divided in fundamental ways that militated against unified class action. In Nicaragua, old regional rivalries between the capital city (first Granada, then Managua) and León had always interfered with true upper-class unity. Progressively in this century, further divisions appeared, most notably between the *Banco Nicaragüense* group, the *Banco de América* group (tied to the Chamorro family, Somoza's old enemies), and the increasing fortunes controlled directly by Somoza Debayle and his allies.[17] In Cuba, there was a fundamental tripartite division that was never successfully transcended, between U.S. businessmen controlling land, capital, and sugar mills; immigrant Spanish landowners and businessmen; and indigenous Cuban landowners and entrepreneurs.[18]

Loosing the State from Civil Society

If the ruling class did not rule in these mafiacracies, who did? As the regimes consolidated their power, the state and government increasingly seemed to free themselves from their moorings in civil society. In a situation in which all class-based forces were markedly weak—a feature that Cuban analysts such as Farber, Blackburn, and Domínguez highlight, and which was true as well of Nicaragua under the Somoza clan—it was possible for the state to loose itself from control by "civil society" once the upper class was eased from power. Since these governments did not generate revenue primarily through direct taxation of the populace, that structural source of discontent was sharply reduced—again, quite unlike France, Russia, or China, but rather like the Shah's rentier state. Most fundamentally, the new Cuban governments worked through a combination of personalized military control and an individualized system of patronage, corruption, and graft. Mark

Falcoff has nicely termed the parallel Nicaraguan result a patrimonial police state. It is the personal character of rule, the extreme personalization of control over the military, and the high levels of corruption that best characterize these mafiacracies. Under such conditions, politics tended to "individualize" rather than to "class-ify" in both Cuba and Nicaragua.

The topic of corruption has been widely discussed in both Cuban and Nicaraguan historiography. While I will not treat it in detail here, the Cuban system revolved around control of the national lottery and around the spoils system of political appointments, each of which supplied literally tens of millions of dollars in graft for the lucky winners. In Nicaragua, the system of corruption existed at the highest levels, with Somoza *père*'s personal enrichment at the expense of the Nicaraguan upper and middle classes, eventually securing Somoza *fils* and his allies as much as one-third of the national patrimony, in some estimates. This pattern was reproduced on an ever smaller scale down through the ranks of the National Guard, until one encounters rank-and-file guardsmen obtaining graft trickling down from their superiors or protection money directly from citizens.[19]

In each nation the dictator converted the armed forces into the personal tool of his rule. Fulgencio Batista led the famed "Sergeants' Revolt" of 1933, taking control of a military whose command structure had already been weakened by President Machado's attempts to suborn the lower ranks against their officers. Batista restructured the military so that it became a personal tool of his rule over Cubans, and Cubans never believed otherwise. Promotion in Batista's armed forces was not for professionalism or excellence, but based rather on personal loyalty to Batista himself. When Batista returned to rule in a 1952 coup, he had lost much of his personal control over the military, which by then was disintegrating from the top down, with loyalties based at the camp level, rather than rooted in national images of defense of the *patria*. Somoza's personal control over the Nicaraguan National Guard was even more striking, a control passed down to his sons. Appointed by the U.S. occupation forces to head the newly formed National Guard around 1925, within a few years Somoza had converted it into a personal tool for maintaining his personal rule. The Guard enjoyed all manner of special privileges and perquisites, as well as the benefits of corruption (all in striking parallel with Batista's army), and the Somozas went to great lengths to isolate them from day-to-day contact with Nicaraguan citizens, even drilling into them the idea that "the people" were the Guard's enemy.

While such personal control over the military gave both Batista and the Somozas decisive military advantage against their domestic enemies, it weakened both armed forces (i.e., the fundamental coercive arm of the state) in the longer term, and each failed utterly to attain the degree of morale, solidarity, and national orientation of the armed forces in such nations as Colombia, Peru, Chile, or Brazil. Thus, when confronted with guerrilla military resistance, Batista's army largely refused to fight, and Somoza's Guard, while it did fight for a while, succumbed eventually to the decay that riddled its internal command structure.[20] Neither armed force fought so well as did the counterinsurgency forces of the 1960s to 1980s in places such as Colombia (usually held up as the model), Argentina, Uruguay, Peru, Guatemala, or Venezuela. It is difficult not to trace their military weaknesses to the personalized and capricious manner in which they were ruled from above. They could not fight "Communist subversion" in the name of the *patria*, for all Cubans and Nicaraguans knew otherwise: the armed forces were the personal tools of Batista and Somoza.[21]

Structural Weakness, National Resistance

In the end each regime succumbed to a resistance that always remained strongest in the universities, but which spread to the middle classes, who could not advance their interests (as in other Latin American nations) through regular or intermittent party politics by which they could elect governments favoring middle-class interests. Government intransigence *grew* in the later years of each regime—as in Brinton's or Pettee's stage-theories of revolution—and the dictator gave fewer crumbs to his middle-class, "respectable" opponents. This attitude is best summed up by the following Somoza anecdote. The dictator was confronted with a co-opted Conservative Party opponent who had lost a clearly fraudulent vote-count; he called Somoza a son of a bitch, and demanded that the dictator admit that the Conservative had won the election. Somoza conceded, "You won the election, but you lost the count. And the bigger son of a bitch is he who loses what he's won." The pattern of Cuban and Nicaraguan politics is well captured by Max Weber's reference to late prerevolutionary Russian politics as an experiment with "sham-constitutionalism." A recurring pattern in middle-class opposition to Batista and Somoza was the joint theme of a return to real constitutional rule and an end to the rampant corruption that offended the civic ideology of the middle class (even though in Cuba other segments of the middle class clearly benefited from the spoils system).

Neither did the dictators ever successfully secure long-term peasant or worker support. Batista did secure a substantial following among the workers and peasantry in the 1930s and 1940s, and actually won the 1940 elections fairly, in Hugh Thomas's estimation.[22] He achieved this because his initial government was revolutionary in its class implications: the elimination of strictly upper- and upper-middle-class party politics in favor of a series of populist programs that aided workers and even *colono* farmers. The most notable feature of his populist rule was Batista's strange alliance with the Cuban Communists (the channel to Cuban workers), which still existed in some degree as late as 1957. Batista's lower-class, Afro-Cuban background secured him a strong following among the cane-cutting lower class as well. These populist elements of Batista's rule virtually disappeared in his second, dictatorial period beginning in 1952, and his support disappeared as the decade progressed. Neither Somoza nor his sons ever had even that degree of support among the Nicaraguan workers or peasants, the one exception being the families of members of the National Guard.

While the upper-class forces could tolerate dictatorial rule that maintained order and did not attack their interests directly, the Somoza dynasty actually did just that for almost half a century. Upper-class property was not secure, in particular, from the younger Somoza's use of the state and National Guard to buy or steal any property he desired. In Cuba, Batista's degree of outright thievery and corruption could only be dwarfed by Somoza Debayle's personal ownership of the national patrimony, yet Batista too enriched himself far beyond tolerable limits. In both cases, though, *status distinctions* may well have been at the cutting edge of upper-class suspicion, resentment, and finally outright opposition to mafiacracy. In both cases the dictator came from the lower orders of society: the elder Somoza was a lower-middle-class used car salesman at one point, while Batista was a mulatto and the son of a cane-cutter. In the first Somoza's Nicaragua, the upper class spoke of his government disparagingly as the triumph of *mala educación* (bad breeding) over the proper pattern of upper-class rule. In Cuba, the upper class criticized Batista more as a mulatto than as a dictator.[23] In both cases, one decisive turning point in upper-class opposition to the dictators came when repressive measures, tortures, and murders came increasingly to touch the children of the upper and upper-middle classes. From that point on, *family* opposition came increasingly to the forefront of the resistance, especially in Nicaragua during the 1970s, as both the upper-class Cubans and Nicaraguans came to agree that someone had to rid society of the thug who ruled it.

In the end, the regimes fell because they saw no need to secure legitimacy among the populace. Since direct taxation did not bind the regimes directly to the people, the dictators had no structural need to legitimate their rule in more formal terms: little taxation, little need for representation or legitimation (although in the last decade of his rule, Somoza sharply increased regressive sales taxes).[24] Because they had decreasing roots of support in the populace at large, the two regimes eventually succumbed to a resistance movement begun in the universities which transplanted itself to the countryside, rooted itself on a base of squatter support, and then spread to the working, middle, and upper classes. The mass opposition to a dictatorial regime then generated sympathy in the United States, as the more radical opposition softened its ideology to retain its more moderate, middle-class allies. In both nations, the mass opposition aligned itself with constitutional and electoral symbols, which the United States government could not ignore under American domestic pressure to withdraw support for the dictator.

The Necessary Contrast: Revolutionary Failures in Latin America

Following Skocpol's example, our approach to revolution must be comparative. Only in Cuba and Nicaragua have revolutionary movements in the region clearly succeeded over the last thirty-five years. On the other hand, many revolutionary movements have failed to come to power, despite having substantial support among the peasantry and appreciable military capability: Venezuela (1962–68), Guatemala (1964–68, 1975–present), Colombia (1964–present), Peru (1980–present), and most notably El Salvador (1975–present). There is very little evidence that the Cuban and Nicaraguan revolutionaries had either more peasant support or more military strength than their failed counterparts.[25] El Salvador is especially noteworthy in this regard. Other failures in the region occurred without deep peasant support or much military might, notably in Peru (1965) and in Ché Guevara's Bolivian *foco* attempt (1966–67).

Given a Skocpolian emphasis on regime-types and their varying strengths, yet still acknowledging the vast sociopolitical gap between the three great revolutions and contemporary Latin America, what can comparative scholars do? We can, from the infinite variety of political reality, specify three ideal types of political regime in Latin America. No sociopolitical reality matches any of these exactly, and one could create other ideal types. However, several regimes come tolerably close to our ideal-typical portraits. By examining these types, perhaps we can "model" the sociopolitical features of "stronger" and "weaker" regimes. We have already examined mafiacracies, so we may now proceed to our other two types.

Type 2: The Democratic or Reformist Regime

A democratic regime is one where different political parties contend openly for political power, and where governments are formed through periodic elections with mass participation. In this manner, democratic regimes can often reach down into the populace for reservoirs of support in times of crisis. Moreover, failures to respond can result in a loss of power. Such regimes are strengthened by their periodic resort to popular reaffirmation; as Lipset argued, popular participation in the electoral process itself tends to legitimate democratic regimes.[26] (This may explain why revolutionaries have tried to disrupt national elections, most notably in Venezuela in 1963; Peru in the 1980s and 1990; and El Salvador in 1982, 1984, 1988, and 1989.) Democratic regimes therefore tend to be reformist ones as well, but many reformist regimes are explicitly nondemocratic in terms of popular controls over governors (e.g., Peru's military-controlled "revolution from above," 1968–75). Ché Guevara was perhaps the first to affirm the futility of guerrilla attacks upon elected governments, and a comparative treatment by Loveman and Davies has largely confirmed this.[27] We should also note the contrast between the structure of such democratic regimes and the regimes in Skocpol's revolutionary scenario: here the state is intertwined with society in a manner that stabilizes the state, rather than weakening it.

Many of the failed revolutionary movements in Latin America have faced democratic regimes and hence states that had been strengthened by recent, and sometimes recurrent, affirmation of popular support for governments. Instead of analyzing those regimes, as Guevara clearly did, revolutionaries often instead chose to abuse them (Debray termed Venezuelan politics "Demo-bourgeois fascism").[28] The clearest case was in Venezuela, where elections in 1958, 1963, and 1968 provided repeated affirmation for the moderate left and the center, and increasingly isolated the Marxist left—the Communists and the MIR—both of whom backed guerrilla struggles. In Colombia, following a massively favorable 1957 plebiscite, National Front governments doled out political posts equally to Liberals and Conservatives from 1958 to 1974, and those two parties (the focus of Colombia's "hereditary hatreds") have also prevailed in continued elections since that time. The bizarre incongruence in the Colombian guerrilla war—over 7,000 guerrillas in the early 1980s, yet virtually no serious *political* challenge to the regime—must be traced to the continued existence of elected governments (including those with support in the lower classes, like Belisario Betancur's), and to traditions of Liberal and Conservative loyalties which "occupy" most spaces in Colombian politics.[29]

Even in Peru and Bolivia in the 1960s, where weak guerrillas had little chance of military victory, the revolutionaries also found themselves facing elected presidents, Fernando Belaúnde in Peru and René Barrientos in Bolivia, who had garnered peasant support in those elections (Belaúnde in the southern Sierra in 1963; Barrientos in many Indian areas, but especially in the Cochabamba Valley in 1966). Each had either previously enacted or had promised to enact reforms. Since that time, Peru's *Sendero Luminoso*, from our perspective, made the strategic mistake of launching its Andean revolution at the very time (1980) that Peru was returning to electoral democracy, including electoral participation by a bewildering array of left-wing and Marxist groups. Those groups undoubtedly absorbed popular discontent through votes for the United Left (*Izquierda Unida*) or for separate parties of the left.

Type 3: The Collective Military Regime

While many now concede that Guevara's analysis was largely correct for democratic and reformist regimes, few have systematically considered the counterrevolutionary strengths of collective military rule. The ideal-typical pattern here is one in which anticommunism is simultaneously strengthened within the armed forces, and helps to solidify a sociopolitical alliance between the military and the upper class. Note how this pattern contrasts with Skocpol's analysis of sharp state and upper-class *conflicts* over fiscal reforms in her analyses of France and China. In this military and upper-class alliance, there is good reason for believing that the upper class may be the junior partner, especially where the military itself comes to rule directly, staffing the government and a good part of the state with professional officers, not with traditional politicians or civilian bureaucrats.

George Black and his colleagues have discussed the prototype for this state, in their aptly titled book *Garrison Guatemala*.[30] From 1954 to 1985—and the jury is still out on the Vinicio Cerezo years—Guatemala provided the single strongest instance in the region of collective, anti-communist, military rule, personified by a series of military presidents: Carlos Castillo Armas, Miguel Ydígoras Fuentes, Enrique Peralta Azurdia, Carlos Arana Osorio, Kjell Laugerud García, Romeo Lucas García, and Efraín Ríos Montt. Under such deeply conservative governments, upper-class property was defended, reclaimed, and extended—especially in reversing the land reforms of 1952–53—and higher officers by the 1970s were enriched by using state power to secure themselves large properties.[31] One is struck throughout by the close alliance between a deeply conservative military and parallel sentiments in the upper class.

El Salvador provides a partial parallel to the Guatemalan case. There, too, the military ruled society in alliance with the upper class from 1932 to 1979. The alliance was more vulnerable than that in Guatemala, with elements of reformism cropping up periodically in the Salvadoran armed forces, yet still far too stable for domestic political opponents to unseat or even seriously challenge.[32]

In El Salvador up until about 1980, and Guatemala to this day, one is struck by the manner in which strong guerrilla movements did not effectively disrupt the unity of the armed forces in their counterinsurgency efforts. Batista's army in Cuba, by contrast, had largely refused to fight the guerrillas, had at times deserted en masse to the rebels, and had spawned several conspiracies and revolts. As Diana Russell has asked, why did armies in certain nations show much greater willingness to defend the old regime ?[33]

Perhaps nation-specific historical events in this century can help us to understand better the fervent anticommunism of the armed forces of

El Salvador, Guatemala, and perhaps Colombia as well (in the last case, wedded to a democratic regime). In each case specific military experiences or events have served to color and harden anticommunism in both the armed forces and the upper class, and to reduce the degree of conflict within and between those two crucial allies. This experience made it most unlikely that even a sustained, large-scale insurgency would produce large cracks in the monolithic, counterrevolutionary edifice.

In El Salvador, the decisive events are clearest: the 1932 Communist-led peasant uprising-*manqué* in the western coffee highlands, and the subsequent government massacre of peasants known as the *matanza*. These events have decisively colored the politics of the far right and the far left to this day, as evidenced by the names given to a death squad (Maximiliano Hernández) and to two separate guerrilla organizations (Farabundo Martí): those men were the main leaders of the 1932 antagonists. The Salvadoran military therefore required no cold war to become strongly anticommunist and stay that way until the present, a half-century later.

In Guatemala, the role of Communists (members of the PGT, or Guatemalan Labor Party) within the Arbenz government of the early 1950s plus the cold war environment nurtured to a fever pitch by the American government plus the secretive shipment of arms to the Arbenz government from Eastern Europe (in order to arm a counter-force against the army), all dovetailed to fortify a solid anticommunism within the Guatemalan military. Thus the army stood aside in face of the U.S.–orchestrated Castillo Armas invasion of 1954, and it also backed the ensuing counterrevolutionary policies—including complete reversal of the land-reform program—in the late 1950s. Remaining "leftist" elements within the junior officer corps were rooted out with suppression of the reformist and nationalist (i.e., anti-Yanqui) military uprising of 13 November 1960.[34] In both countries, the anticommunism of the armed forces was only strengthened by the later counterinsurgency struggles against partly Communist guerrilla forces.

In Colombia, peasant areas of quasi independence began to emerge in the interior as early as the 1930s; they grew in scope and number during *La Violencia* in the 1950s, as areas of self-defense against *pájaros* and other violent groups. Throughout that entire period these peasant zones were closely linked to the Colombian Communist Party

(PCC). During the fight against *La Violencia*'s bandits and guerrillas, Colombia's armed forces became the most effective counterinsurgent army in the region, and anticommunist ideology clearly was sharpened by that experience, especially the retaking of the PCC–linked peasant "republics" in the mid-1960s. Moreover, anticommunism in the armed forces had already been solidified by Colombia's experience as the only Latin American nation to send armed forces to fight along with the United States and the United Nations in Korea in the early 1950s.[35]

El Salvador, 1979–Present: A Mixed Case

Since the 1979 coup, and clearer still with the installation of electoral politics in 1982, Salvadoran politics have displayed a unique blend of "Type 2" and "Type 3" politics, a blend that has befuddled regime defenders and attackers alike: a new electoral democracy to liberal friends at home and abroad, a shadowy continuation of violent, anti-Communist military rule to its enemies. In fact, the regime both benefits and suffers from its curious mixture. The heritage of collective military rule (from 1932 to 1979), in strong alliance with highly conservative upper-class elements (whom Enrique Baloyra terms the "disloyal right"), has resulted in a virulent opposition by both partners to the guerrilla insurgency. They are most unlikely to sunder ranks with each other, as occurred in Cuba and Nicaragua. On the other hand, the successive 1980s elections served to legitimate the government of President José Napoleón Duarte, who received substantial electoral support both from the urban masses and in guerrilla strongholds in the countryside.[36]

However, this blend has a central weakness, which Baloyra has clearly outlined: the disloyal right has the will and the structural capability—given its presence in the state and especially the armed forces—to oppose, block, limit, derail, or sabotage reforms, particularly agrarian reforms. In this respect, it structurally resembles the upper classes of France and China, who staved off state reforms, but only at the final expense of their classes' very privileges and existence.[37] The mixed model of the Salvadoran polity appeared most clearly in the truncated land-reform program initiated by the interim junta. Some have seen it simply as a cover to bring peasant mobilization to light, so as to kill as many claimants as possible. It seems more reasonable to suggest that the reformist elements in the regime (Type 2) pushed through the land reform, while the disloyal right (Type 3) was behind the murders. This paradox is further suggested by the divisions that have come to light within the armed forces themselves, especially between reformist officers in the early versions of the junta, on the one hand, and members of the National Guard and the Treasury Police, who on the other hand have been rather clearly tied to the death squads.[38]

Conclusions

There remains yet one more typical, although not universal, difference in the revolutionary cases in Latin America. Unlike Skocpol's great revolutions, where regimes fell due to external pressures, the Cuban and Nicaraguan regimes fell in the end due to the withdrawal of foreign support, which was more important for its symbolic impact—on the morale of the regimes and their defenders—than for its military or material impact. In the end, it was as Barrington Moore said in *Social Origins of Dictatorship and Democracy*, that the politics of small nations are determined in large part by the actions of the larger nations around them.[39] This was true for the case of small revolutions as well, even though that pattern only held in the special case where the domestic sociopolitical structure was a mafiacracy, with its special sociopolitical vulnerabilities.

Elsewhere in Latin America, even where guerrilla movements gained strong peasant support, classic and bureaucratic authoritarian regimes (as in Guatemala) or electoral democratic regimes (as in Venezuela, Colombia, Peru, and partially in El Salvador) have instead proven themselves remarkably resistant to guerrilla-based revolution.[40] On the other hand, without a strong peasant-based rural resistance movement, even the structural weaknesses of mafiacracies have not led directly to revolutionary outcomes: witness the histories of Haiti (despite Duvalier's fall), Trujillo's Dominican Republic, and perhaps Stroessner's Paraguay. Therefore not only peasant-based insurrection and popular support (which are far more widespread than revolutions) nor only the sociopolitical weaknesses of regimes have been enough to dynamite the traditional order. Yet together they produced revolutionary outcomes in Cuba and Nicaragua.

Notes

1. Jeffery M. Paige, *Agrarian Revolution: Social Movements and Export Agriculture in the Underdeveloped World* (New York: Free Press, 1975).

2. Theda Skocpol, *States and Social Revolutions* (Cambridge: Cambridge University Press, 1979), p. 17.

3. Theda Skocpol, "Rentier State and Shi'a Islam in the Iranian Revolution," *Theory and Society* 11, no. 2 (May 1982), p. 268.

4. Skocpol, "Rentier State and Shi'a Islam," passim.

5. Paige, *Agrarian Revolution*, chapters 1 and 2.

6. Skocpol, *States and Social Revolutions,* pp. 147–53, 252–62. Both of these critical points (conscious agency and the role of the Chinese Communists as peasant mobilizers) were raised in the best careful critique of Skocpol yet to appear: cf. Jerome L. Himmelstein and Michael S. Kimmel's review, in *American Journal of Sociology* 86, no. 5 (March 1981), pp. 1145–55.

7. For details on these processes, see Timothy P. Wickham-Crowley, *Guerrillas and Revolution in Latin America* (Princeton, N.J.: Princeton University Press, 1991 forthcoming), especially chapters 6 and 10. The same argument with far less detail is in my "Winners, Losers, and Also-Rans: Toward a Comparative Sociology of Latin American Guerrilla Movements," in *Power and Popular Protest: Latin American Social Movements*, ed. Susan Eckstein (Berkeley: University of California Press, 1989), chapter 4.

8. Wickham-Crowley, *Guerrillas and Revolution in Latin America*, ch. 6.

9. Skocpol, *States and Social Revolutions*, chapter 3, especially pp. 112–17; Eric R. Wolf, *Peasant Wars of the Twentieth Century* (New York: Harper, 1969), ch. 6 and conclusion, especially pp. 290–94.

10. Ramón Barquín López, *Las luchas guerrilleras en Cuba* (Madrid: Plaza Mayor, 1975), vol. 1, pp. 327–29; Ernesto "Ché" Guevara, *Reminiscences of the Cuban Revolutionary War* (New York: Monthly Review, 1968), pp. 246–47; Ramón L. Bonachea and Marta San Martín, *The Cuban Insurrection, 1952–1959* (New Brunswick, N.J.: Transaction, 1974), p. 271; Fritz René Allemann, *Macht und Ohnmacht der Guerilla* (Munich: R. Piper, 1974), pp. 86, 461; Jorge I. Domínguez, *Cuba: Order and Revolution* (Cambridge, Mass.: Belknap Press of Harvard, 1978), pp. 429–37.

11. See John A. Booth, *The End and the Beginning: The Nicaraguan Revolution* (Boulder, Colo.: Westview, 1982), pp. 117, 149, for maps of guerrilla zones.

12. For a discussion of patrimonial praetorian regimes, a type virtually identical to my concept of mafiacracy, see Alain Rouquié, *The Military and the State in Latin America*, trans. Paul E. Sigmund (Berkeley: University of California Press, 1987), chapter 6. On Cuban export taxes, see Guy Bourdé and Oscar Zanetti, "Le commerce extérieur de Cuba à l'époque de la république neo-coloniale (1897–1958)," *Cahiers des Ameriques Latines* 8 (2d semester, 1973), p. 56.

13. Inter-American Development Bank, *Economic and Social Progress in Latin America: 1986 Report* (Washington, D.C.: 1986), pp. 408–12.

14. On these two traditions, see, respectively, Alfred Stepan, *The State and Society: Peru in Comparative Perspective* (Princeton, N.J.: Princeton University

Press, 1978), and Claudio Véliz, *The Centralist Tradition of Latin America* (Princeton, N.J.: Princeton University Press, 1980). The role of the state in providing or withdrawing subsidies to urban consumers is highlighted in two rather different pieces: see Thomas C. Wright, "The Politics of Urban Provisioning in Latin American History" in *Food, Politics, and Society in Latin America*, ed. John C. Super and Thomas C. Wright, (Lincoln: University of Nebraska Press, 1985), pp. 24–45; on the "IMF riots" of recent years, see John Walton's close analysis in "Debt, Protest, and the State in Latin America," in Eckstein, *Power and Popular Protest*, ch. 10.

15. Domínguez, *Order and Revolution*, esp. pp. 95–109; Robin Blackburn, "Prologue to the Cuban Revolution," *New Left Review* 21 (October 1963), pp. 66–70; Samuel Farber, *Revolution and Reaction in Cuba, 1933–1960* (Middletown, Conn.: Wesleyan University Press, 1976), passim.

16. Harald Jung, "Behind the Nicaraguan Revolution," in *Revolution in Central America*, ed. Stanford Central America Action Network (SCAAN) (Boulder, Colo.: Westview, 1983), p. 25.

17. Jung, "Behind the Nicaraguan Revolution," pp. 22–23; Dennis Gilbert, "The Bourgeoisie in the Nicaraguan Revolution," in *Nicaragua: The First Five Years*, ed. Thomas W. Walker (New York: Praeger, 1985).

18. On this question, see Hugh Thomas, *Cuba: The Pursuit of Freedom* (New York: Harper and Row, 1971), p. 684; Farber, *Revolution and Reaction*, pp. 32–33, 98–101.

19. On corruption in Cuba, see Domínguez, *Order and Revolution*, pp. 93–95; Thomas, *Cuba*, pp. 564–65, 574, 581, 583, 737–38, 763; Hugh Thomas, "Origins of the Cuban Revolution," *World Today* 19 (October 1963), pp. 457–58. For Nicaragua, see Mark Falcoff, "Nicaragua: Somoza, Sandino, and the United States," in *Crisis and Opportunity: U.S. Policy in Central America and the Caribbean*, ed. Mark Falcoff and Robert Royal (Washington, D.C.: Ethics and Public Policy Center, 1984), pp. 338–41; Claribel Alegría and D. J. Flakoll, *Nicaragua: La revolución sandinista—Una crónica política, 1855–1979* (México, D.F.: Era, 1984), pp. 120–26 (where they, like others, compare Somoza's rule directly with the Sicilian mafia); Booth, *The End and the Beginning*, pp. 54–57; George Black, *Triumph of the People: The Sandinista Revolution in Nicaragua* (London: Zed, 1981), p. 209; Jung, "Behind the Nicaraguan Revolution," pp. 22, 26; *Los Sandinistas* (Bogotá: Oveja Negra, 1979), p. 130; "Crisis in Nicaragua," in North American Congress on Latin America (NACLA) *Report on the Americas* 12, no. 6 (November–December 1978), pp. 8–9.

20. The "evaporation" and failure to fight off Batista's army is well-known; one detailed discussion is by Barquín, *Las luchas guerrilleras en Cuba*; less well known is the internal decay within Somoza's National Guard, discussed in some detail by Black, *Triumph of the People*, pp. 51–52, and in NACLA's "Crisis in Nicaragua," pp. 8–9.

21. On the Cuban armed forces, see Thomas, *Cuba*, pp. 583, 637, 679, 725–26; Günter Maschke, *Kritik des Guerillero* (Frankfurt, Germany: S. Fischer, 1973), pp. 65–66; Robert F. Lamberg, *Die castristiche Guerilla in Lateinamerika: Theorie und Praxis eines revolutionären Modells* (Hannover, Germany: Verlag für Literatur und Zeitgeschehen, 1971), p. 14; Allemann, *Macht und Ohnmacht*, p. 65; Theodore Draper, *Castro's Revolution: Myths and Realities* (New York:

Frederick A. Praeger, 1962), p. 14; Farber, *Revolution and Reaction*, pp. 20–22, 148, 168–72.

22. Thomas, *Cuba*, pp. 636–37, 700–701, 706–9, 722.

23. Falcoff, "Somoza, Sandino, and the United States," pp. 353–54; Bonachea and San Martín, *The Cuban Insurrection*, p. 84; Maschke, *Kritik des Guerillero*, p. 77.

24. See Jung, "Behind the Nicaraguan Revolution," p. 26, on the sales tax.

25. Wickham-Crowley, *Guerrillas and Revolution in Latin America*, chs. 4, 6, 10.

26. Seymour Martin Lipset, *Political Man: The Social Bases of Politics*, 2d ed. (Baltimore, Md.: Johns Hopkins University Press, 1981), pp. 12–16 and ch. 3.

27. [Ernesto] Ché Guevara, *Guerrilla Warfare*, with an introduction and case studies by Brian Loveman and Thomas M. Davies, Jr. (Lincoln, Neb.: University of Nebraska Press, 1985).

28. Malcolm Deas, "Guerrillas in Latin America: A Perspective," *World Today* 24 (February 1968), pp. 72–78.

29. The best treatment by far of this period in Venezuela is still Daniel Levine, *Conflict and Political Change in Venezuela* (Princeton, N.J.: Princeton University Press, 1973). For the military and guerrilla aspects of this period in Colombia, the best source is Richard L. Maullin, *Soldiers, Guerrillas, and Politics in Colombia* (Toronto: Lexington, 1973); for coverage of politics, we have an excellent reader in R. Albert Berry, Ronald G. Hellman, and Mauricio Solaún, eds., *Politics of Compromise: Coalition Government in Colombia* (New Brunswick, N.J.: Transaction, 1980). Jacobo Arenas, one of the leaders of the FARC, Colombia's largest guerrilla group by far, candidly confirmed in the early 1980s that his group posed no immediate political threat to the regime; see Carlos Arango Z., *FARC: Veinte años—De Marquetalia a la Uribe* (Bogotá: Ediciones Aurora, 1984), pp. 39–40.

30. George Black, with Milton Jamail and Norma Stoltz Chinchilla, *Garrison Guatemala* (New York: Monthly Review Press, 1984).

31. Black et al., *Garrison Guatemala*, pp. 29–30, 35, 53–54; Concerned Guatemala Scholars, *Guatemala: Dare to Struggle, Dare to Win* (San Francisco, Calif.: Solidarity Publications, 1982), pp. 60–63. On the reclamation of property following the 1954 coup, see the data on land tenure reported by Comité Interamericano para Desarrollo Agrícola (henceforth CIDA), *Guatemala: Tenencia de la tierra y desarrollo socio-económico del sector agrícola* (Washington, D.C.: Pan American Union, 1965), pp. 36–52.

32. On El Salvador in this century, see Alastair White, *El Salvador* (New York: Praeger, 1973), ch. 3; Enrique Baloyra, *El Salvador in Transition* (Chapel Hill, N.C.: University of North Carolina Press, 1982), chs. 1–4, including his comments on military reformism, pp. 17–18, 53–64; Central American Information Office (henceforth CAMINO), *El Salvador: Background to the Crisis* (Cambridge, Mass.: CAMINO, 1982), ch. 2 on the military.

33. Notable in this regard were the arrest of Colonel Ramón Barquín López in 1956 as head of a *puro* anti-Batista conspiracy, and the Cienfuegos Naval Revolt of September 1957. The body count of dead insurgent fighters was actually quite small by the end of the revolution, perhaps fewer than 500; see Thomas, *Cuba*, p. 1044. Such relatively low numbers do not suggest that Batista's armed forces were greatly willing to engage in combat with armed

opponents, which is precisely what many have argued. For a carefully measured analysis of military loyalty and disloyalty, see D. E. H. Russell, *Rebellion, Revolution, and Armed Force* (New York: Academic Press, 1974), esp. pp. 85–89.

34. The facts on El Salvador are widely known, and relatively uncontentious. On PGT influence in the Arbenz government, see Ronald Schneider, *Communism in Guatemala: 1944–54* (New York: Praeger, 1959); on that same topic and the secret arms shipment, as well as the other issues, see Richard N. Adams, *Crucifixion by Power* (Austin, Tex.: University of Texas, 1970), pp. 184–87, 190, 196–97, 266–67; on reversal of the agrarian reforms, see CIDA, *Guatemala*, pp. 36–52.

35. On most of these issues, Maullin, *Soldiers, Guerrillas, and Politics*, is still the best source. For one autobiographical account of an undercover soldier during *La Violencia*, see Evelio Buitrago Salazar, *Zarpazo the Bandit* (Tuscaloosa, Ala.: University of Alabama Press, 1977), also available in the original Spanish.

36. Baloyra, *El Salvador in Transition*, pp. 106–11 on the "disloyal right," and pp. 167–80 on the 1982 election.

37. On this, see Skocpol, *States and Social Revolutions*, pp. 47–81.

38. For the debate on the "real" meaning of the land reform, see the respective submissions by Peter Shiras (chapters 24 and 27) and Roy Prosterman (chapter 25) to Marvin E. Gettleman, Patrick Lacefield, Louis Menashe, David Mermelstein, and Ronald Radosh, eds., *El Salvador: Central America in the New Cold War* (New York: Grove, 1981); on divisions within the military, see Shirley Christian, "El Salvador's Divided Military" *Atlantic Monthly* (June 1983), pp. 50–60, esp. p. 50. For an expanded treatment of the counterrevolutionary strengths of the Salvadoran regime, one that also addresses its weaknesses, see Timothy P. Wickham-Crowley, "Understanding Failed Revolution in El Salvador: A Comparative Analysis of Regime Types and Social Structures" *Politics and Society* 17, no. 4 (December 1989), pp. 511–37.

39. Barrington Moore, Jr., *Social Origins of Dictatorship and Democracy: Lord and Peasant in the Making of the Modern World* (Boston: Beacon, 1966), pp. xii–xiii.

40. This highlights a weakness of Skocpol's Marxisant analysis. She finds so much conflict among political actors, whether states or classes, that she seems to miss patterns of alliances between them.

Index

TIMOTHY P. WICKHAM-CROWLEY is Assistant Professor of Sociology at Georgetown University, where he also advises undergraduates as Associate Director of the Latin American Studies Program. His teaching and research interests lie generally in comparative political sociology and Latin America, with a special focus on social movements, revolutions, development, and inequality.

Wickham-Crowley has published several articles on guerrillas, terror, and revolution, and is the author of the forthcoming work, *Guerrillas and Revolution in Latin America* (1991). He is currently studying and writing on the comparative experience of development and underdevelopment in the New World since 1500.